THE DISTANT ECHO

"Cunningly plotted . . . McDermid administers the venom drop by drop . . . Individually the characters are sensitively drawn. Collectively, they present the inscrutable face of closed-off communities so terrified of change they would kill for peace."

—The New York Times Book Review

"This absorbing psychological novel of revenge shows British author McDermid at the top of her form . . . Outstanding pacing, character and plot development, plus evocative place descriptions, make this another winner."

—Publishers Weekly (starred review)

"If you still haven't absorbed the fact that Val McDermid is writing at the top of anyone's game, here's another chance to join the celebration . . . Her clean, crisp writing, especially about crime science, might just remind you of the early books of P. D. James."

—Chicago Tribune

"McDermid, whose reputation and popularity are growing incrementally with each new book, is very like P. D. James in her masterful mixing of forensic science with brisk plots and in-depth characterization."

—Booklist (starred review)

THE LAST TEMPTATION

"A psychologically chilling and multifaceted thriller . . . With consummate skill and pacing, [McDermid] braids together the complex story lines through surprising revelations, heart-stopping suspense and cruel double-crosses . . . creating even more tension. McDermid's writing and her understanding of the criminal mind get better with each novel. With its European locales, depiction of Nazi-mind experiments, and hints at another Jordan/Hill novel, this may well be her breakout book. She certainly deserves it."

—*Publishers Weekly*

"McDermid's Dr. Tony Hill is so tortured he makes Thomas Harris's troubled heroes seem like lighthearted game-show hosts. McDermid has become a whiz at generating breathless, crosscutting suspense."

—*GQ*

"This well-executed novel has it all: a complex, suspenseful plot, a full cast of interesting characters, and two budding romances."

—*Library Journal*

"Exciting and compassionate."

—Salon.com

"White-knuckle suspense, hot action, and graphic chills. Sure to be a hit with thriller fans."

—*Booklist*

"Irresistible . . . McDermid skillfully controls her cast . . . This is a hugely ambitious novel, involving three police forces, [and] the settings in Berlin are vividly evoked."

—*The Daily Express* (UK)

"More than just a serial killer novel, [*The Last Temptation* is] a masterful examination of evil."

—*The Guardian* (UK)

"Powerful . . . spooky and effective . . . this complex tale will leave you satisfied and hungry for more."
—*Chattanooga Times Free Press*

"McDermid skillfully alternates points of view and creates memorable scenes and complex characters."
—*Publishers Weekly*

"A compelling, intricately plotted page-turner."
—*Library Journal*

"Terrific . . . McDermid's deft mix of the whodunnit, the psychological thriller, some sparkling action and plenty of tension results in a hugely entertaining, gripping read."
—*The Times* (UK)

"As compelling as *A Place of Execution* . . . puts the much-overrated Patricia Cornwell to shame."
—*The Guardian* (UK)

"[McDermid] is still head and shoulders above . . . the competition."
—*The Observer* (UK)

"[*Killing the Shadows*] could rank as McDermid's finest yet crime novel."
—*Publishing News* (UK)

THE MERMAIDS SINGING

"Compelling and shocking."
—Minette Walters

"A dark tale . . . Complex, carefully crafted, and disturbing . . . powerful . . . psychologically terrifying . . . impossible to put down."
—*Publishers Weekly*

"Exciting, rapid-fire . . . A satisfying descent into the territory of a twisted mind."

—Booklist

"[A] terrific chiller from Manchester's answer to Thomas Harris."

—The Guardian (UK)

"Truly, horribly good."

—Mail on Sunday (UK)

THE WIRE IN THE BLOOD

"This book [has] a sense of gravitas and intelligence utterly beyond lesser writers in the field . . . This is a wholly satisfying read which cleverly subverts tradition and expectation."

—Ian Rankin

"This is a shocking book, stunningly exciting, horrifyingly good. It is so convincing that one fears reality may be like this and these events the awful truth."

—Ruth Rendell

"Ye Gods, she's Good"

—Colin Dexter

"A superb psychological thriller."

—Cosmopolitan

"Truly frightening. McDermid's capacity to enter the warped mind of a deviant criminal is shiveringly convincing."

—The Times (UK)

"A modern masterpiece . . . a book that will haunt us forever."

—The Denver Post

"A stunning and cunning novel."

—The Orlando Sentinel

"An extraordinary story [told] with extraordinary skill."
—San Antonio Express-News

"If you only have time to read one mystery this or any other season, make it *A Place of Execution.*"

—Associated Press

"Val McDermid is one of the bright new lights of the mystery field . . . [She] proves herself a lively storyteller."
—The Washington Post Book World

"McDermid can't write an uninteresting sentence."
—Women's Review of Books

"McDermid's a skillful writer—comparisons with such American novelists as Sara Paretsky and Sue Grafton are appropriate. Clever, absorbing and lots of fun."
—Chicago Tribune

"A cleanly written, fast-paced escapade. This tale jumps out of the gate at top speed."

—Publishers Weekly

THE
DISTANT
ECHO

Val McDermid

St. Martin's Paperbacks

First published in Great Britain by HarperCollins*Publishers*.

THE DISTANT ECHO

Library of Congress Catalog Card Number: 2003052902

ISBN: 978-1-250-09315-8

St. Martin's Press hardcover edition / October 2003
St. Martin's Paperbacks edition / October 2004

St. Martin's Paperbacks are published by St. Martin's Press, 175 Fifth Avenue, New York, NY 10010.

P1

For the ones who got away; and for the others,
particularly the Thursday Club, who made the getaway possible

ACKNOWLEDGMENTS

It's a welcome relief to write a book that doesn't take much research. Nevertheless, I'm indebted for their backstage assistance to Sharon at That Café, Wendy at the *St. Andrews Citizen*, Dr. Julia Bray of St. Andrews University and forensic anthropologist Dr. Sue Black.

As always, my efforts were improved by suggestions from my editors, Julia Wisdom and Anne O'Brien, my editorial consultant, Lisanne Radice, my agent, Jane Gregory, and my legal adviser and first reader, Brigid Baillie.

I now describe my country as if to strangers.

—from Deacon Blue's "Orphans,"
lyrics by Ricky Ross

PROLOGUE

November 2003; St. Andrews, Scotland
He always liked the cemetery at dawn. Not because day-break offered any promise of a fresh beginning, but because it was too early for there to be anyone else around. Even in the dead of winter, when the pale light was so late in coming, he could guarantee solitude. No prying eyes to wonder who he was and why he was there, head bowed before that one particular grave. No nosy parkers to question his right to be there.

It had been a long and troublesome journey to reach this destination. But he was very good at uncovering information. Obsessive, some might say. He preferred persistent. He'd learned how to trawl official and unofficial sources, and eventually, after months of searching, he'd found the answers he'd been looking for. Unsatisfactory as they'd been, they had at least provided him with this marker. For some people, a grave represented an ending. Not for him. He saw it as a beginning. Of sorts.

He'd always known it wouldn't be sufficient in itself. So he'd waited, hoping for a sign to show him the way forward. And it had finally come. As the sky changed its color from the outside to the inside of a mussel shell, he reached into his pocket and unfolded the clipping he'd taken from the local paper.

FIFE POLICE IN COLD CASES REVIEW

Unsolved murders in Fife going back as far as thirty years are to be re-examined in a full-scale cold case review, police announced this week.

Chief Constable Sam Haig said that new forensic breakthroughs meant that cases which had lain dormant for many years could now be reopened with some hope of success. Old evidence which has lain in police property stores for decades will be the subject of such methods as DNA analysis to see whether fresh progress can be made.

Assistant Chief Constable (Crime) James Lawson will head the review. He told the *Courier*, "Murder files are never closed. We owe it to the victims and their families to keep working the cases.

"In some instances, we had a strong suspect at the time, though we didn't have enough evidence to tie them to the crime. But with modern forensic techniques, a single hair, a bloodstain or a trace of semen could give us all we need to obtain a conviction. There have been several recent instances in England of cases being successfully prosecuted after twenty years or more.

"A team of senior detectives will now make these cases their number one priority."

ACC Lawson was unwilling to reveal which specific cases will be top of the list for his detectives.

But among them must surely be the tragic murder of local teenager Rosie Duff.

The 19-year-old from Strathkinness was raped, stabbed and left for dead on Hallow Hill almost 25 years ago. No one was ever arrested in connection with her brutal murder.

Her brother Brian, 46, who still lives in the family home, Caberfeidh Cottage, and works at the paper mill in Guardbridge, said last night, "We have never given up hope that Rosie's killer would one day face justice.

There were suspects at the time, but the police were never able to find enough evidence to nail them.

"Sadly, my parents went to their grave not knowing who did this terrible thing to Rosie. But perhaps now we'll get the answer they deserved."

He could recite the article by heart, but he still liked to look at it. It was a talisman, reminding him that his life was no longer aimless. For so long, he'd wanted someone to blame. He'd hardly dared hope for revenge. But now, at long last, vengeance might possibly be his.

PART
ONE

CHAPTER
ONE

1978; St. Andrews, Scotland

Four in the morning, the dead of December. Four bleary out-
lines wavered in the snow flurries that drifted at the beck and
call of the snell northeasterly wind whipping across the
North Sea from the Urals. The eight stumbling feet of the
self-styled Laddies fi' Kirkcaldy traced the familiar path of
their shortcut over Hallow Hill to Fife Park, the most modern of the halls of residence attached to St. Andrews University, where their perpetually unmade beds yawned a
welcome, lolling tongues of sheets and blankets trailing to
the floors.

The conversation staggered along lines as habitual as their
route. "I'm telling you, Bowie is the king," Sigmund
Malkiewicz slurred loudly, his normally impassive face loosened with drink. A few steps behind him, Alex Gilbey yanked
the hood of his parka closer to his face and giggled inwardly
as he silently mouthed the reply he knew would come.

"Bollocks," said Davey Kerr. "Bowie's just a big jessie.
Pink Floyd can run rings round Bowie any day of the week.
Dark Side of the Moon, that's an epic. Bowie's done nothing
to touch that." His long dark curls were loosening under the
weight of melted snowflakes and he pushed them back impatiently from his waiflike face.

And they were off. Like wizards casting combative spells
at each other, Sigmund and Davey threw song titles, lyrics

and guitar riffs back and forth in the ritual dance of an argument they'd been having for the past six or seven years. It didn't matter that, these days, the music rattling the windows of their student rooms was more likely to come from the Clash, the Jam or the Skids. Even their nicknames spoke of their early passions. From the very first afternoon they'd congregated in Alex's bedroom after school to listen to his purchase of *Ziggy Stardust and the Spiders from Mars*, it had been inevitable that the charismatic Sigmund would be Ziggy, the leper messiah, for eternity. And the others would have to settle for being the Spiders. Alex had become Gilly, in spite of his protestations that it was a jessie nickname for someone who aspired to the burly build of a rugby player. But there was no arguing with the accident of his surname. And none of them had a moment's doubt about the appropriateness of christening the fourth member of their quartet Weird. Because Tom Mackie was weird, make no mistake about it. The tallest in their year, his long gangling limbs even looked like a mutation, matching a personality that delighted in being perverse.

That left Davey, loyal to the cause of the Floyd, steadfastly refusing to accept any nickname from the Bowie canon. For a while, he'd been known halfheartedly as Pink, but from the first time they'd all heard "Shine on, You Crazy Diamond" there had been no further debate; Davey was a crazy diamond, right enough, flashing fire in unpredictable directions, edgy and uncomfortable out of the right setting. Diamond soon became Mondo, and Mondo Davey Kerr had remained through the remaining year of high school and on to university.

Alex shook his head in quiet amazement. Even through the blur of far too much beer, he wondered at the glue that had held the four of them fast all those years. The very thought provoked a warm glow that kept the vicious cold at bay as he tripped over a raised root smothered under the soft blanket of snow. "Bugger," he grumbled, cannoning into Weird, who gave him a friendly shove that sent Alex sprawling. Flailing to keep his balance, he let his momentum carry him forward and stumbled up the short slope, suddenly exhilarated with the feel of the snow against his flushed skin. As he reached the summit, he hit an unexpected dip that pulled the feet from under him. Alex found himself crashing head over heels to the ground.

His fall was broken by something soft. Alex struggled to sit up, pushing against whatever it was he had landed on. Spluttering snow, he wiped his eyes with his tingling fingers, breathing hard through his nose in a bid to clear it of the freezing melt. He glanced around to see what had cushioned his landing just as the heads of his three companions appeared on the hillside to gloat over his farcical calamity.

Even in the eerie dimness of snow light, he could see that the bulwark against his fall was no botanical feature. The outline of a human form was unmistakable. The heavy white flakes began to melt as soon as they landed, allowing Alex to see it was a woman, the wet tendrils of her dark hair spread against the snow in Medusa locks. Her skirt was pushed up to her waist, her knee-length black boots looking all the more incongruous against her pale legs. Strange dark patches stained her flesh and the pale blouse that clung to her chest. Alex stared uncomprehendingly for a long moment, then he looked at his hands and saw the same darkness contaminating his own skin.

Blood. The realization dawned at the same instant that the snow in his ears melted and allowed him to hear the faint but stertorous wheeze of her breath.

"Jesus Christ," Alex stuttered, trying to scramble away from the horror that he had stumbled into. But he kept banging into what felt like little stone walls as he squirmed backward. "Jesus Christ." He looked up desperately, as if the sight of his companions would break this spell and make it all go away. He glanced back at the nightmare vision in the snow. It was no drunken hallucination. It was the real thing. He turned again to his friends. "There's a lassie up here," he shouted.

Weird Mackie's voice floated back eerily. "Lucky bastard."

"No, stop messing, she's bleeding."

Weird's laughter split the night. "No' so lucky after all, Gilly."

Alex felt sudden rage well up in him. "I'm not fucking joking. Get up here. Ziggy, come on, man."

Now they could hear the urgency in Alex's voice. Ziggy in the lead as always, they wallowed through the snow to the crest of the hill. Ziggy took the slope at a jerky run, Weird plunged headlong toward Alex, and Mondo brought up the rear, cautiously planting one foot in front of the other.

Weird ended up diving head over heels, landing on top of Alex and driving them both on top of the woman's body. They thrashed around, trying to free themselves, Weird giggling inanely. "Hey, Gilly, this must be the closest you've ever got to a woman."

"You've had too much fucking dope," Ziggy said angrily, pulling him away and crouching down beside the woman, feeling for a pulse in her neck. It was there, but it was terrifyingly weak. Apprehension turned him instantly sober as he took in what he was seeing in the dim light. He was only a final-year medical student, but he knew life-threatening injury when he saw it.

Weird leaned back on his haunches and frowned. "Hey, man, you know where this is?" Nobody was paying him any attention, but he continued anyway. "It's the Pictish cemetery. These humps in the snow, like wee walls? That's the stones they used like coffins. Fuck, Alex found a body in the cemetery." And he began to giggle, an uncanny sound in the snow-muffled air.

"Shut the fuck up, Weird." Ziggy continued to run his hands over her torso, feeling the unnerving give of a deep wound under his searching fingers. He cocked his head to one side, trying to examine her more clearly. "Mondo, got your lighter?"

Mondo moved forward reluctantly and produced his Zippo. He flicked the wheel and moved the feeble light at arm's length over the woman's body and up toward her face. His free hand covered his mouth, ineffectually stifling a groan. His blue eyes widened in horror and the flame trembled in his grasp.

Ziggy inhaled sharply, the planes of his face eerie in the shivering light. "Shit," he gasped. "It's Rosie from the Lammas Bar."

Alex didn't think it was possible to feel worse. But Ziggy's words were like a punch to his heart. With a soft moan, he turned away and vomited a mess of beer, crisps and garlic bread into the snow.

"We've got to get help," Ziggy said firmly. "She's still alive, but she won't be for long in this state. Weird, Mondo—get your coats off." As he spoke, he was stripping off his own sheepskin jacket and wrapping it gently round Rosie's shoulders. "Gilly, you're the fastest. Go and get help. Get a phone. Get somebody out of their bed if you have to. Just get them here, right? Alex?"

Dazed, Alex forced himself to his feet. He scrambled back down the slope, churning the snow beneath his boots as he fought for purchase. He emerged from the straggle of trees into the streetlights that marked the newest cul-de-sac in the new housing estate that had sprung up over the past half-dozen years. Back the way they'd come, that was the quickest route.

Alex tucked his head down and set off at a slithering run up the middle of the road, trying to lose the image of what he'd just witnessed. It was as impossible as maintaining a steady pace on the powdery snow. How could that grievous thing among the Pictish graves be Rosie from the Lammas Bar? They'd been in there drinking that very evening, cheery and boisterous in the warm yellow glow of the public bar, knocking back pints of Tennent's, making the most of the last of their university freedom before they had to return to the stifling constraints of family Christmases thirty miles down the road.

He'd been speaking to Rosie himself, flirting with her in the clumsy way of twenty-one-year-olds uncertain whether they're still daft boys or mature men of the world. Not for the first time, he'd asked her what time she was due to finish.

He'd even told her whose party they were going on to. He'd scribbled the address down on the back of a beer mat and pushed it across the damp wooden bar toward her. She'd given him a pitying smile and picked it up. He suspected it had probably gone straight in the bucket. What would a woman like Rosie want with a callow lad like him, after all? With her looks and her figure, she could take her pick, go for somebody who could show her a good time, not some penniless student trying to eke his grant out till his holiday job stacking supermarket shelves.

So how could that be Rosie lying bleeding in the snow on Hallow Hill? Ziggy must have got it wrong, Alex insisted to himself as he veered left, heading for the main road. Anybody could get confused in the flickering glow of Mondo's Zippo. And it wasn't as if Ziggy had ever paid much attention to the dark-haired barmaid. He'd left that to Alex himself and Mondo. It must just be some poor lassie that looked like Rosie. That would be it, he reassured himself. A mistake, that's what it was.

Alex hesitated for a moment, catching his breath and wondering where to run. There were plenty of houses nearby, but none of them was showing a light. Even if he could rouse someone, Alex doubted whether anyone would be inclined to open their door to a sweaty youth smelling of drink in the middle of a blizzard.

Then he remembered. This time of night, there was regularly a police car parked up by the main entrance to the Botanic Gardens a mere quarter of a mile away. They'd seen it often enough when they'd been staggering home in the small hours of the morning, aware of the car's single occupant giving them the once-over as they attempted to act sober for his benefit. It was a sight that always set Weird off on one of his rants about how corrupt and idle the police were. "Should be out catching the real villains, nailing the gray men in suits that rip the rest of us off, not sitting there all night with a flask of tea and a bag of scones, hoping to score some drunk peeing in a hedge or some eejit driving home too fast. Idle bastards." Well, maybe tonight Weird would get part of his wish. Because it looked like tonight the idle bastard in the car would get more than he bargained for.

Alex turned toward the Canongate and began to run again, the fresh snow creaking beneath his boots. He wished he'd kept up his rugby training as a stitch seized his side, turning his rhythm into a lopsided hop and skip as he fought to pull enough air into his lungs. Only a few dozen more yards, he told himself. He couldn't stop now, when Rosie's life might depend on his speed. He peered ahead, but the snow was falling more heavily and he could barely see farther than a couple of yards.

He was almost upon the police car before he saw it. Even as relief flooded his perspiring body, apprehension clawed at his heart. Sobered by shock and exertion, Alex realized he bore no resemblance to the sort of respectable citizen who normally reported a crime. He was disheveled and sweaty, bloodstained and staggering like a half-shut knife. Somehow, he had to convince the policeman who was already halfway out of his panda car that he was neither imagining things nor playing some kind of prank. He slowed to a halt a couple of feet from the car, trying not to look like a threat, waiting for the driver to emerge.

The policeman set his cap straight on his short dark hair. His head was cocked to one side as he eyed Alex warily. Even masked by the heavy uniform anorak, Alex could see the tension in his body. "What's going on, son?" he asked. In spite of the diminutive form of address, he didn't look much older than Alex himself, and he possessed an air of unease that sat ill with his uniform.

Alex tried to control his breathing, but failed. "There's a lassie on Hallow Hill," he blurted out. "She's been attacked. She's bleeding really badly. She needs help."

The policeman narrowed his eyes against the snow, frowning. "She's been attacked, you say. How do you know that?"

"She's got blood all over her. And . . ." Alex paused for thought. "She's not dressed for the weather. She's not got a coat on. Look, can you get an ambulance or a doctor or something? She's really hurt, man."

"And you just happened to find her in the middle of a blizzard, eh? Have you been drinking, son?" The words were patronizing, but the voice betrayed anxiety.

Alex didn't imagine this was the kind of thing that happened often in the middle of the night in douce, suburban St. Andrews. Somehow he had to convince this plod that he was serious. "Of course I've been drinking," he said, his frustration spilling over. "Why else would I be out at this time in the morning? Look, me and my pals, we were taking a short-cut back to halls and we were messing about and I ran up the top of the hill and tripped and landed right on top of her." His voice rose in a plea. "Please. You've got to help. She could die out there."

The policeman studied him for what felt like minutes, then leaned into his car and launched into an unintelligible conversation over the radio. He stuck his head out of the door. "Get in. We'll drive up to Trinity Place. You better not be playing the goat, son," he said grimly.

The car fishtailed up the street, tires inadequate for the conditions. The few cars that had traveled the road earlier had left tracks that were now only faint depressions in the smooth white surface, testament to the heaviness of the snowfall. The policeman swore under his breath as he avoided skidding into a lamppost at the turning. At the end of Trinity Place, he turned to Alex. "Come on then, show me where she is."

Alex set off at a trot, following his own rapidly disappearing tracks in the snow. He kept glancing back to check if the policeman was still in his wake. He nearly went headlong at one point, his eyes taking a few moments to adjust to the greater darkness where the streetlights were cut off by the tree trunks. The snow seemed to cast its own strange light over the landscape, exaggerating the bulk of bushes and turning the path into a narrower ribbon than it normally appeared. "It's this way," Alex said, swerving off to the left. A quick look over his shoulder reassured him that his companion was right behind him.

The policeman hung back. "Are you sure you're no' on drugs, son?" he said suspiciously.

"Come on," Alex shouted urgently as he caught sight of the dark shapes above him. Without waiting to see if the policeman was following, Alex hurried up the slope. He was almost there when the young officer overtook him, brushing past and stopping abruptly a few feet short of the small group.

Ziggy was still hunkered down beside the woman's body, his shirt plastered to his slim torso with a mixture of snow and sweat. Weird and Mondo stood behind him, arms folded across their chests, hands tucked in their armpits, heads thrust down between their raised shoulders. They were only trying to stay warm in the absence of coats, but they presented an unfortunate image of arrogance.

"What's going on here, then, lads?" the policeman asked, his voice an aggressive attempt to stamp authority in spite of the greater weight of numbers arrayed against him.

Ziggy pushed himself wearily to his feet and shoved his wet hair out of his eyes. "You're too late. She's dead."

CHAPTER
TWO

Nothing in Alex's twenty-one years had prepared him for a police interrogation in the middle of the night. TV cop shows and movies always made it look so regimented. But the very disorganization of the process was somehow more nerve-wracking than military precision would have been. The four of them had arrived at the police station in a flurry of chaos. They'd been hustled off the hill, bathed in the strobing blue lights of panda cars and ambulances, and nobody seemed to have any clear idea of what to do with them.

They'd stood under a streetlamp for what felt like a very long time, shivering under the frowning gaze of the constable Alex had summoned to the scene and one of his colleagues, a grizzled man in uniform with a scowl and a stoop. Neither officer spoke to the four young men, though their eyes never strayed from them.

Eventually, a harassed-looking man huddled into an overcoat that looked two sizes too big for him slithered over to them, his thin-soled shoes no match for the terrain. "Lawson, Mackenzie, take these boys down to the station, keep them apart when you get there. We'll be down in a wee while to talk to them." Then he turned and stumbled back in the direction of their terrible discovery, now hidden behind canvas screens through which an eerie green light emanated, staining the snow.

The younger policeman gave his colleague a worried look. "How are we going to get them back?"

He shrugged. "You'll have to squeeze them in your panda. I came up in the Sherpa van."

"Can we not take them back down in that? Then you could keep an eye on them while I'm driving."

The older man shook his head, pursing his lips. "If you say so, Lawson." He gestured to the Laddies fi' Kirkcaldy. "Come on, youse. Into the van. And no messing about, right?" He herded them toward a police van, calling over his shoulder to Lawson, "You better get the keys off Tam Watt."

Lawson set off up the slope, leaving them with Mackenzie. "I wouldnae like to be in your shoes when the CID get off that hill," he said conversationally as he climbed in behind them. Alex shivered, though not from the cold. It was slowly dawning on him that the police were regarding him and his companions as potential suspects rather than witnesses. They'd been given no opportunity to confer, to get their ducks in a row. The four of them exchanged uneasy looks. Even Weird had straightened out enough to realize this wasn't some daft game.

When Mackenzie hustled them into the van, there had been a few seconds when they'd been left alone. Just sufficient time for Ziggy to mutter loud enough for their ears, "For fuck's sake, don't mention the Land Rover." Instant comprehension had filled their eyes.

"Christ, aye," Weird said, head jerking back in terrified realization. Mondo chewed the skin round his thumbnail, saying nothing. Alex merely nodded.

The police station hadn't felt anymore composed than the crime scene. The desk sergeant complained bitterly when the two uniformed officers arrived with four bodies who were supposed to be prevented from communicating with each other. It turned out there were insufficient interview rooms to keep them separate. Weird and Mondo were taken to wait in unlocked cells, while Alex and Ziggy were left to their own devices in the station's two interview rooms.

The room Alex found himself in was claustrophobically

small. It was barely three paces square, as he established within minutes of being shut in to kick his heels. There were no windows, and the low ceiling with its graying polystyrene tiles made it all the more oppressive. It contained a chipped wooden table and four unmatching wooden chairs that looked exactly as uncomfortable as they felt. Alex tried them all in turn, finally settling for one that didn't dig into his thighs as much as the others.

He wondered if he was allowed to smoke. Judging by the smell of the stale air, he wouldn't have been the first. But he was a well-brought-up lad, and the absence of an ashtray gave him pause. He searched his pockets and found the screwed-up silver paper from a packet of Polo mints. Carefully, he spread it out, folding the edges up to form a rough tray. Then he took out his packet of Bensons and flipped the top open. Nine left. That should see him through, he thought.

Alex lit his cigarette and allowed himself to think about his position for the first time since they'd arrived at the police station. It was obvious, now he thought about it. They'd found a body. They had to be suspects. Everybody knew that the prime candidates for arrest in a murder investigation were either the ones who last saw the victim alive or the ones who found the body. Well, that was them on both counts.

He shook his head. The body. He was starting to think like them. This wasn't just a body, it was Rosie. Somebody he knew, however slightly. He supposed that made it all the more suspicious. But he didn't want to consider that now. He wanted that horror far from his mind. Whenever he closed his eyes, flashbacks to the hill played like a movie before his eyes. Beautiful, sexy Rosie broken and bleeding on the snow. "Think about something else," he said aloud.

He wondered how the others would react to questioning. Weird was off his head, that was for sure. He'd had more than drink tonight. Alex had seen him with a joint in his hand earlier, but with Weird, there was no telling what else he might have indulged in. There had been tabs of acid floating around. Alex had refused it himself a couple of times. He didn't mind dope but he preferred not to fry his brains.

But Weird was definitely in the market for anything that would allegedly expand his consciousness. Alex fervently hoped that whatever he'd swallowed, inhaled or snorted, it would have worn off before it was his turn to be interviewed. Otherwise, Weird was likely to piss the cops off very badly indeed. And any fool knew that was a bad idea in the middle of a murder investigation.

Mondo would be a different kettle of fish. This would freak him out in a totally different way. Mondo was, when you got right down to it, too sensitive for his own good. He'd always been the one picked on at school, called a jessie partly because of the way he looked and partly because he never fought back. His hair hung in tight ringlets round his pixie face, his big sapphire eyes always wide like a mouse keeking out from a divot. The lassies liked it, that was for sure. Alex had once overheard a pair of them giggling that Davey Kerr looked just like Marc Bolan. But in a school like Kirkcaldy High, what won you favor with the lassies could equally earn you a kicking in the cloakroom. If Mondo hadn't had the other three to back him up, he'd have had a pretty thin time of it. To his credit, he knew that, and he repaid their services with interest. Alex knew he'd never have got through Higher French without Mondo's help.

But Mondo would be on his own with the police. Nobody to hide behind. Alex could picture him now, head hung low, tossing the odd glance out from under his brows, picking at the skin round his thumbnail or flicking the lid of his Zippo open and shut. They'd get frustrated with him, think he had something to hide. The thing they'd never suss, not in a million years, was that the big secret with Mondo was that ninety-nine times out of a hundred, there was no secret. There was no mystery wrapped in an enigma. There was just a guy who liked Pink Floyd, fish suppers with lashings of vinegar, Tennent's lager and getting laid. And who, bizarrely, spoke French like he'd learned it at his mother's knee.

Except of course tonight there was a secret. And if anybody was going to blow it, it would be Mondo. *Please God, let him not give up the Land Rover*, Alex thought. At the very least, they'd all be landed with the charge of taking and driving away without the owner's consent. At the very worst, the cops would realize one or all of them had the perfect means to transport a dying girl's body to a quiet hillside.

Weird wouldn't tell; he had most to lose. He'd been the one who'd turned up at the Lammas grinning from ear to ear, dangling Henry Cavendish's key-ring from his finger like the winner at a wife-swapping party.

Alex wouldn't tell, he knew that. Keeping secrets was one of the things he did best. If the price of avoiding suspicion was to keep his mouth shut, he had no doubts he could manage it.

Ziggy wouldn't tell either. It was always safety first with Ziggy. After all, he was the one who had sneaked away from the party to move the Land Rover once he'd realized how off his head Weird was getting. He'd taken Alex to one side and said, "I've taken the keys out of Weird's coat pocket. I'm going to shift the Land Rover, put it out of temptation's way. He's already been taking people for a spin round the block, it's time to put a stop to it before he kills himself or somebody else." Alex had no idea how long he'd been gone, but when he'd returned, Ziggy had told him the Land Rover was safely stowed up behind one of the industrial units off the Largo Road. "We can go and pick it up in the morning," he'd said.

Alex had grinned. "Or we could just leave it there. A nice wee puzzle for Hooray Henry when he comes back next term."

"I don't think so. As soon as he realized his precious wheels weren't parked where he left them, he'd go to the police and drop us right in it. And our fingerprints are all over it."

He'd been right, Alex thought. There was no love lost between the Laddies fi' Kirkcaldy and the two Englishmen who shared their sixroom campus house. There was no way Henry would see the funny side of Weird helping himself to the Land Rover. Henry didn't see the funny side of much that his housemates did. So, Ziggy wouldn't tell. That was for sure.

But Mondo just might. Alex hoped Ziggy's warning had penetrated Mondo's self-absorption enough for him to think through the consequences. Telling the cops about Weird helping himself to someone else's car wouldn't get Mondo off the hook. It would only put all four of them firmly on it. Besides, he'd been driving it himself, taking that lassie home to Guardbridge. *For once in your life, think it through, Mondo.*

Now, if it was a thinker you wanted, Ziggy was your man. Behind the apparent openness, the easy charm and the quick intellect, there was a lot more going on than anyone knew. Alex had been pals with Ziggy for nine and a half years, and he felt as though he'd only scratched the surface. Ziggy was the one who would surprise you with an insight, knock you off balance with a question, make you look at something through fresh eyes because he'd twisted the world like a Rubik's Cube and seen it differently. Alex knew one or two things about Ziggy that he felt pretty sure were still hidden from Mondo and Weird. That was because Ziggy had wanted him to know, and because Ziggy knew his secrets would always be safe with Alex.

He imagined how Ziggy would be with his interrogators. He'd seem relaxed, calm, at ease with himself. If anyone could persuade the cops that their involvement with the body on Hallow Hill was entirely innocent, it was Ziggy.

Detective Inspector Barney Maclennan threw his damp coat over the nearest chair in CID office. It was about the size of a primary school classroom, bigger than they normally needed. St. Andrews wasn't high on Fife Constabulary's list of crime hotspots, and that was reflected in their staffing levels. Maclennan was head of CID out at the edge of the empire not because he lacked ambition but because he was a fully paid-up member of the awkward squad, the sort of bolshie copper senior officers liked best at a distance. Normally, he chafed at the lack of anything interesting to keep him occupied, but that didn't mean he welcomed the murder of a young lassie on his patch.

They'd got an ID right away. The pub Rosie Duff worked in was an occasional drop-in for some of the uniformed boys, and PC Jimmy Lawson, the first man at the locus, had recognized her immediately. Like most of the men at the scene, he'd looked shell-shocked and nauseous. Maclennan couldn't remember the last time they'd had a murder on his patch that hadn't been a straightforward domestic; these lads hadn't seen enough to harden them to the sight they'd come upon on the snowy hilltop. Come to that, he'd only seen a couple of murder victims himself, and never anything quite as pathetic as the abused body of Rosie Duff.

According to the police surgeon, it looked as if she'd been raped and stabbed in the lower abdomen. A single, vicious blow carving its lethal track upward through her gut. And it had probably taken her quite a while to die. Just thinking about it made Maclennan want to lay hands on the man responsible and beat the crap out of him. At times like this, the law felt more like a hindrance than a help when it came to achieving justice.

Maclennan sighed and lit a cigarette. He sat down at his desk and made notes of what little information he'd learned so far. Rosemary Duff. Nineteen years old. Worked in the Lammas Bar. Lived in Strathkinness with her parents and two older brothers. The brothers worked in the paper mill out at Guardbridge, her father was a groundsman up at Craigtoun Park. Maclennan didn't envy Detective Constable Iain Shaw and the WPC he'd sent up to the village to break the news. He'd have to talk to the family himself in due course, he knew that. But he was better employed trying to get this investigation moving. It wasn't as if they were swarming with detectives who had a clue about running a major inquiry. If they were going to avoid being pushed out to the sidelines by the big boys from headquarters, Maclennan had to get the show on the road and make it look good.

He looked impatiently at his watch. He needed another

CID man before he could start interviewing the four students who claimed they'd found the body. He'd told DC Allan Burnside to get back down to the station as soon as he could, but there was still no sign of him. Maclennan sighed. Goons and balloons, that was what he was stuck with out here.

He slipped his feet out of his damp shoes and swiveled round so he could rest them on the radiator. God, but it was a hell of a night to be starting a murder inquiry. The snow had turned the crime scene into a nightmare, masking evidence, making everything a hundred times more difficult. Who could tell which traces had been left by the killer, and which by the witnesses? That was assuming, of course, that those were separate entities. Rubbing the sleep from his eyes, Maclennan thought about his interview strategy.

All the received wisdom indicated he should speak first to the lad who'd actually found the body. Well-built lad, broad-shouldered, hard to see much of his face inside the big snorkel hood of the parka. Maclennan leaned back for his notebook. Alex Gilbey, that was the one. But he had a funny feeling about that one. It wasn't that he'd been exactly shifty, more that he'd not met Maclennan's eyes with the kind of piteous candour that most young lads in his shoes would have shown. And he certainly looked strong enough to carry Rosie's dying body up the gentle slope of Hallow Hill. Maybe there was more going on here than met the eye. It wouldn't be the first time a murderer had engineered the discovery of his victim's body to include himself. No, he'd let young Mr. Gilbey sweat a wee bit longer.

The desk sergeant had told him that the other interview room was occupied by the medical student with the Polish name. He was the one who had been adamant that Rosie had still been alive when they found her, claiming he'd done all he could to keep her that way. He'd seemed pretty cool in the circumstances, cooler than Maclennan would have managed. He thought he'd start there. Just as soon as Burnside showed his face.

· · ·

The interview room that housed Ziggy was the double of Alex's. Somehow, Ziggy managed to look comfortable in it. He slouched in his chair, half-leaning against the wall, his eyes fixed on the middle distance. He was so exhausted he could easily have fallen asleep, except that every time he closed his eyes, the image of Rosie's body flared brilliant in his mind. No amount of theoretical medical study had prepared Ziggy for the brutal reality of a human being so wantonly destroyed. He just hadn't known enough to be any use to Rosie when it mattered, and that galled him. He knew he should feel pity for the dead woman, but his frustration left no room for any other emotion. Not even fear.

But Ziggy was also smart enough to know he should be afraid. He had Rosie Duff's blood all over his clothes, under his fingernails. Probably even in his hair; he remembered pushing his wet fringe out of his eyes as he'd desperately tried to see where the blood was coming from. That was innocent enough, if the police believed his story. But he was also the man without an alibi, thanks to Weird's contrary notions of what constituted a bit of fun. He really couldn't afford for the police to find the best possible vehicle for driving in a blizzard with his fingerprints all over it. Ziggy was usually so circumspect, but now his life could be blown apart by one careless word. It didn't bear thinking about.

It was almost a relief when the door opened and two policemen walked in. He recognized the one who had told the uniforms to bring them to the station. Stripped of his overwhelming overcoat, he was a lean whippet of a man, his mousy hair a little longer than was fashionable. The stubbled cheeks revealed he had been rousted from bed in the middle of the night, though the neat white shirt and the smart suit looked as if they'd come straight from the dry cleaner's hanger. He dropped into the chair opposite Ziggy and said, "I'm Detective Inspector Maclennan and this is Detective Constable Burnside. We need to have a wee chat about what happened tonight." He nodded toward Burnside. "My colleague will take notes and then we'll prepare a statement for you to sign."

Ziggy nodded. "That's fine. Ask away." He straightened up in his seat. "I don't suppose I could get a cup of tea?"

Maclennan turned to Burnside and nodded. Burnside rose and left the room. Maclennan leaned back in his chair and checked out his witness. Funny how the mod haircuts had come back into fashion. The dark-haired lad opposite him wouldn't have looked out of place a dozen years earlier in the Small Faces. He didn't look like a Pole to Maclennan's way of thinking. He had the pale skin and red cheeks of a Fifer, though the brown eyes were a bit unusual with that coloring. Wide cheekbones gave his face a chiseled, exotic air. A bit like that Russian dancer, Rudolph Nearenough, or whatever his name was.

Burnside returned almost immediately. "It's on its way," he said, sitting down and picking up his pen.

Maclennan placed his forearms on the table and locked his fingers together. "Personal details first." They ran through the preliminaries quickly, then the detective said, "A bad business. You must be feeling pretty shaken up."

Ziggy began to feel as if he was trapped in the land of clichés. "You could say that."

"I want you to tell me in your own words what happened tonight."

Ziggy cleared his throat. "We were walking back to Fife Park . . ."

Maclennan stopped him with a raised palm. "Back up a bit. Let's have the whole evening, eh?"

Ziggy's heart sank. He was hoping he might avoid mentioning their earlier visit to the Lammas Bar. "OK. The four of us, we live in the same unit in Fife Park so we usually eat together. Tonight, it was my turn to cook. We had egg and chips and beans and about nine o'clock we went down into the town. We were going to a party later on and we wanted to have a few pints first." He paused to make sure Burnside was getting it down.

"Where did you go for your drinks?"

"The Lammas Bar." The words hung in the air between them.

Maclennan showed no reaction, though he felt his pulse quicken. "Did you often drink there?"

"Pretty regularly. The beer's cheap and they don't mind students, not like some of the places in town."

"So you'll have seen Rosie Duff? The dead girl?"

Ziggy shrugged. "I didn't really pay attention."

"What? A bonnie lassie like that, you didn't notice her?"

"It wasn't her that served me when I went up for my round."

"But you must have spoken to her in the past?"

Ziggy took a deep breath. "Like I said, I never really paid attention. Chatting up barmaids isn't my scene."

"Not good enough for you, eh?" Maclennan said grimly.

"I'm not a snob, Inspector. I come from a council house myself. I just don't get my kicks playing macho man in the pub, OK? Yes, I knew who she was, but I'd never had a conversation with her that went beyond 'Four pints of Tennent's, please.'"

"Did any of your friends take more of an interest in her?"

"Not that I noticed." Ziggy's nonchalance hid a sudden wariness at the line of questioning.

"So, you had a few pints in the Lammas. What then?"

"Like I said, we went on to a party. A third-year mathematician called Pete that Tom Mackie knows. He lives in St. Andrews, in Learmonth Gardens. I don't know what number. His parents were away and he threw a party. We got there about midnight and it was getting on for four o'clock when we left."

"Were you all together at the party?"

Ziggy snorted. "Have you ever been to a student party, Inspector? You know what it's like. You walk through the door together, you get a beer, you drift apart. Then when you've had enough, you see who's still standing and you gather them together and stagger off into the night. The good shepherd, that's me." He gave an ironic smile.

"So the four of you arrived together and the four of you

left together, but you've no idea what the others were doing in between?"

"That's about the size of it, yeah."

"You couldn't even swear that none of them left and came back later?"

If Maclennan had expected alarm from Ziggy, he was disappointed. Instead, he cocked his head to one side, thoughtful. "Probably not, no," he admitted. "I spent most of the time in the conservatory at the back of the house. Me and a couple of English guys. Sorry, I can't remember their names. We were talking about music, politics, that sort of thing. It got quite heated when we got on to Scottish devolution, as you can imagine. I wandered through a few times for another beer, went through to the dining room to grab something to eat, but no, I wasn't being my brothers' keeper."

"Do you usually all end up going back together?" Maclennan wasn't quite sure where he was going with this, but it felt like the right question.

"Depends if anybody's got off with somebody."

He was definitely on the defensive now, the policeman thought. "Does that happen often?"

"Sometimes." Ziggy's smile was a little strained. "Hey, we're healthy, red-blooded young men, you know?"

"But the four of you usually end up going home together? Very cozy."

"You know, Inspector, not all students are obsessed with sex. Some of us know how lucky we are to be here and we don't want to screw it up."

"So you prefer each other's company? Where I come from, people might think you were queer."

Ziggy's composure slipped momentarily. "So what? It's not against the law."

"That depends on what you're doing and who you're doing it with," Maclennan said, any pretense of amiability gone.

"Look, what has any of this got to do with the fact that we stumbled over the dying body of a young woman?" Ziggy demanded, leaning forward. "What are you trying to suggest? We're gay, therefore we raped a lassie and murdered her?"

"Your words, not mine. It's a well-known fact that some homosexuals hate women."

Ziggy shook his head in disbelief. "Well known to whom? The prejudiced and ignorant? Look, just because Alex and Tom and Davey left the party with me doesn't make them gay, right? They could give you a list of girls who could show you just how wrong you are."

"And what about you, Sigmund? Could you do the same thing?"

Ziggy held himself rigid, willing his body not to betray him. There was a world of difference the size of Scotland between legal and comprehended. He'd arrived at a place where the truth was not going to be his friend. "Can we get back on track here, Inspector? I left the party about four o'clock with my three friends. We walked down Learmonth Place, turned left up the Canongate then went down Trinity Place. Hallow Hill is a short cut back to Fife Park . . ."

"Did you see anyone else as you walked down toward the hill?" Maclennan interrupted.

"No. But the visibility wasn't great because of the snow. Anyway, we were walking along the footpath at the bottom of the hill and Alex started running up the hill. I don't know why, I was ahead of him and I didn't see what set him off. When he got to the top, he tripped and fell into the hollow. The next thing I knew was he was shouting to us to come up, that there was a young woman bleeding." Ziggy closed his eyes, but opened them hastily as the dead girl rose before him again. "We climbed up and we found Rosie lying in the snow. I felt her carotid pulse. It was very faint, but it was still there. She seemed to be bleeding from a wound to the abdomen. Quite a large slit, it felt like. Maybe three or four inches long. I told Alex to go and get help. To call the police. We covered her with our coats and I tried to put pressure on the wound. But it was too late. Too much internal damage. Too much blood loss. She died within a couple of minutes." He gave a long exhalation. "There was nothing I could do."

Even Maclennan was momentarily silenced by the intensity of Ziggy's words. He glanced at Burnside, who was scribbling furiously. "Why did you ask Alex Gilbey to go for help?"

"Because Alex was more sober than Tom. And Davey tends to go to pieces in a crisis."

It made perfect sense. Almost too perfect. Maclennan pushed his chair back. "One of my officers will take you home now, Mr. Malkiewicz. We'll want the clothes you're wearing, for forensic analysis. And your fingerprints, for the purposes of elimination. And we'll be wanting to talk to you again." There were things Maclennan wanted to know about Sigmund Malkiewicz. But they could wait. His feeling of unease about these four young men was growing stronger by the minute. He wanted to start pushing. And he had a feeling that the one who went to pieces in a crisis might just be the one to cave in.

CHAPTER
THREE

The poetry of Baudelaire seemed to be doing the trick. Curled into a ball on a mattress so hard it scarcely deserved the name, Mondo was mentally working his way through *Les Fleurs du Mal*. It seemed ironically appropriate in the light of the night's events. The musical flow of the language soothed him, rubbing away the reality of Rosie Duff's death and the police cell it had brought him to. It was transcendent, raising him out of his body and into another place where the smooth sequence of syllables was all his consciousness could accommodate. He didn't want to deal with death, or guilt, or fear, or suspicion.

His hiding place imploded abruptly with the crashing open of the cell door. PC Jimmy Lawson loomed above him. "On your feet, son. You're wanted."

Mondo scrambled back, away from the young policeman who had somehow changed from rescuer to persecutor.

Lawson's smile was far from soothing. "Don't get your bowels in a confusion. Come on, look lively. Inspector Maclennan doesn't like being kept waiting."

Mondo edged to his feet and followed Lawson out of the cell and into a brightly lit corridor. It was all too sharp, too defined for Mondo's taste. He really didn't like it here.

Lawson turned a bend in the corridor then flung a door open. Mondo hesitated on the threshold. Sitting at the table was the man he'd seen up on Hallow Hill. He looked too small to be a copper, Mondo thought. "Mr. Kerr, is it?" the man asked.

Mondo nodded. "Aye," he said. The sound of his own voice surprised him.

"Come in and sit down. I'm DI Maclennan, this is DC Burnside."

Mondo sat down opposite the two men, keeping his eyes on the table top. Burnside took him through the formalities with a politeness that surprised Mondo, who had expected *The Sweeney*: all shouting and macho swaggering.

When Maclennan took over, a note of sharpness entered the conversation. "You knew Rosie Duff," he said.

"Aye." Mondo still didn't look up. "Well, I knew she was the barmaid at the Lammas," he added as the silence grew around them.

"Nice looking lassie," Maclennan said. Mondo did not respond. "You must have noticed that, at least."

Mondo shrugged. "I didn't give her any thought."

"Was she not your type?"

Mondo looked up, his mouth hitched up in one corner in a half-smile. "I think I definitely wasn't her type. She never took any notice of me. There were always other guys she was more interested in. I always had to wait to get served in the Lammas."

"That must have annoyed you."

Panic flashed in Mondo's eyes. He was beginning to understand that Maclennan was sharper than he had expected a copper to be. He was going to have to box clever and keep his wits about him. "Not really. If we were in a hurry, I just used to get Gilly to go up when it was my round."

"Gilly? That would be Alex Gilbey?"

Mondo nodded, dropping his eyes again. He didn't want to let this man see any of the emotions churning inside him. *Death, guilt, fear, suspicion.* He desperately wanted to be out of this, out of the police station, out of the case. He didn't want to drop anyone else in it in the process, but he couldn't take this. He knew he couldn't take it, and he didn't want to end up acting in a way that would make these cops think there was something suspicious about him, something guilty. Because he wasn't the suspicious one. He hadn't chatted up Rosie Duff, much as he might have wanted to. He hadn't stolen a Land Rover. All he'd done was borrow it to drive a lassie home to Guardbridge. He hadn't stumbled over a body in the snow. That was down to Alex. It was thanks to the others he was in the middle of this shit. If keeping himself secure meant making the cops look elsewhere, well, Gilly would never find out. Even if he did, Mondo was sure Gilly would forgive him.

"So she liked Gilly, did she?" Maclennan was relentless.

"I don't know. Far as I'm aware, he was just another customer to her."

"But one she paid more attention to than she did to you."

"Aye, well, that didn't exactly make him unique."

"Are you saying Rosie was a bit of a flirt?"

Mondo shook his head, impatient at himself. "No. Not at all. It was her job. She was a barmaid, she had to be nice to people."

"But not to you."

Mondo tugged nervously at the ringlets falling round his ears. "You're twisting this. Look, she was nothing to me, I was nothing to her. Now, can I go, please?"

"Not quite yet, Mr. Kerr. Whose idea was it tonight to come back via Hallow Hill?"

Mondo frowned. "It wasn't anybody's idea. That's just the quickest route from where we were back to Fife Park. We often walk back that way. Nobody gave it a second thought."

"And did any of you ever feel the need to run up to the Pictish cemetery before?"

Mondo shook his head. "We knew it was there, we went up to look at it when they were excavating it. Like half of St. Andrews. Doesnae make us weirdos, you know."

"I never said it did. But you never made a detour there on the way back to your residence before?"

"Why would we?"

Maclennan shrugged. "I don't know. Daft boys games. Maybe you've watched *Carrie* a few too many times."

Mondo tugged at a lock of his hair. *Death, guilt, fear, suspicion.* "I'm not interested in horror films. Look, Inspector, you're reading this all wrong. We're just four ordinary guys that walked into the middle of something extraordinary. Nothing more, nothing less." He spread his hands in a gesture of innocence that he prayed was convincing. "I'm sorry for what happened to the lassie, but it's got nothing to do with me."

Maclennan leaned back in his chair. "So you say." Mondo said nothing, simply letting his breath out in a long sigh of frustration. "What about the party? What were your movements there?"

Mondo twisted sideways in his seat, his desire for escape obvious in every muscle. Would the lassie talk? He doubted it. She'd had to sneak in to the house, she'd been supposed to be home hours before. And she wasn't a student, had known almost nobody there. With a bit of luck, she'd never be mentioned, never questioned. "Look, why do you care about this? We just found a body, you know?"

"We have to explore all the possibilities."

Mondo sneered. "Just doing your job, eh? Well, you're wasting your time if you think we had anything to do with what happened to her."

Maclennan shrugged. "Nevertheless, I'd like to know about the party."

Stomach churning, Mondo produced an edited version he hoped would pass muster. "I don't know. It's hard to remember every detail. Not long after we arrived, I was chatting up this lassie. Marg, her name was. From Elgin. We danced for a while. I thought I was in there, you know?" He pulled a rueful face. "Then her boyfriend turned up. She hadn't mentioned him before. I was pretty fed up, so I had a couple more beers, then I went upstairs. There was this wee study, just a boxroom really, with a desk and a chair. I sat there feeling sorry for myself for a bit. Not long, just the time it took to drink a can. Then I went back downstairs and mooched around. Ziggy was giving some English guys his Declaration of Arbroath speech in the conservatory, so I didn't hang around there. I've heard it too many times. I didn't really pay attention to anybody else. There wasn't much in the way of talent, and what there was was spoken for, so I just hung around. Tell you the truth, I was ready to go ages before we finally left."

"But you didn't suggest leaving?"

"No."

"Why not? Don't you have a mind of your own?"

Mondo gave him a look of loathing. It wasn't the first time he'd been accused of following the others around like a mindless sheep. "Of course I do. I just couldn't be bothered, OK?"

"Fine," Maclennan said. "We'll be checking your story out. You can go home now. We'll want the clothes you were wearing tonight. There'll be an officer at your residence to take them from you." He stood up, the chair legs grating on the floor in a screech that set Mondo's teeth on edge. "We'll be in touch, Mr. Kerr."

WPC Janice Hogg closed the door of the panda car as quietly as she could. No need to wake the whole street. They'd hear the news soon enough. She flinched as DC Iain Shaw slammed the driver's door without a thought and directed a glare at the back of his balding head. Only twenty-five and already he had an old man's hairline, she thought with a flash of smug pleasure. And him thinking he was such a catch.

As if the tenor of her thoughts had penetrated his skull, Shaw turned and scowled. "Come on, then. Let's get it over with."

Janice gave the cottage the once-over as Shaw pushed open the wooden gate and walked briskly up the short path. It was typical of the area; a low building with a couple of dormer windows thrusting out of the pantile roof, crowstepped gables dressed with snow. A small porch thrust out between the downstairs windows, the harling painted some dun color that was hard to identify in the weak light shed by the street-lamps. It looked well enough kept, she reckoned, wondering which room had been Rosie's.

Janice put the thought from her mind as she prepared herself for the coming ordeal. She'd been brought in to deliver the bad news on more than her fair share of occasions. It came with the gender. She braced herself as Shaw banged the heavy iron knocker on the door. At first, nothing stirred. Then a muted light glowed behind the curtains at the right-hand downstairs window. A hand appeared, pulling the curtain to one side. Next, a face, lit on one side. A man in late middle age, hair graying and tousled, stared open-mouthed at the pair of them.

Shaw produced his warrant card and held it out. There was nomistaking the gesture. The curtain fell back. A couple of moments later, the front door opened to reveal the man, tying the cord of a thick woolen dressing gown round his waist. The legs of his pajamas pooled over faded tartan slippers. "What's going on?" he demanded, hiding apprehension imperfectly behind belligerence.

"Mr. Duff?" Shaw asked.

"Aye, that's me. What are you doing at my door at this hour?"

"I'm Detective Constable Shaw, and this is WPC Hogg. Can we come in, Mr. Duff? We need to talk to you."

"What have they laddies of mine been up to?" He stood back and waved them inside. The inner door gave straight on to the living room. A three-piece suite covered in brown corduroy laid siege to the biggest TV set Janice had ever seen. "Have a seat," he said.

As they made for the sofa, Eileen Duff emerged from the door at the far end of the room. "What's going on, Archie?" she asked. Her naked face was greasy with night cream, her hair covered in a beige chiffon scarf to protect her shampoo and set. Her quilted nylon housecoat was buttoned awry.

"It's the polis," her husband said.

The woman's eyes were wide with anxiety. "What's the matter?"

"Could you come and sit down, Mrs. Duff?" Janice said, crossing to the woman and taking her elbow. She steered her to the sofa and gestured to her husband that he should join her there.

"It's bad news, I can tell," the woman said piteously, clutching at her husband's arm. Archie Duff stared impassively at the blank TV screen, lips pressed tightly together.

"I'm very sorry, Mrs. Duff. But I'm afraid you're right. We do have some very bad news for you." Shaw stood awkwardly, head slightly bowed, eyes on the multicolored swirls of the carpet.

Mrs. Duff pushed her husband. "I told you not to let Brian buy that motorbike. I told you."

Shaw cast a glance of appeal at Janice. She took a step closer to the Duffs and said gently, "It's not Brian. It's Rosie."

A soft mewing noise came from Mrs. Duff.

"That cannae be right," Mr. Duff protested.

Janice forced herself to continue. "Earlier tonight, the body of a young woman was found on Hallow Hill."

"There's been some mistake," Archie Duff said stubbornly.

"I'm afraid not. Some of the officers at the scene recognized Rosie. They knew her from the Lammas Bar. I'm very sorry to have to tell you that your daughter is dead."

Janice had delivered the blow often enough to know that most people fell into one of two reactions. Denial, like Archie Duff. And overwhelming grief that hit the surviving relatives like an elemental force of nature. Eileen Duff threw her head back and roared her pain at the ceiling, her hands twisting and wringing in her lap, her whole body possessed by anguish. Her husband stared at her as if she were a stranger, his brows drawn down in a firm refusal to acknowledge what was happening.

Janice stood there, letting the first wave break over her like a spring tide on the West Sands. Shaw shifted from one foot to the other, unsure what to say next.

Suddenly there were heavy footfalls on the stairs that led

off one end of the room. Legs clad in pajama bottoms appeared, followed by a naked torso then a sleepy face topped with a shock of tousled dark hair. The young man stopped a couple of steps from the bottom and surveyed the scene. "What the hell's going on?" he grunted.

Without turning his head, Archie said, "Your sister's dead, Colin."

Colin Duff's mouth fell open. "What?"

Janice stepped into the breach again. "I'm very sorry, Colin. But your sister's body was found a short while ago."

"Where about? What happened? What do you mean, her body was found?" The words tumbled out as his legs gave way and he crumpled onto the bottom tread of the stairs.

"She was found on Hallow Hill." Janice took a deep breath. "We believe that Rosie was murdered."

Colin dropped his head into his hands. "Oh Jesus," he whispered over and over again.

Shaw leaned forward. "We're going to need to ask you some questions, Mr. Duff. Could we maybe go through to the kitchen?"

Eileen's first paroxysm of grief was easing now. She'd stopped wailing and turned her tear-streaked face to Archie.

"Bide here. I'm no' a bairn that needs to be kept from the truth," she gulped.

"Have you got some brandy?" Janice asked. Archie looked blank. "Or some whiskey?"

Colin stumbled to his feet. "There's a bottle in the scullery. I'll get it."

Eileen turned her swollen eyes to Janice. "What happened to my Rosie?"

"We can't be certain yet. It appears that she was stabbed. But we'll need to wait for the doctor before we can be sure."

At her words, Eileen recoiled as if she herself had been struck. "Who would do a thing like that to Rosie? Her that wouldnae hurt a fly."

"We don't know that yet either," Shaw chipped in. "But we'll find him, Mrs. Duff. We'll find him. I know this is the worst time in the world to be asking you questions, but the sooner we get the information we need, the quicker we can make progress."

"Can I see her?" Eileen asked.

"We'll arrange for that later today," Janice said. She crouched down beside Eileen and put a comforting hand on her arm. "What time did Rosie usually come in?"

Colin emerged from the kitchen carrying a bottle of Bells and three glasses. "The Lammas has last orders at half-past ten. Most nights, she was in by quarter-past eleven." He put the glasses down on the coffee table and poured three stiff measures.

"But some nights she was later?" Shaw asked.

Colin handed his parents a whiskey each. Archie downed half of his in one gulp. Eileen clutched the glass but didn't put it to her lips. "Aye. If she was going to a party or something."

"And last night?"

Colin swallowed some whiskey. "I don't know. Mum? Did she say anything to you?"

Eileen looked up at him, her expression dazed and lost. "She said she was meeting some friends. She didnae say who, and I didnae ask. She's got a right to her own life." There was a defensive tone in her voice that told Janice this had been a bone of contention, probably with Archie.

"How did Rosie usually get home?" Janice asked.

"If me or Brian was in the town, we'd stop by at closing time and give her a lift. One of the other barmaids, Maureen, she'd drop her off if they were on the same shift. If she couldn't get a lift, she'd get a taxi."

"Where's Brian?" Eileen said suddenly, anxious for her chicks.

Colin shrugged. "He's not come home. He must have stayed down in the town."

"He should be here. He shouldnae hear this from strangers."

"He'll be back for his breakfast," Archie said roughly. "He needs to get ready for his work."

"Was Rosie seeing anybody? Did she have a boyfriend?"

Shaw let his eagerness to be away take over and shunt the interview back on the track he wanted.

Archie scowled. "She was never short of boyfriends."

"Was there anyone in particular?"

Eileen took a tiny sip of whiskey. "She's been going out with somebody lately. But she wouldnae tell me anything about him. I asked her, but she said she'd tell me in her own good time."

Colin snorted. "Some married man, by the sounds of it."

Archie glared at his son. "You keep a civil tongue in your heid when you talk about your sister, you hear me?"

"Well, why else would she keep it secret?" The young man's jaw jutted out defiantly.

"Maybe she didnae want you and your brother sticking your oar in again," Archie retorted. He turned to Janice. "They once gave a laddie a battering because they thought he wasnae treating Rosie right."

"Who was that?"

Archie's eyes widened in surprise. "That was years ago. It's got nothing to do with this. The laddie doesnae even live here anymore. He moved down to England not long after it happened."

"We'll still want his name," Shaw insisted.

"John Stobie," Colin said mutinously. "His dad's a greenkeeper at the Old Course. Like Dad says, he wouldnae dare go near Rosie."

"It's not a married man," Eileen said. "I asked her. She said she wouldnae bring trouble like that to our door."

Colin shook his head and turned away, nursing his whiskey. "I never saw her with anybody lately," he said. "But she liked her secrets, did Rosie."

"We'll need to take a look at her room," Shaw said. "Not just now. But later today. So if you could avoid moving anything in there, that would be helpful." He cleared his throat. "If you'd like, WPC Hogg can stay with you?"

Archie shook his head. "We'll manage."

"You might get reporters coming to the door," Shaw said. "It would be easier for you if you had an officer here."

"You heard my dad. We're better left to ourselves," Colin said.

"When can I see Rosie?" Eileen asked.

"We'll send a car up for you later. I'll make sure somebody calls you to arrange it. And if you remember anything Rosie said about where she was going tonight, or who she was seeing, please let us know. It would be helpful if you could make a list of her friends. Especially anyone who might know where she was last night and who she was with. Can you do that for us?" Shaw was gentle now he could see his escape route clear.

Archie nodded and got to his feet. "Later. We'll do it."

Janice stood up, her knees complaining at their prolonged crouch. "We'll see ourselves out."

She followed Shaw to the door. The misery in the room felt like a tangible substance, filling the air and making it hard to breathe. It was always the same. The melancholy seemed to grow incrementally in those first hours after the news arrived.

But that would change. Soon enough, the anger would come.

CHAPTER
FOUR

Weird glared at Maclennan, skinny arms folded across his narrow chest. "I want a smoke," he said. The acid he'd taken earlier had worn off, leaving him jittery and fractious. He didn't want to be here, and he was determined to get out as quickly as he could. But that didn't mean he was going to give an inch.

Maclennan shook his head. "Sorry, son. I don't use them."

Weird turned his head and stared at the door. "You're not supposed to use torture, you know."

Maclennan refused to rise to the bait. "We need to ask you some questions about what happened tonight."

"Not without a lawyer, you don't." Weird gave a small, inward smile.

"Why would you need a lawyer if you've got nothing to hide?"

"Because you're the Man. And you've got a dead lassie on your hands that you need to blame somebody for. And I'm not signing any false confessions, no matter how long you keep me here."

Maclennan sighed. It depressed him that the dubious antics of a few gave smart-arsed boys like this a stick to beat all cops with. He'd bet a week's wages that this self-righteous adolescent had a poster of Che Guevara on his bedroom wall. And that he thought he had first dibs on the role of working-class hero. None of which meant he couldn't have killed Rosie Duff. "You've got a very funny notion of the way we do things round here."

"Tell that to the Birmingham Six and the Guildford Four," Weird said, as if it were a trump card.

"If you don't want to end up where they are, son, I suggest you start cooperating. Now, we can do this the easy way, where I ask a few questions and you answer them, or we can lock you away for a few hours till we can find a lawyer who's that desperate for work."

"Are you denying me the right to legal representation?" There was a note of pomposity in Weird's voice that would have made the hearts of his friends sink if they'd heard it.

But Maclennan reckoned he was more than a match for some student on his high horse. "Please yourself." He pushed back from the table.

"I will," Weird said stubbornly. "I've got nothing to say to you without a lawyer present." Maclennan made for the door, Burnside on his tail. "So you get someone here, right?"

Maclennan turned at the open doorway. "That's not my job, son. You want a lawyer, you make the phone call."

Weird calculated. He didn't know any lawyers. Hell, he couldn't afford a lawyer, even if he'd known one. He could imagine what his dad would say if he phoned home and asked for help with the situation. And it wasn't an appealing thought. Besides, he'd have to tell a lawyer the whole story, and any lawyer paid for by his father would be bound to make a full report back. There were, he thought, far worse things than being nicked for stealing a Land Rover. "I tell you what," he said grudgingly. "You ask your questions. If they're as harmless as you seem to think, I'll answer them. But any hint you're trying to stitch me up, and I'm saying nothing."

Maclennan closed the door and sat down again. He gave Weird a long, hard stare, taking in the intelligent eyes, the sharp beaky nose and the incongruously full lips. He didn't think Rosie Duff would have seen him as a desirable catch. She'd probably have laughed at him if he'd ever propositioned her. That sort of reaction could breed festering resentment. Resentment that might have spilled over into murder. "How well did you know Rosie Duff?" he asked.

Weird cocked his head to one side. "Not well enough to know what her second name was."

"Did you ever ask her out?"

Weird snorted. "You've got to be joking. I'm a wee bit more ambitious than that. Small-town lassies with small-time dreams; that's not my scene."

"What about your friends?"

"Shouldnae think so. We're here precisely because we've got bigger ideas than that."

Maclennan raised his eyebrows. "What? You've come all the way from Kirkcaldy to St. Andrews to broaden your horizons? My, the world must be holding its breath. Listen, son, Rosie Duff has been murdered. Whatever dreams she had have died with her. So think twice before you sit here and patronize her."

Weird held Maclennan's stare. "All I meant was that our lives had nothing in common with hers. If it hadn't been for the fact that we stumbled across her body, you wouldn't even have heard our names in connection with this investigation. And frankly, if we're the best you can do in the way of suspects, you don't deserve to be called detectives."

The air between the two of them was electric with tension. Normally, Maclennan welcomed the raising of the stakes in an interrogation. It was a useful lever to get people to say more than they meant to. And he had a gut feeling that this young man was covering something with his apparent arrogance. It might be nothing of significance, but it might be everything that mattered. Even if all he'd gain by pushing him would be a sinus headache, Maclennan still couldn't resist. Just on the off chance. "Tell me about the party," he said.

Weird cast his eyes upward. "Right enough, I don't suppose you get invited to many. Here's how it goes. Males and females congregate in a house or a flat, they have a few bevvies, they dance to the music. Sometimes they get off with each other. Sometimes they even get laid. And then everybody goes home. That's how it was tonight."

"And sometimes they get stoned," Maclennan said mildly, refusing to let the boy's sarcasm rile him further.

"Not when you're there, I bet." Weird's smile was scornful.

"Did you get stoned tonight?"

"See? There you go. Trying to fit me up."

"Who were you with?"

Weird considered. "You know, I don't really remember. I arrived with the boys, I left with the boys. In between? I can't say I recall. But if you're trying to suggest I slipped away to commit murder, you're barking up the wrong tree. Ask me *where* I was and I can give you an answer. I was in the living room all night except for when I went upstairs for a piss."

"What about the rest of your friends? Where were they?"

"I haven't a clue. I am not my brothers' keeper."

Maclennan immediately noticed the echo of Sigmund Malkiewicz's words. "But you look out for each other, don't you?"

"No reason why you'd know that that's what friends do," Weird sneered.

"So you'd lie for each other?"

"Ah, the trick question. 'When did you stop beating your wife?' There's no call for us to lie for each other where Rosie Duff is concerned. Because we didn't do anything that needs lying about." Weird rubbed his temples. He wanted his bed so badly it was like a deep itch in his bones. "We just got unlucky, that's all."

"Tell me how it happened."

"Alex and me, we were mucking about. Pushing each other in the snow. He kind of lost his balance and carried on up the hill. Like the snow was making him excited. Then he tripped and fell and the next thing was, he was shouting at us to come up quick." For a moment, Weird's cockiness slipped and he looked younger than he was. "And we found her. Ziggy tried . . . but there was nothing he could do to save her." He flicked a smudge of dirt off his trouser leg. "Can I go now?"

"You didn't see anybody else up there? Or on the way there?"

Weird shook his head. "No. The crazed axe-murderer must have gone another way." His defenses were back in place, and Maclennan could see that any further attempts to extract information would likely be fruitless. But there would be another day. And he suspected there would be another way under Tom Mackie's defenses. He just had to figure out what that might be.

Janice Hogg slithered across the car park in Iain Shaw's wake. They'd been more or less silent on the drive back to the police station, each relating the encounter with the Duffs to their own lives with varying levels of relief. As Shaw pushed open the door leading into the welcome warmth of the station, Janice caught up with him. "I'm wondering why she wouldn't let on to her mum about who she was seeing," she said.

Shaw shrugged. "Maybe the brother was right. Maybe he was a married man."

"But what if she was telling the truth? What if it wasn't? Who else would she be secretive about?"

"You're the female here, Janice. What do you think?" Shaw carried on through to the cubbyhole occupied by the officer charged with keeping local intelligence up to date. The office was empty in the middle of the night, but the cabinets with their alphabetically arranged filing cards were unlocked and available.

"Well, if her brothers had a track record of warning off unsuitable men, I suppose I'd have to think about what sort of man Colin and Brian would consider unsuitable," she mused.

"And that would be what?" Shaw asked, pulling open the drawer marked "D." His fingers, surprisingly long and slender, began to riffle through the cards.

"Well, thinking aloud . . . Looking at the family, that buttoned-up, Fife respectability . . . I'd say anybody they considered beneath her or above her."

Shaw glanced round at her. "That really narrows it down."

"I said I was thinking aloud," she muttered. "If it was some toerag, she'd probably think he could hold his own against her brothers. But if it was somebody a bit more rarefied . . ."

"Rarefied? Posh word for a woolly suit, Janice."

"Woolly suit doesn't mean woolly brain, DC Shaw. Don't forget you were in uniform yourself not so long ago."

"OK, OK. Let's stick to rarefied. You mean, like a student?" Shaw asked.

"Exactly."

"Like one of the ones that found her?" He turned back to his search.

"I wouldn't rule it out." Janice leaned against the doorframe. "She had plenty of opportunity to meet students at her work."

"Here we are," Shaw said, pulling a couple of cards out of the drawer. "I thought Colin Duff rang a bell with me." He read the first card, then passed it over to Janice. In neat handwriting, it read, *Colin James Duff. DoB: 5/3/55 LKA: Caberfeidh Cottage, Strathkinness. Employed at Guardbridge paper mill as forklift truck driver. 9/74 Drunk and disorderly, fined £25. 5/76 Breach of the peace, bound over. 6/78 Speeding, fined £37. Known associates: Brian Stuart Duff, brother. Donald Angus Thomson.* Janice turned the card over. In the same handwriting, but in pencil this time so it could be erased if ever called into evidence, she read, *Duff likes a fight when he's had a drink. Handy with his fists, handy at keeping out of the frame. Bit of a bully. Not dishonest, just a handful.*

"Not the sort of guy you'd want mixing it with your sensitive student boyfriend," Janice commented as she took the second file card from Shaw. *Brian Stuart Duff. DoB 27/5/57 LKA Caberfeidh Cottage, Strathkinness. Employed at Guardbridge paper mill as warehouseman. 6/75 Assault, fined £50. 5/76 Assault, three months, served at Perth. 3/78 Breach of the peace, bound over. Known associates: Colin James Duff, brother. Donald Angus Thomson.* When she flipped it over, she read, *Duff junior is a lout who thinks he's a hard man. Record would be a lot longer if big brother didn't drag him away before the trouble really gets going. He started early—John Stobie's broken ribs and arm in 1975 likely down to him, Stobie refused to give a statement, said he'd had an accident on his bike. Duff suspected of involvement in unsolved break-in at the off-license at West Port 8/78. One day he's going to go away for a long time.* Janice always appreciated the personal notes their local record-keeper appended to the official record. It helped when you were going out on an arrest to know if things were likely to turn ugly. And by the looks of it, the Duff boys could turn very ugly indeed. A pity really, she thought. Now she looked back, Colin Duff was rather hunky.

"What do you think?" Shaw asked, surprising her both because of her train of thought but also because she wasn't used to CID expecting her to be capable of joined-up thinking.

"I think Rosie was keeping quiet about who she was seeing because she knew it would provoke her brothers. They seem like a close family. So maybe she was protecting them as much as her boyfriend."

Shaw frowned. "How do you mean?"

"She didn't want them getting into more trouble. With Brian's record especially, another serious assault would get them both jail time. So she kept her mouth shut." Janice put the cards back in the file.

"Good thinking. Look, I'm going up to the CID room to write up the report. You go down to the mortuary and see about arranging a viewing for the family. The day shift can take the Duffs down, but it would be helpful if they know when that's likely to happen."

Janice pulled a face. "How come I get all the good jobs?"

Shaw raised his eyebrows. "You need to ask?"

Janice said nothing. She left Shaw in the intelligence office and headed for the women's locker room, yawning as she went. They had a kettle in there that the guys knew nothing about. Her body craved a hit of caffeine and if she was going to the mortuary, she deserved a treat. After all, Rosie Duff wasn't going anywhere.

Alex was on his fifth cigarette and wondering if the packet was going to last him when the door to his interview room finally opened. He recognized the thin-faced detective he'd seen up on Hallow Hill. The man looked a lot fresher than Alex felt. Hardly surprising, since it was getting on for breakfast time for most people. And Alex doubted very much if the detective was experiencing the dull ache of a fledgling hangover at the base of his skull. He crossed to the chair opposite, never taking his eyes off Alex's face. Alex forced himself to hold the policeman's gaze, determined not to let exhaustion make him look shifty.

"I'm Detective Inspector Maclennan," the man said, his voice clipped and brisk.

Alex wondered what the etiquette was here. "I'm Alex Gilbey," he tried.

"I know that, son. I also know you're the one that fancied Rosie Duff."

Alex felt a blush rising across his cheeks. "That's not a crime," he said. Pointless to deny what Maclennan seemed so certain of. He speculated which of his friends had betrayed his interest in the dead barmaid. Mondo, almost certainly. He'd sell his granny under pressure, then convince himself it was the best possible outcome for the old woman.

"No, it's not. But what happened to her tonight was the worst kind of crime. And it's my job to find out who did it. So far, the only person connected to the dead girl and also connected to the discovery of her body is you, Mr. Gilbey. Now, you're obviously a smart boy. So I don't have to spell it out for you, do I?"

Alex tapped nervously on his cigarette although there was no ash to dislodge. "Coincidences happen."

"Less often than you might think."

"Well, this is one." Maclennan's gaze felt like insects crawling under Alex's skin. "I just got unlucky, finding Rosie like that."

"So you say. But if I'd left Rosie Duff for dead on a freezing cold hillside and I was worried I'd maybe got some blood on me, and I was a smart boy, I'd engineer it so that I was the one who found her. That way, I've got the perfect excuse for being covered in her blood." Maclennan gestured at Alex's shirt, smeared with the dirty rust of dried blood.

"I'm sure you would. But I didn't. I never left the party." Alex was starting to feel genuinely scared. He'd been half expecting some awkward moments in the conversation with the police, but he hadn't expected Maclennan to go in so hard so soon. Clammy sweat coated his palms and he had to struggle against the impulse to wipe them on his jeans.

"Can you provide witnesses to that?"

Alex squeezed his eyes shut, trying to quiet the pounding in his head enough to remember his movements at the party. "When we got there, I was talking to a woman on my course for a while. Penny Jamieson, her name is. She went off for a dance, and I hung around in the dining room, just picking at the food. Various people were in and out, I didn't pay much attention. I was feeling a bit drunk. Later, I went into the back garden to clear my head."

"All by yourself?" Maclennan leaned forward slightly.

Alex had a sudden flash of memory that brought a flicker of relief in its wake. "Yes. But you'll probably be able to find the rose bush I was sick next to."

"You could have been sick any time," Maclennan pointed out. "If you'd just raped and stabbed someone and left her for dead, for example. That might make you sick."

Alex's moment of hope crashed and burned. "Maybe, but that's not what I did," he said defiantly. "If I had blood all over me, don't you think someone would have noticed when I went back into the party? I was feeling better after I'd thrown up. I went back inside and joined in the dancing in the living room. Any number of people must have seen me then."

"And we'll be asking them. We're going to need a list of everyone who was at that party. We'll be speaking to the host. And to everybody else we can trace. And if Rosie Duff showed her face, even for a minute, you and me will be having a much less friendly conversation, Mr. Gilbey."

Alex felt his face betray him again and hurriedly looked

away. Not soon enough, however. Maclennan pounced. "Was she there?"

Alex shook his head. "I never saw her after we left the Lammas Bar." He could see something dawning behind Maclennan's steady gaze.

"But you invited her to the party." The detective's hands gripped the edge of the table as he leaned forward, so close Alex could smell the incongruous drift of shampoo from his hair.

Alex nodded, too riven with anxiety to deny it. "I gave her the address. When we were in the pub. But she never turned up. And I never expected her to." There was a sob in his voice now, his tenuous control slipping as he remembered Rosie behind the bar, animated, teasing, friendly. Tears welled up as he stared at the detective.

"Did that make you angry? That she hadn't turned up?"

Alex shook his head. "No. I never really expected she would. Look, I wish she wasn't dead. I wish I hadn't found her. But you've got to believe me. I had nothing to do with it."

"So you say, son. So you say." Maclennan held his position, inches from Alex's face. All his instincts told him there was something lurking under the surface of these interviews. And one way or another, he was going to find out what it was.

CHAPTER
FIVE

WPC Janice Hogg glanced at her watch as she made for the front counter. Another hour and she'd be off duty, at least in theory. With a murder inquiry in full swing, the chances were she'd be stuck on overtime, particularly since women officers were thin on the ground in St. Andrews. She pushed through the swing doors into the reception area just as the street door was barged open so hard it bounced against the wall.

The force behind the door was a young man with shoulders almost as wide as the doorframe. Snow clung to his dark wavy hair and his face was wet either with tears, sweat or melted flakes. He hurtled toward the front counter, rage a deep growl in his throat. The duty constable reared back in shock, almost toppling off his high stool. "Where are they bastards?" the man roared.

To his credit, the PC managed to find some *sang froid* from the deepest recesses of his training. "Can I help you, sir?" he asked, moving out of reach of the fists that were pounding on the counter top. Janice hung back unnoticed. If this turned as nasty as it promised, she'd be best served by the element of surprise.

"I want those fucking bastards that killed my sister," the man howled.

So, Janice thought. The news had reached Brian Duff.

"Sir, I don't know what you're talking about," the PC said gently.

"My sister. Rosie. She's been murdered. And you've got them here. The bastards that did it." Duff looked as if he was about to clamber over the counter in his desperate desire for vengeance.

"Sir, I think you've been misinformed."

"Don't come it with me, you cunt," Duff screamed. "My sister's lying dead, somebody's going to pay."

Janice chose her moment. "Mr. Duff?" she said quietly, stepping forward.

He whirled round and glared at her, wide-eyed, white spittle at the corners of his mouth. "Where are they?" he snarled.

"I'm very sorry about your sister. But nobody's been arrested in connection with her death. We're still in the early stages of our investigation, and we're questioning witnesses. Not suspects. Witnesses." She put a cautious hand on his forearm. "You'd be better at home. Your mother needs her sons about her."

Duff shook off her hand. "I was told you'd got them locked up. The bastards that did this."

"Whoever told you made a mistake. We're all desperate to catch the person who did this terrible thing, and sometimes that makes people jump to the wrong conclusions. Trust me, Mr. Duff. If we had a suspect in custody, I would tell you." Janice kept her eyes on his, praying that her calm, unemotional approach would work. Otherwise he could break her jaw with a single blow. "Your family will be the first to know when we make an arrest. I promise you that."

Duff looked baffled and angry. Then suddenly, his eyes filled with tears and he slumped into one of the chairs in the waiting area. He wrapped his arms round his head and shook in a paroxysm of violent sobbing. Janice exchanged a helpless look with the PC behind the counter. He mimed the application of handcuffs but she shook her head and sat down next to him.

Gradually, Brian Duff regained his composure. His hands

dropped like stones into his lap and he turned his tear-stained face to Janice. "You'll get him, though? The bastard that's done this?"

"We'll do our best, Mr. Duff. Now, why don't you let me drive you home? Your mum was worried about you earlier. She needs to be reassured that you're all right." She got to her feet and looked down at him expectantly.

The rage had subsided for the moment. Meekly, Duff stood up and nodded. "Aye."

Janice turned to the duty constable and said, "Tell DC Shaw I'm taking Mr. Duff home. I'll catch up with what I'm supposed to be doing when I get back." Nobody was going to give her a hard time for acting on her own initiative for once. Anything that could be discovered about Rosie Duff and her family was grist to the mill right now, and she was perfectly placed to catch Brian Duff with his defenses down. "She was a lovely girl, Rosie," she said conversationally as she led Duff out of the front entrance and round the side to the car park.

"You knew her?"

"I drink in the Lammas sometimes." It was a small lie, expedient in the circumstances. Janice considered the Lammas Bar about as enticing as a bowl of cold porridge. A smoke-flavored one at that.

"I cannae take it in," Duff said. "This is the kind of thing you see on the telly. Not the kind of thing that happens to people like us."

"How did you hear about it?" Janice was genuinely curious. News generally traveled through a small town like St. Andrews at the speed of sound, but not usually in the middle of the night.

"I crashed at one of my pals last night. His girlfriend works the breakfast shift at the greasy spoon on South Street. She heard about it when she turned in for work at six and she got straight on the phone. Fuck," he exploded. "I thought it was some kind of stupid bad-taste joke at first. I mean, you would, wouldn't you?"

Janice unlocked the car, thinking, *No, actually, I don't have the sort of friends who would find that amusing.* She said, "You don't want to think even for a second that it could be the truth."

"Exactly," Duff said, climbing into the passenger seat. "Who would do a thing like that to Rosie, though? I mean, she was a good person, you know? A nice lassie. Not some slut."

"You and your brother kept an eye on her. Did you see anybody hanging around her that you didn't like the look of?" Janice started the engine, shivering as a blast of cold air gusted out of the vents. Christ, but it was a bitter morning.

"There were always lowlifes sniffing around. But everybody knew they'd have me and Colin to answer to if they bothered Rosie. So they kept their distance. We always looked out for her." He suddenly slammed one fist into the palm of his other hand. "So where were we last night when she really needed us?"

"You can't blame yourself, Brian." Janice edged the panda out of the car park on to the glassy compressed snow of the main drag. The Christmas lights looked sickly against the yellowish gray of the sky, the glamorous laser laid on by the university physics department an unremarkable pale scribble against the low clouds.

"I don't blame myself. I blame the bastard that did this. But I just wish I'd been there to stop it happening. Too fucking late, always too fucking late," he muttered obscurely.

"So you didn't know who she was meeting?"

He shook his head. "She lied to me. She said she was going to a Christmas party with Dorothy that she works with. But Dorothy turned up at the party I was at. She said Rosie had gone off to meet some bloke. I was going to give her what for when I saw her. I mean, it's one thing keeping Mum and Dad out of the picture. But me and Colin, we were always on her side." He rubbed his eyes with the back of his hand. "I cannae bear it. Last thing she said to me was a lie."

"When did you see her last?" Janice slewed to a halt at the West Port and edged forward onto the Strathkinness road.

"Yesterday, after I'd finished my work. I met her in the town, we went shopping for Mum's Christmas present. The three of us clubbed together to get her a new hairdrier. Then we went to Boots to get her some nice soap. I walked Rosie to the Lammas and that's when she told me she was going out with Dorothy." He shook his head. "She lied. And now she's dead."

"Maybe she didn't lie, Brian," Janice said. "Maybe she was planning to go to the party but something came up later in the evening." That was probably as truthful as the story Rosie had offered up, but Janice knew from experience that the bereaved would grasp at any straw that kept intact their image of the person they'd lost.

Duff acted true to form. Hope lit his face. "You know, that's probably it. Because Rosie wasn't a liar."

"She had her secrets, though. Like any girl."

He scowled again. "Secrets are trouble. She should have known that." Something struck him suddenly and his body tensed. "Was she . . . you know? Interfered with?"

Nothing Janice could say would offer him any comfort. If the rapport she appeared to have established with Duff was going to survive, she couldn't afford to let him think she too was a liar. "We won't know for sure until after the post mortem, but yes, it looks that way."

Duff smashed his fist into the dashboard. "Bastard," he roared. As the car fishtailed up the hill toward Strathkinness he turned in his seat. "Whoever did this, he better fucking hope you catch him before I do. I swear to God, I'll kill him."

The house felt violated, Alex thought as he opened the door into the self-contained unit the Laddies fi' Kirkcaldy had turned into their personal fiefdom. Cavendish and Greenhalgh, the two English former public schoolboys they shared the house with, spent as little time there as possible, an arrangement that suited everyone perfectly. They'd already gone home for the holidays, but today the braying accents that sounded so stridently posh to Alex would have been far more welcome than the police presence that seemed to dominate the very air he breathed.

Maclennan at his heels, Alex ran upstairs to the room

where he slept. "Don't forget, we want everything you're wearing. That includes underwear," Maclennan reminded him as Alex pushed the door open. The detective stood on the threshold, looking mildly puzzled at the sight of two beds in the tiny room that had clearly been designed for only one. "Who do you share with?" he demanded.

Before Alex could reply, Ziggy's cool tones cut through the atmosphere. "He thinks we're all queer for each other," he said sarcastically. "And that of course is why we murdered Rosie. Never mind the complete absence of logic, that's what's going on in his mind. Actually, Mr. Maclennan, the explanation is far more mundane." Ziggy gestured over his shoulder at the closed door across the landing. "Take a look," he said.

Curious, Maclennan seized Ziggy's invitation. Alex took the opportunity of his turned back to strip himself hastily, grabbing at his dressing gown to cover his embarrassment. He followed the other two across the landing and couldn't help a smug smile when he saw Maclennan's bemused expression.

"You see?" Ziggy said. "There's simply no room for a full drum kit, a Farfisa organ, two guitars and a bed in one of these rabbit hutches. So Weird and Gilly drew the short straws and ended up sharing."

"You boys are in a group, then?" Maclennan sounded like his father, Alex thought with a pang of affection that surprised him.

"We've been making music together for about five years," Ziggy said.

"What? You're going to be the next Beatles?" Maclennan couldn't let it go.

Ziggy cast his eyes heavenward. "There are two reasons why we're not going to be the next Beatles. For one thing, we play purely for our own pleasure. Unlike the Rezillos, we have no desire to be on *Top of the Pops*. The second reason is talent. We're perfectly competent musicians, but we haven't got an original musical thought between us. We used to call ourselves Muse until we realized we didn't have one to call our own. Now we call ourselves The Combine."

"The Combine?" Maclennan echoed faintly, taken aback by Ziggy's sudden access of confidentiality.

"Again, two reasons. Combine harvesters gather in everybody else's crop. Like us. And because of the Jam track of the same name. We just don't stand out from the crowd."

Maclennan turned away, shaking his head. "We'll have to search in there as well, you know."

Ziggy snorted. "The only lawbreaking you'll find evidence of in there is breach of copyright," he said. "Look, we've all cooperated with you and your officers. When are you going to leave us in peace?"

"Just as soon as we've bagged all your clothes. We'd also like any diaries, appointment books, address books."

"Alex, give the man what he wants. We've all handed our stuff over. The sooner we get our space back, the sooner we can get our heads straight." Ziggy turned back to Maclennan. "You see, what you and your minions seem to have taken no notice of is the fact that we have had a terrible experience. We stumbled on the bleeding, dying body of a young woman that we actually knew, however slightly." His voice cracked, revealing the fragility of his cool surface. "If we seem odd to you, Mr. Maclennan, you should bear in mind that it might have something to do with the fact that we've had our heads royally fucked up tonight."

Ziggy pushed past the policeman and took the stairs at a run, wheeling into the kitchen and slamming the door behind him. Maclennan's narrow face took on a pinched look around the mouth.

"He's right," Alex said mildly.

"There's a family up in Strathkinness who've had a far worse night than you, son. And it's my job to find some answers for them. If that means treading on your tender corns, that's just tough. Now, let's have your clothes. And the other stuff."

He stood on the threshold while Alex piled his filthy clothes into a bin liner. "You need my shoes as well?" Alex said, holding them up, his face worried.

"Everything," Maclennan said, making a mental note to tell forensics to take special care with Gilbey's footwear.

"Only, I've not got another decent pair. Just baseball boots, and they're neither use nor ornament in weather like this."

"My heart bleeds. In the bag, son."

Alex threw his shoes on top of the clothes. "You're wasting your time here, you know. Every minute you spend concentrating on us is a minute lost. We've got nothing to hide. We didn't kill Rosie."

"As far as I'm aware, nobody has said you did. But the way you guys keep going on about it is starting to make me wonder." Maclennan grabbed the bag from Alex and took the battered university diary he proffered. "We'll be back, Mr. Gilbey. Don't go anywhere."

"We're supposed to be going home today," Alex protested.

Maclennan stopped two steps down the stairs. "That's the first I've heard of it," he said suspiciously.

"I don't suppose you asked. We're due to get the bus this afternoon. We've all got holiday jobs starting tomorrow. Well, all except Ziggy." His mouth twitched in a sardonic smile. "His dad believes students need to work on their books in the school holidays, not stacking shelves in Safeway."

Maclennan considered. Suspicions based mostly on his gut didn't justify demanding that they remained in St. Andrews. It wasn't as if they were about to flee the jurisdiction. Kirkcaldy was only a short drive away, after all. "You can go home," he said finally. "Just as long as you don't mind me and my team turning up on your parents' doorsteps."

Alex watched him leave, dismay dragging him further into depression. Just what he needed to make the festive season go with a swing.

CHAPTER
SIX

The events of the night had caught up with Weird at least. When Alex went upstairs after a glum cup of coffee with Ziggy, Weird was in his usual position. Flat on his back, his gangling legs and arms thrown out from under the bedclothes, he shattered the relative peace of the morning with grumbling snores that mutated every now and again into a high-pitched whistle. Normally, Alex had no trouble sleeping to the strident soundtrack. His bedroom at home backed onto the railway tracks, so he'd never been accustomed to night silence.

But this morning, Alex knew without even trying that he'd never drop off with Weird's noises as a backdrop to his racing thoughts. Even though he felt light-headed with lack of sleep, he wasn't in the least drowsy. He gathered an armful of clothes from his chair, scrabbled under the bed for his baseball boots and backed out of the room. He dressed in the bathroom and crept downstairs, not wanting to wake Weird or Mondo. He didn't even want Ziggy's company for once. He paused by the coat hooks in the hall. His parka was gone with the police. That only left a denim jacket or a kagoule. He grabbed them both and headed out.

The snow had stopped, but the clouds were still low and heavy. The town seemed smothered in cotton wool. The world had turned monochrome. If he half-closed his eyes, the white buildings of Fife Park disappeared, the purity of the vista defeated only by the rectangles of blank windows. Sound had disappeared too, smothered under the weight of the weather. Alex struck out across what would have been grass toward the main road. Today, it resembled a track in the Cairngorms, flattened snow indicating where occasional vehicles had toiled past. Nobody who didn't absolutely have to was driving in these conditions. By the time he reached the university playing fields, his feet were wet and freezing, and somehow that felt appropriate. Alex turned up the drive and headed out toward the hockey pitches. In the middle of an expanse of white, he brushed a goalmouth backboard clear of snow and perched on it. He sat, elbows on knees, chin cupped in his hands and stared out over the unbroken tablecloth of snow until little lights danced in front of his vision.

Try as he might, Alex couldn't get his mind as blank as the view. Images of Rosie Duff flitted behind his eyes like static. Rosie pulling a pint of Guinness, serious concentration on her face. Rosie half turned away, laughing at some quip from a customer. Rosie raising her eyebrows, teasing him about something he'd said. Those were the memories he could just about cope with. But they wouldn't settle. They were constantly chased away by the other Rosie. Face twisted in pain. Bleeding on the snow. Gasping for her last breaths.

Alex leaned down and grabbed a couple of handfuls of snow, clenching them tight in his fists until his hands started to turn reddish purple with cold and drops of water ran down to his wrists. Cold turned to pain, pain to numbness. He wished there was something he could do to provoke the same response in his head. Turn it off, turn it all off. Leave a blank the brilliant white of the snowfield.

When he felt a hand on his shoulder, he nearly pissed himself. Alex stumbled forward and upward, almost sprawling in the snow but catching himself just in time. He whirled round, hands still fists against his chest. "Ziggy," he shouted. "Christ, you nearly scared the shit out of me."

"Sorry." Ziggy looked on the point of tears. "I said your name, but you didn't react."

"I didn't hear you. Christ, creeping up on people like that, you'll get a bad name, man," Alex said with a shaky laugh, trying to make a joke of his fear.

Ziggy scuffed at the snow with the toe of his wellies. "I know you probably wanted to be on your own, but when I saw you go out, I came after you."

"It's OK, Zig." Alex bent over and swept more snow off the backboard. "Join me on my luxurious couch, where harem girls will feed us sherbet and rose water."

Ziggy managed a faint smile. "I'll pass on the sherbet. It makes my tongue nip. You don't mind?"

"I don't mind, OK?"

"I was worried about you, that's all. You knew her better than any of us. I didn't know if you wanted to talk, away from the others?"

Alex hunched into his jacket and shook his head. "I've nothing much to say. I just keep seeing her face. I didn't think I could sleep." He sighed. "Hell, no. What I mean is, I was too frightened to try. When I was wee, a friend of my dad's was in an accident in the shipyard. Some sort of explosion, I don't know exactly what. Anyway, it left him with half a face. Literally. He had half a face. The other half's a plastic mask he has to wear over the burn tissue. You've probably seen him down the street or at the football. He's hard to miss. My dad took me to see him in the hospital. I was only five. And it freaked me out completely. I kept imagining what was behind the mask. When I went to sleep at night, I'd wake up screaming because he'd be there in my dreams. Sometimes when the mask came off, it was maggots. Sometimes it was a bloody mess, like those illustrations in your anatomy textbooks. The worst one was when the mask came off and there was nothing there, just smooth skin with the echoes of what should be there." He coughed. "That's why I'm frightened to go to sleep."

Ziggy put his arm round Alex's shoulders. "That's a hard

one, Alex. Thing is, though, you're older now. What we saw last night, that was as bad as it gets. There's really nothing much your imagination can do to make it worse. Whatever you dream now, it's not going to be half as bad as seeing Rosie like that."

Alex wished he could take more comfort from Ziggy's words. But he sensed they were only half true. "I guess we're all going to have demons to deal with after last night," he said.

"Some more practical than others," Ziggy said, taking his arm back and clasping his hands. "I don't know how, but Maclennan picked up on me being gay." He bit his lip.

"Oh, shit," Alex said.

"You're the only person I've ever told, you know that?" Ziggy's mouth twisted in a wry smile. "Well, apart from the guys I've been with, obviously."

"Obviously. How did he know?" Alex asked.

"I was being so careful not to lie, he spotted the truth in between the cracks. And now I'm worried that it's going to spread out further."

"Why should it?"

"You know how people love to gossip. I don't suppose cops are any different from anybody else in that respect. They're bound to talk to the university. If they wanted to put pressure on us, that would be one way to do it. And what if they come and see us at home in Kirkcaldy? What if Maclennan thinks it would be a smart move to out me to my parents?"

"He's not going to do that, Ziggy. We're witnesses. There's no mileage for him in alienating us."

Ziggy sighed. "I wish I could believe you. As far as I can see, Maclennan is treating us more like suspects than witnesses. And that means he'll use anything as a pressure point, doesn't it?"

"I think you're being paranoid."

"Maybe. But what if he says something to Weird or Mondo?"

"They're your friends. They're not going to turn their backs on you over that."

Ziggy snorted. "I tell you what I think would happen if Maclennan lets slip that their best mate is a poof. I think Weird will want to fight me and Mondo will never walk into a toilet with me again as long as he lives. They're homophobic, Alex. You know that."

"They've known you half their lives. That's going to count for a lot more than stupid prejudice. I didn't freak out when you told me," Alex said.

"I told you precisely because I knew you wouldn't freak out. You're not a knee-jerk Neanderthal."

Alex pulled a self-deprecating face. "It was a pretty safe bet, telling somebody whose favorite painter is Caravaggio, I suppose. But they're not dinosaurs either, Ziggy. They'd take it on board. Revise their world view in the light of what they know about you. I really don't think you should lose sleep over it."

Ziggy shrugged. "Maybe you're right. I'd prefer not to put it to the test, though. And even if they're all right, what happens if it gets out? How many out gays can you name in this university? All those English public schoolboys who spent their teens buggering each other, they're not out of the closet, are they? They're all running about with Fionas and Fenellas, securing the succession. Look at Jeremy Thorpe. He's standing trial for conspiring to murder his ex-lover, just to keep his homosexuality quiet. This isn't San Francisco, Alex. This is St. Andrews. I've got years before I qualify as a doctor, and I tell you now, my career is dead in the water if Maclennan outs me."

"It's not going to happen, Ziggy. You're getting things out of proportion. You're tired, and you said yourself, we've all had our heads fucked up by what's happened. I tell you what I'm a lot more concerned about."

"What's that?"

"The Land Rover. What the fuck are we going to do about that?"

"We'll have to bring it back. There's no other option. Otherwise it gets reported stolen, and we're in big trouble."

"Sure, I know that. But when?" Alex asked. "We can't do it today. Whoever dumped Rosie there must have had some sort of vehicle, and the one thing that makes us look less like suspects is that none of us has a car. But if we're spotted tooling around in the snow in a Land Rover, we go straight to number one on Maclennan's hit parade."

"Same thing applies if a Land Rover suddenly appears smack bang outside our house," Ziggy said.

"So what do we do?"

Ziggy kicked at the snow between his feet. "I suppose we just have to wait till the heat dies down, then I'll come back and shift it. Thank God I remembered about the keys in time to shove them into the waistband of my underpants. Otherwise we'd have been screwed when Maclennan made us turn out our pockets."

"You're not kidding. You sure you want to move it?"

"The rest of you have got holiday jobs. I can easily get away. All I have to do is make some excuse about needing the university library."

Alex shifted uneasily on his perch. "I suppose it has occurred to you that covering up the fact we had the Land Rover might just be letting a killer off the hook?"

Ziggy looked shocked. "You're not seriously suggesting . . . ?"

"What? That one of us could have done it?" Alex couldn't believe he'd given voice to the insidious suspicions that had wormed their way into his consciousness. Hastily, he tried to cover up. "No. But those keys were floating around at the party. Maybe somebody else saw a chance and took it . . ." His voice tailed off.

"You know that didn't happen. And in your heart, you know you don't really believe one of us could have murdered Rosie," Ziggy said confidently.

Alex wished he could be so sure. Who knew what went on in Weird's head when he was drugged up to the eyeballs? And what about Mondo? He'd driven that girl home, obviously thinking he was in there. But what if she'd knocked him back? He'd have been pissed off and frustrated, and maybe just drunk enough to want to take it out on another lassie who had knocked him back as Rosie had more than once in the Lammas. What if he'd come across her on his way back? He shook his head. It didn't bear thinking about.

As if sensing the thoughts in Alex's head, Ziggy said softly, "If you're thinking about Weird and Mondo, you have to include me in the list. I had just as much chance as them. And I hope you know what a ludicrous idea that is."

"It's insane. You'd never hurt anybody."

"Same goes for the other two. Suspicion's like a virus, Alex. You've picked it up off Maclennan. But you need to shake it off before it takes hold and infects your head and your heart. Remember what you know about us. None of that matches up with a cold-blooded killer."

Ziggy's words didn't quite dispel Alex's unease, but he didn't want to discuss it. Instead, he put his arm round Ziggy's shoulders. "You're a pal, Zig. Come on. Let's go into town. I'll treat you to a pancake."

Ziggy grinned. "Last of the big spenders, huh? I'll pass, if you don't mind. Somehow, I don't feel that hungry. And remember: All for one and one for all. That's not about being blind to each other's faults, but it is about trusting each other. It's a trust that's based on years of solid knowledge. Don't let Maclennan undermine that."

Barney Maclennan looked round the CID room. For once it was packed out. Unusually among plainclothes detectives, Maclennan believed in including the uniformed officers in his briefings on major cases. It gave them a stake in the investigation. Besides, they were so much closer to the ground, they were likely to pick up things detectives might miss. Making them feel part of the team meant they were more inclined to follow those observations through rather than put them to one side as irrelevant.

He stood at the far end of the room, flanked by Burnside and Shaw, one hand in his trouser pocket obsessively turning over coins. He felt brittle with tiredness and strain, but knew that adrenaline would keep him fired for hours to come. It was always the way when he was following his gut. "You know why we're here," he said once they'd settled down. "The body of a young woman was discovered in the early hours of this morning on Hallow Hill. Rosie Duff was killed by a single stab wound to her stomach. It's too early for much detail, but it's likely she was also raped. We don't get many cases like this on our patch, but that's no reason why we can't clear it up. And quickly. There's a family out there that deserves answers.

"So far, we've not got much to go on. Rosie was found by four students on their way back to Fife Park from a party in Learmonth Gardens. Now, they may be innocent bystanders, but equally they might be a hell of a lot more than that. They're the only people we know that were walking around in the middle of the night covered in blood. I want a team to check out the party. Who was there? What did they see? Have our lads really got alibis? Are there any chunks of time unaccounted for? What was their behavior like? DC Shaw will lead this team, and I'd like some of the uniformed officers to work with him. Let's put the fear of God into these partygoers.

"Now, Rosie worked in the Lammas Bar, as I'm sure a few of you know?" He looked around, seeing a handful of nods, including one from PC Jimmy Lawson, the officer who had been first on the scene. He knew Lawson; young and ambitious; he'd respond well to a bit of responsibility. "These four were drinking in there earlier in the evening. So I want DC Burnside to take another team and talk to everybody you can find who was in there last night. Was anybody taking particular notice of Rosie? What were our four lads doing? How were they acting? PC Lawson, you drink in there. I want you to liaise with DC Burnside, give him all the help you can to nail down the regulars." Maclennan paused, looking round the room.

"We also need to do door-to-door in Trinity Place. Rosie didn't walk to Hallow Hill. Whoever did this had some sort of transport. Maybe we'll get lucky and find the local insomniac. Or at least somebody who got up for a pee. Any vehicles seen on the move down that way in the early hours of the morning, I want to know about it."

Maclennan looked round the room. "Chances are Rosie knew the person who did this. Some stranger grabbing her off the street wouldn't have bothered to move her dying body. So we need to go through her life too. Her family and friends aren't going to enjoy that, so we need to be sensitive to their grief. But that doesn't mean we settle for coming back with half a tale. There's somebody out there who killed last night. And I want him brought to book before he gets the chance to do it again." There was a murmur of agreement through the room. "Any questions?"

To his surprise, Lawson raised a hand, looking faintly embarrassed. "Sir? I wondered if there was any significance in the choice of where the body was dumped?"

"How do you mean?" Maclennan asked.

"With it being the Pictish cemetery. Maybe this was some sort of satanic rite? In which case, could it not have been a stranger who just picked on Rosie because she fitted in with what he needed for a human sacrifice?"

Maclennan's skin crawled at the possibility. What was he thinking of, not to have considered this option? If it had occurred to Jimmy Lawson, it might well occur to the press. And the last thing he wanted was headlines proclaiming there was a ritual killer on the loose. "That's an interesting thought. And one we should all bear in mind. But not one we should mention outside these four walls. For now, let's concentrate on what we know for sure. The students, the Lammas Bar and the door-to-door. That doesn't mean closing our eyes to other possibilities. Let's get busy."

The briefing over, Maclennan walked through the room, pausing for a word of encouragement here and there as officers bunched around desks, organizing their tasks. He couldn't help hoping they could tie this to one of the students. That way, they might get a swift result, which was what counted with the public in cases like this. Even better, it wouldn't leave the town with the taste of suspicion on its tongue. It was always easier when the bad guys came from the outside. Even if the outside, in this instance, was a mere thirty miles away.

Ziggy and Alex got back to their residence with an hour to spare before they had to leave for the bus station. They'd walked down to check and had been assured that the country services were running, although the timetable was more honored in the breach than the observance. "You take your chances," the booking clerk had told them. "I can't guarantee a time, but buses there will be."

They found Weird and Mondo hunched over coffee in the kitchen, both looking disgruntled and unshaven. "I thought you were out for the count," Alex said, filling the kettle for a fresh brew.

"Fat fucking chance," Weird grumbled.

"We reckoned without the vultures," Mondo said. "Journalists. They keep knocking at the door and we keep telling them to piss off. Doesn't work, though. Ten minutes go by and there they are again."

"It's like a fucking 'knock, knock' joke in here. I told the last one if he didn't piss off, I'd knock his puss into the middle of next week."

"Mmm," said Alex. "And the winner of this year's Mrs. Joyful Prize for Tact and Diplomacy is . . ."

"What? I should have let them in?" Weird exploded. "These assholes, you have to talk to them in language they understand. They don't take no for an answer, you know."

Ziggy rinsed a couple of mugs and spooned coffee into them. "We didn't see anyone just now, did we, Alex?"

"No. Weird must have persuaded them of the error of their ways. If they come back, though, you don't think we should just give them a statement? It's not like we've got anything to hide."

"It would get them off our backs," Mondo agreed, but in the way that Mondo always agreed. He specialized in a tone of voice that managed to suggest doubt, always leaving himself a way out if he found himself accidentally swimming against the tide. His need to be loved colored everything he said, everything he did. That and his need to protect himself.

"If you think I'm talking to the running dogs of capitalist imperialism, you've another think coming." Weird, on the other hand, never left room for qualms. "They're scum. When did you ever read a match report that bore any resemblance to the game you'd just seen? Look at the way they ripped the piss out of Ally McLeod. Before we went to Argentina, the man was a god, the hero who was going to bring the World Cup home. And now? He's not good enough to wipe your arse with. If they can't get something as straightforward as football right, what chance have we got of getting away without being misquoted?"

"I love it when Weird wakes up in a good mood," Ziggy said. "But he's got a point, Alex. Better to keep our heads down. They'll have moved on to the next big thing by tomorrow." He stirred his coffee and made for the door. "I've got to finish my packing. We better give ourselves a bit of leeway, leave a bit earlier than usual. It's hard going underfoot and, thanks to Maclennan, none of us have got decent shoes. I can't believe I'm walking around in wellies."

"Watch out, the style police'll get you," Weird shouted after him. He yawned and stretched. "I can't believe how tired I am. Has anybody got any dexys?"

"If we did, they'd have been flushed down the toilet hours ago," Mondo said. "Are you forgetting the pigs have been crawling all over the place?"

Weird looked abashed. "Sorry. I'm not thinking straight. You know, when I woke up, I could almost believe last night was nothing more than a bad trip. That would have been enough to put me off acid for life, I tell you." He shook his head. "Poor lassie."

Alex took that as his cue to disappear upstairs and cram a last bundle of books in his holdall. He wasn't sorry to be going home. For the first time since he'd started living with the other three, he felt claustrophobic. He longed for his own bedroom; a door he could close that nobody else would think of opening without permission.

It was time to leave. Three holdalls and Ziggy's towering rucksack were piled in the hall. The Laddies fi' Kirkcaldy were ready to head for home. They shouldered their bags and opened the door, Ziggy leading the way. Unfortunately, the effect of Weird's hard words had apparently worn off. As they emerged on the churned-up slush of their path, five men materialized as if from nowhere. Three carried cameras, and before the foursome even realized what was happening, the air was thick with the sounds of Nikon motor drives.

The two journalists were coming round the flank of the photographers, shouting questions. They managed to make themselves sound like an entire press conference, so quick-fire were their inquiries. "How did you find the girl?" "Which one of you made the discovery?" "What were you doing on Hallow Hill in the middle of the night?" "Was this some sort of satanic rite?" And of course, inevitably, "How do you feel?"

"Fuck off," Weird roared at them, swinging his heavy bag in front of him like an overweight scythe. "We've got nothing to say to you."

"Jesus, Jesus, Jesus," Mondo muttered like a record stuck in the groove.

"Back indoors," Ziggy shouted. "Get back inside."

Alex, bringing up the rear, reversed hastily. Mondo tumbled in, almost tripping over him in his haste to get away from the insistent badgering and the clicking cameras. Weird and Ziggy followed, slamming the door behind them. They looked at each other, hunted and haunted. "What do we do now?" Mondo asked, voicing what they were all wondering. They all looked blank. This was a situation entirely outwith their limited experience of the world.

"We can't sit tight," Mondo continued petulantly. "We've got to get back to Kirkcaldy. I'm supposed to start at Safeway at six tomorrow morning."

"Me and Alex too," said Weird. They all looked expectantly at Ziggy.

"OK. What if we go out the back way?"

"There isn't a back way, Ziggy. We've only got a front door," Weird pointed out.

"There's a toilet window. You three can get out that way, and I'll stay put. I'll move around upstairs, putting lights on and stuff so they'll think we're still here. I can go home tomorrow, when the heat's died down."

The other three exchanged looks. It wasn't a bad idea. "Will you be all right on your own?" Alex asked.

"I'll be fine. As long as one of you rings my mum and dad and explains why I'm still here. I don't want them finding out about this from the papers."

"I'll phone," Alex volunteered. "Thanks, Ziggy."

Ziggy raised his arm and the other three followed suit. They gripped hands in a familiar four-way clasp. "All for one," Weird said.

"And one for all," the others chorused. It made as much sense now as it had when they'd first done it nine years before. For the first time since he'd stumbled over Rosie Duff in the snow, Alex felt a faint flicker of comfort.

CHAPTER
SEVEN

Alex trudged over the railway bridge, turning right into Balsusney Road. Kirkcaldy was like a different country. As the bus had meandered its way along the Fife Coast, the snow had gradually given way to slush, then to this biting gray damp. By the time the northeast wind made it this far, it had dumped its load of snow and had nothing to offer the more sheltered towns farther up the estuary but chilly gusts of rain. He felt like one of Breughel's more miserable peasants plodding wearily home.

Alex lifted the latch on the familiar wrought-iron gate and walked up the short path to the little stone villa where he'd grown up. He fumbled his keys out of his trouser pocket and let himself in. A blast of warmth enveloped him. They'd had central heating installed over the summer, and this was the first time he'd experienced the difference it made. He dumped his bag by the door and shouted, "I'm home."

His mother appeared from the kitchen, wiping her hands on a dishtowel. "Alex, it's lovely to have you back. Come away through, there's soup and there's stew. We've had our tea, I was expecting you earlier. I suppose it was the weather? I saw on the local news you'd had it bad up there."

He let her words wash over him, their familiar tone and content a security blanket. He hauled off his kagoule and walked down the hall to give her a hug. "You look tired, son," she said, concern in her voice.

"I've had a pretty terrible night, Mum," he said, following her back into the tiny kitchen.

From the living room, his father's voice. "Is that you, Alex?"

"Aye, Dad," he called back. "I'll be through in a minute."

His mother was already dishing up a plate of soup, handing him the bowl and a spoon. While there was food to be served, Mary Gilbey had no attention to be spared for minor details like personal grief. "Away and sit with your dad. I'll heat up the stew. There's a baked potato in the oven."

Alex went through to the living room where his father sat in his armchair, the TV facing him. There was a place set at the dining table in the corner and Alex sat down to his soup. "All right, son?" his father asked, not taking his eyes off the game show on the screen.

"No, not really."

That got his father's attention. Jock Gilbey turned and gave his son the sort of scrutiny that schoolteachers are adept at. "You don't look good," he said. "What's bothering you?"

Alex swallowed a spoonful of soup. He hadn't felt hungry, but at the first taste of homemade Scotch broth, he'd realized he was ravenous. The last he'd eaten had been at the party and he'd lost that twice over. All he wanted now was to fill his belly, but he was going to have to sing for his supper. "A terrible thing happened last night," he said between mouthfuls. "There was a girl murdered. And it was us that found her. Well, me, actually, but Ziggy and Weird and Mondo were with me."

His father stared, mouth agape. His mother had walked in on the tail end of Alex's revelation and her hands flew to her face, her eyes wide and horrified. "Oh, Alex, that's . . . Oh, you poor wee soul," she said, rushing to him and taking his hand.

"It was really bad," Alex said. "She'd been stabbed. And she was still alive when we found her." He blinked hard. "We ended up spending the rest of the night at the police station.

They took all our clothes and everything, like they thought we had something to do with it. Because we knew her, you see. Well, not really *knew* her. But she was a barmaid in one of the pubs we sometimes go to." Appetite deserted him at the memory, and he put his spoon down, his head bowed. A tear formed at the corner of his eye and trickled down his cheek.

"I'm awful sorry, son," his father said inadequately. "That must have been a hell of a shock."

Alex tried to swallow the lump in his throat. "Before I forget," he said, pushing his chair back. "I need to phone Mr. Malkiewicz and tell him Ziggy won't be home tonight."

Jock Gilbey's eyes widened in shock. "They've not kept him at the police station?"

"No, no, nothing like that," Alex said, wiping his eyes with the back of his hand. "We had journalists on the doorstep at Fife Park, wanting pictures and interviews. And we didn't want to talk to them. So me and Weird and Mondo climbed out the toilet window and went off the back way. We're all supposed to be working at Safeway tomorrow, see? But Ziggy's not got a job, so he said he'd stay behind and come home tomorrow. We didn't want to leave the window unlocked, you know? So I've got to phone his dad and explain."

Alex gently freed himself from his mother's hand and went through to the hall. He lifted the phone and dialed Ziggy's number from memory. He heard the ringing tone, then the familiar Polish-accented Scots of Karel Malkiewicz. Here we go again, Alex thought. He was going to have to explain last night once more. He had a feeling it wouldn't be the last time either.

"This is what happens when you fritter the nights away drinking and God knows what else," Frank Mackie said bitterly. "You get yourself in bother with the police. I'm a respected man in this town, you know. The police have never been at my door. But all it takes is one useless galloot like you, and we'll be the talk of the steamie."

"If we hadn't been out late, she'd have lain there till morning. She'd have died on her own," Weird protested.

"That's none of my concern," his father said, crossing the room and pouring himself a whiskey from the corner bar he'd had installed in the front room to impress those of his clients deemed respectable enough to be invited into his home. It was fitting, he thought, that an accountant should show the trappings of achievement. All he'd wanted was for his son to show some signs of aspiration, but instead, he had spawned a useless waster of a boy who spent his nights in the pub. What was worse was that Tom clearly had a gift for figures. But instead of harnessing that practically by going in for accountancy, he'd chosen the airy-fairy world of pure mathematics. As if that was the first step on the road to prosperity and decency. "Well, that's that. You're staying in every night, my lad. No parties, no pubs for you this holiday. You're confined to barracks. You go to your work, and you come straight home."

"But Dad, it's Christmas," Weird protested. "Everybody will be out. I want to catch up with my pals."

"You should have thought about that before you got yourself in trouble with the police. You've got exams this year. You can use the time to study. You'll thank me for it, you know."

"But Dad . . ."

"That's my last word on the subject. While you live under my roof, while I'm paying for you to go to the university, you'll do as you're told. When you start earning a living wage of your own, then you can make the rules. Till then, you do as I say. Now get out of my sight."

Fuming, Weird stormed out of the room and ran up the stairs. God, he hated his family. And he hated this house. Raith Estate was supposed to be the last word in modern living, but he thought this was yet another con perpetrated by, the gray men in suits. You didn't have to be smart to recognize that this wasn't a patch on the house they used to live in. Stone walls, solid wooden doors with panels and beading, stained glass in the landing window. That was a house. OK, this box had more rooms, but they were poky, the ceilings and doorways so low that Weird felt he had to stoop constantly to accommodate his six feet and three inches. The walls were paper thin too. You could hear someone fart in the next room. Which was pretty funny, when you thought about it. His parents were so repressed, they wouldn't know an emotion if it bit them on the leg. And yet they'd spent a fortune on a house that stripped everyone of privacy. Sharing a room with Alex felt more privileged than living under his parents' roof.

Why had they never made any attempt to understand the first thing about him? He felt as if he'd spent his whole life in rebellion. Nothing he achieved had ever cut any ice here because it didn't fit the narrow confines of his parents' aspirations. When he'd been crowned school chess champion, his father had harrumphed that he'd have been better off joining the bridge team. When he'd asked to take up a musical instrument, his father had refused point blank, offering to buy him a set of golf clubs instead. When he'd won the mathematics prize every single year in high school, his father had responded by buying him books on accountancy, completely missing the point. Maths to Weird wasn't about totting up figures; it was the beauty of the graph of a quadratic equation, the elegance of calculus, the mysterious language of algebra. If it hadn't been for his pals, he'd have felt like a complete freak. As it was, they'd given him a place to let off steam safely, a chance to spread his wings without crashing and burning.

And all he'd done in return was to give them grief. Guilt washed over him as he remembered his latest madness. This time, he'd gone too far. It had started as a joke, nicking Henry Cavendish's motor. He'd had no idea then where it might lead. None of the others could save him from the consequences if this came out, he realized that. He only hoped he wouldn't bring them down with him.

Weird slotted his new Clash tape into the stereo and threw himself down on the bed. He'd listen to the first side, then he'd get ready for bed. He had to be up at five to meet

Alex and Mondo for their early shift at the supermarket. Normally, the prospect of rising so early would have depressed the hell out of him. But the way things were here, it would be a relief to be out of the house, a mercy to have something to stop his mind spinning in circles. Christ, he wished he had a joint.

At least his father's emotional brutality had pushed the invasive thoughts of Rosie Duff to one side. By the time Joe Strummer sang "Julie's in the Drug Squad," Weird was locked in deep, dreamless sleep.

Karel Malkiewicz drove like an old man at the best of times. Hesitant, slow, entirely unpredictable at junctions. He was also a fair-weather driver. Under normal circumstances, the first sign of fog or frost would mean the car stayed put and he'd walk down the steep hill of Massareene Road to Bennochy, where he could catch a bus that would take him to Factory Road and his work as an electrician in the floor-covering works. It had been a long time since the disappearance of the pall of linseed oil that had given the town its reputation of "the queer-like smell," but although linoleum had plummeted out of fashion, what came out of Nairn's factory still covered the floors of millions of kitchens, bathrooms and hallways. It had given Karel Malkiewicz a decent living since he'd come out of the RAF after the war, and he was grateful.

That didn't mean he'd forgotten the reasons why he'd left Krakow in the first place. Nobody could survive that toxic atmosphere of mistrust and perfidy without scars, especially not a Polish Jew who had been lucky enough to get out before the pogrom that had left him without a family to call his own.

He'd had to rebuild his life, create a new family for himself. His old family had never been particularly observant, so he hadn't felt too bereft by his abandonment of his religion. There were no Jews in Kirkcaldy, he remembered someone telling him a few days after he'd arrived in the town. The sentiment was clear: "That's the way we like it." And so he'd assimilated, even going so far as to marry his wife in a Catholic church. He'd learned how to belong in this strange, insular land that had made him welcome. He'd surprised himself at the fierce possessive pride he'd felt when a Pole had become Pope so recently. He so seldom thought of himself as Polish these days.

He'd been almost forty when the son he'd always dreamed of had finally arrived. It was a cause for rejoicing, but also for a renewal of fear. Now he had so much more to lose. This was a civilized country. The fascists could never gain a hold here. That was the received wisdom, anyway. But Germany too had been a civilized country. No one could predict what might happen in any country when the numbers of the dispossessed reached a critical mass. Anyone who promised salvation would find a following.

And lately, there had been good grounds for fear. The National Front were creeping through the political undergrowth. Strikes and industrial unrest were making the government edgy. The IRA's bombing campaign gave the politicians all the excuses they needed for introducing repressive measures. And that cold bitch who ran the Tory party talked of immigrants swamping the indigenous culture. Oh yes, the seeds were all there.

So when Alex Gilbey had rung and told him his son had spent the night in a police station, Karel Malkiewicz had no choice. He wanted his boy under his roof, under his wing. Nobody would come and take his son away in the night. He wrapped up warmly, instructing his wife to prepare a flask of hot soup and a parcel of sandwiches. Then he set off across Fife to bring his son home.

It took him nearly two hours to negotiate the thirty miles in his elderly Vauxhall. But he was relieved to see lights on in the house Sigmund shared with his friends. He parked the car, picked up his supplies and marched up the path.

There was no answer to his knocking at first. He stepped gingerly on to the snow and looked in through the brightly lit kitchen window. The room was empty. He banged on the window and shouted, "Sigmund! Open up, it's your father."

He heard the sound of feet clattering down stairs, then the

door opened to reveal his handsome son, grinning from ear to ear, his arms spread wide in welcome. "Dad," he said, stepping barefoot into the slush to embrace his father. "I didn't expect to see you."

"Alex called. I didn't want you to be alone. So I came to get you." Karel clasped his son to his chest, the butterfly of fear beating its wings inside his chest. Love, he thought, was a terrible thing.

Mondo sat cross-legged on his bed, within easy reach of his turntable. He was listening, over and over again, to his personal theme, "Shine On, You Crazy Diamond." The swooping guitars, the heartfelt anguish of Roger Waters's voice, the elegiac synths, the breathy saxophone provided the perfect soundtrack for wallowing to.

And wallowing was exactly what Mondo wanted to do. He'd escaped the smother of his mother's concern that had swamped him as soon as he'd explained what had happened. It had been quite pleasant for a while, the familiar cocoon of concern spinning itself around him. But gradually, it had started to stifle him and he'd excused himself with the need to be alone. The Greta Garbo routine always worked with his mother, who thought he was an intellectual because he read books in French. It seemed to escape her notice that that's what you had to do when you were studying the subject at degree level.

Just as well, really. He couldn't have begun to explain the turmoil of emotion that threatened to swamp him. Violence was alien to him, a foreign language whose grammar and vocabulary he'd never assimilated. His recent confrontation with it had left him feeling shaky and strange. He couldn't honestly say he was sorry Rosie Duff was dead; she'd humiliated him in front of his friends more than once when he'd tried on the chat-up lines that seemed to work with other lassies. But he was sorry that her death had plummeted him into this difficult place where he didn't belong.

What he really needed was sex. That would take his mind off the horrors of the night before. It would be a sort of therapy. Like getting back on the horse. Unfortunately, he lacked the amenity of a girlfriend in Kirkcaldy. Maybe he should make a couple of phone calls. One or two of his exes would be more than happy to renew their relationship. They'd be a willing ear for his woes and it would tide him over the holidays at least. Judith, maybe. Or Liz. Yeah, probably Liz. The chubby ones were always so pathetically grateful for a date, they came across with no effort at all. He could feel himself growing hard at the thought.

Just as he was about to get off the bed and go downstairs to the phone, there was a knock at his door. "Come in," he sighed wearily, wondering what his mother wanted now. He shifted his position to hide his budding erection.

But it wasn't his mother. It was his fifteen-year-old sister Lynn. "Mum thought you might like a Coke," she said, waving the glass at him.

"I can think of things I'd rather have," he said.

"You must be really upset," Lynn said. "I can't imagine what that must have been like."

In the absence of a girlfriend, he'd have to make do with impressing his sister. "It was pretty tough," he said. "I wouldn't want to go through that again in a hurry. And the police were Neanderthal imbeciles. Why they felt the need to interrogate us as if we were IRA bombers, I'll never know. It took real guts to stand up to them, I can tell you."

For some reason, Lynn wasn't giving him the unthinking adoration and support he deserved. She leaned against the wall, her expression that of someone waiting for a break in the flow so she could get to what's really on her mind. "It must have," she said mechanically.

"We'll probably have to face more questioning," he added.

"It must have been awful for Alex. How is he?"

"Gilly? Well, he's hardly Mr. Sensitive. He'll get over it."

"Alex is a lot more sensitive than you give him credit for," Lynn said fiercely. "Just because he played rugby, you think he's all muscle and no heart. He must be really torn up about it, especially with him knowing the girl."

Mondo cursed inwardly. He'd momentarily forgotten the crush his sister had on Alex. She wasn't in here to give him Coke and sympathy, she was here because it gave her an excuse to talk about Alex. "It's probably just as well for him that he didn't know her as well as he'd have liked to."

"What do you mean?"

"He fancied her something rotten. He even asked her out. Now, if she'd said yes, then you can bet your bottom dollar that Alex would be the prime suspect."

Lynn flushed. "You're making it up. Alex wouldn't go around chasing barmaids."

Mondo gave a cruel little smile. "Wouldn't he? I don't think you know your precious Alex as well as you think."

"You're a creep, you know that?" Lynn said. "Why are you being so horrible about Alex? He's supposed to be one of your best friends."

She slammed out, leaving him to ponder her question. Why was he being so horrible about Alex, when normally he'd never have heard a word against him?

Slowly, it began to dawn on him that, deep down, he blamed Alex for this whole mess. If they'd just gone straight down the path, somebody else would have found Rosie Duff's body. Somebody else would have had to stand there and listen to her last breaths dragging out of her. Somebody else would feel tainted by the hours they'd spent in a police cell.

That he was now apparently a suspect in a murder inquiry was Alex's fault, there was no getting away from it. Mondo squirmed uncomfortably at the thought. He tried to push it away, but he knew you couldn't close Pandora's box. Once the idea was planted, it couldn't be uprooted and thrown aside to wither. This wasn't the time to be coming up with notions that would drive a wedge between them. They needed each other now as they had never done before. But there was no getting away from it. He wouldn't be in this mess if it wasn't for Alex.

And what if there was worse to come? There was no escaping the fact that Weird had been driving around in that

Land Rover half the night. He'd been taking girls for a spin, trying to impress them. He didn't have an alibi worth a shit, and neither did Ziggy, who had sneaked off and dumped the Land Rover somewhere Weird couldn't find it. And neither did Mondo himself. What had possessed him, borrowing the Land Rover to take that lassie back to Guardbridge? A quick fuck in the back seat wasn't worth the hassle he faced if somebody remembered she'd been at the party. If the police started asking questions of the other partygoers, somebody would shop them. No matter how much the students professed contempt for authority, somebody would lose their bottle and tell tales. The finger would point then.

Suddenly, blaming Alex seemed like the least of his worries. And as he turned over the events of the past few days, Mondo remembered something he'd seen late one night. Something that might just ease him off the hook. Something he was going to keep to himself for now. Never mind all for one and one for all. The first person Mondo owed any duty of care to was himself. Let the others look after their own interests.

CHAPTER
EIGHT

Maclennan closed the door behind him. With WPC Janice Hogg and him both in the room, it felt claustrophobic, the low slant of the roof hemming them in. This was the most pitiful element of sudden death, he thought. Nobody has the chance to tidy up after themselves, to present a picture they'd like the world to see. They're stuck with what they left behind the last time they closed the door. He'd seen some sad sights in his time, but few more poignant than this.

Someone had taken the trouble to make this room look bright and cheerful, in spite of the limited amount of light that came in at the narrow dormer window overlooking the village street. He could see St. Andrews in the distance, still looking white under yesterday's snow, though he knew the truth was different. Already, pavements were filthy with slush, the roads a slippery morass of grit and melt. Beyond the town, the gray smudge of the sea melted imperceptibly into the sky. It must be a fine view on a sunny day, he thought, turning back to the magnolia-painted woodchip and the white candlewick bedspread, still rumpled from where Rosie had last sat on it. There was a single poster on the wall. Some group called Blondie, their lead singer busty and pouting, her skirt impossibly short. Was that what Rosie aspired to, he wondered.

"Where would you like me to start, sir?" Janice asked,

looking around at the 1950s wardrobe and dressing table
which had been painted white in an effort to make them look
more contemporary. There was a small table by the bed with
a single drawer. Other than that, the only place where anything might be concealed was a small laundry hamper
tucked behind the door and a metal wastepaper bin under the
dressing table.

"You do the dressing table," he said. That way, he didn't
have to deal with the makeup that would never be used
again, the second-best bra and the old knickers thrust to the
back of the drawer for laundry emergencies that never happened. Maclennan knew his tender places, and he preferred
to avoid probing them whenever he could.

Janice sat on the end of the bed, where Rosie must have
perched to peer into the mirror and apply her makeup.
Maclennan turned to the dressing table and slid open the
drawer. It contained a fat book called *The Far Pavilions*,
which Maclennan thought was just the sort of thing his ex-
wife had used to keep him at bay in bed. "I'm reading, Barney," she'd say in a tone of patient suffering, brandishing
some doorstop novel under his nose. What was it with
women and books? He lifted out the book, trying not to notice Janice systematically exploring drawers. Underneath
was a diary. Refusing to allow himself optimism, Maclennan
picked it up.

If he'd been hoping for some confessional, he'd have
been sorely disappointed. Rosie Duff hadn't been a "Dear
Diary" sort of girl. The pages listed her shifts at the Lammas
Bar, birthdays of family and friends, and social events such
as, "Bob's party" "Julie's spree." Dates were indicated with
the time and place and the word, "Him," followed by a number. It looked like she'd gone through 14, 15 and 16 in the
course of the past year; 16 was, obviously, the most recent.
He first appeared in early November and soon became a regular feature two or three times a week. Always after work,
Maclennan thought. He'd have to go back to the Lammas
and ask again if anyone had seen Rosie meeting a man after
closing time. He wondered why they met then, instead of on

Rosie's night off, or during the day when she wasn't working. One or other of them seemed determined to keep his identity secret.

He glanced across at Janice. "Anything?"

"Nothing you wouldn't expect. It's all the kind of stuff women buy for themselves. None of the tacky things that guys buy."

"Guys buy tacky things?"

"I'm afraid you do, sir. Scratchy lace. Nylon that makes you sweat. What men want women to wear, not what they'd choose for themselves."

"So that's where I've been going wrong all these years. I should really have been buying big knickers from Marks and Spencer."

Janice grinned. "Gratitude goes a long way, sir."

"Any sign she was on the pill?"

"Nothing so far. Maybe Brian was on the money when he said she was a good girl."

"Not entirely. She wasn't a virgin, according to the pathologist."

"There's more than one way of losing your virginity, sir," Janice pointed out, not quite courageous enough to cast aspersions on a pathologist that everyone knew was more focused on his next drink and his retirement than on whoever ended up on his slab.

"Aye. And the pills are probably in her handbag, which hasn't turned up yet." Maclennan sighed and shut the drawer on the novel and the diary. "I'll take a look at the wardrobe." Half an hour later, he had to concede that Rosie Duff had not been a hoarder. Her wardrobe contained clothes and shoes, all in current styles. In one corner, there was a pile of paperbacks, all thick bricks of paper that promised glamour, wealth and love in equal measure. "We're wasting our time here," he said.

"I've just got one drawer to go. Why don't you have a look in her jewelry box?" Janice passed him a box in the shape of a treasure chest covered in white leatherette. He flipped open the thin brass clasp and opened the lid. The top tray contained a selection of earrings in a range of colors. They were mostly big and bold, but inexpensive. In the lower tray there was a child's Timex watch, a couple of cheap silver chains and a few novelty brooches; one looked like a piece of knitting, complete with miniature needles; one a fishing fly, and the third a brightly enameled creature that looked like a cat from another planet. It was hard to read anything significant into any of it. "She liked her earrings," he said, closing the box. "Whoever she was seeing wasn't the kind who gives expensive jewelry."

Janice reached to the back of her drawer and pulled out a packet of photographs. It looked as if Rosie had raided the family albums and made her own selection. It was a typical mixture of family photos: her parents' wedding picture, Rosie and her brothers growing up, assorted family groups spanning the last three decades, a few baby pictures and some snaps of Rosie with schoolfriends, mugging at the camera in their Madras College uniforms. No photo-booth shots of her with boyfriends. No boyfriends at all, in fact. Maclennan flicked through them then shoved them back in the packet. "Come on, Janice, let's see if we can find something a bit more productive to occupy us." He took a last look round the room that had told him far less than he'd hoped about Rosie Duff. A girl with a craving for something more glamorous than she had. A girl who kept herself to herself. A girl who had taken her secrets to the grave, probably protecting her killer in the process.

As they drove back down to St. Andrews, Maclennan's radio crackled. He fiddled with the knobs, trying to get a clear signal. Seconds later, Burnside's voice came through loud and clear. He sounded excited. "Sir? I think we've got something."

Alex, Mondo and Weird had finished their shift stacking shelves in Safeway, keeping their heads down and hoping nobody would recognize them from the front page of the *Daily Record*. They'd bought a bundle of papers and walked along the High Street to the café where they'd spent their early evenings as teenagers.

"Did you know that one in two adults in Scotland reads the *Record*?" Alex said gloomily.

"The other one can't read," Weird said, looking at the snatched picture of the four of them on the doorstep of their residence. "Christ, look at us. They might as well have captioned it, 'Shifty bastards suspected of rape and murder.' Do you suppose anybody seeing that wouldn't think we'd done it?"

"It's not the most flattering photo I've ever had taken," Alex said.

"It's all right for you. You're right at the back. You can hardly make out your face. And Ziggy's turning away. It's me and Weird that have got it full frontal," Mondo complained. "Let's see what the others have got."

A similar picture appeared in the *Scotsman*, the *Glasgow Herald* and the *Courier*, but thankfully on inside pages. The murder made it to the front page of all of them, however, with the exception of the *Courier*. Nothing as insignificant as a murder could shift the fatstock prices and small ads from their front page.

They sat sipping their frothy coffees, silently poring over the column inches. "I suppose it could be worse," Alex said.

Weird made an incredulous face. "Worse how, exactly?"

"They spelled our names right. Even Ziggy's."

"Big fat hairy deal. OK, I'll grant you they've stopped short of calling us suspects. But that's about all you can say in our favor. This makes us look bad, Alex. You know it does."

"Everybody we know is going to have seen this," Mondo said. "Everybody is going to be into our ribs about it. If this is my fifteen minutes of fame, you can stuff it."

"Everybody was going to know anyway," Alex pointed out. "You know what this town's like. Village mentality. People have got nothing else to keep them occupied but gossiping about their neighbors. It doesn't take the papers to spread the news around here. The plus side is that half the university lives in England, so they're not going to know anything about this. And by the time we get back after the New Year, it'll be history."

"You think so?" Weird folded the *Scotsman* shut with an air of finality. "I tell you something. We better be praying that Maclennan finds out who did this and puts him away."

"Why?" Mondo asked.

"Because if he doesn't, we're going to go through the rest of our lives as the guys that got away with murder."

Mondo looked like a man who's just been told he has terminal cancer. "You're kidding?"

"I've never been more serious in my puff," Weird said. "If they don't arrest anybody for Rosie's murder, all anybody's going to remember is that we're the four who spent the night at the police station. It's obvious, man. We're going to get a not proven verdict without a trial. 'We all know they did it, the police just couldn't prove it,'" he added, mimicking a woman's voice. "Face it, Mondo, you're never going to get laid again." He grinned wickedly, knowing he'd hit his friend where it hurt most.

"Fuck off, Weird. At least I'll have memories," Mondo snapped.

Before any of them could say more, they were interrupted by a new arrival. Ziggy came in, shaking rain from his hair. "I thought I'd find you here," he said.

"Ziggy, Weird says . . ." Mondo began.

"Never mind that. Maclennan's here. He wants to talk to the four of us again."

Alex raised his eyebrows. "He wants to drag us back to St. Andrews?"

Ziggy shook his head. "No. He's here in Kirkcaldy. He wants us to come to the police station."

"Fuck," Weird said. "My old man's going to go mental. I'm supposed to be grounded. He'll think I'm giving him the V-sign. It's not like I can tell him I've been at the cop shop."

"Thank my dad for the fact that we're not having to go to St. Andrews," Ziggy said. "He went spare when Maclennan turned up at the house. Read him the riot act, accusing him of treating us like criminals when we'd done everything we could to save Rosie. I thought at one point he was going to start battering him with the *Record*." He smiled. "I tell you, I was proud of him."

"Good for him," Alex said. "So where's Maclennan?"

"Outside in his car. With my dad's car parked right behind him." Ziggy's shoulders started shaking with laughter. "I don't think Maclennan's ever come up against anything quite like my old man."

"So we've got to go to the police station now?" Alex asked.

Ziggy nodded. "Maclennan's waiting for us. He said my dad could drive us there, but he's not in the mood for hanging around."

Ten minutes later, Ziggy was sitting alone in an interview room. When they'd arrived at the police station, Alex, Weird and Mondo had been taken to a separate interview room under the watchful eye of a uniformed constable. An anxious Karel Malkiewicz had been unceremoniously abandoned in the reception area, told abruptly by Maclennan that he'd have to wait there. And Ziggy had been shepherded off, sandwiched between Maclennan and Burnside, who had promptly left him to kick his heels.

They knew what they were doing, he thought ruefully. Leaving him isolated like this was a sure-fire recipe for unsettling him. And it was working. Although he showed no outward signs of tension, Ziggy felt taut as a piano wire, vibrating with apprehension. The longest five minutes of his life ended when the two detectives returned and sat down opposite him.

Maclennan's eyes burned into his, his narrow face tight with some suppressed emotion. "Lying to the police is a serious business," he said without preamble, his voice clipped and cold. "Not only is it an offense, it also makes us wonder what exactly it is you've got to hide. You've had a night to sleep on things. Would you care to revise your earlier statement?"

A chilly shock of fear spasmed in Ziggy's chest. They knew something. That was clear. But how much? He said nothing, waiting for Maclennan to make his move.

Maclennan opened his file and pulled out the fingerprint sheet that Ziggy had signed the previous day. "These are your fingerprints?"

Ziggy nodded. He knew what was coming now.

"Can you explain how they came to be on the steering wheel and gearstick of a Land Rover registered to a Mr. Henry Cavendish, found abandoned this morning in the parking area of an industrial unit on Largo Road, St. Andrews?"

Ziggy closed his eyes momentarily. "Yes, I can." He paused, trying to gather his thoughts. He'd rehearsed this conversation in bed that morning, but all his lines had deserted him now he was faced with this unnerving reality.

"I'm waiting, Mr. Malkiewicz," Maclennan said.

"The Land Rover belongs to one of the other students who shares the house with us. We borrowed it last night to get to the party."

"You borrowed it? You mean, Mr. Cavendish gave you his permission to ride around in his Land Rover?" Maclennan pounced, refusing to give Ziggy the chance to get into his stride.

"Not exactly, no." Ziggy looked off to one side, unable to meet Maclennan's stare. "Look, I know we shouldn't have taken it, but it was no big deal." As soon as the words were out of his mouth, Ziggy knew they were a mistake.

"It's a criminal offense. Which I'm sure you knew. So, you stole the Land Rover and took it to the party. That doesn't explain how it ended up where it did."

Ziggy's breath was fluttering in his chest like a trapped moth. "I moved it there for safety. We were drinking and I didn't want any of us to be tempted to drive it when we were drunk."

"When exactly did you move it?"

"I don't know exactly. Probably some time between one and two in the morning."

"You must have had quite a lot to drink by then yourself."

Maclennan was on a roll now, his shoulders hunched forward as he leaned into the interrogation.

"I was probably over the limit, yes. But . . ."

"Another criminal offense. So you were lying when you said you never left the party?" Maclennan's eyes felt like surgical probes.

"I was gone for as long as it took to move the Land Rover and walk back. Maybe twenty minutes."

"We've only got your word for that. We've been speaking to some of the other people at the party, and we've not had many sightings of you. I think you were away for a lot longer than that. I think you came across Rosie Duff and you offered her a lift."

"No!"

Maclennan continued relentlessly. "And something happened that made you angry, and you raped her. Then you realized that she could destroy your life if she went to the police. You panicked and you killed her. You knew you had to dump the body, but you had the Land Rover, so that wasn't a big deal. And then you cleaned yourself up and went back to the party. Isn't that how it happened?"

Ziggy shook his head. "No. You've got it all wrong. I never saw her, never touched her. I just got rid of the Land Rover before somebody had an accident."

"What happened to Rosie Duff wasn't an accident. And you were the one who made it happen."

Flushed with fear, Ziggy ran his hands through his hair. "No. You've got to believe me. I had nothing to do with her death."

"Why should I believe you?"

"Because I'm telling you the truth."

"No. What you're telling me is a new version of events that covers what you think I know. I don't think it's anything like the whole truth."

There was a long silence. Ziggy clenched his jaw tight, feeling the muscles bunching in his cheeks.

Maclennan spoke again. This time, his tone was softer. "We're going to find out what happened. You know that.

Right now, we've got a team of forensic experts going over every inch of that Land Rover. If we find one spot of blood, one hair from Rosie Duff's head, one fiber from her clothes, it'll be a very long time before you sleep in your own bed again. You could save yourself and your father a lot of grief if you just tell us everything now."

Ziggy almost burst out laughing. It was so transparent a move, so revealing of the weakness of Maclennan's hand. "I've got nothing more to say."

"Have it your own way, son. I'm arresting you for taking and driving away a motor vehicle without the owner's consent. You'll be bailed to report to the police station in a week's time." Maclennan pushed his chair back. "I suggest you get yourself a lawyer, Mr. Malkiewicz."

Inevitably, Weird was next up. It had to be the Land Rover, he'd decided as they'd sat in silence in the interview room. OK, he'd told himself. He'd hold his hand up, carry the can. He wasn't going to let the others take the blame for his stupidity. They wouldn't send him to jail, not for something so trivial. It would be a fine, and he could pay that off somehow. He could get a part-time job. You could be a mathematician with a criminal record.

He slouched in the chair opposite Maclennan and Burnside, a cigarette dangling from one corner of his mouth, trying to look casual. "How can I help?" he said.

"The truth would be a start," Maclennan said. "Somehow, it slipped your mind that you'd been joyriding in a Land Rover when you were supposed to be partying."

Weird spread his hands. "It's a fair cop. Just youthful high spirits, officer."

Maclennan slammed his hands down on the table. "This isn't a game, son. This is murder. So stop acting the goat."

"But that's all it was, really. Look, the weather was shite. The others went on ahead to the Lammas while I finished doing the dishes. I was standing in the kitchen looking out at the Land Rover, and I thought, why not? Henry's away back to England and nobody would be any the wiser if I borrowed it for a few hours. So I took it down to the pub. The other three were pretty pissed off with me, but when they saw the way the snow was coming down, they decided it wasn't such a bad idea after all. So we took it to the party. Ziggy moved it later, to save me from making a complete arse of myself. And that's all there is to it." He shrugged. "Honest. We didn't tell you before because we didn't want to waste your time over something and nothing."

Maclennan glared at him. "You're wasting my time now." He opened his file. "We've got a statement from Helen Walker that you persuaded her to go for a ride in the Land Rover. According to her, you were trying to grab her as you drove. Your driving became so erratic that the Land Rover went into a skid and stalled against a kerb. She jumped out and ran back to the party. She said, and I'm quoting now, 'He was out of control.'"

Weird's face twitched, tipping the ash from his cigarette down his jumper. "Silly wee lassie," he said, his voice less confident than his words.

"Just how out of control were you, son?"

Weird managed a shaky laugh. "Another one of your trick questions. Look, OK, I was a bit carried away with myself. But there's a big difference between having a bit of fun in a borrowed motor and killing somebody."

Maclennan gave him a look of contempt. "That's your idea of a bit of fun, is it? Molesting a woman and frightening her to the point where running through a blizzard in the middle of the night is better than sitting in a car with you?" Weird looked away, sighing. "You must have been angry. You get a woman into your stolen Land Rover, you think you're going to impress her and get your way with her, but instead she runs away. So what happens next? You see Rosie Duff in the snow, and you think you'll work your magic on her? Only she doesn't want to know, she fights you off, but you overpower her. And then you lose it, because you know she can destroy your life."

Weird jumped to his feet. "I don't have to sit here and listen to this. You're full of shite, you've got nothing on me and you know it."

Burnside was on his feet, obstructing Weird's path to the door while Maclennan leaned back in his chair. "Not so fast, son," Maclennan said. "You're under arrest."

Mondo hunched his shoulders round his ears, a feeble defense against what he knew was coming next. Maclennan gave him a long, cool stare. "Fingerprints," he said. "Your fingerprints on the steering wheel of a stolen Land Rover. Care to comment?"

"It wasn't stolen. Just borrowed. Stolen is when you don't plan to give it back, right?" Mondo sounded petulant.

"I'm waiting," Maclennan said, ignoring the reply.

"I gave somebody a lift home, OK?"

Maclennan leaned forward, a hound with a sniff of prey. "Who?"

"A girl that was at the party. She needed to get home to Guardbridge, so I said I'd take her." Mondo reached inside his jacket and took out a piece of paper. He'd written down the girl's details while he'd been waiting, anticipating just this moment. Somehow, not saying her name out loud made it less real, less significant. Besides, he'd worked out that if he pitched it right, he could make himself look even further in the clear. Never mind that he'd be dropping some girl in the shit with her parents. "There you go. You can ask her, she'll tell you."

"What time was this?"

He shrugged. "I don't know. Two o'clock, maybe?"

Maclennan looked down at the name and address. Neither was familiar to him. "What happened?"

Mondo gave a little smirk, a worldly moment of male complicity. "I drove her home. We had sex. We said goodnight. So you see, Inspector, I had no reason to be interested in Rosie Duff, even if I had seen her. Which I didn't. I'd just got laid. I was feeling pretty pleased with myself."

"You say you had sex. Where, exactly?"

"In the back seat of the Land Rover."

"Did you use a condom?"

"I never believe women when they say they're on the pill. Do you? Of course I used a condom." Now Mondo was more relaxed. This was territory he understood, territory where males colluded with each other in a conspiracy of comprehension.

"What did you do with it afterward?"

"I chucked it out the window. Leaving it in the Land Rover would have been a bit of a giveaway with Henry, you know?" He could see Maclennan was struggling to know where to go next with his questions. He'd been right. His admission had defused their line of questioning. He hadn't been driving round in the snow, frustrated and desperate for sex. So what possible motive could he have had for raping Rosie Duff and killing her?

Maclennan gave a grim smile, not joining in Mondo's assumption of camaraderie. "We'll be checking out your story, Mr. Kerr. Let's see if this young woman backs you up. Because if she doesn't, that paints a very different picture, doesn't it?"

CHAPTER
NINE

It didn't feel like Christmas Eve. Walking to the bakery for a pie at lunchtime, Barney Maclennan had experienced the illusion of having been dropped into a parallel universe. Shop windows blossomed with garish Christmas decorations, fairy lights twinkled in the gloaming and the streets were thronged with shoppers staggering under the weight of bulging carrier bags. But it seemed alien to him. Their concerns were not his; they had something more to look forward to than a Christmas dinner tainted with the sad taste of failure. Eight days since Rosie Duff's murder, and no prospect of an arrest.

He'd been so confident that the discovery of the Land Rover had been the keystone that would support a case against one or more of the four students. Especially after the interviews in Kirkcaldy. Their stories had been plausible enough, but then they'd had a day and a half to perfect them. And he'd still had the sense that he wasn't getting the whole truth, though it was hard to pinpoint where precisely the falsehood lay. He'd believed hardly a word that Tom Mackie said, but Maclennan was honest enough to acknowledge that might have something to do with the deep antipathy he'd felt toward the math student.

Ziggy Malkiewicz was a deep one, that was for sure. If he'd been the killer, Maclennan knew he'd get nowhere until he had solid evidence; the medical student wasn't going to cave in. He thought he'd broken Davey Kerr's story when the lassie in Guardbridge had denied they'd had sex. But Janice Hogg, whom he'd taken with him for the sake of propriety, had been convinced that the girl had been lying, trying misguidedly to protect her reputation. Right enough, when he'd sent Janice back to reinterview the girl alone, she'd broken down and admitted that she had let Kerr have sex with her. It didn't sound as if it was an experience she was keen to repeat. Which, thought Maclennan, was interesting. Maybe Davey Kerr hadn't been quite as satisfied and cheerful afterward as he'd made out.

Alex Gilbey was a likely prospect, if only because there was no evidence that he'd driven the Land Rover. His fingerprints were all over the interior, but not around the driving seat. That didn't let him off the hook, however. If Gilbey had killed Rosie, he would likely have called for help from the others, and they would probably have given it; Maclennan was under no misapprehension about the strength of the bond that united them. And if Gilbey had arranged a date with Rosie Duff that had gone horribly wrong, Maclennan was pretty sure that Malkiewicz wouldn't have hesitated to do everything he could to protect his friend. Whether Gilbey knew it or not, Malkiewicz was in love with him, Maclennan had decided on nothing more than his gut reaction.

But there was more than Maclennan's instinct at play here. After the frustrating series of interviews, he'd been about to head back for St. Andrews when a familiar voice had hailed him. "Hey, Barney, I heard you were in town," echoed across the bleak car park.

Maclennan swung round. "Robin? That you?"

A slim figure in a police constable's uniform emerged into a pool of light. Robin Maclennan was fifteen years younger than his brother, but the resemblance was striking. "Did you think you could sneak off without saying hello?"

"They told me you were out on patrol."

Robin reached his brother and shook his hand. "Just came back for refs. I thought it was you I saw as we pulled up.

Come away and have a coffee with me before you go." He grinned and gave Maclennan a friendly punch on the shoulder. "I've got some information I think you'll appreciate."

Maclennan frowned at his brother's retreating back. Robin, ever sure of his charm, hadn't waited for his brother's reaction, but had turned toward the building and the canteen inside. Maclennan caught up with him by the door. "What do you mean, information?" he asked.

"Those students you've got in the frame for the Rosie Duff murder. I thought I'd do a wee bit of digging, see what the grapevine had to say."

"You shouldn't be involving yourself in this, Robin. It's not your case," Maclennan protested as he followed his brother down the corridor.

"A murder like this, it's everybody's case."

"All the same." If he failed with this one, he didn't want his bright, charismatic brother tarred with the same brush. Robin was a pleaser; he'd go far farther in the force than Maclennan had, which was no less than he deserved. "None of them has a record anyway. I've already checked."

Robin turned as they entered the canteen and gave him the hundred-watt smile again. "Look, this is my patch. I can get people to tell me stuff that they're not going to give up to you."

Intrigued, Maclennan followed his brother to a quiet corner table and waited patiently while Robin fetched the coffees. "So, what do you know?"

"Your boys are not exactly innocents abroad. When they were thirteen or so, they got caught shoplifting."

Maclennan shrugged. "Who didn't shoplift when they were kids?"

"This wasn't just nicking a couple of bars of chocolate or packets of fags. This was what you might call Formula One Challenge Shoplifting. It seems they'd dare each other to nick really difficult things. Just for the hell of it. Mostly from small shops. Nothing they particularly wanted or needed. Everything from secateurs to perfume. It was Kerr who got caught red-handed with a Chinese ginger jar from a licensed grocer. The other three got nabbed standing outside waiting for him. They folded like a bad poker hand as soon as they were brought in. They took us to a shed in Gilbey's garden, where they'd stashed the loot. Everything still in its packaging." Robin shook his head wonderingly. "The guy who arrested them said it was like Aladdin's cave."

"What happened?"

"Strings got pulled. Gilbey's old man's a headmaster, Mackie's dad plays golf with the Chief Super. They got off with a caution and the fear of God."

"Interesting. But it's hardly the Great Train Robbery."

Robin conceded with a nod. "That's not all, though. A couple of years later, there were a series of pranks with parked cars. The owners would come back and find graffiti on the inside of their windscreens, written in lipstick. And the cars would all be locked up tight. It all ended as suddenly as it began, around the time that a stolen car got burned out. There was never anything concrete against them, but our local intelligence officer reckons they were behind it. They seem to have a knack for taking the piss."

Maclennan nodded. "I don't think I could argue with that." He was intrigued by the information about the cars. Maybe the Land Rover hadn't been the only vehicle on the road that night with one of his suspects behind the wheel.

Robin had been eager to find out more details of the investigation, but Maclennan sidestepped neatly. The conversation slipped into familiar channels—family, football, what to get their parents for Christmas—before Maclennan had managed to get away. Robin's information wasn't much, it was true, but it made Maclennan feel there was a pattern to the activities of the Laddies fi' Kirkcaldy that smacked of a love of risk-taking. It was the sort of behavior that could easily tip over into something much more dangerous.

Feelings were all very well, but they were worthless without hard evidence. And hard evidence was what was sorely lacking. The Land Rover had turned into a forensic dead-end. They'd practically dismantled the entire interior but nothing had turned up to prove that Rosie Duff had ever been inside it. Excitement had burned through the team like a fuse when the scene of crime officers had discovered traces of blood, but closer examination had revealed that not only did it not belong to Rosie, it wasn't even human.

The one faint hope on the horizon had emerged only a day ago. A householder in Trinity Place had been doing some seasonal tidying in his garden when he'd found a sodden bundle of material thrust into his hedge. Mrs. Duff had identified it as belonging to Rosie. Now it had gone off to the lab for testing, but Maclennan knew that in spite of his marking it urgent, nothing would happen now until after the New Year. Just another frustration to add to the list.

He couldn't even decide whether to charge Mackie, Kerr and Malkiewicz with taking and driving away. They'd answered their bail requirements religiously and he'd been on the point of charging them when he'd overheard a conversation in the police social club. He'd been shielded from the officers talking by the back of a banquette, but he'd recognized the voices of Jimmy Lawson and Iain Shaw. Shaw had advocated throwing every charge they could come up with at the students. But to Maclennan's surprise, Lawson had disagreed. "It just makes us look bad," the uniformed constable had said. "We look petty and vindictive. It's like putting up a billboard saying, Hey, we can't get them for murder, but we're going to make their lives a misery anyway."

"So what's wrong with that?" Iain Shaw had replied. "If they're guilty, they should suffer."

"But maybe they're not guilty," Lawson said urgently. "We're supposed to care about justice, aren't we? That's not just about nailing the guilty, it's also about protecting the innocent. OK, so they lied to Maclennan about the Land Rover. But that doesn't make them killers."

"If it wasn't one of them, who was it, then?" Shaw challenged.

"I still think it's tied in to Hallow Hill. Some pagan rite or other. You know as well as me that we get reports every year from Tentsmuir Forest about animals that look like they've been the victims of some sort of ritual slaughter. And we never pay any attention to it, because it's no big deal in the great scheme of things. But what if some weirdo has been building up to this for years? It was pretty near to Saturnalia, after all."

"Saturnalia?"

"The Romans celebrated the winter solstice on December seventeenth. But it was a pretty moveable feast."

Shaw snorted incredulity. "Christ, Jimmy, you've been doing your research."

"All I did was ask down at the library. You know I want to join CID, I'm just trying to show willing."

"So you think it was some satanic nutter that offed Rosie?"

"I don't know. It's a theory, that's all. But we're going to look very fucking stupid if we point the finger at these four students and then there's another human sacrifice come Beltane."

"Beltane?" Shaw said faintly.

"End of April, beginning of May. Big pagan festival. So I think we should stand back from hitting these kids too hard until we've got a better case against them. After all, if they hadn't stumbled across Rosie's body, the Land Rover would have been returned, nobody any the wiser, no damage done. They just got unlucky."

Then they'd finished their drinks and left. But Lawson's words stuck in Maclennan's mind. He was a fair man, and he couldn't help acknowledging that the PC had a point. If they'd known from the start the identity of the mystery man Rosie had been seeing, they'd barely have looked twice at the quartet from Kirkcaldy. Maybe he was going in hard against the students simply because he had nothing else to focus on. Uncomfortable though it was to be reminded of his obligations by a woolly suit, Lawson had persuaded Maclennan he should hold back on charging Malkiewicz and Mackie.

For now, at least.

In the meanwhile, he'd put out one or two feelers. See if anybody knew anything about satanic rituals in the area. The trouble was, he didn't have a clue where to start. Maybe he'd get Burnside to have a word with some of the local ministers. He smiled grimly. That would take their minds off the baby Jesus, that was for sure.

Weird waved good-bye to Alex and Mondo at the end of their shift and headed down toward the prom. He hunched his shoulders against the chill wind, burying his chin in his scarf. He was supposed to be finishing off his Christmas shopping, but he needed some time on his own before he could face the relentless festive cheer of the High Street.

The tide was out, so he made his way down the slimy steps from the esplanade to the beach. The wet sand was the color of old putty in the low gray light of the afternoon and it sucked at his feet unpleasantly as he walked. It fit his mood perfectly. He couldn't remember ever having felt so depressed about his life.

Things at home were even more confrontational than usual. He'd had to tell his father about his arrest, and his revelation had provoked a constant barrage of criticism and digs about his failure to live up to what a good son should be. He had to account for every minute spent outside the house, as if he was ten years old all over again. The worst of it was that Weird couldn't even manage to take the moral high ground. He knew he was in the wrong. He almost felt as if his father's contempt was deserved, and that was the most depressing thing of all. He'd always been able to console himself that his way was the better way. But this time, he'd placed himself outside the limits.

Work was no better. Boring, repetitive and undignified. Once upon a time, he'd have turned it into a big joke, an opportunity for mayhem and mischief. The person who would have relished winding up his supervisors and enlisting the support of Alex and Mondo in a series of pranks felt like a distant stranger to Weird now. What had happened to Rosie Duff and his involvement in the case had forced him to acknowledge that he was indeed the waster that his father had always believed him to be. And it wasn't a comfortable realization.

There was no consolation for him in friendship either. For once, being with the others didn't feel like being absorbed into a support system. It felt like a reminder of all his failings. He couldn't escape his guilt with them, because they were the ones he'd implicated in his actions, even though they never seemed to blame him for it.

He didn't know how he was going to face the new term. Bladderwrack popped and slithered under his feet as he reached the end of the beach and started to climb the broad steps toward the Port Brae. Like the seaweed, everything about him felt slimed and unstable.

As the light faded in the west, Weird turned toward the shops. Time to pretend to be part of the world again.

CHAPTER
TEN

New Year's Eve, 1978; Kirkcaldy, Scotland

They'd made a pact, back when they were fifteen, when their parents were first persuaded that they could be allowed out first-footing. At the year's midnight, the four Laddies fi' Kirkcaldy would gather in the Town Square and bring in the New Year together. Every year so far, they'd kept their word, standing around jostling each other as the hands of the town clock crept toward twelve. Ziggy would bring his transistor radio to make sure they heard the bells, and they'd pass around whatever drink they'd managed to acquire. They'd celebrated the first year with a bottle of sweet sherry and four cans of Carlsberg Special. These days, they'd graduated to a bottle of Famous Grouse.

There was no official celebration in the square, but over recent years groups of young people had taken to congregating there. It wasn't a particularly attractive place, mostly because the Town House looked like one of the less alluring products of Soviet architecture, its clock tower greened with verdigris. But it was the only open space in the town center apart from the bus station, which was even more charmless. The square also boasted a Christmas tree and fairy lights, which made it marginally more festive than the bus station.

That year, Alex and Ziggy arrived together. Ziggy had called round to the house to collect him, charming Mary Gilbey into giving them both a tot of Scotch to keep out the cold. Pockets stuffed with home-made shortbread, black bun that nobody would eat, and sultana cake, they'd walked down past the station and the library, past the Adam Smith Center with its posters advertising *Babes in the Wood* starring Russell Hunter and the Patton Brothers, past the Memorial Gardens. Their conversation kicked off with speculation as to whether Weird would manage to persuade his father to let him off the leash for Hogmanay.

"He's been acting pretty strange lately," Alex said.

"Gilly, he's always strange. That's why we call him Weird."

"I know, but he's been different. I've noticed it, working beside him. He's been kind of subdued. He's not had much to say for himself."

"Probably something to do with his current lack of access to alcohol and substances," Ziggy said wryly.

"He's not even been stroppy, though. That's the clincher. You know Weird. The minute he thinks anybody might be taking the piss, he erupts. But he's been keeping his head down, not arguing when the supervisors have a go. He just stands and takes it, then gets on with whatever they want him to do. You think it's the business with Rosie that's got to him?"

Ziggy shrugged. "Could be. He took it pretty lightly at the time, but then he was off his head. To tell you the truth, I've hardly spoken to him since the day Maclennan came over."

"I've only seen him at work. Soon as we clock off, he's out of there. He won't even come for a coffee with me and Mondo."

Ziggy pulled a face. "I'm surprised Mondo's got the time for coffee."

"Go easy on him. It's his way of dealing with it. When he's getting his end away with some lassie, he can't be thinking about the murder. Which is why he's going for the all-comer's record," Alex added with a grin.

They crossed the road and walked down Wemyssfield, the short street that led to the town square. They had the confident stride of men on their home turf, a place so familiar that it conferred a kind of ownership. It was ten to twelve when they trotted down the wide, shallow steps that led to the paved area outside the Town House. There were already several groups of people passing bottles from hand to hand. Alex looked around to see if he could spot the others.

"Over there, up at the Post Office end," Ziggy said. "Mondo's brought the latest lay. Oh, and Lynn's there with them too." He pointed to his left, and they set off to join the others.

After the exchange of greetings, and the general agreement that it didn't look like Weird was going to make it, Alex found himself standing next to Lynn. She was growing up, he thought. Not a kid anymore. With her elfin features and dark curls, she was a feminine version of Mondo. But paradoxically, the elements that made his face seem weak had the opposite effect with Lynn. There was nothing remotely fragile about her. "So, how's it going?" Alex said. It wasn't much of a line, but then, he didn't want to be thought to be chatting up fifteen-year-olds.

"Great. You have a good Christmas?"

"Not bad." He screwed up his face. "It was hard not to think about . . . you know."

"I know. I couldn't get her out of my mind either. I kept wondering what it must be like for her family. They'd have probably bought her Christmas presents by the time she died. What a horrible reminder, having them in the house."

"I suppose practically everything must be a horrible reminder. Come on, let's talk about something different. How are you getting on at school?"

Her face fell. She didn't want to be reminded of the age gap between them, he realized. "Fine. I've got my O grades this year. Then my Highers. I can't wait to get them out of the way so I can start my life properly."

"Do you know what you're going to do?" Alex asked.

"Edinburgh College of Art. I want to do a Fine Art degree and then go to the Courtauld in London and learn how to be a picture restorer."

Her confidence was beautiful to behold, he thought. Had he ever been so sure of himself? He'd more or less drifted into History of Art, because he'd never had the confidence in his talent as a practitioner. He whistled softly. "Seven years studying? That's a big commitment."

"It's what I want to do, and that's what it takes."

"What made you want to restore pictures?" He was genuinely curious.

"It fascinates me. First the research and then the science, and then that leap in the dark where you have to get in tune with what the artist really wanted to let us see. It's exciting, Alex."

Before he could respond, a shout went up from the others. "He made it!"

Alex turned round to see Weird outlined against the gray Scottish baronial Sheriff Court, his arms windmilling like a disarticulated scarecrow. As he ran, he let out a whooping cry. Alex looked up at the clock. Only a minute to spare.

Then Weird was upon them, hugging them, grinning. "I just thought, this is stupid. I'm a grown man and my father's trying to keep me from my friends on Hogmanay. What's that about?" He shook his head. "If he throws me out, I can bunk up with you, right, Alex?"

Alex punched him on the shoulder. "Why not? I'm used to your disgusting snoring."

"Quiet, everybody," Ziggy shouted over the hubbub. "It's the bells."

A hush fell over them as they strained to hear the tinny translation of Big Ben coming from Ziggy's transistor. As the chimes began, the Laddies fi' Kirkcaldy looked at each other. Their arms rose as if drawn by a common thread and they clasped their hands on the final stroke of twelve. "Happy New Year," they chorused. Alex could see his friends were as choked with emotion as he was himself.

Then they broke away from each other and the moment was gone. He turned to Lynn and kissed her chastely on the lips. "Happy New Year," he said.

"I think it might be," she said, a rosy blush on her cheeks.

Ziggy cracked open the bottle of Grouse and it passed from hand to hand. Already the groups in the square were breaking up, everyone mingling and wishing strangers a guid New Year with whiskey breath and generous embraces. A few people who knew them from school commiserated with their hard luck at stumbling on a dying girl in the snow. There was no malice in their words, but Alex could see from the eyes of his friends that they hated it as much as he did. A bunch of girls were dancing an impromptu eightsome reel by the Christmas tree. Alex looked around, unable to articulate the emotions swelling in his breast.

Lynn sneaked her hand into his. "What are you thinking, Alex?"

He looked down at her and forced a tired smile. "I was just thinking how easy it would be if time froze now. If I never had to see St. Andrews again as long as I live."

"It won't be as bad as you think. You've only got six months to go anyway, and then you'll be free."

"I could come back at weekends." The words were out before Alex knew he was going to say them. They both knew what he meant.

"I'd like that," she said. "We'll just not mention it to my horrible brother, though."

Another New Year, another pact.

At the police social club in St. Andrews, the drink had been flowing for some time. The bells were almost lost in the raucous bonhomie of the Hogmanay dance. The only curb on the boisterousness of those who suffered restraint as a condition of their employment was the presence of spouses, fiancées and anyone who could be inveigled into coming along to save the faces of the unattached.

Flushed with exertion, Jimmy Lawson was flanked by the two middle-aged women who operated the station switchboard in a Dashing White Sergeant set. The pretty dental receptionist he'd arrived with had escaped to the toilets, worn out by his apparently boundless enthusiasm for Scottish country dancing. He didn't care; there were always plenty of women up for a turn on the floor on Hogmanay, and Lawson liked to let off steam. It made up for the intensity he brought to his work.

Barney Maclennan leaned on the bar, flanked by Iain Shaw and Allan Burnside, each holding a substantial whiskey. "Oh God, look at them," he groaned. "If the Dashing White Sergeant comes, can Strip the Willow be far behind?"

"Nights like this, it's good to be single," Burnside said. "Nobody dragging you away from your drink and on to the dance floor."

Maclennan said nothing. He'd lost count of the number of times he'd tried to convince himself he was better off without Elaine. He'd never managed it for more than a few hours at a time. They'd still been together last Hogmanay, though only just. They were hanging on to each other with rather less determination than the sets of dancers birling in circles on the floor. Only a few weeks into the year, she'd told him she was off. She was tired of his job coming before her.

With a flash of irony, Maclennan remembered one of her rants. "I wouldn't mind so much if it was important crimes you were solving, like rape or murder. But you're out there all the hours God sends on tuppeny-ha'penny burglaries and car thefts. How do you think it feels to play second fiddle to some middle-aged old fart's Austin Maxi?" Well, her wish had come true. Here he was, a year later, mired in the biggest case of his career. And all he was doing was spinning his wheels.

Every avenue they'd pursued had turned into a cul-de-sac. Not a single witness who could put Rosie with a man after the beginning of November. Lucky for the mystery man that it had been a hard winter, when folk were more interested in the square yard of pavement in front of them than in who was hanging about with somebody they shouldn't. Lucky for him, but unlucky for the police. They'd tracked down her two previous boyfriends. One had dumped her in favor of the girl he was still going out with. He'd had no axe to grind with the dead barmaid. Rosie had chucked the other in early November, and at first he'd seemed a promising prospect. He'd been reluctant to take no for an answer, turning up a couple of times to make trouble at the bar. But he had a rock-solid alibi for the night in question. He'd been at his office Christmas party till gone midnight, then he'd gone home with his boss's secretary and spent the rest of the night with her. He admitted he'd been sore about Rosie ending their relationship at the time, but, frankly, he was having a lot more fun with a woman who was a bit more generous with her sexual favors.

When pressed by Maclennan as to what he meant by that, male pride had kicked in and he'd clammed up. But under pressure, he'd admitted they'd never actually had intercourse. They'd played around plenty; it wasn't that Rosie was a prude. Just that she wouldn't go all the way. He'd mumbled about blow jobs and hand jobs, but said that was the extent of it.

So Brian had been right, sort of, when he said his sister was a nice girl. Maclennan understood that, in the hierarchy of these things, Rosie was a long way from a good-time girl. But an intimate knowledge of her sexual proclivities didn't take him any nearer finding her killer. In his heart, he knew the chances were that the man she'd met that night had also been the man who had taken what he wanted from her and then taken her life. It might have been Alex Gilbey or one of his friends. But it might not.

His fellow detectives had argued that there could be a good reason why her date hadn't come forward. "Maybe he's married," Burnside had said. "Maybe he's scared we're going to fit him up," Shaw had added cynically. They were valid explanations, Maclennan supposed. They didn't alter his personal conviction, however. Never mind Jimmy Lawson's theories about satanic rites. None of the ministers Burnside had spoken to had even heard a whisper of anything like that happening locally. And Maclennan believed they were the most likely vessels for such information. He was relieved in a way; he didn't need any red herrings. He was sure that Rosie had known her killer, and she'd walked into the night confidently with him.

Just like thousands of other women all over the country

would tonight. Maclennan hoped fervently they'd all end up safe in their own beds.

Three miles away in Strathkinness, the New Year had arrived in a very different atmosphere. Here, there were no Christmas decorations. Cards sat in an unheeded pile on a shelf. The television, which normally hanselled in the first of January, was blank and silent in the corner. Eileen and Archie Duff sat huddled in their chairs, untouched glasses of whiskey at their sides. The oppressive stillness carried the weight of grief and depression. The Duffs knew in their hearts they would never have another happy New Year. The festive season would forever be tainted by their daughter's death. Others might celebrate; they could only mourn.

In the scullery, Brian and Colin sat slumped on a pair of plastic-covered kitchen chairs. Unlike their parents, they were having no difficulty drinking the New Year in. Since Rosie's death, they'd found it easy to pour alcohol down their throats till they couldn't find their mouths any longer. Their response to tragedy had not been to retreat into themselves but to become more expansively themselves. The publicans of St. Andrews had grown resigned to the drunken antics of the Duff brothers. They didn't have much alternative, not unless they wanted to face the wrath of their volatile clientele who reckoned Colin and Brian deserved all the sympathy that was going.

Tonight, the bottle of Bells was already past the halfway mark. Colin looked at his watch. "We missed it," he said.

Brian looked at him blearily. "Why should I care? Rosie's going to miss it every year."

"Aye. But somewhere out there, whoever killed her is probably raising a glass to getting away with it."

"It was them. I'm sure it was them. You see that picture? Did you ever see anybody look more guilty?"

Colin drained his glass and reached for the bottle, nodding agreement. "There was nobody else about. And they said she was still breathing. So if it wasn't them, where did the murderer disappear to? He didnae just vanish into thin air."

"We should make a New Year's resolution."

"Like what? You're not going to give up smoking again, are you?"

"I'm serious. We should make a solemn promise. It's the least we can do for Rosie."

"What do you mean? What kind of a solemn promise?"

"It's simple enough, Col." Brian topped up his glass. He held it up expectantly. "If the cops can't get a confession, then we will."

Colin considered for a moment. Then he raised his glass and chinked it against his brother's. "If the cops can't get a confession, then we will."

CHAPTER
ELEVEN

The substantial remains of Ravenscraig Castle stand on a rocky promontory between two sandy bays, commanding a magisterial view of the Forth estuary and its approaches. To the east, a long stone wall provides a defense against the sea and against any marauders. It runs all the way to Dysart harbor, now largely silted up but once a prosperous and thriving port. At the tip of the bay that curves along from the castle, past the dovecot that still houses pigeons and seabirds, where the wall comes to a V-shaped point, there is a small lookout with a steeply pitched roof and arrow slits in the walls.

Since their early teens, the Laddies fi' Kirkcaldy had regarded this as their personal fiefdom. One of the best ways to escape adult supervision was invariably to go for walks. It was deemed to be healthy and unlikely to lead to them falling into Bad Ways. So when they promised to be gone all day, exploring the coast and the woods, they were always heartily supplied with picnics.

Sometimes, they headed in the opposite direction, along Invertiel and out past the ugliness of Seafield pit toward Kinghorn. But mostly, they came to Ravenscraig, not least because it wasn't far to the ice cream van in the nearby park. On hot days, they lay on the grass and indulged in wild fantasies of what their lives would be, both in the near and the distant futures. They retold stories of their term-time adventures, embellishing and spinning off into might-have-beens. They played cards, endless games of pontoon for matches. They smoked their first cigarettes here, Ziggy turning green and throwing up ignominiously into a gorse bush.

Sometimes they'd clamber up the high wall and watch the shipping in the estuary, the wind cooling them down and making them feel they were standing in the prow of some sailing ship, creaking and wallowing beneath their feet. And when it rained, they'd shelter inside the lookout post. Ziggy had a groundsheet they could spread over the mud. Even now, when they considered themselves to be grown-ups, they still liked to descend the stone stairs leading down from the castle to the beach, meandering among the coal dirt and seashells to the lookout.

The day before they were due to return to St. Andrews, they met up in the Harbor Bar for a lunchtime pint. Flush with their Christmas earnings, Alex, Mondo and Weird would have been happy to make a session of it. But Ziggy talked them out into the day. It was crisp and clear, the sun watery in a pale blue sky. They walked through the harbor, cutting between the tall silos of the grain mill and out on to the west beach. Weird hung back a little behind the other three, his eyes on the distant horizon as if seeking inspiration.

As they approached the castle, Alex peeled off and scrambled up the rocky outcropping that would be almost submerged at high tide. "Tell me again, how much did he get?"

Mondo didn't even have to pause for thought. "Magister David Boys, master mason, was paid by the order of Queen Mary of Gueldres, widow of James the Second of Scotland, the sum of six hundred pounds Scots for the building of a castle at Ravenscraig. Mind you, he had to pay for materials out of that."

"Which wasn't cheap. In 1461, fourteen timber joists were felled from the banks of the River Allan then transported to Stirling at the cost of seven shillings. And one

Andrew Balfour was then paid two pounds and ten shillings for cutting, planing and transporting these joists to Ravenscraig," Ziggy recited.

"I'm glad I decided to take the job at Safeway," Alex joked. "The money's so much better." He leaned back and looked up the cliff to the castle. "I think the Sinclairs made it much prettier than it would have been if old Queen Mary hadn't kicked the bucket before it was finished."

"Pretty isn't what castles are for," Weird said, joining them. "They're supposed to be a refuge and a strength."

"So utilitarian," Alex complained, jumping off into the sand. The others followed him, scuffing through the flotsam along the high-water mark.

Halfway along the beach, Weird spoke as seriously as any of them had ever heard. "I've got something to tell you," he said.

Alex turned to face him, walking backward. The others turned in to look at Weird. "That sounds ominous," Mondo said.

"I know you're not going to like it, but I hope you can respect it."

Alex could see the wariness in Ziggy's eyes. But he didn't think his friend had anything to worry about. Whatever Weird was about to tell them came out of self-absorption, not the need to expose another. "Come on then, Weird. Let's hear it," Alex said, trying to sound encouraging.

Weird dug his hands into the pockets of his jeans. "I've become a Christian," he said gruffly. Alex stared openmouthed. He thought he might have been marginally less surprised if Weird had announced he'd killed Rosie Duff.

Ziggy roared with laughter. "Jesus, Weird, I thought it was going to be some terrible revelation. A Christian?"

Weird's jaw took on a stubborn cast. "It was a revelation. And I've accepted Jesus into my life as my savior. And I'd appreciate it if you wouldn't mock."

Ziggy was doubled up with mirth, clutching his stomach. "This is the funniest thing I've heard in years . . . Oh God, I think I'm going to piss myself." He leaned against Mondo, who was grinning from ear to ear.

"And I'd appreciate it if you wouldn't take the Lord's name in vain," Weird said.

Ziggy erupted in fresh snorts of laughter. "Oh my. What is it they say? There is more rejoicing in heaven over one sinner who repents? I tell you, they'll be dancing in the streets of paradise, snagging a sinner like you."

Weird looked offended. "I'm not trying to deny I've done bad things in the past. But that's behind me now. I'm born again, and that means the slate is wiped clean."

"That must have been some blackboard duster. When did this happen?" Mondo said.

"I went to the Watch Night service on Christmas Eve," Weird said. "And something just clicked. I realized I wanted to be washed in the blood of the lamb. I wanted to be cleansed."

"Wild," Mondo said.

"You never said anything on Hogmanay," Alex said.

"I wanted you to be sober when I told you. It's a big step, giving your life to Christ."

"I'm sorry," Ziggy said, composing himself. "But you're the last person on the planet I expected to say those words."

"I know," Weird said. "But I mean them."

"We'll still be your pals," Ziggy said, trying to keep the smirk off his lips.

"Just so long as you don't try and convert us," Mondo said. "I mean, I love you like a brother, Weird, but not enough to give up sex and drink."

"That's not what loving Jesus is about, Mondo."

"Come on," Ziggy interrupted. "I'm freezing, standing here. Let's go up to the lookout." He set off, Mondo at his side. Alex fell into step beside Weird. He felt curiously sorry for his friend. It must have been terrible to have experienced a sense of isolation so profound that he'd had to turn to the happy clappies for solace. *I should have been there for him,* Alex thought with a twinge of guilt. Maybe it wasn't too late.

"It must have felt pretty strange," he said.

Weird shook his head. "Just the opposite. I felt at peace. Like I'd finally stopped being a square peg in a round hole and I'd found the place I belonged all along. I can't describe it any better than that. I only went to the service to keep my mum company. And I was sitting there in Abbotshall Kirk, the candles flickering all around like they do at the Watch Night service. And Ruby Christie was singing "Silent Night" solo, unaccompanied. And all the hairs on my body stood on end and suddenly it all made sense. I understood that God gave his only son for the sins of the world. And that meant me. It meant I could be redeemed."

"Big stuff." Alex was embarrassed by this emotional candour. For all their years of friendship, he'd never had a conversation like this with Weird. Weird, of all people, whose only tenet of faith had apparently been to consume as many mind-altering substances as he could reasonably ingest before he died. "So what did you do?" He had a sudden vision of Weird running down to the front of the church and demanding he be forgiven his sins. That would be truly mortifying, he thought. The kind of thing that would bring you out in a cold sweat to remember once you'd come out of the other side of the God-bothering phase and resumed normal life.

"Nothing. I sat through the service and went home. I thought it was just a one-off, some kind of bizarre mystical experience. Maybe to do with all the stuff that Rosie's death churned up. Maybe even some kind of acid flashback. But when I woke up in the morning, I felt the same. So I looked in the paper to see who had a Christmas Day service and I ended up at an evangelical gig down the Links."

Uh-oh. "I bet you had the place to yourself on Christmas morning."

Weird laughed. "Are you kidding? The place was full to the doors. It was brilliant. The music was great, the people treated me like we'd been friends for years. And after the service, I went and spoke to the minister." Weird bowed his head. "It was a pretty emotional encounter. Anyway, the upshot is he baptised me last week. And he's given me the name of a sister congregation in St. Andrews." He gave Alex a beatific smile. "That's why I needed to tell you guys today. Because I'll be going to church just after we get back to Fife Park tomorrow."

The first opportunity the others had to discuss Weird's drama-scene conversion was the following evening after he'd packed his electric acoustic guitar into its case and set off to walk across town to the evangelical service down near the harbor. They sat in the kitchen and watched him stride off into the night. "Well, that's the end of the band," Mondo said decisively. "I'm not playing fucking spirituals and 'Jesus Loves Me' for anybody."

"Elvis has now left the building," Ziggy said. "I tell you, he's lost any connection to reality he ever had."

"He means it, guys." Alex said.

"You think that makes it better? We're in for a rough ride, boys," Ziggy said. "He'll be bringing the beardie weirdies back here. They'll be determined to save us whether we want to be saved or not. Losing the band is going to be the least of our worries. No more, 'All for one and one for all.' "

"I feel bad about this," Alex said.

"Why?" Mondo said. "You didn't drag him off and make him listen to Ruby Christie."

"He wouldn't have gone off like this if he hadn't been feeling really shit. I know he seemed to be the most cool of all of us about Rosie's murder, but I think deep down it must have affected him. And we were all so wrapped up in our own reactions, we didn't pick up on it."

"Maybe there's more to it than that," Mondo said.

"How do you mean?" Ziggy asked.

Mondo scuffed the toes of his boots against the floor. "Come on, guys. We don't know what the fuck Weird was doing running around in that Land Rover the night Rosie died. We've only got his word for it that he never saw her."

Alex felt the ground shift beneath his feet. Ever since he'd hinted at suspicion with Ziggy, Alex had forced himself to suppress such treacherous thoughts. But now Mondo had given fresh shape to the unthinkable. "That's a terrible thing to say," Alex said.

"I bet you've thought it, though," Mondo said defiantly.

"You can't think Weird would rape somebody, never mind kill them," Alex protested.

"He was off his face that night. You can't say what he could or couldn't do when he's in that state," Mondo said.

"Enough." Ziggy's voice cut through the atmosphere of mistrust and discomfort like a blade. "You start that and where do you stop? I was out there too that night. Alex actually invited Rosie to the party. And come to that, you took a hell of a long time taking that lassie back to Guardbridge. What kept you, Mondo?" He glared at his friend. "Is that the kind of shit you want to hear, Mondo?"

"I never said anything about you two. There's no call for you to have a go at me."

"But it's all right for you to have a go at Weird when he's not here to defend himself? Some friend you are."

"Aye well, now he's got a friend in Jesus," Mondo sneered. "Which, when you think about it, is a pretty extreme reaction. Looks like guilt to me."

"Stop it," Alex shouted. "Listen to yourselves. There's going to be plenty of other people ready to spread the poison without us turning on each other. We need to stick together or we're sunk."

"Alex is right," Ziggy said wearily. "No more accusing each other, OK? Maclennan's just dying to drive a wedge between us. He doesn't care who he gets for this murder as long as he gets somebody. We need to make sure it's not one of us. Mondo, you keep your poisonous notions to yourself in future." Ziggy got to his feet. "I'm going down to the late shop to buy some milk and bread so we can all have a cup of coffee before those hairy-arsed Tories get back and clutter the place up with their English accents."

"I'll come down with you. I need to get some fags," Alex said.

When they returned half an hour later, the world had turned upside down. The police were back in force, and their two fellow residents were on the doorstep with their luggage, their faces a study in disbelief. "Evening, Harry. Evening, Eddie," Ziggy said affably, peering over their shoulders into the hallway where Mondo was being sulky with a WPC. "Just as well I bought the two pints."

"What the hell is going on here?" Henry Cavendish demanded. "Don't tell me that cretin Mackie's been done for drugs."

"Nothing so prosaic," Ziggy said. "I don't suppose the murder made the *Tatler* or *Horse and Hounds*."

Cavendish groaned. "Oh for God's sake, don't be so pathetic. I thought you'd grown out of the working-class hero rubbish."

"Watch your mouth, we've got a Christian among us now."

"What are you talking about? Murder? Christians?" Edward Greenhalgh said.

"Weird's got God," Alex said succinctly. "Not your High Church Anglican sort, but the tambourines and praise the Lord sort. He'll be holding prayer meetings in the kitchen." Alex believed there was no greater sport than baiting those who believed in their privilege. And St. Andrews offered plenty of opportunity for that.

"What has that to do with the fact that the house is full of policemen?" Cavendish asked.

"I think you'll find the one in the hall is a woman," Ziggy said. "Unless of course Fife Police have started recruiting particularly attractive transvestites."

Cavendish ground his teeth. He hated the way the Laddies fi' Kirkcaldy persisted in treating him like a caricature. It was the main reason why he spent so little time in the house. "Why the police?" he said.

Ziggy smiled sweetly at Cavendish. "The police are here because we're murder suspects."

"What he means to say," Alex added hastily, "is that we're witnesses. One of the barmaids from the Lammas Bar was murdered just before Christmas. And we happened to find the body."

"That's appalling," Cavendish said. "I had no idea. Her poor family. Pretty grim for you too."

"It wasn't a lot of fun," Alex said.

Cavendish peered into the house again, looking discomfited. "Look, this is a bad time for you. It's probably easier all round if we find somewhere else to stay for now. Come on, Ed. We can crash with Tony and Simon tonight. We'll see if we can get transferred to another residence in the morning." He turned away, then looked back, frowning. "Where's my Land Rover?"

"Ah," Ziggy said. "It's a bit complicated. See, we borrowed it and . . ."

"You *borrowed* it?" Cavendish sounded outraged.

"I'm sorry. But the weather was terrible. We didn't think you'd mind."

"So where is it now?"

Ziggy looked embarrassed. "You'll need to ask the police about that. The night we borrowed it, that was the night of the murder."

Cavendish's sympathy had evaporated now. "I don't believe you people," he snarled. "My Land Rover is part of a murder investigation?"

"Afraid so. Sorry about that."

Cavendish looked furious. "You'll be hearing from me about this."

Alex and Ziggy watched in grim silence as the other two staggered back down the path with their suitcases. Before they could say more, they had to step aside to let the police leave. There were four uniformed officers and a couple of men in plain clothes. They ignored Alex and Ziggy and headed for their cars.

"What was all that about?" Alex asked as they finally made it indoors.

Mondo shrugged. "They didn't say. They were taking paint samples from the walls and the ceilings and the woodwork," he said. "I overheard one of them say something about a cardigan, but they didn't seem to be looking at our clothes. They poked around everywhere, asked if we'd decorated recently."

Ziggy snorted with laughter. "As if that's going to happen. And they wonder why they get called plods."

"I don't like the sound of this," Alex said. "I thought they'd given up on us. But here they are again, turning the place upside down. They must have some new evidence."

"Well, whatever it is, it's nothing for us to worry about," Ziggy said.

"If you say so," Mondo said sarcastically. "Me, I'll stick with worrying for now. Like Alex says, they've left us alone, but now they're back. I don't think that's something we can just shrug off."

"Mondo, we're innocent, remember? That means we've nothing to worry about."

"Yeah, right. So what's with Henry and Eddie?" Mondo asked.

"They don't want to live with mad axe-murderers," Ziggy said over his shoulder as he went through to the kitchen.

Alex followed. "I wish you hadn't said that," he said.

"What? Mad axe-murderers?"

"No. I wish you hadn't told Harry and Eddie we're murder suspects."

Ziggy shrugged. "It was a joke. Harry's more interested in his precious Land Rover than in anything we might have done. Except that it gives him the excuse he's always wanted to move out of here. Besides, you're the one who benefits. With an extra couple of rooms, you're not going to have to share with Weird anymore."

Alex reached for the kettle. "All the same, I wish you hadn't planted the seed. I've got a horrible feeling we're all going to catch the harvest."

CHAPTER

TWELVE

Alex's prediction came true a lot sooner than he'd expected. A couple of days later, walking down North Street toward the History of Art Department, he saw Henry Cavendish and a bunch of his cronies approaching, swaggering along in their red flannel gowns as if they owned the place. He saw Henry nudge one of them and say something. As they came face-to-face, Alex found himself surrounded by young men in the standard uniform of tweed jackets and twill trousers, their faces leering at him.

"I'm surprised you've got the nerve to show your face round here, Gilbey," Cavendish sneered.

"I think I've got more right to walk these streets than you and your pals," Alex said mildly. "This is my country, not yours."

"Some country, where people get to steal cars with impunity. I can't believe you lot aren't up in court for what you did," Cavendish said. "If you used my Land Rover to cover up a murder, you'll have more than the police to worry about."

Alex tried to push past, but he was hemmed in on all sides, jostled by their elbows and hands. "Fuck off, will you, Henry? We had nothing to do with Rosie Duff's murder. We're the ones who went for help. We're the ones who tried to keep her alive."

"And the police believe that, do they?" Cavendish said. "They must be more stupid than I thought." A fist flashed out and caught Alex hard under the ribs. "Steal my wheels, would you?"

"I didn't know you could do thinking," Alex gasped, unable to keep himself from goading his tormentor.

"It's a disgrace that you're still a member of this university," another shouted, prodding Alex in the chest with a bony finger. "At the very least, you're a shitty little thief."

"God, just listen to yourselves. You sound like a bad comedy sketch." Alex said, suddenly angry. He lowered his head and thrust forward, his body remembering countless rucks on the rugby field. "Now, get out of my road," he yelled. Panting, he emerged on the far side of the group and turned back, his lip curled in a sneer. "I've got a lecture to go to."

Taken aback by his outburst, they let him go. As he stalked off, Cavendish called after him, "I'd have thought you'd have been going to the funeral, not a lecture. Isn't that what murderers are supposed to do?"

Alex turned around. "What?"

"Didn't they tell you? They're burying Rosie Duff today."

Alex stormed up the street, shaking with anger. He'd been scared, he had to admit. For a moment there, he'd been scared. He couldn't believe Cavendish had taunted him about Rosie's funeral. Nor could he credit the fact that nobody had told them it was today. Not that he would have wanted to go. But it would have been nice to have been warned.

He wondered how the others were faring and wished yet again that Ziggy had kept his smart mouth shut.

Ziggy walked in to an anatomy class and was immediately greeted with cries of, "Here comes the body snatcher."

He threw his hands up, acknowledging the good-natured ribbing from his fellow medics. If anybody was going to find the black humor in Rosie's death, it would be them. "What's wrong with the cadavers they give us to practice on?" one shouted across the room.

"Too old and ugly for Ziggy," came the reply from another. "He had to go out and get some quality meat for himself."

"All right, leave it out," Ziggy said. "You're just jealous that I got to go into practice before any of the rest of you."

A handful of his colleagues gathered around him. "What was it like, Ziggy? We hear she was still alive when you found her. Were you scared?"

"Yeah, I was scared. But I was more frustrated because I couldn't keep her alive."

"Hey, man, you did your best," one reassured him.

"It was a pretty crap best. We spend years cramming our heads with knowledge, but, faced with the real thing, I didn't know where to start. Any ambulance driver would have had a better chance of saving Rosie's life than I did." Ziggy shrugged out of his coat and dropped it over a chair. "I felt useless. It made me realize that you don't start becoming a doctor till you get out there and start treating living, breathing patients."

A voice behind them said, "That's a very valuable lesson to have learned, Mr. Malkiewicz." Unnoticed, their tutor had walked in on the conversation. "I know it's no consolation, but the police surgeon told me that she was beyond saving by the time you found her. She'd lost far too much blood." He clapped Ziggy on the shoulder. "We can't work miracles, I'm afraid. Now, gentlemen and ladies, let's all settle down. We've got important work to get through this term."

Ziggy went to his place, his head somewhere else altogether. He could feel the blood slick on his hands, the feeble, irregular heartbeat, the chill of her flesh. He could hear her failing breath. He could taste the coppery taint on his tongue. He wondered if he could ever get past that. He wondered if he could ever become a doctor, knowing that failure would always be the ultimate outcome of his actions.

A couple of miles away, Rosie's family were preparing to lay their daughter to rest. The police had released the body at last, and the Duffs could take the first formal step on the long journey of grieving. Eileen straightened her hat in the mirror, oblivious to the pinched, raw look of her face. She couldn't be bothered with makeup these days. What was the point? Her eyes were dull and heavy. The pills the doctor had given her didn't take the pain away; they simply moved it out of her immediate reach, turning it into something she contemplated rather than experienced.

Archie stood at the window, waiting for the hearse. Strathkinness Parish Church was only a couple of hundred yards away. They'd decided the family would walk behind the coffin, keeping Rosie company on her last journey. His broad shoulders drooped. He had become an old man in the previous few weeks, an old man who had lost the will to engage with the world.

Brian and Colin, spruced as nobody had ever seen them before, were in the scullery, bracing themselves with a whiskey. "I hope the four of them have the good sense to stay away," Colin said.

"Let them come. I'm ready for them," Brian said, his handsome face set in dourness.

"Not today. For fuck's sake, Brian. Have some dignity, will you?" Colin drained his glass and slammed it down on the draining board.

"They're here," his father called through.

Colin and Brian exchanged a look, a promise to each other that they'd make it through the day without doing anything to shame themselves or their sister's memory. They squared their shoulders and went through.

The hearse was parked outside the house. The Duffs walked down the path, heads bowed, Eileen leaning heavily on her husband's arm. They took up their places behind the coffin. Behind them, friends and relatives gathered in somber groupings. Bringing up the rear were the police. Maclennan led the detachment, proud that several of the team had turned up on their time off. For once, the press were discreet, agreeing among themselves on pool coverage.

Villagers lined the street to the church, many of them falling in behind the cortege as it moved at a slow walk down to the gray stone building that sat four square on the hill, brooding over St. Andrews below. When everyone had filed in, the small church was packed. Some mourners had to stand in the side aisles and at the back.

It was a short and formal service. Eileen had been beyond thinking of details, and Archie had asked for it to be kept to the bare minimum. "It's something we've to get through," he'd explained to the minister. "It's not what we're going to be remembering Rosie by."

Maclennan found the simple words of the funeral service unbearably poignant. These were words that should be spoken over people who had lived their lives to the full, not a young woman who'd barely begun to scratch the surface of what her life could be. He bowed his head for the prayer, knowing this service would bring no resolution to anyone who had known Rosie. There would be no peace for any of them until he did his job.

And it was looking less and less likely that he would be able to satisfy their need. The investigation had almost ground to a halt. The only recent forensic evidence had come from the cardigan. All that had yielded were some paint fragments. But none of the samples taken from inside the student house in Fife Park had come anywhere near a match. Headquarters had sent a superintendent down to review the work he and his team had done, the implication being that they'd somehow fallen down on the job. But the man had had to concede that Maclennan had done a commendable job. He hadn't been able to make a single suggestion that might lead to fresh progress.

Maclennan found himself coming back again and again to the four students. Their alibis were so flimsy they hardly deserved the name. Gilbey and Kerr had fancied her. Dorothy, one of the other barmaids, had mentioned it more than once when giving her statement. "The big one that looks a bit like a dark-haired Ryan O'Neal," she'd put it. Not how he would have described Gilbey himself, but he knew what she meant. "He fancied her something rotten," she'd said. "And the wee one that looks like him out of T Rex. He was always mooning after Rosie. Not that she gave him the time of day, mind you. She said he fancied himself too much for her liking. The other one, though, the big one. She said she wouldn't mind a night out with him if he was five years older."

So there was the shadow of a motive. And of course, they'd had access to the perfect vehicle for transporting the dying body of a young woman. Just because there were no forensic traces didn't mean they hadn't used the Land Rover. A tarpaulin, a groundsheet, even a thick plastic sheet would have contained the blood and left the interior clean. There was no doubt that whoever had killed Rosie must have had a car.

Either that or he was one of the respectable householders on Trinity Place. The trouble was, every male resident between fourteen and seventy was accounted for. They were either away from home, or asleep in their beds, alibied to the hilt. They'd looked closely at a couple of teenage boys, but there was nothing to link them to Rosie or to the crime.

The other thing that made Gilbey look less likely as a suspect was the forensics. The sperm they'd found on Rosie's clothes had been deposited by a secretor, someone whose blood group was present in his other bodily fluids. Their rapist and presumably their killer had blood group O. Alex Gilbey was AB, which meant he hadn't raped her unless he'd used a condom. But Malkiewicz, Kerr and Mackie were all group O. So theoretically, it could have been one of them.

He really didn't think Kerr had it in him. But Mackie was possible, that was for sure. Maclennan had heard about the young man's sudden conversion to Christianity. To him, it sounded like a desperate act born of guilt. And Malkiewicz was another story altogether. Maclennan had accidentally stumbled into the issue of the lad's sexuality, but if he was in love with Gilbey, he might have wanted to get rid of what he saw as the competition. It had the ring of possibility.

Maclennan was so deep in thought, he was taken aback to find the service over, the congregation shuffling to their feet. The coffin was being carried up the aisle, Colin and Brian Duff the lead pall-bearers. Brian's face was streaked with tears, and Colin looked as if it was taking every ounce of his strength not to weep.

Maclennan looked around at his team, nodding them outside as the coffin disappeared. The family would be driven down the hill to Western Cemetery for a private internment. He slipped outside, standing by the door and watching the mourners disperse. He had no conviction that his killer was among the congregation; that was too glib a conclusion for him to be comfortable with. His officers gathered behind him, speaking softly among themselves.

Hidden by a corner of the building, Janice Hogg lit a cigarette. She wasn't on duty, after all, and she needed a blast of nicotine after that harrowing. She'd only had a couple of drags when Jimmy Lawson appeared. "I thought I smelled smoke," he said. "Mind if I join you?"

He lit up, leaning against the wall, his hair falling over his forehead and shading his eyes. She thought he'd lost weight recently, and it suited him, hollowing his cheeks and defining his jawline. "I wouldn't want to go through that again in a hurry," he said.

"Me neither. I felt like all those eyes were looking to us for an answer we haven't got."

"And no sign of getting one either. CID haven't got anything you could call a decent suspect," Lawson said, his voice as bitter as the east wind that whipped the smoke from their mouths.

"It's not like *Starsky and Hutch*, is it?"

"Thank God for that. I mean, would you want to wear those cardies?"

Janice sniggered, in spite of herself. "When you put it like that . . ."

Lawson inhaled deeply. "Janice . . . do you fancy going out for a drink sometime?"

Janice looked at him in astonishment. She'd never imagined for a moment that Jimmy Lawson had noticed she was a woman except when it came to making tea or breaking bad news. "Are you asking me out?"

"Looks like it. What do you say?"

"I don't know, Jimmy. I'm not sure if it's a good idea to get involved with somebody in the job."

"And when do we get the chance to meet anybody else unless we're arresting them? Come on, Janice. Just a wee drink. See how we get on?" His smile gave him a charm she'd never noticed before.

She looked at him, considering. He wasn't exactly a dreamboat, but he wasn't bad looking. He had a reputation for being a bit of a ladies' man, somebody who usually got what he wanted without having to work too hard for it. But he'd always treated her with courtesy, unlike so many of her colleagues whose contempt was seldom far from the surface. And she hadn't been out with anyone interesting for longer than she could remember. "OK," she said.

"I'll look at the rosters when we come on tonight. See when we're both off." He dropped his cigarette end and ground it out with his toe. She watched him walk round the corner of the church to join the others. It seemed she had a date. It was the last thing she'd expected from Rosie Duff's funeral. Maybe the minister had been right. This should be a time for looking forward as well as backward.

CHAPTER
THIRTEEN

None of his three friends would ever have described Weird as sensible, even before he got God. He'd always been an unstable mixture of cynicism and naïveté. Unfortunately, his new-found spirituality had stripped away the cynicism without providing any complementary access of *nous*. So when his new friends in Jesus announced that there was no better occasion to evangelize than the evening of Rosie Duff's funeral, Weird had gone along with the suggestion. People would be thinking about their mortality, the reasoning went. This was the best possible time to remind them that Jesus offered the one direct route to the kingdom of heaven. The notion of offering his witness to strangers would have had him rolling on the floor with laughter a few weeks previously, but now it seemed the most natural thing in the world.

They gathered in the home of their pastor, an eager young Welshman whose enthusiasm was almost pathological. Even in the first flush of his conversion, Weird found him slightly overwhelming. Lloyd genuinely believed that the only reason the whole of St. Andrews hadn't accepted Christ into their lives was the inadequacy of the proselytizing of himself and his flock. Clearly, Weird thought, he'd never met Ziggy, the atheist's atheist. Nearly every meal he'd eaten in Fife Park since they'd returned had included passionate discussion about faith and religion. Weird was weary of it. He didn't know enough yet to counter all the arguments, and he knew instinctively it wasn't enough to respond with, "That's where your faith comes in." Bible study would solve that in time, he knew. Till then, he was praying for patience and the right lines.

Lloyd thrust leaflets into his hand. "These give a brief introduction to the Lord, along with a short selection of passages from the Bible," he explained. "Try to engage people in conversation, then ask them if they'd give five minutes of their time to save themselves from disaster. That's when you give them this and ask them to read it. Tell them if they want to ask you any questions about it, they can meet you at the service on Sunday." Lloyd spread his hands as if to indicate that was all there was to it.

"Right," Weird said. He looked around at their little group. There were half a dozen of them. Apart from Lloyd, there was only one other man. He carried a guitar and wore an expression of eagerness. Sadly, his zeal wasn't matched by his talent. Weird knew he wasn't supposed to judge, but he reckoned that, even on his worst day, he could play this geek under the table. But he didn't know the songs yet, so he wasn't going to be busking for Christ tonight.

"We'll set up the music on North Street. There's plenty of people around there. The rest of you, go round the pubs. You don't have to go in. Just catch people as they're entering or leaving. Now, we'll just have a quick prayer before we go about the Lord's business." They held hands and bowed their heads. Weird felt the newly familiar sense of peace wash over him as he entrusted himself to his savior.

It was funny how different things were now, he thought later as he ambled along from one pub to the next. In the past, he'd never have considered approaching complete strangers for anything other than directions. But he was actually enjoying himself. Most people brushed him off, but several had accepted his leaflets and he was confident that he'd see some of them again. He was convinced they couldn't miss the tranquillity and joy that must be emanating from him.

It was nearly ten o'clock when he walked through the massive stone archway of the West Port toward the Lammas Bar. It shocked him now to think of how much time he'd wasted in there over the years. He wasn't ashamed of his past; Lloyd had taught him that that was the wrong way to look at it. His past was a comparison point that revealed just how glorious his new life was. But he regretted that he hadn't found this peace and sanctuary sooner.

He crossed the road and stationed himself by the door of the Lammas. In the first ten minutes, he handed out a single tract to one of the regulars who gave him a curious stare as he pushed the door open. Seconds later, the door swung back violently. Brian and Colin Duff hurtled into the street, followed by a couple of other young men. They were all red in the face and fueled by drink.

"What the fuck do you think you're doing?" Brian roared, grabbing Weird by the front of his parka. He pushed him back against the wall hard.

"I just . . ."

"Shut your puss, you wee shite," Colin shouted. "We buried my sister today, thanks to you and your vicious wee pals. And you've got the nerve to turn up here preaching about Jesus?"

"Call yourself a fucking Christian? You killed my sister, you cunt." Brian was banging him rhythmically against the wall. Weird tried to force his hands away, but the other man was far stronger.

"I never touched her," Weird howled. "It wasnae us."

"Well, who the fuck was it? Youse were the only ones there," Brian raged. He released Weird's parka and raised his fist. "Let's see how you like it, cunt." He smashed a right hook into Weird's jaw and followed it with a crushing left to his face. Weird's knees gave way. He thought the bottom half of his face was going to come away in his hands.

It was only the beginning. Suddenly feet and fists were flying, thumping cruelly into his body. Blood, tears and mucus streamed down his face. Time slowed to a trickle, distorting words and intensifying every agonizing contact.

He'd never been in a grown-up fight before, and the naked violence of it terrified him. "Jesus, Jesus," he sobbed.

"He's not going to help you now, you big streak of piss," somebody shouted.

Then, blessedly, it stopped. As suddenly as the blows ended, silence fell. "What's going on here?" he heard a woman say. He lifted his head out of the fetal crouch he'd adopted. A WPC was standing over him. Behind her, he could see the constable Alex had fetched through the snow. His assailants stood around, sullen, hands in their pockets.

"Just a bit of fun," Brian Duff said.

"Doesn't look very funny to me, Brian. Lucky for him the landlord had the good sense to call this one in," the woman said, bending down to peer at Weird's face. He pushed himself into a sitting position and coughed up a mouthful of snot and blood. "You're Tom Mackie, aren't you?" she said, understanding dawning.

"Aye," he groaned.

"I'll radio for an ambulance," she said.

"No," Weird said, somehow getting his feet under him and tottering upright. "I'll be fine. Just a bit of fun." Speaking, he discovered, took an effort. It felt like he'd had a jaw transplant that he hadn't learned how to work yet.

"I think your nose is broken, son," the male cop said. What was his name? Morton? Lawton? Lawson, that was it.

"It's OK. I live with a doctor."

"He was a medical student the last I heard," Lawson said.

"We'll give you a lift home in the patrol car," the woman said. "I'm Constable Hogg, and this is Constable Lawson. Jimmy, keep an eye on him, will you? I need to have a word with these morons. Colin, Brian? Over here. You others? Make yourselves scarce." She led Colin and Brian to one side. She was careful to stay close enough to Lawson for him to dive in if things got out of hand.

"What the hell was that about?" she demanded. "Look at the state of him."

Slack-jawed, glassy-eyed and sweating with exertion, Brian gave a drunken sneer. "Less than he deserves. You know what that was about. We're just doing your job for you because you're a bunch of useless twats who couldn't detect your way out of a paper bag."

"Shut up, Brian," Colin urged. He was only marginally more sober than his brother, but he had always had more of an instinct for staying out of trouble. "Look, we're sorry, OK? Things just got a bit out of hand."

"I'll say. You've half-killed him."

"Aye well, him and his pals didnae leave the job half-done when they started it," Brian said pugnaciously. Suddenly, his face crumpled and hot tears trickled down his cheeks. "My wee sister. My Rosie. You wouldnae treat a dog the way they treated her."

"You've got it wrong, Brian. They're witnesses, not suspects," Janice said wearily. "I told you that the night it happened."

"You're the only ones round here that think that," Brian said.

"Will you shut up?" Colin said. He turned to Janice. "You arresting us, or what?"

Janice sighed. "I know you buried Rosie today. I was there. I saw how upset your parents were. For their sake, I'm willing to turn a blind eye. I don't think Mr. Mackie will want to press charges." As Colin went to speak, she held up a cautionary finger. "This only works provided you and Cassius Clay here keep your hands to yourself. Leave this to us, Colin."

He nodded. "OK, Janice."

Brian looked astonished. "When did you start calling her Janice? She's not on our side, you know."

"Shut the fuck up, Brian," Colin said, syllable by pointed syllable. "I apologize for my brother. He's had a wee bit too much to drink."

"Don't worry about it. But you're not stupid, Colin. You know I meant what I said. Mackie and his pals are off limits to you two. Is that clear?"

Brian sniggered. "I think she fancies you, Colin."

The idea clearly tickled the drunk part of Colin Duff's

brain. "Is that right? Well, what do you say, Janice? Why don't you keep me on the straight and narrow? You fancy a night out? I'll show you a good time."

Janice caught a movement out of the corner of her eye and glanced round in time to see Jimmy Lawson draw his truncheon and move toward Colin Duff. She raised a hand to ward him off, but the threat was enough to leave Duff backing away, wide-eyed and apprehensive. "Hey," he protested.

"Wash your mouth out, you sad sack of shite," Lawson said. His face was set and angry. "Don't you ever, ever speak to a police officer like that. Now get out of our sight before I get Constable Hogg to change her mind about locking you two up for a very long time." He spoke savagely, his lips tight against his teeth. Janice bridled. She hated it when male officers thought they had to demonstrate their manhood by defending her honor.

Colin grabbed Brian's arm. "Come on. We've got a pint waiting for us inside." He led his leering brother away before he could cause anymore bother.

Janice turned to Lawson. "There was no call for that, Jimmy."

"No call for it? He was making a pass at you. He's not fit to shine your shoes." His voice was thick with contempt.

"I'm perfectly capable of taking care of myself, Jimmy. I've dealt with a lot worse than Colin Duff without you playing the knight in shining armor. Now, let's get this lad home."

Between them, they helped Weird to their car and eased him into the back seat. As Lawson walked round to the driver's door, Janice spoke. "And Jimmy . . . About that drink? I think I'll pass."

Lawson gave her a long, hard stare. "Please yourself."

They drove back to Fife Park in stony silence. They helped Weird to the front door then headed back to the car. "Look, Janice, I'm sorry if you thought I came on too heavy back there. But Duff was well out of line. You can't talk to a police officer like that," Lawson said.

Janice leaned on the roof of the car. "He was out of line. But you didn't react like that because he was insulting the uniform. You drew your truncheon because somewhere in your head, you'd decided I was your property just because I agreed to go out for a drink with you. And he was stepping on your territory. I'm sorry, Jimmy, I don't need that in my life just now."

"That's not how it was, Janice," Lawson protested.

"Let's leave it, Jimmy. No hard feelings, eh?"

He shrugged, petulant. "Your loss. It's not like I'm stuck for female company." He got into the driver's seat.

Janice shook her head, unable to keep a smile from her face. They were so predictable, men. The first sniff of feminism and they headed straight for the hills.

Inside the house in Fife Park, Ziggy was examining Weird. "I told you it would end in tears," he said, his fingers gently probing the swollen tissue around Weird's ribs and abdomen. "You go out for a bit of light evangelism and you came back looking like an extra from *Oh! What a Lovely War*. Onward, Christian soldiers."

"It was nothing to do with giving my witness," Weird said, wincing at the effort. "It was Rosie's brothers."

Ziggy stopped what he was doing. "Rosie's brothers did this to you?" he said, a worried frown on his face.

"I was outside the Lammas. Somebody must have told them. They came out and set about me."

"Shit." Ziggy went to the door. "Gilly," he shouted upstairs. Mondo was out, as he had been most evenings since their return. Sometimes he was there for breakfast, but mostly he wasn't.

Alex came thundering downstairs, stopping short at the sight of Weird's ravaged face. "What the fuck happened to you?"

"Rosie's brothers," Ziggy said tersely. He filled a bowl with warm water and started gently cleaning Weird's face with balls of cotton wool.

"They beat you up?" Alex couldn't make sense of this.

"They think we did it," Weird said. "Ow! Can you be a bit more careful?"

"Your nose is broken. You should go to the hospital," Ziggy said.

"I hate hospitals. You fix it."

Ziggy raised his eyebrows. "I don't know what kind of a job I'll make of it. You could end up looking like a bad boxer."

"I'll take my chances."

"At least you've not got a broken jaw," he said, bending over Weird's face. He took his nose in both hands and twisted it, trying not to feel nauseous at the grinding crepitation of cartilage. Weird screamed, but Ziggy carried on. There was sweat on his lip. "There you go," he said. "Best I can do."

"It was Rosie's funeral today," Alex said.

"Nobody told us," Ziggy complained. "That explains why feelings were running so high."

"You don't think they're coming after us, then?" Alex asked.

"Cops warned them off," Weird said. It was getting harder and harder to speak as his jaw stiffened.

Ziggy studied his patient. "Well, Weird, looking at the state of you, I hope to Christ they were listening."

CHAPTER
FOURTEEN

Any hopes they'd had of Rosie's death being a nine-day wonder were dashed by the newspaper coverage of the funeral. It was all over the front pages again, and anyone in the town who had missed the initial coverage would have been hard pressed to avoid the reprise.

Again, it was Alex who was the first victim. Walking home from the supermarket a couple of days later, he was taking a short cut along the bottom of the Botanic Gardens when Henry Cavendish and his chums ran up in a ragged bunch, dressed for rugby training. As soon as they spotted Alex, they started catcalling, then surrounded him, pushing and shoving. They formed a loose ruck around him, dragging him to the grass verge and throwing him to the slushy ground. Alex rolled around, trying to escape the prodding of their boots. There was little danger of real violence such as Weird had experienced, and he was more angry than frightened. A stray boot caught his nose and he felt the spurt of blood.

"Fuck off," he shouted, wiping mud, blood and slush from his face. "Why don't you all just fuck off?"

"You're the ones who should fuck off, killer boy," Cavendish shouted. "You're not wanted here."

A quiet voice interjected. "And what makes you think you are?"

Alex rubbed his eyes clear and saw Jimmy Lawson standing on the fringe of the group. It took him a moment to recognize him out of uniform, but his heart lifted when he did.

"Push off," Edward Greenhalgh said. "This is none of your business."

Lawson reached inside his anorak and pulled out his warrant card. He flipped it open negligently and said, "I believe you'll find it is, sir. Now, if I could just take your names? I think this is a matter for the university authorities."

At once, they were small boys again. They shuffled their feet and stared at the ground, muttering and mumbling their details for Lawson to write down in his notebook. Meanwhile, Alex got to his feet, sodden and filthy, contemplating the wreckage of the shopping. A bottle of milk had erupted all over his trousers, a burst plastic jar of lemon curd was smeared down one sleeve of his parka.

Lawson dismissed his tormentors and stood looking at Alex, a smile on his face. "You look terrible," he said. "Lucky for you I was passing."

"You're not working?" Alex said.

"No. I live round the corner. I just popped out to catch the post. Come on, come back to my place, we'll get you cleaned up."

"That's very kind of you, but there's no need."

Lawson grinned. "You can't walk the streets of St. Andrews looking like that. You'd probably get arrested for frightening the golfers. Besides, you're shivering. You need a cup of tea."

Alex wasn't going to argue. The temperature was dropping back toward freezing point and he didn't fancy walking home soaking wet. "Thanks," he said.

They turned into a brand new street, so new it still didn't have pavements. The first few plots were completed, but after that, they petered into building sites. Lawson carried on past the finished homes and stopped by a caravan parked on what would one day be a front garden. Behind it, four walls and roof timbers covered in tarpaulin offered a promise of something rather more palatial than the four-berth caravan.

"I'm doing a self-build," he said, unlocking the door of the caravan. "The whole street's doing it. We all contribute labor and skills to each other's houses. That way, I get a chief superintendent's house on a constable's salary." He climbed up into the caravan. "But for now, I live here."

Alex followed. The caravan was cozy, a portable gas heater blasting out dry warmth into the confined space. He was impressed by its neatness. Most single men he knew lived in pigsties, but Lawson's home was spotless. All the chrome gleamed. The paintwork was clean and fresh. The curtains were bright and tied back neatly. There was no clutter. Everything was neatly stowed; books on shelves, cups on hooks, cassettes in a box, architect's drawings framed on the bulkheads. The only sign of habitation was a pan simmering on the stove. The smell of lentil soup went round Alex's heart. "Very nice," he said, taking it all in.

"It's a bit cramped, but if you keep it tidy, it doesn't get too claustrophobic. Take your jacket off, we'll hang it over the heater. You'll need to wash your face and hands—that's the toilet, just past the cooker."

Alex let himself into the tiny cubicle. He looked in the mirror above the doll's house sink. God, but he was a mess. Dried blood, mud. And lemon curd spiking his hair. No wonder Lawson had made him come back and clean up. He ran a basin of water and scrubbed himself clean. When he emerged, Lawson was leaning against the stove.

"That's better. Sit near the heater, you'll soon dry off. Now, a cup of tea? Or I've got home-made soup if you fancy that."

"Soup would be great." Alex did as he was told while Lawson ladled out a steaming bowl of golden yellow soup with chunks of ham hock floating in it. He put it in front of Alex and handed him a spoon. "I don't mean to sound rude, but why are you being so nice to me?" he asked.

Lawson sat down opposite him and lit a cigarette. "Because I feel sorry for you and your pals. All you did was act like responsible citizens, but you've been made to look like the bad guys. And I suppose I feel partly responsible. If I'd been out on patrol instead of sitting tucked up in my car, I'd maybe have caught the guy red-handed." He tilted his head back and sighed a stream of smoke into the air. "That's what makes me think it wasn't somebody local that did this. Anybody who knew that area at night would know that there's often a patrol car sitting there." Lawson grimaced. "We don't get enough petrol allowance to drive around all night, so we have to park up somewhere."

"Does Maclennan still think it might have been us?" Alex asked.

"I don't know what he thinks, son. I'll be honest with you. We're stuck. And so you four have ended up in the firing line. You've got the Duffs baying for your blood, and from the looks of what I've just seen, your own pals have turned on you too."

Alex snorted. "They're no pals of mine. Are you really going to report them?"

"Do you want me to?"

"Not really. They'd just find a way to get their own back. I don't think they'll be bothering us anymore. Too frightened that Mummy and Daddy might get to hear about it and stop their allowances. I'm more worried about the Duffs."

"I think they'll leave you alone too. My colleague gave them the hard word. Your pal Mackie just caught them on the raw. They were pretty chewed up after the funeral."

"I don't blame them. I just don't want a doing like Weird got."

"Weird? You mean Mr. Mackie?" Lawson frowned.

"Aye. It's a nickname from school. From a David Bowie song."

Lawson grinned. "Of course. *Ziggy Stardust and the Spiders from Mars*. That makes you Gilly, right? And Sigmund's Ziggy."

"Well done."

"I'm not that much older than you. So where does Mr. Kerr fit in?"

"He's not a big Bowie fan. He's into Floyd. So he's Mondo. Crazy diamond? Get it?"

Lawson nodded.

"Great soup, by the way."

"My mother's recipe. You go back a long way, then?"

"We met on our first day at high school. We've been best mates ever since."

"Everybody needs their pals. It's like this job. You work with the same people over a period of time, they're like brothers. You'd lay down your life for them if you had to."

Alex smiled understanding. "I know what you mean. It's the same for us." *Or it used to be*, he thought with a pang. This term, things were different. Weird was off with the God Squad more often than not. And God alone knew where Mondo was half the time. The Duffs weren't the only ones paying an emotional price for Rosie's death, he suddenly realized.

"So you'd lie for each other if you thought you had to?"

The spoon stopped halfway to Alex's mouth. So that was what this was about. He pushed the bowl away from him and stood up, reaching for his jacket. "Thanks for the soup," he said. "I'm fine now."

Ziggy seldom felt lonely. An only child, he was accustomed to his own company and never lacked diversion. His mother had always looked at other parents as if they were mad when they complained about their children being bored in the school holidays. Boredom had never been a problem she'd had to contend with.

But tonight, loneliness had seeped into the little house on Fife Park. He had plenty of work to keep him busy, but for once Ziggy craved company. Weird was off with his guitar, learning how to praise the Lord in three chords. Alex had come home in a foul mood after a rumble with the Right and an encounter with that copper Lawson that had turned very sour. He'd got changed then gone off to some slide lecture on Venetian painters. And Mondo was out somewhere, probably getting laid.

Now that was an idea. The last time he'd had sex had been quite a while before they'd stumbled over Rosie Duff.

He'd gone to Edinburgh for the evening, to the one pub he'd ever been in that welcomed gays. He'd stood at the bar, nursing a pint of lager, surreptitiously glancing to either side, carefully not making eye contact. After half an hour or so, he'd been joined by a man in his late twenties. Denim jeans, shirt and jacket. Good looking, in a tough guy sort of way. He'd struck up a conversation, and they'd ended up having fast but satisfying sex against the toilet wall. It had been all over well before the last train home.

Ziggy hankered after something more than the anonymous encounters with strangers that were his only experience of sex. He wanted what his straight friends seemed to slip into with ease. He wanted courtship and romance. He wanted someone with whom he could share an intimacy that went beyond the exchange of body fluids. He wanted a boyfriend, a lover, a partner. And he had no idea how to find one.

There was a Gay Soc at the university, he knew that much. But as far as he could gather, it consisted of half a dozen guys who seemed almost to relish the controversy of being seen to be gay. The politics of Gay Liberation interested Ziggy, but from what he'd seen of these guys posturing round the campus, they had no serious political engagement. They just liked being notorious. Ziggy wasn't ashamed of being gay, but he didn't want it to be the only thing people knew about him. Besides, he wanted to be a doctor, and he had a shrewd suspicion that a career as a gay activist wouldn't help him achieve his ambition.

So for now, the only outlet for his feelings was the casual encounter. As far as he knew, there were no pubs in St. Andrews where he was likely to find what he was looking for. But there were a couple of places where men hung out, ready for anonymous sex with a stranger. The drawback was that they were in the open air, and in this weather, there wouldn't be many braving the elements. Still, he couldn't be the only guy in St. Andrews wanting sex tonight.

Ziggy pulled on his sheepskin jacket, laced up his boots and walked out into the freezing cold night air. A brisk fifteen minute walk brought him to the back of the ruined cathedral. He crossed over to The Scores, making for what remained of St. Mary's Church. In the shadow of the broken walls, men often lurked, trying to look as if they were out for an evening stroll that encompassed a bit of architectural heritage. Ziggy squared his shoulders and tried to look casual.

Down by the harbor, Brian Duff was drinking with his cronies. They were bored. And they were just drunk enough to want to do something about it. "This is no fucking fun," his best pal Donny complained. "And we're too skint to go somewhere you can get a decent night out."

The complaint ran back and forth across the group for a while. Then Kenny had his brainwave. "I ken what we can do. Fun, and money. And no comebacks."

"What's that, then?" Brian demanded.

"Let's go and mug a few nancy boys."

They looked at him as if he was speaking Swahili. "What?" Donny said.

"It'll be a laugh. And they'll have money on them. They're not going to put up much of a fight, are they? They're a bunch of jessies."

"You're talking about going and robbing people?" Donny said, doubt in his voice.

Kenny shrugged. "They're poofs. They don't count. And they're not going to go running to the polis, are they? Otherwise they'd have to explain what they were doing hanging about St. Mary's Church in the dark."

"Could be a laugh," Brian slurred. "Scare the shit out of the shirtlifters." He giggled. "Scare the shit out of them. That could be bad news for somebody." He drained his pint and got to his feet. "Come on, then. What's keeping you?"

They lurched out into the night, nudging each other in the ribs and guffawing. It was a short walk up The Shore to the church ruins. A half-moon peeped out from fitful clouds, silvering the sea and lighting their way. As they approached they fell silent, prowling on the balls of their feet. They rounded the corner of the building. Nothing. They crept up the side and through the remains of a doorway. And there, in an alcove, they found what they were looking for.

A man leaned against the wall, head back, small noises of pleasure spilling from his lips. In front of him, another knelt, head bobbing back and forward.

"Well, well, well," Donny slurred. "What have we here?"

Startled, Ziggy pulled his head away and gazed in horror at his worst nightmare.

Brian Duff stepped forward. "I'm really going to enjoy this."

CHAPTER
FIFTEEN

Ziggy had never been so scared. He stumbled to his feet and backed away. But Brian was upon him, his hand grabbing at the lapel of the sheepskin. Brian threw him against the wall, knocking the breath from him. Donny and Kenny stood uncertain as the other man hastily zipped himself up and took to his heels. "Brian, you want us to go after the other one?" Kenny said.

"No, this is perfect. You know who this creepy little fairy is?"

"Naw," Donny said. "Who is he?"

"He's only one of those bastards that killed Rosie." His hands bunched into fists, his eyes daring Ziggy to make an attempt at escape.

"We didn't kill Rosie," Ziggy said, unable to keep the tremor of fear out of his voice. "I'm the one who tried to save her."

"Aye, after you'd raped and stabbed her first. Were you trying to prove to your mates that you were a real man and not a poof?" Brian shouted. "Well, son, it's confession time. You're going to tell me the truth about what happened to my sister."

"I'm telling you the truth. We never harmed a hair on her head."

"I don't believe you. And I'm going to make you tell the

truth. I know the very thing." Without taking his eyes off Ziggy, he said, "Kenny, away down the harbor and get me a rope. A good long length, mind."

Ziggy had no idea what lay ahead, but he knew it wasn't going to be pleasant. The only chance he had was to talk his way out. "This isn't a good idea," he said. "I didn't kill your sister. And I know the cops have already warned you to leave us alone. Don't think I'm not going to report this."

Brian laughed. "You think I'm stupid? You're going to go to the police and say, 'Please, sir, I was sucking some cunt's cock and Brian Duff came along and gave me a slap?' You must think I came up the Forth on a biscuit. You're not going to tell anybody about this. Because then they'd all know you're an arse bandit."

"I don't care," Ziggy said. And at this point, it seemed a fate less terrible than whatever an uncurbed Brian Duff might mete out. "I'll take my chances. Do you really want another load of grief dumped on your mother's doorstep?"

As soon as the words were out, Ziggy knew he'd miscalculated. Brian's face closed down. He raised his hand and slapped Ziggy so hard he heard the vertebrae in his neck crack. "Don't you mention my mother, cocksucker. She never knew grief before you bastards killed my sister." He slapped him again. "Admit it. You know you're going to have to pay sooner or later."

"I'm not admitting something I didn't do," Ziggy choked out. He could taste blood; the inside of his cheek had torn on the sharp edge of a tooth.

Brian pulled his hand back and gut-punched him with all his considerable strength. Ziggy folded, staggering. Hot vomit cascaded to the ground, splashing his feet. Gasping for breath, he felt the rough stone at his back, the only thing that was holding him upright.

"Tell me," Brian hissed.

Ziggy closed his eyes. "Nothing to tell," he squeezed out.

By the time Kenny returned, he'd taken a few more blows. He didn't know it was possible to feel this much pain without passing out. Blood covered his chin from a split lip, and his kidneys were sending sharp stabs of agony through his body.

"What kept you?" Brian demanded. He yanked Ziggy's hands in front of him. "Tie one end round his wrists," he ordered Kenny.

"What are you going to do to me?" Ziggy asked through swollen lips.

Brian grinned. "Make you talk, cocksucker."

When Kenny had finished, Brian took the rope. He wound a loop round Ziggy's waist, tying it tightly. Now his hands were held firm against his body. Brian yanked on the rope. "Come on, we've got business to attend to." Ziggy dug his heels in, but Donny grabbed the rope with Brian and yanked so hard they nearly pulled him off his feet. "Kenny, check it's all clear."

Kenny ran ahead to the archway. He looked up The Scores. There was no sign of life. It was too cold to be out walking for pleasure, and still too early for the last-minute dog walkers. "Nobody around, Bri," he called softly.

Hauling on the rope, Brian and Donny set off. "Faster," Brian said to Donny. They trotted up The Scores, Ziggy desperately trying to keep his balance while also tugging at his hands to see if he could free himself. What the hell were they going to do to him? It was high tide. Surely they weren't going to lower him into the sea? People died in the North Sea in a matter of minutes. Whatever they had planned, he knew instinctively it was going to be worse than anything he could imagine.

The ground fell away under his feet without warning and Ziggy tumbled to the ground, rolling over and over, crashing into Brian and Donny's legs. A storm of swearing, then hands on his body, pulling him roughly to his feet, shoving him face first into a wall. Ziggy slowly orientated himself. They were standing on the path that ran alongside the wall that surrounded the castle. This wasn't a medieval rampart, just a modern barrier to deter vandals and lovers. Were they going to take him inside and hang him from the battlements?

"What are we doing here?" Donny asked uneasily. He

wasn't sure he had the stomach for whatever Brian had planned.

"Kenny, over the wall," Brian said.

Accustomed to Brian's leadership, Kenny did as he was told, scrambling up the six feet and disappearing over the other side. "I'm throwing the rope over, Kenny," Brian shouted. "Grab a hold of it."

He turned to Donny. "We're going to have to hoist him over. Like tossing the caber, only two-handed."

"You'll break my neck," Ziggy protested.

"Not if you're careful. We'll give you a leg up. You can turn yourself around when you get to the top and drop down."

"I can't do that."

Brian shrugged. "It's your choice. You can go head first or feet first, but you're going. Unless, that is, you're ready to tell me the truth?"

"I've told you the truth," Ziggy yelled. "You've got to believe me."

Brian shook his head. "I'll know the truth when I hear it. You right, Donny?"

Ziggy tried to make a break for it, but they were on him. They whirled him round to face the wall then, taking a leg each, they heaved Ziggy precariously aloft. He didn't dare struggle; he knew how fragile the spinal cord's protection was at the base of the skull and he didn't want to end up paraplegic. He ended up bent over the wall like a sack of potatoes. Slowly, with infinite caution, he worked his way round till he had one leg on either side of the wall. Then, even more slowly, he inched round till the other leg was on top of the wall. His scraped knuckles seared fresh pain up his arms. "Come on, cocksucker," Brian shouted impatiently.

He launched himself at the wall and within seconds, he was alongside Ziggy's foot. He shoved it roughly to the side, throwing him off balance. Ziggy's bladder gave up its contents as he fell backward through the air, alarm pumping his adrenaline levels even higher. He landed heavily on his feet, knees and ankles collapsing under the strain. He lay huddled on the ground, tears of shame and pain stinging his eyes. Brian jumped down beside him. "Nice one, Kenny," he said, taking the rope back.

Donny's face appeared over the top of the wall. "Are you going to tell me what's going on?" he demanded.

"And spoil the surprise? No way." Brian jerked on the rope. "Come on, cocksucker. Let's go for a walk."

They clambered up the grassy slope toward the low stub of the ruined castle's east wall. Ziggy stumbled and fell a few times, but there were always hands at the ready to haul him upright. They crossed the wall and they were in the courtyard. The moon slid out from behind a cloud, bathing them in an eerie radiance. "Me and my brother used to love coming here when we were kids," Brian said as he slowed to a stroll. "It was the church that built this castle. Not a king. Did you know that, cocksucker?"

Ziggy shook his head. "I've never been here before."

"You should have. It's great. The mine and the counter-mine. Two of the greatest siege works anywhere in the world." They were heading toward the north range, the Kitchen Tower to the right of them and the Sea Tower to the left. "It was some place, this. It was a residence, it was a fortress." He turned to face Ziggy, walking backward. "And it was a prison."

"Why are you telling me this?" Ziggy said.

"Because it's interesting. They murdered a cardinal here too. They killed him, then they hung his naked body from the castle walls. I bet you never thought of that, did you, cocksucker?"

"I didn't kill your sister," Ziggy repeated.

By now, they were at the entrance to the Sea Tower. "There are two vaulted chambers in the lower story here," Brian said conversationally, leading the way inside. "The eastern one contains something almost as interesting as the mine and countermine. Do you know what that is?"

Ziggy stood mute. But Kenny answered the question for him. "You're not going to put him down the Bottle Dungeon?"

Brian grinned. "Well done, Kenny. Go to the top of the class." He reached into his pocket and produced a cigarette lighter. "Donny, give me your paper."

Donny produced a copy of the *Evening Telegraph* from his inside pocket. Brian rolled it tightly and lit one end of it as he walked into the eastern chamber. By the flare of the makeshift torch, Ziggy could see a hole in the floor covered with a heavy iron grille. "They cut a hole in the rock. It's in the shape of a bottle. And it's a long way down."

Donny and Kenny looked at each other. This was growing a bit too serious for their taste. "Hang on, Brian," Donny protested.

"What? You're the ones that said poofters don't count. Come on, give me a hand." He tied the end of Ziggy's rope to the grille. "It'll take the three of us to get this off."

They gripped the grille, hunkering down to the task. They grunted and strained. For a long, happy minute Ziggy thought they weren't going to be able to raise it. But eventually, with a harsh grating of metal on stone, it shifted. They moved it to one side and turned as one to Ziggy.

"You got anything to say to me?" Brian Duff demanded.

"I didn't kill your sister," Ziggy said, desperate now. "Do you really think you can get away with dropping me down a fucking dungeon and leaving me to die?"

"The castle's open at the weekends in the winter. That's only a couple of days away. You willnae die. Well, probably not, anyway." He dug Donny in the ribs and laughed. "OK, boys, bombs away."

They rushed Ziggy in a group and manhandled him toward the narrow opening. He kicked out furiously, twisting in their grasp. But three to one, six hands to none, he never had a chance. In seconds, he was sitting on the edge of the circular hole, his legs dangling into space. "Don't do this," he said. "Please, don't do this. They'll send you to jail for a very long time for this. Don't do it. Please." He sniffed, trying not to give way to the panicked tears that choked his throat. "I'm begging you."

"Just tell me the truth," Brian said. "It's your last chance."

"I never," Ziggy sobbed. "I never."

Brian kicked the small of his back, sending him hurtling down for a few feet, his shoulders bouncing painfully against the stone walls of the narrow funnel. Then he jerked to a halt, the rope biting cruelly into his stomach. Brian's laughter echoed around him. "Did you think we were going to drop you all the way?"

"Please," Ziggy sobbed. "I never killed her. I don't know who killed her. Please . . ."

Now he was moving again, the rope lowering him in short spurts. He thought it would cut him in half. He could hear the heavy breathing of the men above him, the occasional curse as the rope burned a careless hand. Every foot took him further into darkness, the faint flickers from above fading in the dank, freezing air.

It seemed to go on forever. Eventually, he felt a difference in the quality of the air around him and he stopped bumping the sides. The bottle was widening from the neck. They were really going to do it. They were really going to abandon him here. "No," he shouted at the top of his lungs. "No."

His toes scraped solid ground and blessedly took the strain off the rope biting into his gut. The rope above him slackened. A dissonant, disembodied voice echoed from above. "Last chance, cocksucker. Confess and we'll pull you out."

It would have been so easy. But it would have been a lie that would lead him into impossible places. Even to save himself, Ziggy couldn't name himself a murderer. "You're wrong," he shouted from the bottom of his battered lungs.

The rope landed on his head, its whipping coils surprisingly heavy. He heard a last jeering laugh, then silence. Total, overwhelming silence. The glimmer of light from the top of the shaft died. He was immured in blackness. No matter how hard he strained his eyes, he could see nothing at all. He had been cast into outer darkness.

Ziggy edged sideways. There was no way of telling how far he was from the walls, and he didn't want to walk his tender face into solid rock. He remembered reading about blind white crabs that had evolved in an underground cave. Some-where in the Canary Islands, he thought. Generations of darkness had made eyes redundant. That was what he had become, a blind white crab sidewinding in impenetrability.

The wall came sooner than he expected. He turned and let his fingertips feel the grainy sandstone. He was struggling to keep his panic at bay, concentrating on his physical environ-ment. He couldn't let himself speculate on how long he would be here. He'd go mad, fall to pieces, dash his brains out on the stone if he thought about the possibilities. Surely they wouldn't leave him to die? Brian Duff might, but he didn't think his friends would take that chance.

Ziggy turned his back to the wall and slowly slid down till he was sitting on the chill floor. He ached all over. He didn't think anything was broken, but he knew now that you didn't have to have fractures to suffer the sort of pain that de-manded serious analgesia.

He knew he couldn't afford just to sit there and do noth-ing. His body was going to stiffen, his joints cramp if he didn't keep moving. He'd die of exposure in these tempera-tures if he couldn't keep his circulation going, and he wasn't about to give those barbaric bastards the satisfaction. He had to get his hands free. Ziggy bent his head as low as possible, wincing at the pain from his bruised ribs and spine. If he pulled his hands up to the limit of the rope, he could just get his teeth on the knotted end.

As silent tears of pain and self-pity dripped down his nose, Ziggy began the most crucial battle of his life.

CHAPTER
SIXTEEN

Alex was surprised to find the house empty when he arrived home. Ziggy hadn't said anything about going out and Alex presumed he'd planned an evening working. Maybe he'd gone round to see one of his fellow medics. Maybe Mondo had come back and they'd gone for a drink together. Not that he was worried. Just because he'd been rousted by Cavendish and his crew was no reason to believe anything bad had happened to Ziggy.

Alex made himself a cup of coffee and a pile of toast. He sat at the kitchen table, his notes from the lecture in front of him. He'd always struggled to hold the Venetian painters distinct in his head, but tonight's slideshow had clarified certain elements he wanted to be sure he'd grasped. He was scribbling in the margin when Weird bounced in, full of earnest bonhomie. "Wow, what a night I've had," he enthused. "Lloyd did an absolutely inspirational Bible study on the Letter to the Ephesians. It's awesome how much he draws out from the text."

"I'm glad you had a good time," Alex said absently. Weird's entrances were as repetitive as they were dramatic ever since he'd started hanging out with the Christians. Alex had long since stopped paying attention.

"Where's Zig? He working?"

"He's out. Don't know where. If you're putting the kettle on, I'll have another coffee."

The kettle had barely boiled when they heard the front door open. To their surprise, it was Mondo who walked in, not Ziggy. "Hello, stranger," Alex said. "She throw you out?"

"She's got an essay crisis," Mondo said, reaching for a mug and tipping coffee into it. "If I hang around, she'll only keep me awake moaning about it. So I thought I'd grace you guys with my presence. Where's Ziggy?"

"I don't know. Am I my brother's keeper?"

"Genesis chapter four, verse nine," Weird said smugly.

"For fuck's sake, Weird," Mondo said. "Are you not over it yet?"

"You don't get over Jesus, Mondo. I don't expect someone as shallow as you to understand that. False gods, that's what you're worshiping."

Mondo grinned. "Maybe. But she gives great head."

Alex groaned. "I can't take anymore. I'm going to bed." He left them to their sparring, luxuriating in the peace of a room of his own again. Nobody had been sent to replace Cavendish and Greenhalgh, so he'd moved into what had been Cavendish's bedroom. He paused on the threshold, glancing into the music room. He couldn't remember the last time they'd sat down and played together. Until this term, hardly a day had gone by when they hadn't sat down and jammed for half an hour or more. But that had disappeared too, along with the closeness.

Maybe that was what happened anyway when you grew up. But Alex suspected it had more to do with what Rosie Duff's death had taught them about themselves and each other. It hadn't been a very edifying journey so far. Mondo had retreated into selfishness and sex; Weird had disappeared to a distant planet where even the language was incomprehensible. Only Ziggy had stayed his intimate. And even he seemed to have taken to disappearing without a trace. And underneath it all, a dissonant counterpoint to everyday life, suspicion and uncertainty gnawed away. Mondo had been the one to utter the poisonous words, but

Alex had already been providing an ample feast for the worm in the bud.

Part of Alex hoped that things would settle down and return to normal. But the other part of him knew that some things, once broken, can never be restored. Thinking of restoration summoned Lynn to his mind, making him smile. He was going home on the weekend. They were going to Edinburgh to see a film. *Heaven Can Wait*, with Julie Christie and Warren Beatty. Romantic comedy seemed like a good place to start. It was an unspoken understanding between them that they wouldn't go out in Kirkcaldy. Too many wagging tongues quick to judgment.

He thought he'd tell Ziggy, though. He'd been going to tell him tonight. But, like heaven, that could wait. It wasn't as if either of them was going anywhere.

Ziggy would have given all he possessed to be anywhere else. It seemed like hours since he'd been dumped in the dungeon. He was chilled to the bone. The damp patch where he'd pissed himself felt icy, his prick and balls shriveled to infant size. And still he hadn't managed to untie his hands. Cramp had shot through his arms and legs in spasms, making him cry out with the excruciating pain of it. But at last, he thought he could feel the knot starting to give.

He gripped his aching jaw over the nylon rope once more and jiggled his head this way and that. Yes, there was definitely more movement. Either that or he was so desperate he was hallucinating progress. A tug to the left, then a jerk backward. He repeated the motion several times. When the rope end finally curled free and whipped against his face, Ziggy burst into tears.

Once that first turn was undone, the rest came away easily. All at once, his hands were free. Numb, but free. His fingers felt as swollen and cold as supermarket sausages. He thrust them inside his jacket, into his armpits. Axillae, he thought, remembering that cold was an enemy of thought, slowing the brain down. "Think anatomy," he said out loud, recalling the giggles he'd shared with a fellow student when reading how to rearticulate a dislocated shoulder. "Place a stockinged foot in the axilla," the text had said. "Cross-dressing for doctors," his friend had said. "I must remember to put a black silk stocking in my bag in case I come across a dislocation."

That was how to stay alive, he thought. Memory and movement. Now he had his arms for balance, he could move around. He could jog on the spot. A minute jogging, two minutes resting. Which would be fine if he could see his watch, he thought stupidly. For once, he wished he smoked. Then he'd have matches, a lighter. Something to breach this appalling blank darkness. "Sensory deprivation," he said. "Break the silence. Talk to yourself. Sing."

Pins and needles in his hands made him twitch. He took his hands out and shook them vigorously from the wrists. He massaged them clumsily against each other, and gradually the feeling came back. He touched the wall, glad of the sedimentary roughness of the sandstone. He'd begun to worry about permanent damage because of the circulatory cut-off. His fingers were still swollen and stiff, but at least he could feel them again.

He pushed himself to his feet and began to lift his feet in a gentle jog. He'd let his pulse-rate rise, then stop till it returned to normal. He thought about all the afternoons he'd spent hating PE. Sadistic gym teachers and endless circuit training, cross country and rugby. Movement and memory.

He was going to make it out alive. Wasn't he?

Morning came, and there was no Ziggy in the kitchen. Concerned now, Alex stuck his head round Ziggy's door. No Ziggy. It was hard to tell whether his bed had been slept in, since Alex doubted he'd made it since the beginning of term. He returned to the kitchen, where Mondo was tucking into a vast bowl of Coco Pops. "I'm worried about Ziggy. I don't think he came back last night."

"You're such an old woman, Gilly. Did you ever consider he might have got laid?"

"I think he might have mentioned the possibility."

Mondo snorted. "Not Ziggy. If he didn't want you to know, you'd never find out. He's not transparent, like you and me."

"Mondo, how long have we been sharing a house?"

"Three and a half years," Mondo said, casting his eyes to the ceiling.

"And how many nights has Ziggy stayed out?"

"I don't know, Gilly. In case you hadn't noticed, I tend to be away from base quite a lot myself. Unlike you, I have a life outside these four walls."

"I'm not exactly a monk, Mondo. But as far as I'm aware, Ziggy has never stayed out all night. And it worries me because it's not that long since Weird had the crap beaten out of him by the Duff brothers. And yesterday I got into a ruck with Cavendish and his Tory cronies. What if he got into a fight? What if he's in the hospital?"

"And what if he got laid? Listen to yourself, Gilly, you sound like my mother."

"Up yours, Mondo." Alex grabbed his jacket from the hall and made for the door.

"Where are you going?"

"I'm going to phone Maclennan. If he tells me I sound like his mother, then I'll shut up, OK?" Alex slammed the door on the way out. He had another fear he hadn't mentioned to Mondo. What if Ziggy had gone out cruising for sex and been arrested? That was the nightmare scenario.

He walked across to the phone booths in the admin building and dialed the police station. To his surprise, he was put straight through to Maclennan. "It's Alex Gilbey, Inspector," he said. "I know this is probably going to sound like a right waste of your time, but I'm worried about Ziggy Malkiewicz. He didn't come home last night, which he's never done before . . ."

"And after what happened to Mr. Mackie, you felt a bit uneasy?" Maclennan finished.

"That's right."

"Are you at Fife Park now?"

"Aye."

"Stay put. I'm coming over."

Alex didn't know whether to be relieved or concerned that the detective had taken him seriously. He trudged back to the house and told Mondo to expect a visit from the police.

"He'll really thank you for that when he walks in with that just-fucked look on his face," Mondo said.

By the time Maclennan arrived, Weird had joined them. He rubbed his tender, half-healed nose and said, "I'm with Gilly on this one. If Ziggy's fallen foul of the Duff brothers, he could be in intensive care by now."

Maclennan took Alex through the events of the previous evening. "And you've no idea where he might have gone?"

Alex shook his head. "He didn't say he was going out."

Maclennan gave Alex a shrewd look. "Does he go in for cottaging, do you know?"

"What's cottaging?" Weird asked.

Mondo ignored him and glared at Maclennan. "What are you saying? You calling my pal a queer?"

Weird looked even more baffled. "What's cottaging? What do you mean, queer?"

Furious, Mondo rounded on Weird. "Cottaging is what poofs do. Picking up strangers in toilets and having sex with them." He gestured with his thumb at Maclennan. "For some reason, the plod thinks Ziggy's a poof."

"Mondo, shut up," Alex said. "We'll talk about this later." The other two were taken aback by Alex's sudden access of authority, bewildered by the turn of events. Alex turned back to Maclennan. "He sometimes goes to a bar in Edinburgh. He's never said anything about here in St. Andrews. You think he's been arrested?"

"I checked the cells before I came out. He's not been through our hands." His radio crackled into life and he moved into the hall to answer it. His words drifted back into the kitchen. "The castle? You're kidding . . . Actually, I've got an idea who it might be. Get the Fire Brigade in. I'll see you down there."

He came back in, looking worried. "I think he might have turned up. We've had a report from one of the guides at the castle. He checks the place over every morning. He rang us to say there's somebody in the Bottle Dungeon."

"The Bottle Dungeon?" all three of them chorused.

"It's a chamber dug out of the rock under one of the towers. Shaped like a bottle. Once you're in, you can't get out. I need to go over there and see what's what. I'll have somebody let you know what's going on."

"No. We're coming too," Alex insisted. "If he's been stuck in there all night, he deserves to see a friendly face."

"Sorry, lads. No can do. If you want to make your own way over there, I'll leave word that you're to be let in. But I don't want you cluttering up a rescue operation." And he was gone.

The moment the door closed, Mondo laid into Alex. "What the hell was all that about? Shutting us up like that? Cottaging?"

Alex looked away. "Ziggy's gay," he said.

Weird looked incredulous. "No, he's not. How can he be gay? We're his best friends, we'd know."

"I know," Alex said. "He told me a couple of years ago."

"Great," Mondo said. "Thanks for sharing that with us, Gilly. So much for, 'All for one and one for all.' We weren't good enough to hear the news, huh? It's all right for you to know, but we haven't got the right to be told our so-called best mate is a poof."

Alex stared Mondo down. "Well, judging by your tolerant and relaxed reaction, I'd say Ziggy made the right judgment call."

"You must have got it wrong," Weird said stubbornly. "Ziggy's not gay. He's normal. Gays are sick. They're an abomination. Ziggy's not like that."

Suddenly, Alex had had enough. His temper flared rarely, but when it did, it was a breathtaking spectacle. His face flushed dark red and he slammed the flat of his hand against the wall. "Shut up, the pair of you. You make me ashamed to be your friend. I don't want to hear another bigoted word from either of you. Ziggy's taken care of the three of us for the best part of ten years. He's been our friend, he's always been there for us and he's never let us down. So what if he fancies men instead of women? I don't give a shit. It doesn't mean he fancies me, or you, anymore than I fancy every woman with a pair of tits. It doesn't mean I've got to watch my back in the shower, for fuck's sake. He's still the same person. I still love him like a brother. I'd still trust him with my life, and so should you. And you—" he added, stabbing a finger into Weird's chest. "You call yourself a Christian? How dare you sit in judgment on a man who's worth a dozen of you and your happy-clappy nutters? You don't deserve a friend like Ziggy." He snatched up his coat. "I'm going to the castle. And I don't want to see you two there unless you've got your fucking acts together."

This time when he slammed the door, even the windows rattled.

When Ziggy saw the faint glow of light, he thought at first he was hallucinating again. He'd been drifting in and out of a kind of delirium, and he had enough insight in his lucid moments to realize he was beginning to go into hypothermia. In spite of his best efforts to keep moving, lethargy was a hard adversary to combat. From time to time, he'd slumped to the floor, in a dwam, his mind rambling in the strangest of directions. Once, he'd thought his father was with him, having a conversation about Raith Rovers's chances of achieving promotion. Now, that was surreal.

He had no idea how long he'd been down there. But when the glimmer of light appeared, he knew what he had to do. He jumped up and down, shouting at the top of his lungs. "Help! Help! I'm down here. Help me!"

For a long moment, nothing happened. Then the light became painful. Ziggy shielded his eyes from its brightness. "Hello?" echoed down the shaft and filled the chamber.

"Get me out of here," Ziggy screamed. "Please, get me out."

"I'm going for help," the disembodied voice called. "If I drop the torch, can you catch it?"

"Wait," Ziggy shouted. He didn't trust his hands. Besides,

a torch would come down the shaft like a bullet. He stripped off his jacket and his sweater, folded them and placed them in the middle of the faint pool of light. "OK, do it now," he called up.

The light juddered and bounced on the walls of the passage, flashing crazy patterns against his startled retinas. It spiraled suddenly out of the shaft and then a heavy rubber torch plopped neatly onto the soft sheepskin. Tears stung Ziggy's eyes, a physiological and emotional reaction rolled into one. He grabbed the torch, holding it to his chest like a talisman. "Thank you," he sobbed. "Thank you, thank you, thank you."

"I'll be as quick as I can," the voice said, tailing off as its owner moved away.

He could bear it now, Ziggy thought. He had light. He played the torch over the walls. The rough red sandstone was worn smooth in places, the roof and walls blackened in patches with soot and tallow. It must have felt like the anteroom to hell for the prisoners kept down here. At least he knew he was going to be freed, and soon. But for them, light must only have brought increase to their despair, a recognition of the futility of any hope of escape.

When Alex arrived at the castle, two police cars, a fire engine and an ambulance sat outside. The sight of the ambulance made his heart pound. What had happened to Ziggy? He had no difficulty gaining access; Maclennan had been true to his word. One of the firemen pointed him across the grassy courtyard to the Sea Tower, where he found a scene of calm efficiency. The fire officers had set up a portable generator to run powerful arc lights and a winch. A rope led down into the hole in the middle of the floor. Alex shivered at the sight.

"It's Ziggy, right enough. The fireman's just gone down in a sort of hoist. Like a breeches buoy, if you know what that is?" Maclennan said.

"I think so. What happened?"

Maclennan shrugged. "We don't know yet."

As he spoke, a voice trickled up from below. "Bring her up."

The fireman on the winch pressed a button and the machinery howled into action. The rope coiled on a drum, inch by tantalizing inch. It seemed to go on forever. Then Ziggy's familiar head rose into sight. He looked a mess. His face was streaked with blood and dirt. One eye was swollen and bruised, his lip split and crusted. He was blinking at the lights, but as soon as his sight cleared and he saw Alex, he managed a smile. "Hey, Gilly," he said. "Nice of you to stop by."

As his torso cleared the funnel, willing hands pulled him clear, helping him out of the canvas sling. Ziggy staggered, disorientated and exhausted. Impulsively, Alex rushed forward and took his friend in his arms. The acrid smell of sweat and urine clung to him, overlaid by the earthy smell of dirt. "You're OK," Alex said, holding him close. "You're OK now."

Ziggy hung on to him as if his life depended on it. "I was afraid I was going to die there," he whispered. "I couldn't let myself think like that, but I was so afraid I was going to die."

CHAPTER
SEVENTEEN

Maclennan stormed out of the hospital. When he got to the car, he slammed his hands against the roof. This case was a nightmare. Nothing had gone right since the night Rosie Duff had died. And now he had the victim of abduction, assault and false imprisonment refusing to give a statement about his attackers. According to Ziggy, he'd been set on by three men. It was dark, he didn't get a proper look at them. He didn't recognize their voices, they didn't call each other by name. And for no good reason, they'd dropped him down the Bottle Dungeon. Maclennan had threatened him with arrest for police obstruction, but a pale and tired Ziggy had looked him straight in the eye and said, "I'm not asking you to carry out an investigation, so how can I be obstructing you? It was a just a prank that went too far, that's all."

He wrenched open the passenger door and threw himself into the car. Janice Hogg, who was in the driver's seat, looked a question at him.

"He says it was a prank that went too far. He doesn't want to make a statement, he doesn't know who did it."

"Brian Duff," Janice said decisively.

"On what basis?"

"While you were inside, waiting for them to give Malkiewicz the once-over, I made a few inquiries. Duff and his two bosom buddies were drinking down at the harbor last night. Just down the road from the castle. They took off about half-past nine. According to the landlord, they looked like they were up to something."

"Well done, Janice. But it's still a bit thin."

"Why do you think Malkiewicz won't give a statement? You think he's frightened of reprisals?"

Maclennan sighed. "Not the kind you're thinking of. I think he was cottaging down by the church. He's scared that if he gives us Duff and his pals, they'll stand up in court and tell the world Ziggy Malkiewicz is a poof. The lad wants to be a doctor. He's not going to take any chances with that. God, I hate this case. Everywhere I turn, it ends up going nowhere."

"You could always lean on Duff, sir."

"And say what?"

"I don't know, sir. But it might make you feel better."

Maclennan looked at Janice in surprise. Then he grinned. "You're right, Janice. Malkiewicz might still be a suspect, but if anybody's going to beat him up, it should be us. Let's go to Guardbridge. I've not been to the paper mill in a very long time."

Brian Duff strode into the manager's office with the cocky strut of a man who thinks he has the keys to the kingdom. He leaned against the wall and swept Maclennan with an arrogant stare. "I don't like being interrupted at my work," he said.

"Shut your puss, Brian," Maclennan said contemptuously.

"That's no way to speak to a member of the public, Inspector."

"I'm not speaking to a member of the public, I'm speaking to a piece of shite. I know what you and your moronic pals did last night, Brian. And I know you think you'll get away with it because of what you know about Ziggy Malkiewicz. Well, I'm here to tell you different." He moved closer to Duff, only inches away from him now. "From now on, Brian, you and your brother are marked men. You go one mile an hour over the speed limit on that bike of yours and you're pulled. You have one drink over the limit, and you're breathalyzed. You so much as breathe on any of those four lads and you're under arrest. And with your record, that means you're going away again. And this time, it'll be for a damn sight more than three months." Maclennan paused for breath.

"That's police harassment," Brian said, his complacency only slightly dented.

"No, it's not. Police harassment is when you accidentally fall down the stairs on the way to the cells. When you trip over and break your nose when you hit the wall." In a sudden, lightning moment, Maclennan's hand shot out and grabbed Duff's crotch. He squeezed as tightly as he could, then twisted his wrist sharply.

Duff screamed, the color draining from his face. Maclennan let him go and stepped back smartly. Duff doubled over, spitting curses. "That's police harassment, Brian. Get fucking used to it." Maclennan yanked open the door. "Oh dear. Brian seems to have banged into the desk and hurt himself," he said to the startled secretary in the anteroom. He smiled as he walked past her, out the door and into the cold sunlight. He got into the car.

"You were right, Janice. I feel a lot better now," he said, smiling broadly.

No work was being done in the small house in Fife Park that day. Mondo and Weird mooched around the music room, but guitar and drums didn't make for a great combo and Alex was clearly not about to join them. He lay on his bed, trying to work out his feelings about what had happened to them all. He'd always wondered why Ziggy had been so reluctant to share his secret with the other two. Deep down, Alex believed they would accept it because they knew Ziggy too well not to. But he'd underestimated the power of knee-jerk bigotry. He didn't like what their reaction said about his friends. And that called into question his own judgment. What was he doing, investing so much time and energy in people who were, at bottom, as narrow-minded as scum like

Brian Duff? On their way to the ambulance, Ziggy had whispered in Alex's ear what had happened. What scared Alex was the thought that his friends shared the same prejudices.

OK, Weird and Mondo weren't about to go out and beat up gay men for want of something better to do of an evening. But not everyone in Berlin had been part of Kristallnacht. And look where that had led. By sharing the same position of intolerance, you gave tacit support to the extremists. In order for evil to triumph, Alex remembered, it is necessary only that good men do nothing.

He could almost understand Weird's position. He'd dug himself in with a bunch of fundamentalists who required that you had to swallow the entire doctrine whole. You couldn't opt out of the bits that didn't suit you.

But there was no excuse for Mondo. The way he felt right now, Alex didn't even want to sit down at the same table with him.

It was all coming apart at the seams, and he didn't know how to stop it.

He heard the sound of the front door opening, and he was out of bed and down the stairs in seconds. Ziggy leaned against the wall, a wobbly smile on his face. "Shouldn't you be in the hospital?" Alex asked.

"They wanted to keep me in for observation. But I can do my own obs. There's no need for me to be cluttering up a bed."

Alex helped him through to the kitchen and put the kettle on. "I thought you had hypothermia?"

"Only very mildly. It's not like I had frostbite or anything. They got my core temperature back up, so that's OK. I've not got any broken bones, just bruises. I'm not passing blood, so my kidneys are fine. I'd rather suffer in my own bed than have doctors and nurses poking at me, making jokes about medics who can't heal themselves."

Footsteps on the stairs, then Mondo and Weird appeared in the doorway, looking sheepish. "Good to see you, man," Weird said.

"Aye," Mondo agreed. "What the hell happened?"

"They know, Ziggy," Alex cut in.

"You told them?" The accusation came out sounding tired rather than angry.

"Maclennan told us," Mondo said sharply. "He just confirmed it."

"Fine," Ziggy said. "I don't expect Duff and his Neanderthal buddies were looking for me in particular. I think they'd just gone out for a bit of queer-bashing and they happened to come across me and this other guy down by St. Mary's Church."

"You were having sex in the church?" Weird sounded appalled.

"It's a ruin," Alex said. "It's not exactly consecrated ground." Weird looked as if he was going to say more, but the look on Alex's face stopped him in his tracks.

"You were having sex with a total stranger out in the open on a freezing winter night?" Mondo spoke with a mixture of disgust and contempt.

Ziggy gave him a long considering look. "Would you rather I'd brought him back here?" Mondo said nothing. "No, I thought not. Unlike the stream of strange women you inflict on us on a regular basis."

"That's different," Mondo said, shifting from one foot to the other.

"Why?"

"Well, it's not illegal, for a start," he said.

"Thanks for your support, Mondo." Ziggy got to his feet, slowly and precariously, like an old man. "I'm going to bed."

"You still haven't told us what happened," Weird said, sensitive to atmosphere as ever.

"When they realized it was me, Duff wanted me to confess. When I wouldn't confess, they tied me up and lowered me down the Bottle Dungeon. It was not the best night of my life. Now, if you'll excuse me?"

Mondo and Weird stepped aside to let him pass. The stairs were too narrow for two, so Alex didn't offer to help. He didn't think Ziggy would accept help right now anyway, not even from him. "Why don't you two just move in with the people you're comfortable with?" Alex said, pushing past them. He picked up his book bag and his coat. "I'm going to the library. It would be really nice if you two were gone when I got back."

A couple of weeks passed in what appeared to be an uneasy truce. Weird spent most of his time either working in the library or with his evangelical friends. Ziggy seemed to recover his sangfroid as his physical injuries healed, but Alex noticed he didn't like being out after dark alone. Alex got his head down to work, but made sure he was around when Ziggy needed company. He went to Kirkcaldy for a weekend, taking Lynn to Edinburgh. They ate in a small Italian restaurant with cheery décor and went to the pictures. They walked all the way from the station to her home three miles away at the back of the town. As they cut through the stand of trees that masked the Dunnikier Estate from the main road, she pulled him into the shadows and kissed him as if her life depended on it. He'd walked home singing.

The person most affected by the recent events, paradoxically, seemed to be Mondo. The story of Ziggy's attack spread round the university like wildfire. The version that went public conveniently left out the first part of the story, so his privacy remained intact. But a sizable majority were talking about the four of them as if they were suspects, as if there was some sort of justification for what had been done to Ziggy. They had become pariahs.

Mondo's girlfriend dumped him unceremoniously. She was worried for her reputation, she said. He didn't find a new one easy to come by either. Girls wouldn't meet his eye anymore. They sidled away when he went to talk to them in pubs and discos.

His fellow students on his French course also made it clear they didn't want him around. He was isolated in a way that none of the others was. Weird had the Christians; Ziggy's fellow medics were firmly on his side; Alex didn't give a shit what anyone else thought; he had Ziggy and, although Mondo didn't know it, he had Lynn.

Mondo had wondered if he still had an ace up his sleeve, but he was nervous about exposing his hand in case it turned into a joker. It wasn't exactly easy to waylay the person he needed to talk to, and so far he'd failed dismally to make contact. He couldn't even manage to set up an exercise in mutual self-interest. Because that's what he'd persuaded himself it was. Not blackmail. Just a little reciprocity. But even that was beyond him right now. He really was a total failure; everything he touched turned to dross.

The world had been his oyster and now all Mondo could taste was the grit. He'd always been the most emotionally fragile of the quartet, and without their support, he crumbled. Depression set in like a heavy blanket, muffling the world outside. He even walked like a man with a burden on his back. He couldn't work, couldn't sleep. He stopped showering and shaving, only changing his clothes occasionally. He spent endless hours lying on his bed, staring at the ceiling and listening to Pink Floyd tapes. He'd go off to pubs where he knew nobody and drink morosely. Then he'd stumble into the night and wander through the town until the small hours.

Ziggy tried to talk to him, but Mondo would have none of it. Somewhere in his heart, he blamed Ziggy, Weird and Alex for what had happened to him, and he didn't want what he saw as their pity. That would be the final indignity. He wanted proper friends who would appreciate him, not people who felt sorry for him. He wanted friends he could trust, not ones who made him worry about what knowing them might mean for him.

One afternoon, his pub crawl took him to a small hotel on The Scores. He trudged up to the bar and slurred an order for a pint. The barman looked at him with thinly disguised contempt and said, "Sorry, son. I'm not serving you."

"What do you mean, you're not serving me?"

"This is a respectable establishment, and you look like a tramp. I have the right to refuse service to anyone I don't want drinking in here." He jerked a thumb toward a notice by the till which backed up his words. "On your bike."

Mondo stared at him in disbelief. He looked around, seeking support from other customers. Everyone studiously avoided meeting his eye. "Fuck you, pal," he said, sweeping an ashtray to the floor and storming out.

In the short time he'd been inside, the heavy rain that had been threatening all day had broken over the town, scouring the streets under the impetus of a strong east wind. In no time at all, he was soaked to the skin. Mondo wiped the rain from his face and realized he was crying. He'd had enough of this. He couldn't take another day of misery and pointlessness. He had no friends, women despised him and he just knew he was going to fail his finals because he hadn't done any work. Nobody cared because nobody understood.

Drunk and depressed, he staggered along The Scores toward the castle. He'd had enough. He'd show them. He'd make them see his point of view. He climbed over the railing by the footpath and stood swaying at the edge of the cliff. Below, the sea pounded angrily against the rocks, sending fountains of spume high into the air. Mondo breathed in the salt spray and felt curiously at peace as he stared down at the raging water. He spread his arms wide, raised his face to the rain and screamed his pain at the sky.

CHAPTER
EIGHTEEN

Maclennan was walking past the radio room when the call went out. He translated the numbers in the code. Potential suicide on the cliffs above the Castle Sands. Not really a CID matter, and anyway, it was his day off. He'd only come in to clear up some paperwork. He could carry on out the door, be home in ten minutes, a can of lager in his hand and the sports pages open on his lap. Like almost every other day off since Elaine walked out the door.

No contest.

He stuck his head in the radioroom door. "Tell them I'm on my way," he said. "And send for the lifeboat from Anstruther."

The operator looked at him in surprise, but gave him the thumbs up. Maclennan carried on through to the car park. God, but it was a rough afternoon. The bloody weather alone was enough to make you suicidal. He drove to the scene, his wipers barely slapping the windscreen clear between gouts of rain.

The cliffs were a favorite spot for attempted suicides. Mostly, they succeeded if the tide was right. There was a vicious undertow that swept the unsuspecting out into the sea in a matter of minutes. And nobody lasted long in the North Sea in winter. There had been some spectacular failures, too. He remembered a janitor from one of the local primary schools who had completely mistimed the attempt. He came crashing down into two feet of water, missed the rocks altogether and ended up hitting the sand. He broke both his ankles and was so mortified at this farcical fiasco that he caught a bus to Leuchars the day he was released from hospital, tottered on his crutches along the railway track and threw himself under the Aberdeen express.

That wouldn't happen today, though. Maclennan was pretty sure the tide was in, and the east wind would whip the sea into a pounding maelstrom beneath the cliffs. He hoped they'd get there in time.

There was a panda car there already when he arrived. Janice Hogg and another uniformed officer were standing uncertainly by the low railing, watching a young man lean into the wind, his arms spread like Christ on the cross. "Don't just stand there," Maclennan said, turning his collar up against the rain. "There's a lifebelt further along. One of those ones with a rope. Get it, now."

The male constable sprinted off in the direction Maclennan was pointing in. The detective climbed over the railing and took a couple of steps forward. "All right, son," he said gently.

The young man turned and Maclennan realized that it was Davey Kerr. A wrecked and ruined Davey Kerr, to be sure. But there was no mistaking that elfin face, those terrified Bambi eyes. "You're too late," he slurred, his body wavering drunkenly.

"It's never too late," Maclennan said. "Whatever's wrong, we can fix it."

Mondo turned to face Maclennan. He dropped his arms to his side. "Fix it?" His eyes blazed. "You're ones that broke it in the first place. Thanks to you lot, everybody thinks I'm a killer. I've got no friends, I've got no future."

"Of course you've got friends. Alex, Ziggy, Tom. They're your friends." The wind howled and the rain battered his face, but Maclennan was oblivious to everything except the frightened face before him.

"Some friends. They don't want me, because I tell the

truth." Mondo's hand came up to his mouth and he chewed at a fingernail. "They hate me."

"I don't think so." Maclennan took a small step nearer. Another couple of feet and he'd be within grabbing distance.

"No closer. You stay back. This is my business. Not yours."

"Think about what you're doing here, Davey. Think about the people who love you. This is going to tear up your family."

Mondo shook his head. "They don't care about me. They've always loved my sister more than me."

"Tell me what's bothering you." *Keep him talking, keep him alive*, Maclennan willed himself. Let this not be another nightmare fuck-up.

"Are you deaf, man? I already told you," Mondo shouted, his face a rictus of pain. "You've ruined my life."

"That's not true. You've got a great future."

"Not anymore, I haven't." He spread his arms like wings again. "Nobody understands what I'm going through."

"Let me understand." Maclennan edged forward. Mondo tried to step sideways but his drunken feet slithered on the thin wet grass. His face was a mask of shocked horror. In a terrible pantomimic cartwheel, he struggled against the pull of gravity. For a few drawn-out seconds, it looked as if he would succeed. Then his feet went from under him and he disappeared from sight in one shocking moment.

Maclennan lunged forward, but far too late. He teetered on the edge, but the wind was on his side and held him till he had his balance again. He looked down. He thought he saw the splash. Then he saw Mondo's white face through a break in the white froth of water. He whirled round as Janice and the other constable reached his side. Another police car drew up, disgorging Jimmy Lawson and two other uniformed officers. "The lifebelt," Maclennan shouted. "Hold on to the rope."

Already, he was tearing off his coat and jacket, slipping out of his shoes. Maclennan grabbed the lifebelt and looked down again. This time, he saw an arm black against the foam. He took a deep breath and launched himself into space.

The drop was heart-stopping in its suddenness. Buffeted by the wind, Maclennan felt weightless and insignificant. It was over in seconds. Hitting the water was like falling on to solid ground. It knocked the breath from him. Gasping and swallowing great mouthfuls of freezing salt water, Maclennan struggled to the surface. All he could see was water, spray and spume. He kicked out with his legs, trying to orientate himself.

Then, in a trough between the waves, he caught a glimpse of Mondo. The lad was a few yards farther out, over to his left. Maclennan struck out toward him, hampered by the lifebelt round his arm. The sea lifted him and brought him crashing down again, carrying him right into Mondo. He grabbed him by the scruff of his neck.

Mondo flailed in his grip. At first, Maclennan thought he was determined to break free and drown himself. But then he understood that Mondo was fighting him for the lifebelt. Maclennan knew he couldn't hang on indefinitely. He let go of the lifebelt but managed to cling on to Mondo.

Mondo grabbed at the belt. He thrust one arm through it and tried to get it over his head. But Maclennan was still gripping his collar, knowing his life depended on it. There was only one thing for it. Mondo thrust back as hard as he could with his free elbow. Suddenly, he was clear.

He pulled the lifebelt over his body, desperately gasping for breath in the saturated air. Behind him, Maclennan struggled closer, somehow managing to get a hand on the rope attached to the lifebelt. It took a superhuman effort, his waterlogged clothes fighting him every inch of the way. Cold was eating into Maclennan now, making his fingers numb. He clung to the rope with one arm, waving the other above their heads to signal to the team on the cliff to bring them up.

He could feel the pull on the rope. Would five be enough to get them both up the cliff? Had somebody had the *nous* to get a boat round from the harbor? They'd be dead from cold long before the lifeboat arrived from Anstruther.

They closed in on the cliffs. One minute, Maclennan was aware of the buoyancy of the water. Then all he felt was drag as he rose out of the water, holding on to the lifebelt and Mondo for dear life. He stared upward, gratefully seeing the pale face of the front man on the rope, his features a blur through the rain and spray.

They were six feet up the cliff when Mondo, terrified that Maclennan was going to pull him back into the maelstrom, kicked backward. Maclennan's fingers gave up the fight. He plunged back helpless into the water. Again he went under, again he struggled to the surface. He could see Mondo's body rising slowly up the cliff face. He couldn't believe it. The bastard had kicked him free to save himself. He hadn't been trying to kill himself at all. It had just been posturing, attention-seeking.

Maclennan spat out another mouthful of water. He was determined now to hang on, if only to make Davey Kerr wish he had drowned after all. All he had to do now was keep his head above water. They'd get the lifebelt back down to him. They'd send a boat round. Wouldn't they?

His strength was fading fast. He couldn't fight the water, so he let it carry him. He'd concentrate on keeping his face out of the sea.

Easier said than done. The undertow sucked at him, the swell smashing black walls of water into his mouth and nose. He didn't feel cold anymore, which was nice. Vaguely, he heard the *pocka-pocka* of a helicopter. He was drifting now, in a place where everything felt very calm. Air/Sea Rescue, that would be the noise he could hear. *Swing low, sweet chariot. Coming for to carry me home. Funny the things that go through your mind.* He giggled and swallowed another mouthful of water.

He felt very light now, the sea a bed rocking him gently to sleep. Barney Maclennan, asleep on the ocean wave.

The helicopter spotlight swept the sea for an hour. Nothing. Rosie Duff's killer had claimed a second victim.

PART
TWO

CHAPTER
NINETEEN

November 2003; Glenrothes, Scotland

ACC James Lawson eased his car into the slot that bore his name in the police HQ car park. Not a day went by when he didn't congratulate himself on his achievement. Not bad for the illegitimate son of a miner who'd grown up in a poky council flat in a dump of a village thrown up in the 1950s to house displaced workers whose only possibility of a job was in the expanding Fife coalfield. What a joke that had been. Within twenty-five years, the industry had shrunk beyond recognition, stranding its former employees in ugly oases of redundancy. His pals had all laughed at him when he'd turned his back on the pit to join what they perceived as the bosses' side. *Who had the last laugh now?* Lawson thought with a grim little smile as he pulled the key out of the ignition of his official Rover. Thatcher had seen off the miners and turned the police into her personal New Model Army. The Left had died and the phoenix risen from its ashes loved to wave the big stick almost as much as the Tories did. It had been a good time to be a career copper. His pension would bear testament to that.

He picked up his briefcase from the passenger seat and walked briskly toward the building, head down against a bitter East Coast wind that promised stinging showers of rain before the morning was out. He punched his security code into the keypad by the back door and headed for the lift. Instead of going straight to his office, he made for the fourth-floor room where the cold cases squad was based. There weren't many unsolved murders on Fife's books, so any success would be seen as spectacular. Lawson knew this operation had the potential to enhance his reputation if it was handled correctly. What he was determined to avoid was a botched job. None of them could afford that.

The room he'd requisitioned for the squad was a decent size. There was space for the half-dozen computer work stations, and although there was no natural light, that meant plenty of room for each of the ongoing cases to be displayed on large corkboards that went all round the walls. Alongside each case was a printed list of actions to be carried out. As the officers worked their way through these tasks, new handwritten actions were added to the lists. Boxes of files were stacked to waist level along two walls. Lawson liked to keep a close eye on progress; although this was a high-profile operation, that didn't mean it wasn't tightly constrained by budgetary controls. Most of the new forensic tests were expensive to commission, and he was determined not to allow his squad to be so seduced by the glamour of technology that they squandered all of their resources on lab bills, leaving nothing for the sheer slog of routine investigative tasks.

With one exception, Lawson had handpicked the team of half a dozen detectives, choosing those with a reputation for meticulous attention to detail and the intelligence to connect disparate pieces of information. That exception was an officer whose presence in the room troubled Lawson. Not because he was an inadequate copper, but because he had far too much at stake. Detective Inspector Robin Maclennan's brother Barney had died in the course of investigating one of these cold cases, and if it had been up to Lawson, he'd have been allowed nowhere near the review. But Maclennan had appealed over his head to the Chief Constable, who had overruled Lawson.

The one thing he'd managed to achieve was to keep

Maclennan away from the Rosie Duff case itself. After Barney's death, Robin had transferred out of Fife down south. He'd only returned after his father's death the previous year, wanting to work out his last years before his pension close to his mother. By chance, Maclennan had a loose operational link to one of the other cases, so Lawson had persuaded his boss to let him assign the DI to the case of Lesley Cameron, a student who had been raped and murdered in St. Andrews eighteen years ago. Back then, Robin Maclennan had been based near her parents' home and he'd been the designated liaison officer with Lesley's family, probably because of his own connections in the Fife force. Lawson thought Maclennan was likely looking over the shoulder of the detective assigned to the Rosie Duff case, but at least his personal feelings couldn't interfere directly with that investigation.

That November morning, only two officers were at their desks. Detective Constable Phil Parhatka had what was probably the most sensitive case in the review. His victim was a young man found murdered in his home. His best friend had been charged and convicted of the crime, but a series of embarrassing revelations about the police investigation had led to the overturning of the conviction on appeal. The repercussions had holed several careers below the waterline, and now the pressure was on to find the real killer. Lawson had partly chosen Parhatka because of his reputation for sensitivity and discretion. But what Lawson had also seen in the young DC was the same hunger for success that had driven him at that age. Parhatka wanted a result so badly Lawson could almost see the desire smoking off him.

As Lawson walked in, the other officer was getting to her feet. DC Karen Pirie yanked an unfashionable but functional sheepskin coat off the back of her chair and shrugged into it. She glanced up, sensing a new presence in the room, and gave Lawson a weary smile. "There's nothing else for it. I'm going to have to talk to the original witnesses."

"There's no point in that until you've dealt with the physical evidence," Lawson said.

"But, sir . . ."

"You're going to have to go down there and do a manual search."

Karen looked appalled. "That could take weeks."

"I know, but that's all there is for it."

"But, sir . . . what about the budget?"

Lawson sighed. "Let me worry about the budget. I don't see what alternative you've got. We need that evidence to apply pressure. It isn't in the box it's supposed to be in. The only suggestion the evidence custody team can come up with is that somehow it got 'mislaid' during the move to the new storage facility. They haven't got the bodies to do a search, so you'll have to."

Karen hefted her bag on to her shoulder. "Right you are, sir."

"I've said right from the beginning that, if we're going to make any progress with this one, the physical evidence is going to be the key. If anyone can find it, you can. Do your best, Karen." He watched her leave, her very walk a simulacrum of the doggedness that had instigated his matching of Karen Pirie with the twenty-five-year-old murder of Rosemary Duff. With a few words of encouragement to Parhatka, Lawson set off for his own office on the third floor.

He settled himself behind his expansive desk and felt a niggle of worry that things might not work out as he had hoped in the cold case review. It would never be enough merely to say they'd done their best. They needed at least one result. He sipped his sweet, strong tea and reached for his in-tray. He scanned a couple of memos, ticking off his initials at the top of the pages and consigning them to the internal mail tray. The next item was a letter from a member of the public, addressed to him personally. That was unusual in itself. But its contents jerked James Lawson to attention in his chair.

12 Carlton Way
St. Monans
Fife

Assistant Chief Constable James Lawson
Fife Constabulary Headquarters
Detroit Road
Glenrothes
KY6 2RJ

8 November 2003

Dear ACC Lawson,
I read with interest a newspaper report that Fife Police
have instigated a cold case review on unsolved murders. I
presume that, among these cases, you will be looking
again at the murder of Rosemary Duff. I would like to
arrange a meeting with you to discuss this case. I have information which, while perhaps not directly relevant, may
contribute to your understanding of the background.
Please do not dismiss this letter as the work of some crank.
I have reason to believe that the police were not aware of
this information at the time of the original investigation.
   I look forward to hearing from you.

Graham Macfadyen
Yours sincerely,
Graham Macfadyen

Graham Macfadyen dressed carefully. He wanted to make
the right impression on ACC Lawson. He'd been afraid the
policeman would write off his letter as the work of some
attention-seeking nutter. But to his surprise, he'd had a reply
by return of post. What was even more surprising was that
Lawson himself had written, asking him to call to arrange an
appointment. He'd expected the ACC would pass his letter
on to whichever of his minions was dealing with the case. It

impressed him that the police were clearly taking the matter so seriously. When he'd rung, Lawson had suggested they meet at Macfadyen's home in St. Monans. "More informal than here at headquarters," he'd said. Macfadyen suspected that Lawson wanted to see him on his home turf, the better to make an assessment of his mental state. But he had been happy to accept the suggestion, not least because he always hated negotiating the labyrinth of roundabouts which Glenrothes seemed to consist of.

Macfadyen had spent the previous evening cleaning his living room. He always thought of himself as a relatively tidy man, and it invariably surprised him that there was so much to clear up on those occasions involving the presence of another in his home. Perhaps that was because he so seldom took the opportunity to extend his hospitality. He'd never seen the point of dating and, if he was honest, he didn't feel the lack of a woman in his life. Dealing with his colleagues seemed to use up all the energy he had for social interaction, and he seldom mixed with them out of working hours; just enough not to stand out. He'd learned as a child it was always better to be invisible than to be noticed. But no matter how much time he spent in software development, he never tired of working with the machines. Whether it was surfing the net, exchanging information in newsgroups or playing multi-user games online, Macfadyen was happiest when there was a barrier of silicon between him and the rest of the world. The computer never judged, never found him wanting. People thought computers were complicated and hard to understand, but they were wrong. Computers were predictable and safe. Computers did not let you down. You knew exactly where you were with a computer.

He studied himself in the mirror. He'd learned that blending in was the perfect way to avoid unwanted attention. Today he wanted to look relaxed, average, unthreatening. Not weird. He knew most people thought anyone who worked in IT was automatically weird, and he didn't want Lawson to jump to the same conclusion. He wasn't weird. Just different. But that was definitely something he didn't want Lawson to pick up on. Slip under their radar, that was the way to get what you wanted.

He'd settled on a pair of Levis and a Guinness polo shirt. Nothing there to frighten the horses. He ran a comb through his thick dark hair, scowling slightly at his reflection. A woman had once told him he resembled James Dean, but he'd dismissed it as a pathetic attempt to get him to take an interest in her. He slipped on a pair of black leather loafers and glanced at his watch. Ten minutes to kill. Macfadyen walked through to the spare bedroom and sat down at one of the three computers. He had one lie to tell, and if he was going to be convincing, he needed to be calm.

James Lawson drove slowly up Carlton Way. It was a crescent of small detached homes, built in the 1990s to resemble the traditional East Neuk style of houses. The harled walls, steep tiled roofs and crow-stepped gables were all trademarks of the local vernacular architecture, and the houses were individual enough to blend innocuously with their surroundings. About half a mile inland from the fishing village of St. Monans, the houses were perfect for young professionals who couldn't afford the more traditional homes that had been snapped up by incomers who wanted something quaint either to retire to or to let out to holidaymakers.

Graham Macfadyen's house was one of the smaller ones. Two recep, two beds, Lawson thought. No garage, but enough of a drive to accommodate a couple of small cars. An elderly silver VW Golf sat there presently. Lawson parked on the street and walked up the path, the trousers of his lounge suit flapping against his legs in the stiff breeze from the Firth of Forth. He rang the bell and waited impatiently. He didn't think he'd fancy living somewhere this bleak. Pretty enough in the summer, but grim and dreich on a cold November evening.

The door opened, revealing a man in his late twenties. Medium height, slim build, Lawson thought automatically. A mop of dark hair, the kind with a wave that's almost impossible to keep looking neat. Blue eyes, deep set, wide cheekbones and a full, almost feminine mouth. No criminal convictions, he knew from his background check. But far too young to have any personal knowledge of the Rosie Duff case. "Mr. Macfadyen?" Lawson said.

The man nodded. "You must be Assistant Chief Constable Lawson. Is that what I call you?"

Lawson smiled reassuringly. "No need for rank, Mr. Lawson is fine."

Macfadyen stepped back. "Come in."

Lawson followed him down a narrow hallway into a neat living room. A three-piece suite in brown leather faced a TV set next to a video and a DVD player. Shelves on either side held video tapes and DVD boxes. The only other furniture in the room was a cabinet containing glasses and several bottles of malt whiskey. But Lawson only took that in later. What hit him between the eyes was the only picture on the walls. An atmospheric photograph blown up to 20" by 30", it was instantly recognizable to anyone involved with the Rosie Duff case. Taken with the sun low in the sky, it showed the exposed long cists of the Pictish cemetery on Hallow Hill where her dying body had been discovered. Lawson was transfixed. Macfadyen's voice dragged him back to the present.

"Can I offer you a drink?" he asked. He stood just inside the doorway, still as prey caught in the gaze of the hunter.

Lawson shook his head, as much to disperse the image as to refuse the offer. "No thanks." He sat down, the assurance of years as a police officer granting him permission.

Macfadyen came into the room and settled in the armchair opposite. Lawson couldn't read him at all, which he found faintly unsettling. "You said in your letter that you have some information on the Rosemary Duff case?" he began cautiously.

"That's right." Macfadyen leaned forward slightly. "Rosie Duff was my mother."

CHAPTER
TWENTY

December 2003

The cannibalized timer from a video recorder; a paint tin; quarter of a liter of petrol; odds and ends of fuse wire. Nothing remarkable, nothing that might not be found in any jumbled collection of domestic flotsam in any cellar or garden shed. Innocuous enough.

Except when combined in one particular configuration. Then it becomes something entirely undomesticated.

The timer reached the set date and time; a spark crossed a gap of wire and ignited the petrol vapor. The lid of the tin exploded upward, spraying the surrounding waste paper and offcuts of wood with flaming petrol. A textbook operation, perfect and deadly.

Flames found fresh fodder in rolls of discarded carpet, half-empty paint pots, the varnished hull of a dinghy. Fiberglass and outboard fuel, garden furniture and aerosol cans turned into torches and flame-throwers as the fire built in intensity. Cinders skyrocketed upward, like a cheapskate's firework display.

Above it all, smoke gathered. While the fire roared at the darkness below, the fumes drifted through the house, lazily at first and then growing in intensity. The outriders were invisible, thin vapors oozing through floorboards and wafting upward on drafts of hot air. They were enough to make the sleeping man cough uneasily but not sufficiently acrid to waken him. As the smoke followed, it became perceptible, wraiths of mist eerie in the patches of moonlight cast by uncurtained windows. The smell, too, became palpable, an alert for anyone in a position to heed it. However, the smoke had already dulled the responses of the sleeping man. If someone had shaken his shoulder, he might have been able to rouse himself and stagger to the window and its promise of safety. But he was beyond self-help. Sleep was becoming unconsciousness. And soon, unconsciousness would give way to death.

The fire crackled and sparked, sending scarlet and golden comet trails into the sky. Timbers groaned and crashed to the ground. It was about as spectacular and painless as murder gets.

In spite of the climate-controlled warmth of his office, Alex Gilbey shivered. Gray sky, gray slates, gray stone. The hoar frost that coated the roofs on the other side of the street had scarcely diminished all day. Either they had terrific insulation across the road, or the temperature hadn't climbed above freezing since the late December dawn. He looked down at Dundas Street below. Exhaust fumes billowed like the ghosts of Christmas past from the traffic that made the routes into the city center even more clogged than usual. Out-of-towners in to do their Christmas shopping, not realizing that finding a parking space in the center of Edinburgh in the weeks leading up to the festive season was harder than finding the perfect gift for a fussy teenage girl.

Alex looked back up at the sky. Leaden and low, it was advertising snow with all the subtlety of a furniture showroom January sales TV commercial. His spirits sank further. He'd been doing pretty well so far this year. But if it snowed, all his determination would unravel and he'd be back in his usual seasonal gloom. Today of all days, he could do without the snow. Exactly twenty-five years ago, he'd stumbled across something that had turned every Christmas since into a maelstrom of bad memories. No amount of goodwill from all men, or women for that matter, could erase the anniversary of Rosie Duff's death from Alex's mental calendar.

He must, he thought, be the only manufacturer of greetings cards who hated the most profitable season of the year. In the offices down the hall, the telesales team would be taking last-minute orders from wholesalers replenishing stock, and using the opportunity to bump up the orders for Valentine's Day, Mother's Day and Easter. At the warehouse, staff would be starting to relax, knowing the worst of the rush was well over now, taking the opportunity to review the successes and failures of the past few weeks. And in the accounts department, they'd be smiling for once. This year's figures were up almost eight percent on the previous year, thanks in part to a new range of cards Alex had developed himself. Even though it had been more than ten years since he'd moved on from earning his living with his pens and inks, Alex liked to make the occasional contribution to the product range. Nothing like it to keep the rest of the team on their toes.

But it had been back in April when he'd designed those cards, well clear of the shadow of the past. It was odd how seasonal this malaise was. As soon as Twelfth Night saw the Christmas decorations consigned to storage once more, the shade of Rosie Duff would grow insubstantial again, leaving his mind clear and unclouded by memory. He'd be able to take pleasure in his life again. For now, he'd just have to endure.

He'd tried a variety of strategies over the years to make it all go away. On the second anniversary, he'd drunk himself into oblivion. He still had no idea who had delivered him back to his bedsit in Glasgow, nor which bar he had ended up in. But all that achieved was to ensure that the night's sweaty paranoid dreams featured Rosie's ironic smile and easy laugh in a constant mad kaleidoscope he couldn't waken from.

The year after that, he'd visited her grave in the Western Cemetery in St. Andrews, right on the edge of the town. He'd waited till dusk to avoid anyone spotting his face. He'd parked his anonymous clapped-out Ford Escort as near to the gate as he could manage, pulled a tweed cap low over his eyes, turned up his coat collar and skulked into the damp gloom. The problem was, he didn't know exactly where Rosie was buried. He'd only ever seen the pictures of the funeral that the local paper had splashed all over the front page, and all that told him was that it was somewhere up toward the back of the graveyard.

He stole head down among the gravestones, feeling like a freak, wishing he'd brought a torch and then realizing there was no better way to draw attention to himself. A little light leaked in from the streetlamps as they came on, just enough to read most of the inscriptions. Alex had been on the point of giving up when he'd finally come upon it, in a secluded corner right against the wall.

It was a simple black granite block. The letters were incised in gold and still looked as fresh as the day they'd been cut. At first, Alex took refuge in his role as an artist, dealing with what was before him as a purely aesthetic object. In those terms, it satisfied. But he couldn't hide for long from the import of the words he'd been trying to see only as shapes in the stone. "Rosemary Margaret Duff. Born 25 May 1959. Cruelly snatched from us 16 December 1978. A loving daughter and sister lost to us forever. May she rest in peace." Alex remembered the police had set up a collection to pay for the headstone. They must have done well, to afford so lengthy a message, he thought, still trying to avoid engaging with what those words connected to.

The other element it was impossible to ignore was the assortment of floral tributes carefully placed at the foot of the stone. There must have been a dozen bunches and sprays of flowers, several in the squat urns that florists sold for the purpose. The overflow lay on the grass, a potent reminder of how many hearts Rosie Duff still inhabited.

Alex unbuttoned his overcoat and took out the single white rose he'd brought with him. He'd crouched down to place it unobtrusively with the others when he nearly pissed himself. The hand on his shoulder came out of nowhere. The wet grass had absorbed the footsteps and he'd been too engrossed in his own thoughts for his animal instincts to have warned him.

Alex spun round and away from the hand, slipping on the grass and sprawling on his back in a nauseating mimicry of that December night three years before. He cringed, expecting a kick or a blow as whoever had disturbed him realized who he was. He was completely unprepared for a concerned inquiry from a familiar voice addressing him by a nickname only ever used by his closest circle.

"Hey, Gilly, you OK?" Sigmund Malkiewicz extended a hand to help Alex to his feet. "I didn't mean to give you a fright."

"Christ, Ziggy, what else did you think you were going to do, creeping up on me in a dark graveyard?" Alex protested, scrambling upright under his own steam.

"Sorry." He indicated the rose with a jerk of his head. "Nice touch. I could never think what might be appropriate."

"You've been here before?" Alex brushed himself down and turned to face his oldest friend. Ziggy looked ghostly in the dim light, his pale skin seeming to glow from within.

He nodded. "Only on the anniversaries. Never saw you before, though."

Alex shrugged. "My first time. Anything to try and make it go away, you know?"

"I don't think I'll ever manage that."

"Me neither." Without another word, they turned and walked back toward the entrance, each locked into his own bad memories. By unspoken agreement, once they'd left university, they'd avoided speaking about the event that had changed their lives so profoundly. The shadow was always there; but these days it remained unacknowledged between them. Perhaps it had been the avoidance of those conversations without resolution that had allowed their friendship to survive as strongly as it had. They didn't manage to see each other so often now that Ziggy was living the hellish schedule of a junior doctor in Edinburgh, but when they did arrange a night out together, the old intimacy was still as strong.

At the gate, Ziggy paused and said, "Fancy a pint?"

Alex shook his head. "If I start, I'll not want to stop. And this isn't a good part of the world for you and me to be pissed in. There are still too many people round here who think we got away with murder. No, I'll get away back to Glasgow."

Ziggy pulled him into a tight hug. "We'll see each other over the New Year, right? Town Square, midnight?"

"Aye. Me and Lynn, we'll be there."

Ziggy nodded, understanding everything contained in those few words. He raised a hand in a mock-salute and walked away into the gathering dark.

Alex hadn't been back to the grave since. It hadn't helped, nor was that how he wanted to encounter Ziggy. It was too raw, too loaded with stuff they both wanted to avoid coming between them.

At least he didn't have to suffer in secret, the way he believed the others did. Lynn had known everything about the death of Rosie Duff right from the word go. They'd been together since that winter. He sometimes wondered if that was the single thing that had made it possible for him to love her, that his biggest secret was already common currency between them.

It was hard not to feel that the circumstances of that night had somehow robbed him of a different future. It was his personal albatross, a stain on the memory that left him feeling permanently tainted. Nobody would want to be his friend if they knew what lay in his past, what suspicions still hung over him in the minds of so many. And yet Lynn knew, and she loved him in spite of it.

She'd demonstrated it in so many ways over the years. And soon, the ultimate proof would come. In two short months, please God, she'd be delivered of the child they'd both desired for so long. They'd both wanted to wait till they were settled before they started a family, and then it had begun to look as if they'd left it too late. Three years of trying, the appointment already set up at the fertility clinic, then out of the blue Lynn had become pregnant. It felt like the first fresh start he'd had in twenty-five years.

Alex turned away from the window. His life was going to change. And maybe, if he made a determined effort, he could loosen the grip of the past. Starting tonight. He'd book a table at the restaurant on the roof of the Museum of Scotland. Take Lynn out for a special meal, instead of sitting at home and brooding.

As he reached out for the phone, it began to ring. Startled, Alex stared stupidly at it for a moment before he reached for it. "Alex Gilbey speaking."

It took him a while to connect the voice on the other end with its owner. Not a stranger, but not someone he expected to call any afternoon, never mind this one in particular. "Alex, it's Paul. Paul Martin." The recognition was made all the more difficult by the caller's obvious agitation.

Paul. Ziggy's Paul. A particle physicist, whatever that was, with the build of a quarterback. The man who'd been bringing a dazzle to Ziggy's face for the past ten years. "Hi, Paul. This is a surprise."

"Alex, I don't know how to say this . . ." Paul's voice cracked. "I got bad news."

"Ziggy?"

"He's dead, Alex. Ziggy's dead."

Alex nearly shook the phone, as if something mechanical had caused him to misapprehend Paul's words. "No," he said. "No, there must be some mistake."

"I wish," Paul said. "There's no mistake, Alex. The house, it went on fire in the night. Burned to the ground. My Ziggy . . . he's dead."

Alex stared at the wall, seeing nothing. Ziggy played guitar, his brain hummed pointlessly.

Not anymore he didn't.

CHAPTER
TWENTY-ONE

Although he'd spent half the day scribbling the date on assorted pieces of paper alongside his initials, James Lawson had managed entirely to avoid its significance. Then he came across a request from DC Parhatka for authorization of a DNA test on an emerging suspect in his inquiry. The combination of the date and the cold case review team made the tumblers of his mind clatter into place. There was no escape from the knowledge. Today was the twenty-fifth anniversary of Rosie Duff's death.

He wondered how Graham Macfadyen was dealing with it, and the memory of their uncomfortable interview made Lawson shift in his seat. At first, he'd been incredulous. No mention of a child had ever been made during the investigation into Rosie's death. Neither friends nor family had even hinted at such a secret. But Macfadyen was adamant.

"You must have known she had a child," he'd insisted. "Surely the pathologist noted it at the post mortem?"

Lawson's mind instantly summoned up the shambling figure of Dr. Kenneth Fraser. He'd already been semiretired by the time of the murder and generally smelled more of whiskey than of formalin. Most of the work he'd done in his long career had been straightforward; he had little experience of murder, and he remembered Barney Maclennan wondering aloud whether they should have brought in someone whose experience was more current. "It never came out," he said, avoiding any further comment.

"That's incredible," Macfadyen said.

"Maybe the wound obscured the evidence."

"I suppose that's possible," Macfadyen said dubiously. "I assumed you knew about me but had never been able to trace me. I always knew I was adopted," he said. "But I thought it was only fair to my adopted parents to wait till they'd both died before I carried out any research into my birth mother. My dad died three years ago. And my mother . . . well, she's in a home. She's got Alzheimer's. She might as well be dead for all the difference it'll make to her. So a few months ago, I started making inquiries." He left the room and returned almost immediately with a blue cardboard folder. "There you go," he said, handing it over to Lawson.

The policeman felt as if he'd been handed a jar of nitroglycerine. He didn't quite understand the faint feeling of disgust that crept through him, but he didn't let that prevent him from opening the folder. The bundle of papers inside was arranged in chronological order. First came Macfadyen's letter of inquiry. Lawson flicked on through, absorbing the gist of the correspondence. He arrived at a birth certificate and paused. There, in the space reserved for the mother's name, familiar information leaped off the page. Rosemary Margaret Duff. Date of birth, 25 May 1959. Mother's occupation: unemployed. Where the father's name should have been, the word, "unknown" sat like the scarlet letter on a Puritan dress. But the address was unfamiliar.

Lawson looked up. Macfadyen was gripping the arms of his chair tight, his knuckles like gravel chips under stretched latex. "Livingstone House, Saline?" he asked.

"It's all in there. A Church of Scotland home where young women in trouble were sent to have their babies. It's a children's home now, but back then, it was where women were sent to hide their shame from the neighbors. I managed to track down the woman who ran the place then. Ina Dryburgh. She's in her seventies now, but she's in full possession of all her marbles. I was surprised how willing she was to talk to me. I thought it would be harder. But she said it was too far in the past to hurt anybody now. Let the dead bury their dead, that seems to be her philosophy."

"What did she tell you?" Lawson leaned forward in his seat, willing Macfadyen to reveal the secret that had miraculously withstood a full-scale murder inquiry.

The young man relaxed slightly, now it appeared he was being taken seriously. "Rosie got pregnant when she was fifteen. She found the courage to tell her mother when she was about three months gone, before anybody had guessed. Her mother acted fast. She went to see the minister and he put her in touch with Livingstone House. Mrs. Duff got on the bus the next morning and went to see Mrs. Dryburgh. She agreed to take Rosie, and suggested that Mrs. Duff put it about that Rosie had gone off to stay with a relative who'd had an operation and needed an extra pair of hands round the house to help with her children. Rosie left Strathkinness that weekend and went to Saline. She spent the rest of the pregnancy under Mrs. Dryburgh's wing." Macfadyen swallowed hard.

"She never held me. Never even saw me. She had a photo, that was all. They did things differently back then. I was taken off and handed over to my parents that same day. And by the end of the week, Rosie was back in Strathkinness as if nothing had happened. Mrs. Dryburgh said the next time she heard Rosie's name was on the television news." He gave a short, sharp exhalation.

"And that's when she told me that my mother had been dead for twenty-five years. Murdered. With nobody ever brought to book. I didn't know what to do. I wanted to contact the rest of my family. I managed to find out that my grandparents were both dead. But I've got two uncles, apparently."

"You haven't made contact with them?"

"I didn't know whether I should. And then I saw the article in the paper about the cold case review, and I thought I'd speak to you first."

Lawson looked at the floor. "Unless they've changed a lot since I knew them, I'd say you might be well advised to let sleeping dogs lie." He felt Macfadyen's eyes on him and raised his head. "Brian and Colin were always very protective of Rosie. They were always ready with their hands too. My guess is that they'd take what you have to say as a slur on her character. I don't think it would make for a happy family reunion."

"I thought, you know . . . maybe they'd see me as some part of Rosie that lived on?"

"I wouldn't bank on it," Lawson said firmly.

Macfadyen looked stubbornly unconvinced. "But if this information helped your new inquiry? They might see it differently then, don't you think? Surely they want to see her killer caught at last?"

Lawson shrugged. "To be honest, I don't see how this takes us any further forward. You were born nearly four years before your mother died."

"But what if she was still seeing my father? What if that had something to do with her murder?"

"There was no evidence of that sort of long-term relationship in Rosie's past. She'd had several boyfriends in the year before she died, none of them very serious. But that didn't leave room for anybody else."

"Well, what if he'd gone away and come back? I read the newspaper reports of her murder, and there was some suggestion there that she was seeing somebody, but nobody knew who it was. Maybe my father came back, and she didn't want her parents to know she was seeing the boy who'd got her pregnant." Macfadyen's voice was urgent.

"It's a theory, I suppose. But if nobody knew who the father of her child was, it still doesn't take us anywhere."

"But you didn't know then that she'd had a child. I bet you never asked who she was going out with four years before her murder. Maybe her brothers knew who my father was."

Lawson sighed. "I'm not going to hold out false hope to you, Mr. Macfadyen. For one thing, Brian and Colin Duff were desperate for us to find Rosie's killer." He enumerated the points he was making on his fingers. "If the father of Rosie's child had still been around, or if he'd reappeared, you can lay money that they'd have been knocking on our door and screaming at us to arrest him. And if we hadn't obliged, they'd probably have broken his legs themselves. At the very least."

Macfadyen compressed his lips into a thin line. "So you're not going to pursue this line of inquiry?"

"If I may, I'd like to take this folder away with me and have a copy made to pass on to the detective who's dealing with your mother's case. It can't hurt to include it in our inquiry and it might just be helpful."

The light of triumph danced briefly in Macfadyen's eyes, as if he'd scored a major victory. "So you accept what I'm saying? That Rosie was my mother?"

"It looks that way. Though of course we'll have to make further inquiries ourselves."

"So you'll be wanting a blood sample from me?"

Lawson frowned. "A blood sample?"

Macfadyen jumped to his feet in a sudden access of energy. "Wait a minute," he said, leaving the room again. When he returned, he was grasping a thick paperback which fell open in line with its cracked spine. "I've read everything I could find about my mother's murder," he said, thrusting the book at Lawson.

Lawson glanced at the cover. *Getting Away With Murder: The Greatest Unsolved Cases of the Twentieth Century.* Rosie Duff merited five pages. Lawson skimmed it, impressed that the authors seemed to have got so little wrong. It brought back in uncomfortably sharp focus the terrible moment when he'd stood looking down at Rosie's body in the snow. "I'm still not with you," he said.

"It says that there were traces of semen on her body and on her clothing. That in spite of the primitive levels of forensic analysis back then, you were able to establish that three of the students who found her were possible candidates for having deposited it. But surely, with what you can do now, you can compare the DNA in the semen to my DNA? If it belonged to my father, you'd be able to tell."

Lawson was beginning to feel as if he'd stumbled through

the looking glass. That Macfadyen would be eager to find out anything he could about his father was entirely understandable. But to carry that obsession to the point where finding him guilty of murder was better than never finding him at all was unhealthy. "If we were going to make comparisons with anyone, it wouldn't be you, Graham," he said as kindly as he could manage. "It would be with the four lads referred to in this book. The ones who found her."

Macfadyen pounced. "You said, 'if.' "

"If?"

"You said, '*If* we were going to make comparisons.' Not, when. If."

Wrong book. It was definitely *Alice in Wonderland*. Lawson felt just like someone who has tumbled headlong down a steep, dark burrow, no safe ground beneath his feet. His lower back pain throbbed into action. Some people's aches and pains responded to the weather; Lawson's sciatic nerve was an acute barometer of stress. "This is very embarrassing for us, Mr. Macfadyen," he said, retreating behind the phalanx of formality. "At some point in the past twenty-five years, the physical evidence relating to your mother's murder has been mislaid."

Macfadyen's face screwed up in an expression of angry incredulity. "What do you mean, mislaid?"

"Exactly what I say. The evidence has been moved three times. Once, when the police station in St. Andrews moved to a new site. Then it was sent to central storage at headquarters. Recently, we moved to a new storage facility. And at some point the evidence bags that contained your mother's clothes were mislaid. When we went looking for them, they weren't in the box where they should have been."

Macfadyen looked as if he wanted to hit someone. "How could that happen?"

"The only explanation I can offer is human error." Lawson squirmed under the young man's look of furious contempt. "We're not infallible."

Macfadyen shook his head. "It's not the only explanation. Someone could have removed it deliberately."

"Why would anyone do that?"

"Well, it's obvious. The killer wouldn't want it found now, would he? Everybody knows about DNA. As soon as you announced a cold case review, he must have known he was living on borrowed time."

"The evidence was locked up in police storage. And we've not had any break-ins reported."

Macfadyen snorted. "You wouldn't need to break in. You'd just need to wave enough money under the right nose. Everybody has their price, even police officers. You can hardly open a paper or turn on the TV without seeing evidence of police corruption. Maybe you should be checking out which one of your officers has had a sudden dose of prosperity."

Lawson felt uneasy. Macfadyen's reasonable persona had slipped to one side, revealing an edge of paranoia that had been previously invisible. "That's a very serious allegation," he said. "And one for which there is no foundation whatsoever. Take it from me, whatever happened to the evidence in this case, it's down to human error."

Macfadyen glared mutinously. "Is that it, then? You're just going to stage a cover-up?"

Lawson tried to arrange his face in a conciliatory expression. "There's nothing to cover up, Mr. Macfadyen. I can assure you that the officer in charge of the case is conducting a search of the storage facility. It's possible she may yet find the evidence."

"But not very likely," he said heavily.

"No," Lawson agreed. "Not very likely."

A few days had passed before James Lawson had a chance to follow up his trying interview with Rosie Duff's illegitimate son. He'd had a quick word with Karen Pirie, but she'd been gloomily pessimistic about getting a result from the evidence warehouse. "Needle in a haystack, sir," she'd said. "I've already found three misfiled bags of evidence. If the public knew . . ."

"Let's make sure they never do," Lawson had said grimly.

Karen had looked horrified. "Oh God, aye."

Lawson had hoped the cock-up with the evidence in the Duff case could be buried. But that hope had died thanks to his own carelessness with Macfadyen. And now he was going to have to confess it all over again. If it ever came out that he'd kept this particular piece of information from the family, his name would be smeared across the headlines. And that would benefit nobody.

Strathkinness hadn't changed much in twenty-five years, Lawson realized as he parked the car outside Caberfeidh Cottage. There were a few new houses, but mostly the village had resisted the blandishments of developers. Surprising really, he thought. With those views, it was a natural location for some boutique country house hotel catering to the golf trade. However much the residents might have changed, it still felt like a working village.

He pushed open the gate, noticing the front garden was as neat as it ever had been when Archie Duff had been alive. Maybe Brian was confounding the prophets of doom and turning into his father. Lawson rang the bell and waited.

The man who opened the door was in good shape. Lawson knew he was in his mid-forties, but Brian Duff looked ten years younger. His skin had the healthy glow of a man who enjoys the outdoors, his short hair showed little sign of receding, and his T-shirt revealed a wide chest and the barest covering of fat over a taut abdomen. He made Lawson feel like an old man. Brian looked him up and down and indulged in a look of disdain. "Oh, it's you," he said.

"Withholding evidence could be construed as police obstruction. And that's a crime." Lawson wasn't going to be put on the back foot by Brian Duff.

"I don't know what you're on about. But I've kept my nose clean for over twenty years. You've no call to come knocking on my door, slinging your accusations about."

"I'm going back more than twenty years, Brian. I'm talking about your sister's murder."

Brian Duff didn't flinch. "I heard you were trying to go

out in a blaze of glory, getting your foot soldiers to try and
solve your old failures."

"Hardly my failure. I was just a bobby on the beat back
then. Are you going to invite me in, or are we going to do
this here for the whole world to see?"

Duff shrugged. "I've got nothing to hide. You might as
well come in."

The cottage had been transformed inside. Uncluttered
and pastel, the living room showed the handiwork of someone with an eye for design. "I've never met your wife," Lawson said as he followed Duff into a modern kitchen, its size
doubled by a conservatory-style extension.

"That's not likely to change. She'll not be home for an
hour yet." Duff opened the fridge and took out a can of lager.
He popped the top and leaned against the cooker. "So what
are you on about? Withholding evidence?" His attention was
ostensibly on the can of beer, but Lawson sensed that Duff
was alert as a cat in a strange garden.

"None of you ever mentioned Rosie's son," he said.

The bald statement provoked no visible response. "That
would be because it had nothing to do with her murder,"
Duff said, flexing his shoulders restlessly.

"Don't you think that was for us to decide?"

"No. It was private. It happened years before. The boy she
was going out with then didn't even live round here anymore.
And nobody knew about the baby outside the family. How
could it have had anything to do with her death? We didn't
want her name dragged through the mud, the way it would
have been if your lot had got hold of it. You'd have made her
look like some slag who got what was coming to her. Anything
to take the heat off the fact that you couldn't do your job."

"That's not true, Brian."

"Aye, it is. You'd have leaked it to the papers. And they'd
have turned Rosie into the village bike. She wasn't like that,
and you know it."

Lawson conceded the point with a faint grimace. "I know
she wasn't. But you should have told us. It might have had
some bearing on the investigation."

"It would have been a wild-goose chase." Duff took a long swig of his lager. "How come you found out about it after all this time?"

"Rosie's son has more of a social conscience than you. He came to us when he saw the story in the papers about the cold case review."

This time, there was a reaction. Duff froze halfway through raising the can to his mouth. He put it down abruptly on a worktop. "Christ," he swore. "What's that about, then?"

"He tracked down the woman who ran the home where Rosie had the baby. She told him about the murder. He wants to find his mother's killer as much as you do."

Duff shook his head. "I doubt that very much. Does he know where me and Colin live?"

"He knows you live here. He knows Colin's got a house in Kingsbarns, though he's mostly out in the Gulf. He says he traced you both via public records. Which is probably true. There's no reason why he should lie. I told him I didn't think you'd be very pleased to meet him."

"You're right about that at least. Maybe it would have been different if you'd managed to put her killer away. But I for one don't want to be reminded of that part of Rosie's life." He rubbed the back of his hand against his eye. "So, are you finally going to nail those fucking students?"

Lawson shifted his weight. "We don't know it was them, Brian. I always thought it was an outsider."

"Don't give me that shite. You know they were in the frame. You've got to be looking at them again."

"We're doing our best. But it's not looking promising."

"You've got DNA now. Surely that makes a difference? You had semen on her clothes."

Lawson looked away. His eye was caught by a fridge magnet made from a photograph. Rosie Duff's smile beamed out at him across the years, a needle of guilt that pierced deep. "There's a problem," he said, dreading what he knew would come next.

"What kind of a problem?"

"The evidence has been mislaid."

Duff pushed himself upright, tense on the balls of his feet. "You've lost the evidence?" His eyes blazed the rage Lawson remembered across the gulf of years.

"I didn't say lost. I said mislaid. It's not where it should be. We're pulling out all the stops to track it down, and I'm hopeful it'll turn up. But right now, we're stymied."

Duff's fists clenched. "So those four bastards are still safe?"

A month later, in spite of his supposedly relaxing fishing holiday, the memory of Duff's fury still reverberated in Lawson's chest. He'd heard nothing from Rosie's brother since then. But her son had been a regular caller. And the knowledge of their righteous anger made Lawson doubly conscious of the need for a result somewhere in the cold case review. The anniversary of Rosie's death somehow made that need more pressing. With a sigh, he pushed back his chair and headed for the squadroom.

CHAPTER
TWENTY-TWO

Alex stared at the entrance to his drive as if he'd never seen it before. He had no recollection of the drive out of Edinburgh, across the Forth Bridge and down into North Queensferry. Dazed, he eased the car in and parked at the far edge of the cobbled area, leaving plenty of space for Lynn's car nearer the house.

The square stone house sat on a bluff near the massive pilings of the cantilevered rail bridge. This close to the sea, the snow was fighting a losing battle with the salt air. The slush was treacherous underfoot, and Alex almost lost his footing a couple of times between the car and the front door. The first thing he did after wiping his feet and slamming the door closed against the elements was to call Lynn's mobile and leave a message warning her to be careful when she got home.

He glanced at the long case clock as he crossed the hall, snapping lights on as he went. It wasn't often that he was home on a weekday in winter when it was still technically daylight, but the sky was so low today, it felt later than it was. It would be at least an hour before Lynn returned. He needed company, but he'd have to make do with the sort that came out of a bottle till then.

In the dining room, Alex poured himself a brandy. Not too much, he cautioned himself. Getting pissed would make it worse, not better. He took his glass and continued through to the large conservatory that commanded a panoramic view of the Firth of Forth and sat in the gray gloom, oblivious to the shipping lights twinkling on the water. He didn't know how to begin to deal with the afternoon's news.

Nobody makes it to forty-six without loss. But Alex had been luckier than most. OK, he'd been to all four funerals of his grandparents in his twenties. But that was what you expected of people in their late seventies and eighties, and one way or another all four deaths had been what the living referred to as "a welcome release." Both his parents and his in-laws were still alive. So, until today, had been all his close friends. The nearest he'd come to intimacy with the dead had been a couple of years before, when his head printer had died in a car crash. Alex had been sad at the loss of a man he'd liked as well as relied on professionally, but he couldn't pretend to a grief he hadn't felt.

This was different. Ziggy had been part of his life for over thirty years. They'd shared every rite of passage; they were the touchstones for each other's memories. Without Ziggy, he felt cast adrift from his own history. Alex cast his mind back to their last meeting. He and Lynn had spent two weeks in California in the late summer. Ziggy and Paul had joined them for three days hiking in Yosemite. The sky had blazed blue, the sunlight casting the astonishing mountains into sharp relief, their every detail clear as the acid etching on a printing plate. On their final evening together, they'd driven cross country to the coast, checking in to a hotel on a bluff overlooking the Pacific. After dinner, Alex and Ziggy had retired to a hot tub with a six-pack from the local micro-brewery and congratulated themselves on having their lives so well sorted. They'd talked about Lynn's pregnancy and Alex had been gratified by Ziggy's obvious delight.

"You going to let me be the godfather?" he'd demanded, chinking his amber ale bottle against Alex's.

"I don't think we'll be doing the christening thing," Alex said. "But if the parents push us into it, there's nobody I'd rather have."

"You won't regret it," Ziggy said.

And Alex knew he wouldn't have. Not for a second. But that was something that would never happen now.

The following morning, Ziggy and Paul had left early for the long drive back to Seattle. They'd stood on the deck of their cabin in the pearly dawn light, hugging farewell. Another thing that would never happen again.

What was the last thing Ziggy had called out of the window of their SUV as they'd set off down the trail? Something about making sure Alex indulged Lynn's every whim because it would get him into practice for parenthood. He couldn't remember the exact words, nor what he'd shouted in reply. But it was typical of Ziggy that their last exchange had been about taking care of someone else. Because Ziggy had always been the one who took care.

In any group, there's always one person who ends up as the rock, who provides the shelter that allows the weaker members of the tribe to grow into their own strengths. For the Laddies fi' Kirkcaldy, that had always been Ziggy. It wasn't that he was bossy, or a control freak. He just had a natural aptitude for the role, and the other three had been the constant beneficiaries of Ziggy's capacity for getting things sorted. Even in their adult lives, it had always been Ziggy that Alex had turned to when he needed a sounding board. When he'd been considering the huge jump of shifting from gainful employment to taking a chance on setting up his own company, they'd spent a weekend in New York thrashing out the pros and cons, and Ziggy's confidence in his abilities had, if Alex was honest, been more of a clincher than Lynn's conviction he could make a go of it.

That was something else that would never happen again.

"Alex?" His wife's voice cut into his numb reverie. He'd been so locked inside himself, he hadn't noticed her car arrive, nor the sound of her footfalls. He half turned toward the faint waft of her perfume.

"Why are you sitting in the dark? And why are you home so early?" There was no accusation in her voice, just concern.

Alex shook his head. He didn't want to share the news.

"Something's wrong," Lynn insisted, covering the distance between them and dropping into the chair next to him. She put a hand on his arm. "Alex? What is it?"

At the sound of her disquiet, the anesthetic of shock vanished abruptly. A searing pain knifed through him, taking his breath away momentarily. He met Lynn's worried eyes and flinched. Without words, he put his hand out and laid it gently on the swell of her stomach.

Lynn covered his hand with hers. "Alex . . . tell me what's happened."

His voice sounded alien to him, a cracked and broken simulacrum of his normal articulation. "Ziggy," he managed. "Ziggy's dead."

Lynn's mouth opened. A frown of incredulity gathered. "Ziggy?"

Alex cleared his throat. "It's true," he said. "There was a fire. At the house. In the night."

Lynn shivered. "No. Not Ziggy. There's been a mistake."

"No mistake. Paul told me. He phoned to tell me."

"How could that be? Him and Ziggy, they shared a bed. How can Paul be all right and Ziggy dead?" Lynn's voice was loud, her disbelief echoing around the conservatory.

"Paul wasn't there. He was giving a guest lecture at Stanford." Alex closed his eyes at the thought of it. "He flew back in the morning. Drove straight home from the airport. And found the firemen and the cops poking through what used to be their house."

Silent tears sparkled on Lynn's eyelashes. "That must have been . . . oh, dear God. I can't take it in."

Alex folded his arms across his chest. "You don't think of the people you love being so fragile. One minute they're there, the next minute they're not."

"Do they have any idea what happened?"

"They told Paul it was too early to say. But he said they were asking him some pretty sharp questions. He thinks it maybe looks suspicious, and they're thinking him being away was a bit too convenient."

"Oh God, poor Paul." Lynn's fingers worried at each

other in her lap. "Losing Ziggy, that's hellish enough. But to have the police on his back, too . . . Poor, poor Paul."

"He asked me if I'd tell Weird and Mondo." Alex shook his head. "I haven't been able to do it yet."

"I'll call Mondo," Lynn said. "But later. It's not as if anybody else is going to tell him first."

"No, I should call him. I told Paul . . ."

"He's my brother. I know how he is. But you'll have to deal with Weird. I don't think I could handle being told that Jesus loves me right now."

"I know. But somebody should tell him." Alex managed a bitter smile. "He'll probably want to preach a sermon at the funeral."

Lynn looked appalled. "Oh, no. You can't let that happen."

"I know." Alex leaned forward and lifted his glass. He swallowed the last few drops of brandy. "You know what day it is?"

Lynn froze. "Oh, Jesus Christ Almighty."

The Reverend Tom Mackie replaced the phone in its cradle and caressed the silver gilt cross that lay on his purple silk cassock. His American congregation loved that they had a British minister and, since they could never distinguish between Scots and English, he satisfied their desire for display with the most lavish trappings of High Anglicanism. It was a vanity, he acknowledged, but essentially a harmless one.

However, his secretary had left for the day and the solitude of his empty office allowed him space to confront his confused emotional reaction to the shock of Ziggy Malkiewicz's death without having to assume a public face. While there was no lack of cynical manipulation in the way Weird dealt with the practice of ministry, the beliefs that underpinned his evangelical regime were sincerely and deeply held. And he knew in his heart that Ziggy was a sinner, tainted irrevocably by the stain of his homosexuality. There was no room for doubt on that point in Weird's fundamentalist universe. The Bible was clear in its prohibition and its abhorrence of the sin. Salvation would have been hard to come by even if Ziggy had earnestly repented, but, as far as Weird was aware, Ziggy had died as he had lived, embracing his sin with enthusiasm. Doubtless the manner of his death would somehow connect back to the transgression of his lifestyle. The link would have been more obvious if the Lord had visited the plague of AIDS upon him. But Weird had already mentally created a scenario that would lay the blame at the door of Ziggy's own perilous choice. Perhaps some casual pickup had waited till Ziggy was asleep to rob him and then set a fire to cover his crime. Perhaps they had been smoking marijuana and a smoldering joint had been the source of the burning.

However it had happened, Ziggy's death was nevertheless a powerful reminder to Weird that it was possible to hate the sin and yet love the sinner. There was no denying the reality of the friendship that had sustained him through his teenage years, when his own wild spirit had blinded him to the light, when he truly had been Weird. Without Ziggy, he'd never have made it through his adolescence without ending up in serious trouble. Or worse.

Without prompting, his memory played a flashback sequence. Winter, 1972. The year of their O Grade exams. Alex had acquired a talent for breaking into cars without damaging the locks. It involved a flexible strip of metal and a lot of dexterity. It gave them scope to be anarchic without really being criminal. The routine was simple. A couple of illicit Carlsberg Specials in the Harbor Bar, then they'd sally forth into the night. They'd pick half a dozen cars at random between the pub and the bus station. Alex would shoogle his metal band inside the car door and pop the lock. Then Ziggy or Weird would climb into the car and scribble their message across the inside of the windscreen. In red lipstick, previously shoplifted from Boots the Chemist and which was a bugger to clean off, they'd scribble the chorus from Bowie's "Laughing Gnome." It always reduced the four of them to helpless mirth.

Then they'd stagger off, giggling like fools, being careful to lock the car door behind them. It was a game that managed to be simultaneously stupid and brilliant.

One night, Weird had climbed behind the wheel of a Ford Escort. While Ziggy was writing, he'd flipped open the ashtray and gazed with delight at a spare key. Knowing that larceny wasn't on the agenda and that Ziggy would manage to stop him having his fun, Weird had waited till his friend got out of the car, then he'd fumbled the key into the ignition and started the engine. He flicked the lights on, revealing shock on the faces of the other three. His first idea had simply been to give his friends a surprise. But confronted with the possibility of mayhem, Weird had let himself be carried away. He'd never driven before, but knew the theory and he'd watched his dad often enough to be convinced he could pull it off. He crashed the car into gear, released the handbrake and juddered forward.

He kangarooed out of the parking space and headed for the exit that would bring him on to the Prom, the two-mile strip that ran alongside the sea wall. The streetlights were an orange blur, the scarlet letters of the message turned black on the windscreen as he careered along, crunching up through the gears as he went. He could hardly steer straight, he was laughing so hard.

The end of the Prom was upon him unbelievably quickly. He wrenched the wheel to the right, somehow managing to keep control as he rounded the bend past the bus garage. Thankfully there were few cars on the road, most people having elected to stay at home on a cold and frosty February night. He jammed his foot on the accelerator, shooting up Invertiel Road, under the railway bridge and past Jawbanes Road.

His speed was his undoing. As the road climbed toward a left-hand bend, Weird hit an ice-covered puddle and found himself spinning. Time decelerated and the car whirled in a slow waltz through three hundred and sixty degrees. He yanked on the wheel, but it only seemed to make things worse. The windscreen was filled with a steep grassy bank, then suddenly the car was on its side and he was slammed against the door, the window-winder smashing into his ribs.

He had no idea how long he lay there, dazed and in pain,

listening to the *tick, tick* of the stalled engine as it cooled in the night air. The next thing he knew was the door above his head disappearing, to be replaced by Alex and Ziggy staring down with frightened faces. "You fucking moron," Ziggy shouted, as soon as he realized Weird was more or less OK.

Somehow, he managed to struggle upright as they hauled him out, screaming in pain as his broken ribs protested. He lay panting on the frosted grass, each breath a knife of agony. It took a minute or so to realize that an Austin Allegro was parked on the road behind the wrecked Escort, its lights cutting through the darkness and casting strange shadows.

Ziggy had dragged him to his feet and down the verge. "You fucking moron," he kept repeating as he shoved him into the backseat of the Allegro. Through a daze of pain, Weird heard the negotiation.

"What are we going to do now?" Mondo asked.

"Alex is going to drive you all back to the Prom and you're going to put this car back where you found it. Then you're going home. OK?"

"But Weird's hurt," Mondo protested. "He needs to go to the hospital."

"Yeah, right. Let's advertise the fact that he's been in a car crash." Ziggy leaned into the car and held his hand in front of Weird's face. "How many fingers, moron?"

Woozily, Weird focused. "Two," he groaned.

"See? He's not even concussed. Amazing. I always thought he had concrete between his ears. It's just his ribs, Mondo. All the hospital will do is give him some painkillers."

"But he's in agony. What's he going to say when he gets home?"

"That's his problem. He can say he fell down some stairs. Anything." He leaned in again. "You're just going to have to grin and bear it, moron."

Weird pushed himself upright, wincing. "I'll manage."

"And what are you going to be doing?" Alex demanded as he slid behind the wheel of the Allegro.

"I'll give you five minutes to get clear. Then I'm going to set fire to the car."

Thirty years on, Weird could still remember the look of shock on Alex's face. "What?"

Ziggy rubbed a hand over his face. "It's covered in our fingerprints. It's got our trademark all over the windscreen. When we were just scribbling on windscreens, the police weren't going to bother with us. But here's a stolen, wrecked car. You think they're going to treat that like a joke? We've got to burn it out. It's totalled anyway."

There was no possible argument. Alex started the engine and drove off without a hitch, looking for a side road to turn around in. It was days later when Weird finally thought to ask: "Where did you learn to drive?"

"Last summer. On the beach on Barra. My cousin showed me how."

"And how did you get the Allegro started without keys?"

"Did you not recognize the car?"

Weird shook his head.

"It belongs to 'Sammy' Seale."

"The metalwork teacher?"

"Exactly."

Weird grinned. The first thing they'd made in metalwork was a magnetized box to stick to a car chassis to hold a spare set of keys. "Lucky break."

"Lucky for you, moron. It was Ziggy that spotted it."

How different it all could have been, Weird mused. Without Ziggy coming to the rescue, he'd have ended up in custody, with a police record, his life blown apart. Instead of abandoning him to the consequences of his own stupidity, Ziggy had found the means to save him. And he'd put himself on the line in the process. Setting a car ablaze was a big deal for an essentially law-abiding, ambitious lad. But Ziggy hadn't hesitated.

So now Weird had to return that and many other favors. He'd speak at Ziggy's funeral. He'd preach repentance and forgiveness. It was too late to save Ziggy, but with God's good grace he might just save another benighted soul.

CHAPTER
TWENTY-THREE

Waiting was one of the things Graham Macfadyen did best. His adopted father had been a passionate amateur ornithologist, and the boy had been forced to spend long tracts of his youth killing time between sightings of birds sufficiently interesting to warrant the raise of binoculars to eyes. He'd learned stillness at an early age; anything to avoid the vicious edge of his father's sarcasm. The wounds of blame cut just as deep as physical blows and Macfadyen would do anything in his limited power to dodge them. The secret, he'd learned early on, was to dress for the weather. So although he'd spend most of the day enduring snow flurries and cold gusts of northerly wind, he was still comfortable in his down parka, his waterproof fleece-lined trousers and his stout walking boots. He was most grateful for the shooting stick he'd brought with him, for his observation post offered nowhere to sit except gravestones. And that felt like bad manners.

He'd taken time off work. It had meant lying, but that couldn't be helped. He knew he was letting people down, that his absence might mean missing a crucial deadline. But some things were more important than hitting a contract payment date. And nobody would suspect someone as conscientious as him of faking it. Lying, like blending in and stillness, was something he did well. He didn't think Lawson had entertained the slightest flicker of doubt when he'd claimed to have loved his adopted parents. God knows, he'd tried to love them. But their emotional distance coupled with the constant attrition of their disapproval and disappointment had worn away his affections, leaving him numb and isolated. It would have been so different with his real mother, he felt sure. But he'd been deprived of the chance to find out, leaving him with nothing but a fantasy of somehow being instrumental in making someone pay for that. He'd had such high hopes of his interview with Lawson, but the incompetence of the police had yanked the ground from under his feet. Still, just because the obvious route had been closed off to him didn't mean he should give up his quest. He'd learned that persistence from years of writing program code.

He wasn't sure whether his vigil would pay off, but he'd felt driven to come here. If it didn't work, he'd find another way to get what he wanted. He'd arrived just after seven and made his way to the grave. He'd been there before, disappointed that it didn't make him feel any closer to the mother he'd never known. This time, he laid the discreet floral tribute at the foot of the headstone then made his way to the vantage point he'd scouted on his last visit. He would be mostly obscured by an ornate memorial to a former town councillor, but with a clear line of sight to Rosie's last resting place.

Someone would come. He'd felt sure of it. But now, as the hands of his watch moved toward seven o'clock, he began to wonder. To hell with what Lawson had told him about staying away from his uncles. He was going to make contact. He'd reckoned that approaching them in such a highly charged place might cut through their hostility and allow them to see him as someone who, like them, had a right to be considered part of Rosie's family. Now it was starting to look as if he'd miscalculated. The thought angered him.

Just then, he saw a darker shape against the graves. It resolved itself to the outline of a man, walking briskly along the path toward him. Macfadyen drew his breath in sharply.

Head down against the weather, the man left the path and picked his way confidently through the grave markers. As he grew closer, Macfadyen could see he carried a small posy of flowers. The man slowed down and came to a halt five feet from Rosie's gravestone. He bowed his head and stood for a long moment. As he bent to place the flowers, Macfadyen moved forward, the snow muffling his steps.

The man straightened and took a step backward, cannoning into Macfadyen. "What the . . ." he exclaimed, swinging round on his heel.

Macfadyen held up his hands in a placatory gesture. "Sorry. I didn't mean to startle you." He pushed back the hood of his parka, to appear less intimidating.

The man scowled at him, head to one side, staring intently at his face. "Do I know you?" he said, his voice as belligerent as his stance.

Macfadyen didn't hesitate. "I think you're my uncle," he said.

Lynn left Alex to make his phone call. Her sorrow felt like a solid uncomfortable lump in her chest. Distracted, she went through to the kitchen and diced chicken on automatic pilot, tossing it into a cast-iron casserole with some roughly chopped onions and peppers. She poured over a jar of ready-made sauce, added a slug of white wine and shoved it in the oven. As usual, she'd forgotten to preheat it. She pricked a couple of baking potatoes with a fork and placed them on the shelf above the casserole. Alex should have finished his call to Weird by now, she thought. She couldn't postpone talking to her brother any longer.

When she stopped to think about it, it seemed slightly odd to Lynn that, despite the blood ties, despite her contempt for Weird's brand of hellfire and damnation, Mondo had become the most disengaged member of the original quartet. She often thought that if it weren't for the fact that they were brother and sister, he'd have disappeared completely from Alex's radar. He was geographically closest, over in Glasgow. But by the end of their university career, it seemed he wanted to shed all the ties that bound him to his childhood and adolescence.

He'd been first to leave the country, heading off to France after graduation to pursue his ambition for a career in academe. He'd scarcely returned to Scotland in the following three years, not even showing up for their grandmother's funeral. She doubted whether he'd have bothered to attend her wedding to Alex if he hadn't been back in the UK by then, lecturing at Manchester University. Whenever Lynn had tried to discover the reason for his absence, he'd always evaded the issue. He'd always been good at avoidance, her big brother.

Lynn, who had stayed firmly anchored to her roots, couldn't understand why anyone would want to sever himself from his personal history. It wasn't as if Mondo had had a shitty childhood and a horrible adolescence. Sure, he'd always been a bit of a jessie, but once he'd hooked up with Alex, Weird and Ziggy, he'd had a bulwark against the bullies. She remembered how she'd envied the four boys their rock-solid friendship, the casual way they'd always created a good time for themselves. Their terrible music, their subversive edge, their complete disregard for the opinion of their peers. It seemed to her entirely masochistic to turn his back on such a support system.

He'd always been weak, she knew that. When trouble walked in the door, Mondo had always been straight out the window. All the more reason, in Lynn's world view, why he should have wanted to cling to the friendships that had sustained him through so much difficulty. She'd asked Alex what he'd thought and he'd shrugged. "That last year at St. Andrews—it was tough. Maybe he just doesn't want to be reminded of it."

It made a kind of sense. She knew Mondo well enough to understand the shame and guilt he'd felt over Barney Maclennan's death. He'd endured the bitter taunts of the barroom bullies who suggested next time he wanted to kill himself, he do it properly. He'd suffered the personal anguish of knowing a piece of selfish grandstanding had robbed someone else of his life. He'd had to put up with counseling that served mostly to remind him of that terrible moment when a bid for attention had turned into the worst of nightmares. She supposed the presence of the other three served only as a cue for memories he wanted to erase. She also knew that, although he never said so, Alex had not been able entirely to shrug off a lingering suspicion that Mondo might know more than he'd told about Rosie Duff's death. Which was nonsense, really. If any of them had been capable of committing that particular crime on that particular night, it had been Weird, off his head on a mixture of drink and drugs, frustrated that his antics with the Land Rover hadn't impressed the girls as much as he'd hoped. She'd always wondered about that sudden damascene conversion of his.

But whatever the underlying reasons, she'd missed her brother over the past twenty years or so. When she was younger, she'd always imagined that he'd marry some girl who would become her best friend; that they'd be brought even closer with the arrival of children; that they'd develop into one of those comfortable extended families who live in each other's pockets. But none of it had come true. After a string of semiserious relationships, Mondo had finally married Hélène, a French student ten years his junior who scarcely bothered to hide her contempt for anyone who couldn't discourse with equal ease on Foucault or couture. Alex she openly despised for choosing commerce over art. Lynn she patronized with lukewarm enthusiasm for her career as a fine art restorer. Like her and Alex, they were childless thus far, but Lynn suspected that was from choice and that they would remain that way.

She supposed distance should make the passing on of this news easier somehow. But still, lifting the phone was one of the hardest things she'd ever done. The call was answered on the second ring by Hélène. "Hallo, Lynn. How nice to hear from you. I'll just get David," she said, her almost perfect English a reproach in itself. Before Lynn could utter a warning about the reason for her call, Hélène was gone. A long minute passed, then her brother's familiar voice sounded in her ear.

"Lynn," he said. "How are you doing?" Just like someone who cared.

"Mondo, I'm afraid I've got some bad news."

"Not the parents?" He jumped in before she could say more.

"No, they're fine. I spoke to Mum last night. This is going to come as a bit of a shock. Alex got a call this afternoon from Seattle." Lynn felt her throat closing at the thought of it. "Ziggy's dead." Silence. She couldn't tell if it was the silence of shock or of uncertainty as to the appropriate response. "I'm sorry," she said.

"I didn't know he was ill," Mondo finally said.

"He wasn't ill. The house went on fire in the night. Ziggy was in bed, asleep. He died in the fire."

"That's terrible. Jesus. Poor Ziggy. I can't believe it. He was always so careful." He made a strange sound, almost like a snort of laughter. "If any of us was going to go up in flames, you'd have to have put your money on Weird. He's always been accident prone. But Ziggy?"

"I know. It's hard to take it in."

"God. Poor Ziggy."

"I know. We had such a lovely time with him and Paul in California in September. It feels so unreal."

"And Paul? Is he dead, too?"

"No. He was away overnight. He came back to find the house burned down and Ziggy dead."

"God. That's going to point the finger at him."

"I'm sure that's the last thing on his mind right now," Lynn snapped.

"No, you misunderstand me. I just meant it would make it all so much worse for him. Christ, Lynn, I know what it means to have everybody looking at you as if you're a murderer," Mondo flashed back.

There was a brief silence while both retreated from confrontation. "Alex is going over for the funeral," Lynn offered as an olive branch.

"Oh, I don't think I'll be able to manage that," Mondo said hastily. "We're off to France in a couple of days. We've got the flights booked and everything. Besides, it's not like I've been as close to Ziggy recently as you and Alex."

Lynn stared at the wall in disbelief. "You four were like blood brothers. Isn't that worth a bit of disruption to your travel plans?"

There was a long silence. Then Mondo said, "I don't want to go, Lynn. It doesn't mean that I don't care about Ziggy. It's just that I hate funerals. I'll write to Paul, of course. What's the point of going halfway across the world for a funeral that will only upset me? It won't bring Ziggy back."

Lynn felt suddenly worn out, grateful that she had taken the burden of this wounding conversation from Alex. The worst of it was that she could still find it in her heart to sympathize with her oversensitive brother. "None of us would want you to be upset," she sighed. "Well, I'll let you go, Mondo."

"Just a minute, Lynn," he said. "Was it today Ziggy died?"

"The early hours of the morning, yes."

A sharp suck of breath. "That's pretty spooky. You know it's twenty-five years today since Rosie Duff died?"

"We hadn't forgotten. I'm surprised you remembered."

He gave a bitter laugh. "You think I could forget the day my life was destroyed? It's carved on my heart."

"Yeah, well, at least you'll always remember the anniversary of Ziggy's death," Lynn said, spite rising as she realized that, yet again, Mondo was turning the kaleidoscope so that everything was about him. Sometimes she really wished you could dissolve family ties.

Lawson glared at the phone as he replaced it in its cradle. He hated politicians. He'd had to listen to the MSP who represented Phil Parhatka's new chief suspect droning on for ten minutes about the scumbag's human rights. Lawson had wanted to shout, "What about the human rights of the poor bastard he killed?" but he'd had far more sense than to give voice to his irritation. Instead, he'd made soothing noises and a mental note to himself to have a word with the parents of the dead man, to get them to remind their MSP that his loyalties should lie with the victims, not the perpetrators. All the same, he'd better warn Phil Parhatka to watch his back.

He glanced at his watch, surprised at the lateness of the hour. He might as well stick his head round the door of the cold case squadroom on his way out, on the off chance that Phil was still at his desk.

But the only person there at this late hour was Robin Maclennan. He was poring over a file of witness statements, his brow furrowed in concentration. In the pool of light cast by his desk lamp, the resemblance to his brother was uncanny. Lawson shivered involuntarily. It was like seeing a ghost, but a ghost who had aged a dozen years since he'd last walked on earth.

Lawson cleared his throat and Robin looked up, the illusion shattered as his own mannerisms superimposed themselves on the fraternal resemblance. "Hello, sir," he said.

"You're late at it," Lawson said.

Robin shrugged. "Diane's taken the kids to the pictures. I thought I might as well be sitting here as in an empty house."

"I know what you mean. I often feel the same myself since Marian died last year."

"Is your boy not at home?"

Lawson snorted. "My boy's twenty-two now, Robin. Michael graduated in the summer. MA in economics. And now he's working as a motorbike courier in Sydney, Australia. Sometimes I wonder what the hell I worked so hard for. You fancy a pint?"

Robin looked mildly surprised. "Aye, OK," he said, closing the file and getting to his feet.

They agreed on a small pub on the outskirts of Kirkcaldy, a short journey home for both of them afterward. The place was buzzing, a thrum of conversation battling the selection of Christmas hits that seemed inescapable at that time of year. Strands of tinsel festooned the gantry and a garish fiber-optic Christmas tree leaned drunkenly at one end of the bar. As Wizzard wished it could be Christmas every day, Lawson bought a couple of pints and whiskey chasers while Robin found a relatively quiet table in the furthest corner of the room. Robin looked faintly startled at the two drinks in front of him. "Thanks, sir," he said cautiously.

"Forget the rank, Robin. Just for tonight, eh?" Lawson took a long draft of his beer. "To tell you the truth, I was glad to see you sitting there. I wanted a drink tonight, and I didn't want to drink alone." He eyed him curiously. "You know what today is?"

Robin's face suddenly grew cautious. "It's the sixteenth of December."

"I think you can do better than that."

Robin picked up his whiskey and knocked it back in one. "It's twenty-five years since Rosie Duff was murdered. Is that what you want me to say?"

"I thought you'd know." Neither could think of what to say next, so they drank in uneasy silence for a few minutes.

"How's Karen getting on with it?" Robin asked.

"I thought you'd know better than me. The boss is always the last to know, isn't that how it goes?"

Robin gave a wry smile. "Not in this case. Karen's hardly been in the office lately. She seems to spend all her time down at the property store. And when she is at her desk, I'm the last person she wants to talk to. Like everybody else, she's embarrassed to talk about Barney's big failure." He swallowed the last of his pint and got to his feet. "Same again?"

Lawson nodded. When Robin returned, he said, "Is that how you see it? Barney's big failure?"

Robin shook his head impatiently. "That's how Barney saw it. I remember that Christmas. I'd never seen him like that. Beating himself up. He blamed himself for the fact that there hadn't been an arrest. He was convinced he was missing something obvious, something vital. It was eating him alive."

"I remember he took it very personally."

"You could say that." Robin stared into his whiskey. "I wanted to help. I only ever went into the police because Barney was like a god to me. I wanted to be like him. I asked for a transfer to St. Andrews to get on the squad. But he put the black on it." He sighed. "I can't help thinking that maybe if I'd been there . . ."

"You couldn't have saved him, Robin," Lawson said.

Robin threw his second whiskey back. "I know. But I can't help wondering."

Lawson nodded. "Barney was a great cop. A hard act to follow. And the way he died, it made me sick to my stomach. I always thought we should have charged Davey Kerr."

Robin looked up, puzzled. "Charged him? What with? Attempting suicide's not a crime."

Lawson looked startled. "But . . . Right enough, Robin. What was I thinking about?" he stammered. "Forget what I said."

Robin leaned forward. "Tell me what you were going to say."

"Nothing, really. Nothing." Lawson tried to cover his confusion by taking a drink. He coughed and choked, spluttering whiskey down his chin.

"You were going to say something about the way Barney died." Robin's eyes pinned Lawson to the seat.

Lawson wiped his mouth and sighed. "I thought you knew."

"Knew what?"

"Culpable homicide, that's what the charge sheet against Davey Kerr should have read."

Robin frowned. "That would never have stood up in court. Kerr didn't mean to go over the edge, it was an accident. He was just drawing attention to himself, not seriously trying to commit suicide."

Lawson looked uncomfortable. He pushed his chair back and said, "You need another whiskey." This time, he came back with a double. He sat down and eyed Robin. "Christ," he said softly. "I know we decided to keep it quiet, but I was sure you would have heard."

"I still don't know what you're talking about," Robin said, his face intense with interest. "But I think I deserve an explanation."

"I was the front man on the rope," Lawson said. "I saw it with my own eyes. When we were pulling them back up the cliff, Kerr panicked and kicked Barney off him."

Robin's face screwed up in an expression of incredulity. "You're saying Kerr pushed him back into the sea to save his own skin?" Robin sounded incredulous. "How come I'm just hearing this now?"

Lawson shrugged. "I don't know. When I told the superintendent what I'd seen, he was shocked. But he said there was no point in pursuing it. The fiscal's office would never have gone through with a prosecution. The defense would have argued that in those conditions I couldn't have seen what I saw. That we were being vindictive because Barney died trying to save Kerr. That we were being vexatious in alleging culpable homicide of Barney because we couldn't nail Kerr and his pals for Rosie Duff. So they decided to keep the lid on it."

Robin picked up his glass, his hand shaking so much it chattered against his teeth. All color had drained from his face, leaving him gray and sweaty. "I don't believe this."

"I know what I saw, Robin. I'm sorry, I assumed you knew."

"This is the first . . ." He looked around him, as if he couldn't understand where he was or how he'd got here. "I'm sorry, I've got to get out of here." Abruptly he got to his feet and headed for the door, ignoring the complaints of fellow drinkers as he jostled them in passing.

Lawson closed his eyes and exhaled. Nearly thirty years on the force and he still hadn't grown accustomed to the hollow feeling that imparting bad news left in his stomach. A worm of anxiety gnawed at his insides. What had he done, revealing the truth to Robin Maclennan after all these years?

CHAPTER
TWENTY-FOUR

The wheels of his suitcase rumbled behind Alex as he emerged into the concourse of SeaTac airport. It was hard to focus on the people waiting to meet the passengers, and if Paul hadn't waved, he might have missed him. Alex hurried toward him and the two men embraced without self-consciousness. "Thanks for coming," Paul said quietly.

"Lynn sends her love," Alex said. "She really wanted to be here, but . . ."

"I know. You've wanted this baby so long, you can't take chances." Paul reached for Alex's suitcase and led the way toward the terminal exit. "How was the flight?"

"I slept most of the way across the Atlantic. But I couldn't seem to settle on the second flight. I kept thinking about Ziggy, and the fire. What a hellish way to go."

Paul stared straight ahead. "I keep thinking it was my fault."

"How could that be?" Alex asked, following him out to the car park.

"You know we converted the whole of the attic into one big bedroom and bathroom for us? We should have had an external fire escape. I kept meaning to get the builder to come back and put one in, but there was always something more important to be done . . ." Paul came to a stop by his

SUV and stowed Alex's suitcase in the luggage space, his broad shoulders straining against his plaid jacket.

"We all put things off," Alex said, his hand on Paul's back. "You know Ziggy wouldn't blame you for that. It was just as much his responsibility."

Paul shrugged and climbed behind the wheel. "There's a decent motel about ten minutes from the house. I'm staying there. I booked you in too, if that's OK? If you'd rather be in the city, we can change it."

"No. I'd rather be with you." He gave Paul a wan smile. "That way we can get maudlin together, right?"

"Right."

They fell silent as Paul headed out on the highway toward Seattle. They skirted the city and continued north. Ziggy and Paul's home had been outside the city limits, a two-story wooden house built on a hillside with breathtaking views of Puget Sound, Possession Sound and, in the distance, Mount Walker. When they'd first visited, Alex had thought they'd been dropped into a corner of paradise. "Wait till it starts raining," Ziggy had said.

Today it was overcast, with the clear light that accompanies high cloud. Alex wanted rain, to match his mood. But the weather seemed reluctant to oblige. He stared out of the window, catching occasional glimpses of the snow caps on the Olympics and the Cascades. The roadside was lined with gray slush, ice crystals glittering occasionally as they caught the light. He was glad he'd only ever previously visited in summer. The view from the window was different enough not to bring too many painful memories flooding back.

Paul turned off the main highway a couple of miles before the exit that led to his former home. The road led through pine trees to a bluff that looked across toward Whidbey Island. The motel had gone for the log cabin style, which Alex thought looked ridiculous on a building as large as the one that housed the reception, bar and restaurant. But the individual cabins set back in a row at the edge of the trees were attractive enough. Paul, whose cabin was next to

Alex's, left him to unpack. "I'll see you in the bar in half an hour, OK?"

Alex hung up his funeral suit and shirt, leaving the rest of his clothes in the suitcase. He'd spent most of the transcontinental flight sketching, and he tore out the one sheet he was satisfied with and propped it up against the mirror. Ziggy stared out at him in three-quarter profile, a crooked smile creasing his eyes. Not a bad likeness from memory, Alex thought sadly. He checked his watch. Almost midnight at home. Lynn wouldn't mind the lateness of the hour. He dialed the number. Their short conversation eased the sharpness of the grief that had threatened to overwhelm him momentarily.

Alex ran a basin of cold water and dashed it over his face. Feeling slightly more alert, he trudged across to the bar, its Christmas decorations seeming incongruous in the face of his sadness. Johnny Mathis crooned saccharine in the background and Alex wanted to muffle the speakers as horses hooves had once been muffled in funeral processions. He found Paul in a booth nursing a bottle of Pyramid ale. He signaled to the barman for another of the same and slid in opposite Paul. Now he had the chance to look at him properly, he could see the signs of strain and grief. Paul's light brown hair was rumpled and unwashed, his blue eyes weary and red-rimmed. A patch of stubble under his left ear showed uncharacteristic carelessness in a man who was always neat and tidy.

"I called Lynn," he said. "She was asking after you."

"She's got a good heart," Paul said. "I feel like I got to know her a lot better this year. It seemed like being pregnant made her open up more."

"I know what you mean. I thought she'd be paralyzed with anxiety throughout this pregnancy. But she's been really relaxed." Alex's drink arrived.

Paul raised his glass. "Let's drink to the future," he said. "Right now, I don't feel like it has much to offer, but I know Ziggy would give me hell for dwelling in the past."

"To the future," Alex echoed. He swallowed a mouthful of beer and said, "How are you holding up?"

Paul shook his head. "I don't think it's hit me yet. There's been so much to take care of. Letting people know, making the funeral arrangements and stuff. Which reminds me. Your friend Tom, the one Ziggy called Weird? He's coming in tomorrow."

The news provoked a mixed reaction from Alex. Part of him longed for the connection to his past that Weird would provide. Part of him acknowledged the unease that still wriggled inside him when he recalled the night Rosie Duff died. And part of him dreaded the aggravation Weird would trail in his wake if he went off on his fundamentalist homophobia. "He's not going to preach at the funeral, is he?"

"No. We're having a humanist service. But Ziggy's friends will have the opportunity to get up and talk about him. If Tom wants to say something then, he's welcome."

Alex groaned. "You know he's a fundamentalist bigot who preaches hellfire and damnation?"

Paul gave a wry smile. "He should be careful. It's not just the South that does lynch mobs."

"I'll have a word with him beforehand." Which would be about as effective as a twig in the path of a runaway train, Alex thought.

They sipped their beers in silence for a few minutes. Then Paul cleared his throat and said, "There's something I need to tell you, Alex. It's about the fire."

Alex looked puzzled. "The fire?"

Paul massaged the bridge of his nose. "The fire wasn't an accident, Alex. It was set. Deliberately."

"Are they sure?"

Paul sighed. "They've had arson investigators crawling all over the place ever since it cooled down enough."

"But that's terrible. Who would do something like that to Ziggy?"

"Alex, I'm the cops' first pick."

"But that's insane. You loved Ziggy."

"Which is exactly why I'm the prime suspect. They always look at the spouse first, right?" Paul's tone was harsh.

Alex shook his head. "Nobody who knew you two would entertain that idea for a minute."

"But the cops didn't know us. And however hard they try to pretend different, most cops like gays about as much as your friend Tom does." He swallowed a mouthful of beer, as if to take the taste of his sentiment away. "I spent most of yesterday at the police station, answering questions."

"I don't get it. You were hundreds of miles away. How are you supposed to have burned your house down when you were in California?"

"You remember the layout of the house?" Alex nodded and Paul continued. "They're saying the fire started in the basement, by the heating-oil tank. According to the fire department guy, it looked like someone had stacked up cans of paint and gasoline at one end of the tank, then piled up paper and wood around them. Which we certainly didn't do. But they also found what looks like the remains of a fire bomb. A pretty simple device, they said."

"Wasn't it destroyed in the fire?"

"These guys are good at reconstructing what happens in a fire. From the bits and pieces they've found, they think it went like this. They found the fragments of a sealed paint can. Fixed to the inside of the lid, the remains of an electronic timer. How they think it worked was that the can had gasoline or some other accelerant in it. Something that would give off fumes. Most of the space inside the can would have been occupied by the fumes. Then when the timer went off, the spark would've ignited the vapor, the can would've exploded, cascading burning accelerant on the other flammable materials. And because the house is wooden, it would have gone up like a torch." The blank recital wavered and Paul's mouth trembled. "Ziggy didn't stand a chance."

"And they think you did this?" Alex was incredulous. At the same time, he felt profound pity for Paul. He knew better than anyone the consequences of baseless suspicion and the toll they exacted.

"They've got no other suspects. Ziggy wasn't exactly a guy who made enemies. And I'm the main beneficiary of his will. What's more, I'm a physicist."

"And that means you know how to make a firebomb?"

"They seem to think so. It's kinda hard to explain what I actually do, but they seem to figure, 'Hey, this guy's a scientist, he must know how to blow people up.' If it wasn't so fucking tragic, I'd have to laugh."

Alex signaled to the barman to bring them fresh drinks. "So they think you set a firebomb and went off to California to give a lecture?"

"That seems to be the way their minds are working. I thought the fact that I'd been away for three nights would put me in the clear, but apparently not. The arson investigator told my lawyer that the timer the killer used could have been set anything up to a week in advance. So I'm still on the hook."

"Wouldn't you have been taking a hell of a chance? What if Ziggy had gone down to the basement and seen it?"

"We almost never went down there in the winter. It was full of summer stuff—the dinghies, the sailboards, the garden furniture. We kept our skis in the garage. Which is another strike against me. How would anybody else know their setup was secure?"

Alex dismissed the point with a wave of his hand. "How many people go down into their basements regularly in the winter? It's not as if your washing machine was down there. How hard would it have been to break in?"

"Not too hard," Paul said. "It wasn't wired into the security system because the guy who does our yard work in the summer has to get in and out. That way, we didn't have to give him details of the alarm system on the house. I guess anyone who was determined to get in wouldn't have found it too hard."

"And of course, any evidence of a break-in would have been destroyed by the fire," Alex sighed.

"So you see, it looks pretty black against me."

"That's insane. Like I said, anybody who knows you would realize you could never have hurt Ziggy, far less killed him."

Paul's smile barely twitched his mustache. "I appreciate your confidence, Alex. And I'm not even going to dignify their accusations with a denial. But I wanted you to know what's being said. I know you understand how terrible it is to be suspected of something you had nothing to do with."

Alex shuddered in spite of the warmth of the cozy bar. "I wouldn't wish that on my worst enemy, never mind my friend. It's horrible. Christ, Paul, I hope they find out who did this, for your sake. What happened to us poisoned my life."

"Ziggy, too. He never forgot how fast the human race could turn hostile. It made him real careful in the way he dealt with the world. Which is why the whole thing is so insane. He went out of his way not to make enemies of people. It's not that he was a pushover—"

"Nobody could ever have accused him of that," Alex agreed. "But you're right. A soft answer turns away wrath. That was his motto. But what about his work? I mean, things go wrong in hospitals. Kids die or they don't get better like they should. Parents need somebody to blame."

"This is America, Alex," Paul said ironically. "Doctors don't take any unnecessary risks. They're too scared of being sued. Sure, Ziggy lost patients from time to time. And sometimes things didn't work out as well as he'd hoped. But one of the reasons he was such a successful pediatrician was that he made his patients and their families his friends. They trusted him, and they were right to do that. Because he was a good doctor."

"I know that. But sometimes when kids die, logic goes out the window."

"There was nothing like that. If there had been, I'd have known about it. We talked to each other, Alex. Even after ten years, we talked to each other about everything."

"What about colleagues? Had he pissed anybody off?"

Paul shook his head. "I don't think so. He had high standards, and I guess not everybody he worked with could keep up to the mark all the time. But he chose his staff pretty carefully. There's a great atmosphere at the clinic. I don't think there's one single person there who didn't respect him. Hell, these people are our friends. They come to the house for barbecues, we baby-sit their kids. Without Ziggy to run the clinic, they've got to feel less secure about their futures."

"You're making him sound like Mr. Perfect," Alex said. "And we both know he wasn't that."

This time, Paul's smile made it to his eyes. "No, he wasn't perfect. Perfectionist, maybe. That could drive you crazy. Last time we went skiing, I thought I was going to have to drag him off the mountain. There was one turn on the run he just couldn't get right. Every time, he screwed up. And that meant we had to go back one more time. But you don't kill somebody because they have anally retentive tendencies. If I'd wanted Ziggy out of my life, I'd just have left him. You know? I wouldn't have had to kill him."

"But you didn't want him out of your life, that's the point."

Paul bit his lip and stared down at the rings of split beer on the table top. "I'd give anything to have him back," he said softly. Alex gave him a moment to collect himself.

"They'll find who did this," he said eventually.

"You think? I wish I agreed with you. What keeps going through my head is what you guys went through all those years ago. They never found who killed that girl. And everybody looked at you with different eyes because of it." He looked up at Alex. "I'm not strong like Ziggy was. I don't know if I can live with that."

CHAPTER
TWENTY-FIVE

Through a mist of tears, Alex tried to focus on the words printed on the order of service. If he'd been asked which of the music on the list might have moved him to tears at Ziggy's funeral, he'd probably have settled on Bowie's "Rock and Roll Suicide" with its final defiant denial of isolation. But he'd made it through that, sustained to the point of elation by the vivid images of a youthful Ziggy projected on the big screen at the end of the crematorium. What had done it for him was the San Francisco Gay Male Choir singing Brahms's setting of the passage from St. Paul's letter to the Corinthians about faith, hope, and love. *Wir sehen jetzt durch einen Spiegel in einem dunkeln Worte*; for now we see through a glass, darkly. The words seemed painfully appropriate. Nothing he'd heard about Ziggy's death made any kind of sense, neither logically nor metaphysically.

Tears cascaded down his cheeks, and he didn't care. He wasn't the only one weeping in the crowded crematorium, and being far from home seemed to liberate him from his usual emotional reticence. Beside him, Weird loomed in an immaculately tailored cassock that made him look far more of a peacock than any of the gay men paying their last respects. He wasn't crying, of course. His lips were moving constantly. Alex presumed this was meant to be a sign of devoutness rather than of mental illness, since Weird's hand regularly strayed to the ridiculously ostentatious silver gilt cross on his chest. When he'd first seen it at SeaTac airport, Alex had almost laughed out loud. Weird had strode confidently toward him, dropping his suit carrier to pull his old friend into a theatrical embrace. Alex noticed how smooth his skin appeared and speculated about plastic surgery.

"It was good of you to come," Alex said, leading the way to the hire car he'd picked up that morning.

"Ziggy was my oldest friend. Along with you and Mondo. I know our lives have moved in very different directions, but nothing could change that. The life I have now I owe in part to the friendship we shared. I'd be a very poor Christian to turn my back on that."

Alex couldn't work out why it was that everything Weird said sounded as if it was for public consumption. Whenever he spoke, it was as if there was an unseen congregation hanging on his every word. They'd only met a handful of times over the past twenty years, but on each occasion it had been the same. Creeping Jesus, Lynn had christened him the first time they'd visited him in the small Georgia town where he'd based his ministry. The nickname felt as appropriate now as it had then.

"And how is Lynn?" Weird asked as he settled himself in the passenger seat, smoothing down his perfectly cut clerical suit.

"Seven months pregnant and blooming," Alex said.

"Praise the Lord! I know how much you two have longed for this." Weird's face lit up in what appeared a genuine smile. But then, he spent enough time in front of the cameras for his television mission via a local channel, it was hard to distinguish the assumed from the real. "I thank the Lord for the blessing of children. The happiest memories I hold are of my five. The love a man feels for his children is deeper and more pure than anything else in this world. Alex, I know you're going to delight in this life change."

"Thanks, Weird."

The reverend winced. "Gonnae no' do that," he said, reverting to a teenage catchphrase. "I don't think it's an appropriate form of address these days."

"Sorry. Old habits die hard. You'll always be Weird to me."

"And who exactly calls you Gilly these days?"

Alex shook his head. "You're right. I'll try to remember. Tom."

"I appreciate that, Alex. And if you want to have the child baptized, I'd be happy to officiate."

"Somehow, I don't think we'll be going down that road. The bairn can make it's own mind up when it's old enough."

Weird pursed his lips. "That's your choice, of course." The subtext was loud and clear. *Damn your child to eternal perdition if you must.* He gazed out of the window at the passing landscape. "Where are we headed?"

"Paul has booked you a cabin at the motel where we're staying."

"Is it near the scene of the fire?"

"About ten minutes away. Why?"

"I'd like to go there first."

"Why?"

"I want to say a prayer."

Alex exhaled noisily. "Fine. Look, there's something you should know. The police believe the fire was arson."

Weird bowed his head ponderously. "I feared as much."

"You did? How come?"

"Ziggy chose a perilous path. Who knows what sort of person he brought into his home? Who knows what damaged soul he drove to desperate measures?"

Alex thumped the steering wheel with his fist. "For fuck's sake, Weird. I thought the Bible said 'Judge not, that ye be not judged?' Who the hell do you think you are, coming out with rubbish like that? Whatever preconceptions you have about Ziggy's lifestyle, drop them right now. Ziggy and Paul were monogamous. Neither of them has had sex with anybody else for the past ten years."

Weird gave a small, condescending smile that made Alex

want to smack him. "You always believed everything Ziggy said."

Alex didn't want to fight. He bit back a sharp retort and said, "What I was trying to tell you is that the police have got some daft notion in their heads that it was Paul who set the fire. So try to be a tad sensitive around him, eh?"

"Why do you think it's a daft notion? I don't know much about the way the police work, but I've been told that the majority of homicides that aren't gang-related are committed by spouses. And since you've asked me to be sensitive, I suppose we should regard Paul as Ziggy's spouse. If I were a police officer, I would consider myself derelict in my duty not to consider the possibility."

"Fine. That's their job. But we're Ziggy's friends. Lynn and I spent plenty of time with the pair of them over the years. And take it from me, that was never a relationship that was heading toward murder. You should remember what it feels like to be suspected of something you haven't done. Imagine how much worse it must be if the person who's dead is the person you loved. Well, that's what Paul's going through. And it's him that deserves our support, not the police."

"OK, OK," Weird muttered uneasily, the façade slipping momentarily as memory kicked in and he remembered the primal fear that had driven him into the arms of the church in the first place. He held his peace for the remainder of the journey, turning his head to stare out at the passing landscape to avoid Alex's occasional glances in his direction.

Alex took the familiar exit off the freeway and headed west toward Ziggy and Paul's former home. His stomach tightened as he turned up the narrow metaled road that wound through the trees. His imagination had already run riot with images of the fire. But when he rounded the final bend and saw what remained of the house, he knew his powers of invention had been woefully inadequate. He'd expected a blackened and scarred shell. But this was almost total destruction.

Speechless, Alex let the car glide to a halt. He climbed

out and took a few slow steps toward the ruin. To his surprise, the smell of burning still hung in the air, cloying in the throat and nostrils. He gazed at the charred mess before him, scarcely able to superimpose his memory of the house on this wreckage. A few heavy beams stuck up at crazy angles, but there was almost nothing else that was recognizable. The house must have gone up like a burning brand dipped in pitch. The trees nearest the house had also been engulfed by the fire, their twisted skeletons stark against the view of the sea and the islands beyond.

He barely registered Weird walking past him. Head bowed, the minister stopped right at the edge of the crime-scene tapes that ringed the burned-out debris. Then he threw his head back, his thick mane of silvered hair shimmering in the light. "Oh Lord," he began, his voice sonorous in the open air.

Alex fought the giggle rising in his chest. He knew it was partly a nervous reaction to the intensity of emotion the ruin had provoked in him. But he couldn't help it. No one who had seen Weird off his face on hallucinogenics, or throwing up in a gutter after closing time could take this performance seriously. He turned on his heel and walked back to the car, slamming the door to seal himself off from whatever clap-trap Weird was spouting at the clouds. He was tempted to drive off and leave the preacher to the elements. But Ziggy had never abandoned Weird—or any of the rest of them, for that matter. And right now, the best Alex could do for Ziggy was to keep the faith. So he stayed put.

A series of vivid visual images projected themselves against his mind's eye. Ziggy asleep in bed; a sudden flare of fire; the tongues of flame licking at the wood; the drift of smoke through familiar rooms; Ziggy stirring vaguely as the insidious fumes crept into his respiratory tract; the blurred shape of the house wavering behind a haze of heat and smoke; and Ziggy, unconscious, at the heart of the blaze. It was almost unbearable, and Alex wanted desperately to disperse the pictures in his head. He tried to conjure up a vision of Lynn, but he couldn't hold onto it. All he wanted was to be out of there, anywhere his mind could focus on a different vista.

After about ten minutes, Weird returned to the car, bringing a blast of chill air with him. "Brrr," he said. "I've never been convinced that hell is hot. If it was up to me, I'd make it colder than a meat freezer."

"I'm sure you could have a word with God when you get to heaven. OK to go back to the motel now?"

The journey seemed to have satisfied Weird's desire for Alex's company. Once he had checked in at the motel, he announced he'd called a cab to take him into Seattle. "I have a colleague here I want to spend some time with." He'd arranged to meet Alex the following morning to drive to the funeral, and he seemed strangely subdued. Still, Alex dreaded what Weird would come out with at the funeral.

The Brahms died away and Paul walked up to the lectern. "We're all here because Ziggy meant something special to us," he said, clearly fighting to keep control of his voice. "If I spoke all day, I still couldn't convey half of what he meant to me. So I'm not even going to try. But if any of you have memories of Ziggy you'd like to share, I know we'd all like to hear them."

Almost before he'd stopped speaking, an elderly man stood up in the front row and walked stiffly to the podium. As he turned to face them, Alex realized the toll that burying a child took. Karel Malkiewicz seemed to have shrunk, his broad shoulders stooped and his dark eyes shrunk back into his skull. He hadn't seen Ziggy's widowed father for a couple of years, but the change was depressing. "I miss my son," he said, his Polish accent still audible beneath the Scots. "He made me proud all his life. Even as a child, he cared for other people. He was always ambitious, but not for personal glory. He wanted to be the best he could be, because that was how he could do his best for other people. Ziggy never cared much about what other people thought of him. He always said he would be judged by what he did, not by other people's opinions. I am glad to see so many of you here today, because that tells me that you all understood that about him." The old man took a sip of water from the glass on the lectern. "I loved my son. Maybe I didn't tell him that enough. But I hope he died knowing it." He bowed his head and returned to his seat.

Alex pinched the bridge of his nose, trying to hold his tears at bay. One after another, Ziggy's friends and colleagues came forward. Some said little more than how much they'd loved him and how much they would miss him. Others told anecdotes of their relationship, many of them warm and funny. Alex wanted to get up and say something, but he couldn't trust his voice not to betray him. Then the moment he had dreaded. He felt Weird shift in his seat and rise to his feet. Alex groaned inwardly.

Watching him stride to the podium, Alex wondered at the presence Weird had managed to acquire over the years. Ziggy had always been the one with charisma, Weird the awkward gangling one who could be relied on to say the wrong thing, make the wrong move, find the wrong note. But he'd learned his lesson well. A pin dropping would have sounded like the last trump as Weird composed himself to speak.

"Ziggy was my oldest friend," he intoned. "I thought the road he chose was misguided. He thought I was, to use a word for which there is no American-English equivalent, a pillock. Maybe even a charlatan. But that never mattered. The bond that existed between us was strong enough to survive that pressure. That's because the years we spent in each other's pockets were the hardest years in any man's life, the years when he grows from childhood to manhood. We all struggle through those years, trying to figure out who we are and what we have to offer the world. Some of us are lucky enough to have a friend like Ziggy to pick us up off the floor when we screw up."

Alex stared in disbelief. He couldn't quite believe his ears. He'd expected hellfire and damnation, and instead what he was hearing was unmistakably love. He found himself smiling, against all the odds.

"There were four of us," Weird continued. "The Laddies

fi' Kirkcaldy. We met on our first day at high school and
something magical happened. We bonded. We shared our
deepest fears and our greatest triumphs. For years, we were
the worst band in the world, and we didn't care. In any
group, everybody takes on a role. I was the klutz. The fool.
The one who always took things too far." He gave a small,
self-deprecating shrug. "Some might say I still do. Ziggy
was the one who saved me from myself. Ziggy was the one
who kept me from destruction. He preserved me from the
worst excesses of my personality until I found a greater Savior. But even then, Ziggy didn't let me go.

"We didn't see much of each other in recent years. Our
lives were too full of the present. But that didn't mean we
threw away the past. Ziggy still remained a touchstone for
me in many ways. I won't pretend I approved of all the
choices he made. You'd recognize me as a hypocrite if I pretended otherwise. But here, today, none of that matters.
What counts is that my friend is dead and, with his death, a
light has gone from my life. None of us can afford to lose
the light. And so today, I mourn the passing of a man who
made my way to salvation so much easier. All I can do for
Ziggy's memory is to try to do the same thing for anyone
else who crosses my path in need. If I can help any one of
you today, don't hesitate to make yourself known to me. For
Ziggy's sake." Weird looked round the room with a beatific
smile. "I thank the Lord for the gift of Sigmund Malkiewicz.
Amen."

OK, Alex thought. He reverted to type at the end. But
Weird had done Ziggy proud in his own way. When his
friend sat down again, Alex reached across and squeezed his
hand. And Weird didn't let go.

Afterward, they filed out, pausing to shake hands with Paul
and with Karel Malkiewicz. They emerged into weak sunshine, letting the flow of the crowd carry them past the floral
tributes. In spite of Paul's request that only family should
send flowers, there were a couple of dozen bouquets and

wreaths. "He had a way of making us all feel like family," Alex said to himself.

"We were blood brothers," Weird said softly.

"That was good, what you said in there."

Weird smiled. "Not what you expected, was it? I could tell from your face."

Alex said nothing. He bent down to read a card. *Dearest Ziggy, the world's too big without you. With love from all your friends at the clinic.* He knew the feeling. He browsed the rest of the cards, then paused at the final wreath. It was small and discreet, a tight circlet of white roses and rosemary. Alex read the card and frowned. *Rosemary for remembrance.*

"You see this?" he asked Weird.

"Tasteful," Weird said approvingly.

"You don't think it's a bit . . . I don't know. Too close for comfort?"

Weird frowned. "I think you're seeing ghosts where none exist. It's a perfectly appropriate tribute."

"Weird, he died on the twenty-fifth anniversary of Rosie Duff's death. This card isn't signed. You don't think this is a bit heavy?"

"Alex, that's history." Weird spread his hand in a gesture that encompassed the mourners. "Do you seriously think there's anybody here but us who even knows Rosie Duff's name? It's just a slightly theatrical gesture, which should hardly come as a surprise, given the crowd that's here."

"They've reopened the case, you know." Alex could be as stubborn as Ziggy when the mood took him.

Weird looked surprised. "No, I didn't know."

"I read about it in the papers. They're doing a review of unsolved murders in the light of new technological advances. DNA and that."

Weird's hand went to his cross. "Thank the Lord."

Puzzled, Alex said. "You're not worried about all the old lies being taken out for an airing?"

"Why? We've nothing to fear. At last our names will be cleared."

Alex looked troubled. "I wish I thought it would be that easy."

Dr. David Kerr pushed his laptop away from him with a sharp exhalation of annoyance. He'd been trying to polish the first draft of an article on contemporary French poetry for the past hour, but the words had been making less and less sense the longer he glared at the screen. He took off his glasses and rubbed his eyes, trying to convince himself there was nothing more bothering him than end-of-term exhaustion. But he knew he was kidding himself.

However hard he tried to escape the knowledge, he couldn't get away from the realization that, while he sat fiddling with his prose, Ziggy's friends and family were saying their final farewells half a world away. He wasn't sorry that he hadn't gone; Ziggy represented a part of his history so distant it felt like a past-life experience and he believed he didn't owe his old friend enough to counterbalance the hassle and upset of traveling to Seattle for a funeral. But the news of his death had rekindled memories David Kerr had worked hard to submerge so deep they seldom surfaced to trouble him. They were not memories that made for comfort.

Yet when the phone rang, he reached for it without any sense of apprehension. "Dr. Kerr?" The voice was unfamiliar.

"Yes. Who's this?"

"Detective Inspector Robin Maclennan of Fife Police." He spoke slowly and distinctly, like a man who knows he's had one more drink than was wise.

David shivered involuntarily, suddenly as cold as if submerged in the North Sea once more. "And why are you calling me?" he asked, hiding behind belligerence.

"I'm a member of the cold case review team. You may have read about it in the papers?"

"That doesn't answer my question," David snapped.

"I wanted to talk to you about the circumstances of my brother's death. That would be DI Barney Maclennan."

David was taken aback, left speechless by the directness of the approach. He'd always dreaded a moment like this, but after nearly twenty-five years he'd persuaded himself it would never come.

"Are you there?" Robin said. "I said, I wanted to talk to you about . . ."

"I heard you," David said harshly. "I have nothing to say to you. Not now, not ever. Not even if you arrest me. You people ruined my life once. I will not give you the opportunity to do it again." He slammed the phone down, his breath coming in short pants, his hands shaking. He folded his arms across his chest and hugged himself. What was going on here? He'd had no idea that Barney Maclennan had had a brother. Why had he left it so long to challenge David about that terrible afternoon? And why was he raising it now? When he'd mentioned the cold case review, David had felt sure Maclennan wanted to talk about Rosie Duff, which would have been enough of an outrage. But Barney Maclennan? Surely Fife Police hadn't decided after twenty-five years to call it murder after all?

He shivered again, staring out into the night. The twinkling lights of the Christmas trees in the houses along the street seemed a thousand eyes, staring back at him. He jumped to his feet and yanked the study curtains closed. Then he leaned against the wall, eyes shut, heart pounding. David Kerr had done his best to bury the past. He'd done everything he could to keep it from his door. Clearly, that hadn't been enough. That left only one option. The question was, did he have the nerve to take it?

CHAPTER
TWENTY-SIX

The light from the study was suddenly obscured by heavy curtains. The watcher frowned. That was a break in the routine. He didn't like that. He worried over what might have provoked the change. But eventually, things went back to normal. The lights went off downstairs. He knew the pattern by now. A lamp would come on in the big bedroom at the front of the Bearsden villa, then David Kerr's wife would appear in silhouette at the window. She'd draw the heavy drapes that shut out all but the barest glimmer of light from within. Almost simultaneously, an oblong of light would shine down on the garage roof. The bathroom, he presumed. David Kerr going about his bedtime ablutions. Like Lady Macbeth, he'd never get his hands clean. About twenty minutes later, the bedroom lights would go out. Nothing else would happen tonight.

Graham Macfadyen turned the key in the ignition and drove off into the night. He was beginning to get a feel for David Kerr's life, but he wanted to know so much more. Why, for example, he hadn't done what Alex Gilbey had, and caught a plane for Seattle. That was cold. How could you not pay your respects to someone who was not only one of your oldest friends but also your partner in crime?

Unless of course there had been some sort of estrangement. People talked about thieves falling out. How much more natural it would be for murderers to do the same. It must have taken time and distance to create such a rift. There had been nothing obvious in the immediate aftermath of their crime. He knew that now, thanks to his Uncle Brian.

The memory of that conversation ticked over in the back of his mind during most of his waking hours, a mental string of worry beads whose movement reinforced his determination. All he'd wanted was to find his parents; he'd never expected to be consumed by this search for a higher truth. But consumed he was. Others might dismiss it as obsession but that was typical of people who didn't understand the nature of commitment and the need for justice. He was convinced that his mother's unquiet shade was watching him, spurring him on to do whatever was necessary. It was the last thing he thought about before sleep consumed him and his first conscious thought on waking. Somebody had to pay.

His uncle had been less than thrilled by their encounter in the graveyard. At first, Macfadyen had thought the older man was going to attack him physically. His hands had bunched into fists and his head had gone down like a bull about to charge.

Macfadyen had stood his ground. "I only want to talk about my mother," he said.

"I've got nothing to say to you," Brian Duff snarled.

"I just want to know what she was like."

"I thought Jimmy Lawson told you to stay away?"

"Lawson came to see you about me?"

"Don't flatter yourself, son. He came to see me to talk about the new investigation into my sister's murder."

Macfadyen nodded, understanding. "So he told you about the missing evidence?"

Duff nodded. "Aye." His hands dropped and he looked away. "Useless twats."

"If you won't talk about my mother, will you at least tell me what went on when she was killed? I need to know what happened. And you were there."

Duff recognized persistence when he saw it. It was, after all, a trait this stranger shared with him and his brother. "You're not going to go away, are you?" he said sourly.

"No. I'm not. Look, I never expected to be welcomed into my biological family with open arms. I know you probably feel I don't belong. But I've got a right to know where I came from and what happened to my mother."

"If I talk to you, will you go away and leave us alone?"

Macfadyen considered for a moment. It was better than nothing. And maybe he could find a way under Brian Duff's defenses that would leave the door ajar for the future. "OK," he said.

"Do you know the Lammas Bar?"

"I've been in a few times."

Duff's eyebrows rose. "I'll meet you there in half an hour." He turned on his heel and stalked off. As the darkness swallowed his uncle, Macfadyen felt excitement rise like bile in his throat. He'd been looking for answers for so long, and the prospect of finally finding some was almost too much.

He hurried back to his car and drove straight to the Lammas Bar, finding a quiet corner table where they could talk in peace. His eyes drifted around, wondering how much had changed since Rosie had worked behind the bar. It looked as if the place had had a major makeover in the early nineties, but judging by the scuffed paintwork and the general air of depression, it had never made the grade as a fun pub.

Macfadyen was halfway down his pint when Brian Duff pushed the door open and strode straight to the bar. He was clearly a familiar face, the barmaid reaching for the glass before he even ordered. Armed with a pint of Eighty Shilling, he joined Macfadyen at the table. "Right then," he said. "How much do you know?"

"I looked up the newspaper archives. And there was a bit about the case in a true-crime book I found. But that just told me the bare facts."

Duff took a long draft of his beer, never taking his eyes off Macfadyen. "Facts, maybe. The truth? No way. Because you're not allowed to call people murderers unless a jury said so first."

Macfadyen's pulse quickened. It sounded as if what he'd suspected was on the money. "What do you mean?" he said.

Duff took a deep breath and exhaled slowly. It was obvious that he didn't want to have the conversation. "Let me tell you the story. The night she died, Rosie was working here. Behind that bar. Sometimes I'd give her a lift home, but not that night. She said she was going to a party, but the truth of it was she was meeting somebody after work. We all knew she'd been seeing someone, but she wouldn't let on who it was. She liked her secrets, did Rosie. But me and Colin, we reckoned she was keeping quiet about the boyfriend because she thought we wouldn't approve of him." Duff scratched his chin. "We were maybe a bit heavy-handed when it came to looking out for Rosie. After she got pregnant . . . well, let's just say we didn't want her getting mixed up with another loser.

"Anyway, she left after closing time, and nobody saw who she met up with. It's like she just disappeared off the face of the earth for four hours." He gripped his glass tightly, his knuckles white. "Round about four o'clock in the morning, four students staggering home drunk from a party found her lying in the snow on Hallow Hill. The official version was that they stumbled on her." He shook his head. "But where she was, you wouldn't just find her by chance. That's the first thing you need to remember.

"She'd been stabbed once in the stomach. But it was a hell of a wound. Deep and long." Duff's shoulders rose protectively. "She bled to death. Whoever killed her carried her up there in the snow and dumped her like she was a sack of shite. That's the second thing you need to remember." His voice was tight and clipped, the emotion still possessing him twenty-five years on.

"They said she'd likely been raped. They tried to say it might just have been rough sex, but I never believed that. Rosie had learned her lesson. She didn't sleep with the guys she went out with. The cops made out that she was spinning me and Colin a line about that. But we had a word with a couple of the guys she'd dated, and they swore they never had sex with her. And I believe them, because we weren't gentle with them. Sure, they messed about. Blow jobs, hand jobs. But she wouldn't have sex. So she had to have been raped. There was semen on her clothes." He gave an angry snort of disbelief. "I can't believe those useless fuckers have lost the evidence. That was all they needed, DNA testing would have done the rest." He swallowed more beer. Macfadyen waited, tense as a hunting dog on point. He didn't want to say a word and break the spell.

"So that was what happened to my sister. And we wanted to know who did this to her. The police didn't have a fucking clue. They took a look at the four students who found her, but they never really worked them over. See this town? Nobody wants to upset the University. And it was worse back then.

"Remember these names. Alex Gilbey, Sigmund Malkiewicz, Davey Kerr, Tom Mackie. That's the four who found her. The four who ended up covered in her blood, but with a so-called legitimate excuse. And where were they during the missing four hours? They were at a party. Some drunken student party, where nobody keeps tabs on anybody else. They could have come and gone without anybody being any the wiser. Who's to say they were ever there for more than half an hour at the beginning and maybe half an hour at the end? Plus, they had access to a Land Rover."

Macfadyen looked startled. "That wasn't in anything I read."

"No, it wouldn't have been. They stole a Land Rover belonging to one of their mates. They were driving about in it that night."

"Why weren't they charged with it?" Macfadyen demanded.

"Good question. And one we never got an answer to. Probably what I was saying before. Nobody wants to upset the University. Maybe the cops didn't want to bother with minor charges if they couldn't prove the big one. It would have made them look pretty pathetic."

He let go his glass and ticked off the points on his fingers. "So, they've got no real alibi. They had the perfect vehicle for driving around with a body in a blizzard. They drank in here. They knew Rosie. Me and Colin thought students were a bunch of lowlifes who used lassies like Rosie then chucked them when the proper wife material came along, and she knew that, so she'd never have let on if she was going out with a student. One of them actually admitted that he'd invited Rosie along to that party. And according to what I was told, the sperm on Rosie's clothes could have come from either Sigmund Malkiewicz, Davey Kerr or Tom Mackie." He leaned back, momentarily worn out by the intensity of his monologue.

"There were no other suspects?"

Duff shrugged. "There was the mystery boyfriend. But, like I said, that could easily have been one of those four. Jimmy Lawson had some daft notion that she'd been picked up by some nutter for a satanic ritual. That's why she was left where she was. But there was never any evidence of that. Besides, how would he find her? She wouldn't have been walking the streets in that weather."

"What do you think happened that night?" Macfadyen couldn't help the question.

"I think she was going out with one of them. I think he was fed up with not getting his way with her. I think he raped her. Christ, maybe they all did, I don't know for sure. When they realized what they'd done, they knew they were fucked if they let her go free to tell. That would be the end of their degrees, the end of their brilliant futures. So they killed her." There was a long silence.

Macfadyen was the first to speak. "I never knew which three the sperm pointed to."

"It was never public knowledge. But it's kosher, all the same. One of my pals was going out with a lassie that worked for the police. She was a civilian, but she knew what was going on. With what they had on those four, it was criminal, how the police just let it slip away."

"They were never arrested?"

Duff shook his head. "They were questioned, but nothing ever came of it. No, they're still walking the streets. Free as birds." He finished his pint. "So, now you know what happened." He pushed his chair back, as if to leave.

"Wait," Macfadyen said urgently.

Duff paused, looking impatient.

"How come you never did anything about it?"

Duff reared back as if he'd been struck. "Who says we didn't?"

"Well, you're the one who just said they're walking the streets, free as birds."

Duff sighed so deeply the stale beer on his breath washed over Macfadyen. "There wasn't much we could do. We had a pop at a couple of them, but we got our cards marked. The police more or less told us that if anything happened to any of the four of them, we'd be the ones who'd end up behind bars. If it had just been me and Colin, we'd have taken no notice. But we couldn't put our mother through that. Not after what she'd already suffered. So we backed off." He bit his lip. "Jimmy Lawson always said the case would never be closed. One day, he said, whoever killed Rosie would get what they deserved. And I really believed that the time had come, with this new inquiry." He shook his head. "More fool me." This time, he stood up. "I've kept my end of the bargain. Now you keep yours. Stay away from me and mine."

"Just one more thing. Please?"

Duff hesitated, his hand on the back of his chair, one step away from escape. "What?"

"My father. Who was my father?"

"You're better off not knowing, son. He was a useless waste of space."

"Even so. Half my genes came from him." Macfadyen could see the uncertainty in Duff's eyes. He pushed the point. "Give me my father and you'll never see me again."

Duff shrugged. "His name's John Stobie. He moved to England three years before Rosie died." He turned on his heel and walked.

Macfadyen sat for a while staring into space, ignoring his beer. A name. Something to start running a trace on. At last, he had a name. But more than that. He had justification for the decision he'd made after James Lawson's admission of incompetence. The names of the students hadn't been news to him. They'd been there, in the newspaper reports of the murder. He'd known about them for months. Everything he'd read had reinforced his desperate need to find someone to blame for what had happened to his mother. When he'd started his search to unearth the whereabouts of the four men he'd convinced himself had destroyed his chance of ever knowing his real mother, he'd been disappointed to discover that all four of them were leading successful, respectable and respected existences. That wasn't any kind of justice.

He'd immediately set up an Internet alert for any information about the four of them. And when Lawson had delivered his revelation, it had only reinforced Macfadyen's decision that they shouldn't get away with it. If Fife Police couldn't bring them to book for what they'd done, then another way had to be found to make them pay.

The morning after his meeting with his uncle, Macfadyen woke early. He hadn't been to work for over a week now. Writing program code was what he excelled at, and it had always been the one thing that made him feel relaxed. But these days the idea of sitting in front of a screen and working through the complex structures of his current project simply made him feel impatient. Compared to all the other stuff fizzing in his brain, everything else felt petty, irrelevant and pointless. Nothing in his life had prepared him for this quest, and he'd realized it needed all of him, not what was left after a day in the computer lab. He'd gone to the doctor and claimed he was suffering from stress. It wasn't exactly a lie, and he'd been convincing enough to be signed off until after the New Year.

He crawled out of bed and staggered into the bathroom, feeling as if he'd been asleep for minutes instead of hours. He barely glanced in the mirror, not registering the shadows under his eyes or the hollows in his cheeks. He had things to do. Getting to know his mother's killers was more important than remembering to eat properly.

Without pausing to dress or even make coffee, he went straight through to his computer room. He clicked the mouse on one of the PCs. A flashing message in the corner of the screen said <Mail waiting>. He called up his message screen. Two items. He opened the first. David Kerr had an article in the latest issue of an academic journal. Some tripe about a French writer Macfadyen had never heard of. He couldn't have been less interested. Still, it showed that he had set up the parameters of his Internet alert properly. David Kerr wasn't exactly an uncommon name and, until he'd refined the search, he'd been getting dozens of hits every day. Which had been a pain in the arse.

The next message was far more interesting. It directed him to the Web pages of the *Seattle Post Intelligencer*. As he read the article, a slow smile spread across his face.

PROMINENT PEDIATRICIAN DIES IN SUSPICIOUS BLAZE

The founder of the prestigious Fife Clinic has perished in a suspected arson at his King County home.

Dr. Sigmund Malkiewicz, known as Doctor Ziggy to patients and colleagues alike, died in the blaze which destroyed his isolated house in the early hours of yesterday morning.

Three fire trucks attended the scene, but the flames had already destroyed the main part of the wood-built house. Fire Marshall Jonathan Ardiles said, "The house was thoroughly ablaze by the time we were alerted by Dr. Malkiewicz's nearest neighbor. There was very little we could do other than try to prevent it spreading to the nearby woodland."

Detective Aaron Bronstein revealed today that police are treating the fire as suspicious. He said, "Arson investigators are working the site. We can't say more at this stage."

Born and raised in Scotland, Dr. Malkiewicz, 45, had worked in the Seattle area for over 15 years. He was a pediatrician in King County General before leaving nine years ago to set up his own clinic. He had established a reputation in the field of pediatric oncology, specializing in the treatment of leukemia.

Dr. Angela Redmond, who worked alongside Dr. Malkiewicz at the clinic, said, "We are all in shock at this tragic news. Doctor Ziggy was a supportive and generous colleague who was devoted to his patients. Everyone who knew him will be devastated by this."

The words danced before him, leaving him feeling a strange mixture of exhilaration and frustration. With what he knew now about the sperm, it seemed appropriate that Malkiewicz should be the first to die. Macfadyen was disappointed that the journalist hadn't been smart enough to dig up the sordid details of Malkiewicz's life. The article read as if Malkiewicz had been some kind of Mother Teresa, when Macfadyen knew the truth was very different. Maybe he should e-mail the journalist, put him right on a few points.

But that might not be such a bright idea. It would be harder to keep on watching the killers if they thought anyone was interested in what had happened to Rosie Duff twenty-five years before. No, better to keep his own counsel for now. Still, he could always find out about the funeral arrangements and make a small point there, if they had eyes to see. It wouldn't hurt to plant the seed of unease in their hearts, to make them start to suffer a little. They'd caused enough suffering over the years.

He checked the time on his computer. If he left now, he'd make it to North Queensferry in time to pick up Alex Gilbey on his way to work. A morning in Edinburgh, and then he'd drive on to Glasgow, to see what David Kerr was up to. But before that, it was time to start searching for John Stobie.

Two days later, he'd followed Alex to the airport and watched him check in for a flight to Seattle. Twenty-five years on, and murder still tied them to each other. He'd half expected to see David Kerr meet up with him. But there had been no sign. And when he'd hurried through to Glasgow to check if he'd maybe missed his prey there, he'd found Kerr in a lecture theater, delivering as advertised.

That was cold, right enough.

CHAPTER
TWENTY-SEVEN

Alex had never been happier to see the landing lights at Edinburgh airport. Rain lashed against the windows of the plane, but he didn't care. He just wanted to be home again, to sit quietly with Lynn, his hand on her belly, feeling the life within. The future. Like everything else that crossed his mind, that thought brought him up short against Ziggy's death. A child his best friend would never see, never hold.

Lynn was waiting for him in the arrivals area. She looked tired, he thought. He wished she'd just give up work. It wasn't as if they needed the money. But she was adamant that she would keep going until the last month. "I want to use my maternity leave to spend time with the baby, not to sit around and wait for it to arrive," she'd said. She was still determined to return to work after six months, but Alex wondered whether that would change.

He waved as he hurried toward her. Then they were in each other's arms, clinging as if they'd been separated for weeks instead of days. "I missed you," he mumbled into her hair.

"I missed you, too." They stepped apart and headed for the car park, Lynn slipping her arm through his. "Are you OK?"

Alex shook his head. "Not really. I feel gutted. Literally. It's like there's a hole inside of me. Christ knows how Paul's getting through the days."

"How's he doing?"

"It's like he's been cast adrift. Arranging the funeral gave him something to concentrate on, take his mind off what he's lost. But last night, after everybody had gone home, he was like a lost soul. I don't know how he's going to get through this."

"Has he got much support?"

"They've got a lot of friends. He's not going to be isolated. But when it comes down to it, you're on your own, aren't you?" He sighed. "It made me realize how lucky I am. Having you, and the baby on the way. I don't know what I'd do if anything happened to you, Lynn."

She squeezed his arm. "It's only natural you're thinking like that. A death like Ziggy's, it makes us all feel vulnerable. But nothing's going to happen to me."

They reached the car and Alex got into the driving seat. "Home, then," he said. "I can't believe tomorrow's Christmas Eve. I'm dying for a quiet night in, just the two of us."

"Ah," Lynn said, adjusting her seatbelt round the bump.

"Oh no. Not your mother. Not tonight."

Lynn grinned. "No, not my mother. Nearly as bad, though. Mondo's here."

Alex frowned. "Mondo? I thought he was supposed to be in France?"

"Change of plans. They were supposed to spend a few days with Hélène's brother in Paris, but his wife's come down with flu. So they changed their flights."

"So what's he doing, coming to see us?"

"He says he had some business through in Fife, but I think he's feeling guilty about not going to Seattle with you."

Alex snorted. "Aye, he was always good at trotting out the guilt after the event. It never stopped him doing what he was guilty about in the first place, though."

Lynn put a hand on his thigh. There was nothing sexual in the gesture. "You've never really forgiven him, have you?"

"I suppose not. Mostly, it's forgotten. But when things come together like they have this past week . . . No, I don't suppose I have ever forgiven him. Partly for dropping me in the shite all those years ago just to get himself off the hook with the cops. If he hadn't told Maclennan about me fancying Rosie, I don't think we'd have been considered so seriously as suspects. But mostly I can't forgive him for that stupid stunt that cost Maclennan his life."

"You think Mondo doesn't blame himself for that?"

"So he should. But if he hadn't made a major contribution to putting us in the frame in the first place, he'd never have ended up feeling like he needed to make such a ridiculous point. And I wouldn't have had to contend with other people pointing the finger everywhere I went for the remains of my university career. I can't help holding Mondo responsible for that."

Lynn opened her bag and dug out change for the bridge toll. "I think he's always known that."

"Which might be why he's worked so hard at putting so much distance between us." Alex sighed. "I'm sorry that meant you lost out."

"Don't be daft," she said, handing him the coins as they sped down the approach road to the Forth Road Bridge, its majestic sweep offering the best possible view of the three cantilevered diamonds of the railway bridge spanning the estuary. "His loss, Alex. I knew when I married you that Mondo was never going to be comfortable with the idea. I still think I got the best bargain. I'd much rather have you at the center of my life than my neurotic big brother."

"I'm sorry about the way things worked out, Lynn. I still care about him, you know. I've got a lot of good memories that he's part of."

"I know. So try to remember that when you feel like strangling him tonight."

Alex opened the window, shivering at the scatter of rain that hit the side of his face. He handed over the toll and accelerated away, feeling the tug of home as he always did on the approach to Fife. He glanced at the clock on the dashboard. "When's he getting here?"

"He's here already."

Alex grimaced. No chance to decompress. No hiding place.

. . .

Detective Constable Karen Pirie scuttled into the shelter of the pub doorway and pushed the door open gratefully. A blast of warm, sour air flavored with stale beer and smoke flowed over her. It was the smell of release. In the background, she recognized St. Germain's *Tourist* playing. Nice one. She craned her neck, peering through the early-evening drinkers to see who was in. Over by the bar, she spotted Phil Parhatka, his shoulders hunched over a pint and a packet of crisps. She pushed through the crowd and pulled up a stool next to him. "Mine's a Bacardi Breezer," she said, digging him in the ribs.

Phil roused himself and caught the eye of the harassed barman. He ordered, then lounged against the bar. Phil was always happier in company than on his own, Karen reminded herself. Nobody could be further from the TV cliché of the maverick lone cop, taking on the world singlehanded. He wasn't what you'd call the life and soul of the party; he just preferred to hang out with the gang. And she didn't mind in the least standing in for the crowd. One to one, he might just notice that she was a woman. Karen seized her drink as soon as it arrived and took a hearty swig. "That's better," she gasped. "I needed that."

"Thirsty work, raking through the evidence boxes. I didn't expect to see you in here tonight, I thought you'd be straight home."

"No, I needed to come back and check out a couple of things on the computer. Pain in the arse, but there you go." She drank some more and leaned conspiratorially toward her colleague. "And you'll never guess who I caught poking about in my files."

"ACC Lawson," Phil said, without even a pretense at guessing.

Karen sat back, peeved. "How did you know that?"

"Who else gives a shit about what we're up to? Besides, he's been on your back far more than anybody else's since this review began. He seems to be taking it personally."

"Well, he was the first officer on the scene."

"Yeah, but he was only a woolly suit at the time. It's not like it was his case or anything." He pushed the crisps toward Karen and finished his first pint.

"I know. But I suppose he feels connected to it more than the other cases in the review. Still, it was funny to walk in on him poring over my files. He's usually long gone by this time of night. I thought he was going to jump out of his skin when I spoke to him. He was that engrossed he didn't hear me come in."

Phil picked up his fresh pint and took a sip. "He went to see the brother a while back, didn't he? To tell him about the fuck-up with the evidence?"

Karen shook her fingers, the gesture of someone ridding herself of something unpleasantly clinging. "Let me tell you, I was more than happy to let him handle that. Not an interview I'd have enjoyed. 'Hello, sir. Sorry we lost the evidence that might have finally convicted your sister's killer. Oh well, that's how it goes.'" She pulled a face. "So, how are you getting on?"

Phil shrugged. "I don't know. I thought I was on to something, but it looks like another dead-end. Plus I've got the local MSP blethering on about human rights. It's a balls-acher, this job."

"Got a suspect?"

"I've got three. What I've not got is decent evidence. I'm still waiting for the lab to come back with the DNA. That's the only real chance I've got to take it any further. How about you? Who do you think killed Rosie Duff?"

Karen spread her hands. "Perm any one from four."

"You really think it was one of the students who found her?"

Karen nodded. "All the circumstantial points that way. And there's something else besides." She paused, waiting for the prompt.

"OK, Sherlock. I'll buy it. What's the something else?"

"The psychology of it. Whether this was a ritual killing or a sexual homicide, we're told by the shrinks that murders like this don't come on their own. You'd expect a couple of attempts first."

"Like with Peter Sutcliffe?"

"Exactly. He didn't get to be the Yorkshire Ripper overnight. Which leads me neatly on to the next point. Sex killers are a bit like my gran. They repeat themselves."

Phil groaned. "Oh, very good."

"Don't clap, just throw money. They repeat themselves because they get off on the killing like normal people get off on porn. Anyway, my point is that we never see another sign of this particular killer anywhere in Scotland."

"Maybe he moved away."

"Maybe. And maybe what we were presented with was a stage set. Maybe this wasn't that kind of killer at all. Maybe one or all of our boys raped Rosie and panicked. They don't want a live witness. And so they kill her. But they make it look like the work of a crazed sex beast. They didn't get off on the murder at all, so there was never any question of repetition."

"You think four half-cut lads could manage to be that cool with a dead lassie on their hands?"

Karen crossed her legs and smoothed down her skirt. She noticed him notice and felt a warm glow that had nothing to do with white rum. "That's the question, isn't it?"

"And what's the answer?"

"When you read the statements, there's one of them that sticks out. The medical student, Malkiewicz. He kept his head at the scene, and his statement reads pretty clinical. The placing of his prints indicated he was the last one to drive the Land Rover. And he was one of the three Group O secretors among the four of them. It could have been his sperm."

"Well, it's a nice theory."

"Deserves another drink, I think." This time, Karen got the round in. "The trouble with theory," she continued once her glass was refreshed, "is that it needs evidence to back it up. Evidence which I don't have."

"What about the illegitimate kid? Doesn't he have a father somewhere? What if it was him?"

"We don't know who he was. Brian Duff is keeping his mouth zipped on that one. I've not been able to talk to Colin yet. But Lawson tipped me the wink that it was probably a lad called John Stobie. He left town round about the right time."

"He might have come back."

"That's what Lawson was looking for in the file. To see if I'd got anywhere with that angle." Karen shrugged. "But even if he did come back, why kill Rosie?"

"Maybe he still carried a torch for her, only she didn't want to know."

"I don't think so. This is a kid who left town because Brian and Colin gave him a doing. He doesn't strike me as the hero who comes back to reclaim his lost love. But, no stone unturned. I've got a request in to our brothers in arms down where he lives now. They're going to go and have a wee chat with him."

"Aye, right. He's going to remember where he was on a December night twenty-five years ago."

Karen sighed. "I know. But at least the guys that interview him will get a sense of whether he's a likely lad. My money's still on Malkiewicz working alone or with his pals. Anyway. Enough shop. D'you fancy a last curry before the turkey and sprouts get a grip?"

Mondo jumped to his feet as soon as Alex walked into the conservatory, almost knocking over his glass of red wine. "Alex," he said, a tinge of nervousness in his voice.

How abruptly we shift back in time when we're knocked out of our daily lives and into the company of those who make up our past, Alex thought, surprised by the insight. Mondo, he was sure, was assured and competent in his professional life. He had a cultured and sophisticated wife with whom he did cultured and sophisticated things that Alex could only guess at. But confronted by the confidant of his adolescence, Mondo was that nervy teenager again, exuding vulnerability and need. "Hi, Mondo," Alex said wearily, slumping into the opposite chair and reaching over to pour himself some wine.

"Good flight?" The smile was just on the edge of be-seeching.

"No such thing. I made it home in one piece, which is the best you can say about any flight. Lynn's sorting out the dinner, she'll be through in a minute."

"I'm sorry to descend on you this evening, but I had to come through to Fife to see somebody, and then we're off to France tomorrow and this was the only chance . . ."

You're not a bit sorry, Alex thought. *You just want to assuage your conscience at my expense.* "Pity you didn't find out about your sister-in-law's flu a bit sooner. Then you could have come to Seattle with me. Weird was there." Alex's voice was matter-of-fact, but he meant his words to sting.

Mondo straightened up in his seat, refusing to meet Alex's gaze. "I know you think I should have been there, too."

"I do, actually. Ziggy was one of your best friends for nearly ten years. He put himself out for you. Actually, he put himself out for all of us. I wanted to acknowledge that and I think you should have, too."

Mondo ran a hand through his hair. It was still luxuriant and curly, though shot with silver now. It gave him the look of an exotic among everyday Scottish manhood. "Whatever. I'm just not good at that sort of thing."

"You always were the sensitive one."

Mondo shot him a look of annoyance. "I happen to think that sensitivity is a virtue, not a vice. And I won't apologize for possessing it."

"Then you should be sensitive to all the reasons why I'm pissed off with you. OK, I can just about grasp why you avoid us all like we've got some contagious disease. You wanted to get as far away as possible from anything and anyone that would remind you of Rosie Duff's murder and Barney Maclennan's death. But you should have been there, Mondo. You really should."

Mondo reached for his glass and clutched it as if it would save him from this awkwardness. "You're probably right, Alex."

"So what brings you here now?"

Mondo looked away. "I suppose this review that Fife Police are doing into Rosie Duff's murder brought a lot of stuff to the surface. I realized I couldn't just ignore this. I needed to talk to somebody who understood that time. And what Ziggy meant to all of us." To Alex's astonishment, Mondo's eyes were suddenly wet. He blinked furiously, but tears spilled over. He put down his glass and covered his face with his hands.

Then Alex realized that he too wasn't immune from time travel. He wanted to jump to his feet and pull Mondo into his arms. His friend was shaking with the effort of containing his grief. But he held back, the twinge of old suspicion kicking in.

"I'm sorry, Alex," Mondo sobbed. "I'm so, so sorry."

"Sorry for what?" Alex said softly.

Mondo looked up, his eyes blurred with tears. "Everything. Everything I did that was wrong or stupid."

"That doesn't really narrow it down," Alex said, his voice gentler than the ironic words.

Mondo flinched, his expression wounded. He had grown accustomed to his imperfections being accepted without comment or criticism. "Mostly, I'm sorry about Barney Maclennan. Did you know his brother is working on the cold case review?"

Alex shook his head. "How would I know that? Come to that, how do you know?"

"He called me up. Wanted to talk about Barney. I hung up on him." Mondo heaved a huge sigh. "It's history, you know? OK, I did a stupid thing, but I was only a kid. Christ, if I'd been done for murder, I'd be walking the streets again by now. Why can't we just be left alone?"

"What do you mean, if you'd been done for murder?" Alex demanded.

Mondo shifted in his chair. "Figure of speech. That's all." He drained his glass. "Look, I'd better be off," he said, getting to his feet. "I'll say cheerio to Lynn on the way out." He pushed past Alex, who stared after him, bemused. Whatever Mondo had come for, it didn't look like he'd found it.

CHAPTER
TWENTY-EIGHT

It hadn't been easy, finding a vantage point that afforded a good view of Alex Gilbey's house. But Macfadyen had persevered, clambering over rocks and scrambling across tussocks of rough grass beneath the massive iron cantilevers of the rail bridge. At last, he'd found the perfect spot, at least for night watching. During the day, it would have been horribly exposed, but Gilbey was never around during daylight hours. But once darkness fell, Macfadyen was lost in the black depths of the bridge's shadow, looking straight down on the conservatory where Gilbey and his wife always sat in the evening, taking advantage of their magnificent panorama.

It wasn't right. If Gilbey had paid the price for his actions, he'd either still be languishing behind bars or living the sort of shitty life most long-term prisoners came out to. A scummy council flat surrounded by junkies and small-time hoods, with a stairwell that smelled of piss and vomit, that's the best he deserved. Not this valuable piece of real estate with its spectacular vista and its triple glazing to keep out the sound of the trains that rattled over the bridge all day and most of the night. Macfadyen wanted to take it all away from him, to make him understand what he'd stolen when he'd taken part in the murder of Rosie Duff.

But that was for another day. Tonight, he was keeping

vigil. He'd been in Glasgow earlier, waiting patiently for a shopper to vacate the parking space that experience had taught him gave the perfect perspective on Kerr's slot in the university car park. When his quarry had emerged just after four, Macfadyen had been surprised that he hadn't headed for Bearsden. Instead, their destination had been the motorway that snaked through the middle of Glasgow before striking out across country to Edinburgh. When Kerr had turned off for the Forth Bridge, Macfadyen had smiled in anticipation. It looked like the conspirators were getting together after all.

His prediction turned out to be spot on. But not quite immediately. Kerr left the motorway on the north side of the estuary and, instead of heading down into North Queensferry, he turned off toward the modern hotel that commanded prime views from the sandstone bluff above the estuary. He parked his car and hurried inside. By the time Macfadyen entered the hotel less than a minute behind him, there was no trace of his quarry. He wasn't in the bar or the restaurant area. Macfadyen hurried to and fro through the public areas, his anxious flurry of movement attracting curious glances from staff and customers alike. But Kerr was nowhere to be seen. Furious that he'd lost his man, Macfadyen stormed back outside, slamming the flat of his hand on his car roof. Christ, this wasn't how it was supposed to be. What was Kerr playing at? Had he realized he was being followed and deliberately shaken off his pursuer? Macfadyen hastily whirled round. No, Kerr's car was still where it should be.

What was going on? Obviously, Kerr was meeting someone and they didn't want their meeting to be observed. But who could it be? Could Alex Gilbey have returned from the States and decided to meet his co-conspirator on neutral ground to keep their meeting from his wife? There was no obvious way to find out. Cursing softly, he climbed back into his car and fixed his gaze on the hotel entrance.

He didn't have long to wait. About twenty minutes after Kerr had entered the hotel, he returned to his car. This time, he drove down into North Queensferry. That answered one question. Whoever he'd met, it hadn't been Gilbey. Macfadyen hung back by the corner of the street until Kerr's car turned into Gilbey's drive. Within ten minutes, he was taking up his station under the bridge, grateful that the rain had eased off. He raised his powerful binoculars to his eyes and focused on the house below. A dim glow from inside trickled into the conservatory, but he couldn't see anything else. He moved his field of vision along the wall, finding the oblong of light from the kitchen.

He saw Lynn Gilbey pass, a bottle of red wine in her hand. Nothing for a long couple of minutes, then the lamps in the conservatory flickered into brightness. David Kerr followed the woman in and sat down while she opened the wine and poured two glasses. They were, he knew, brother and sister. Gilbey had married her six years after Rosie's death, when he'd been twenty-seven and she twenty-one. He wondered if she knew the truth about what her brother and her husband had been involved with. Somehow, he doubted it. She would have been spun a web of lies, and it had suited her to believe it. Just like it had suited the police. They'd all been happy to take the easy way out back then. Well, he wasn't going to let that happen a second time.

And now she was pregnant. Gilbey was going to be a father. It infuriated him that their child would have the privilege of knowing its parents, of being wanted and loved instead of blamed and reproached. Kerr and his friends had taken that chance from him all those years before.

There wasn't much conversation going on down there, he noted. Which meant one of two things. Either they were so close they didn't need chatter to fill the space. Or else there was a distance between them that small talk couldn't bridge. He wondered which it was; impossible to gauge from this distance. After ten minutes or so, the woman glanced at her watch and stood up, one hand in the small of her back, the other on her belly. She walked back into the house.

When she hadn't reappeared after ten minutes, he began to wonder if she'd left the house. Of course, it made sense. Gilbey would be returning from the funeral. Meeting up with

Kerr for a debriefing. Talking through the questions raised by Malkiewicz's mysterious death. The murderers reunited.

He hunkered down and took a thermos from his backpack. Strong, sweet coffee to keep him awake and energized. Not that he needed it. Since he'd begun stalking the men he believed responsible for his mother's death, he seemed fired with vigor. And when he fell into bed at night, he slept more deeply than he had since childhood. It was further justification, if any were needed, that the path he had chosen was the right one.

More than an hour passed. Kerr kept jumping up and pacing back and forth, occasionally going back into the house then coming back almost immediately. He wasn't comfortable, that was for sure. Then suddenly, Gilbey walked in. There was no handshake, and it was soon clear to Macfadyen that this was no easy, relaxed encounter. Even through the binoculars, he could tell the conversation wasn't one either man relished.

Nevertheless, he wasn't expecting Kerr to go to pieces as he did. One minute, he was fine, then he was in tears. The dialogue that followed seemed intense, but it didn't last long. Kerr got to his feet abruptly and pushed past Gilbey. Whatever had passed between them, it hadn't made either of them happy.

Macfadyen hesitated for a moment. Should he keep watch here? Or should he follow Kerr? His feet started moving before he was aware of having decided. Gilbey wasn't going anywhere. But David Kerr had broken his pattern once. He might just do it again.

He ran back to his car, reaching the corner just as Kerr pulled out of the quiet side street. Cursing, Macfadyen dived behind the wheel and gunned the engine, taking off with a screech of rubber. But he needn't have worried. Kerr's silver Audi was still at the intersection with the main road, waiting to turn right. Instead of heading for the bridge and home, he chose the M90 going north. There wasn't much traffic, and Macfadyen had no trouble keeping him in sight. Within twenty minutes, he had a pretty good idea where his quarry was making for. He'd bypassed Kirkcaldy and his parents' home and taken the Standing Stone road east. It had to be St. Andrews.

As they reached the outskirts of the town, Macfadyen crept closer. He didn't want to lose Kerr now. The Audi signaled a left turn, heading up toward the Botanic Gardens. "You just couldn't stay away, could you?" Macfadyen muttered. "Couldn't leave her alone."

As he expected, the Audi turned into Trinity Place. Macfadyen parked on the main road and hurried down the quiet suburban street. Lights were on behind curtained windows, but there was no other sign of life. The Audi was parked at the end of the cul-de-sac, sidelights still glowing. Macfadyen walked past, noting the empty driver's seat. He took the path that skirted the bottom of the hill, wondering how many times that same mud had been trampled by those four students before the night they took their fatal decision. Looking up to his left, he saw what he expected. On the brow of the hill, silhouetted against the night, Kerr stood, head bowed. Macfadyen slowed down. It was strange how everything kept coming together to confirm his conviction that the four men who had found his mother's body knew far more about her death than they'd ever been forced to admit. It was hard to understand how the police had failed all those years ago. To have bungled something so straightforward defied belief. He'd done more for the cause of justice in a few months than they'd achieved in twenty-five years with all their resources and manpower. Just as well he wasn't relying on Lawson and his trained monkeys to avenge his mother.

Maybe his uncle had been right and they'd been in thrall to the University. Or maybe he'd been closer to the mark when he'd accused the police of corruption. Wherever the truth lay, it was a different world now. The old servility was dead. Nobody was afraid of the University anymore. And people understood now that the police were just as likely to be crooked as anybody else. So it still fell to individuals like him to make sure justice was done.

As he watched, Kerr straightened up and headed back toward his car. Another entry in the ledger of guilt, Macfadyen thought. Just another brick in the wall.

Alex shifted onto his side and checked the time. Ten to three. Five minutes since he'd last looked at it. It was no use. His body was disorientated by flight and the shift of time zones. All he would achieve if he kept trying to sleep would be to wake Lynn. And given how disturbed her sleep pattern had been by the pregnancy, he didn't want to risk that. Alex slipped out from under the duvet, shivering a little as the chill air hit his skin. He grabbed his dressing gown on his way out of the room and closed the door softly behind him.

It had been a hell of a day. Taking his farewell of Paul at the airport had felt like an abandonment, his natural desire to be home with Lynn a selfishness. On his first flight, he'd been crammed in a bulkhead seat with no window, next to a woman so large he felt certain the whole bank of seats would leave with her when she attempted to rise. He'd fared a little better on the second leg, but he'd been too tired to sleep by then. Thoughts of Ziggy had plagued him, infusing his heart with regrets at all the opportunities missed over the past twenty years. And instead of a restful evening with Lynn, he'd had to deal with Mondo's emotional outburst. He'd have to go to the office in the morning, but already he knew he'd be good for nothing. Sighing, he made for the kitchen and put the kettle on. Maybe a cup of tea would soothe him back to sleepiness.

Carrying his mug, he wandered through the house, touching familiar objects as if they were talismans that would ground him safely. He found himself standing in the nursery, leaning on the cot. This was the future, he told himself. A future worth having, a future that offered him the opportunity to make something of his life that was more than getting and spending.

The door opened and Lynn stood silhouetted against the warm light of the hall.

"I didn't wake you, did I?" he asked.

"No, I managed that all by myself. Jet lag?" She came in and put an arm round his waist.

"Probably."

"And Mondo didn't help, right?"

Alex nodded. "I could have done without that."

"I don't suppose he considered that for a moment. My selfish brother thinks we're all on the planet for his convenience. I did try to put him off, you know."

"I don't doubt it. He's always had the knack of not hearing what he doesn't want to hear. But he's not a bad man, Lynn. Weak and self-centered, sure. But not malicious."

She rubbed her head against his shoulder. "It comes from being so handsome. He was such a beautiful child, he was indulged by everybody, wherever he went. I used to hate him for it when we were wee. He was the object of adoration, a little Donatello angel. People were dazzled by him. And then they'd look at me and you could see the bafflement. How could a stunner like him have such a plain sister?"

Alex chuckled. "And then the ugly duckling turned into a stunner herself."

Lynn dug him in the ribs. "One of the things I've always loved about you is your ability to lie convincingly about the really unimportant things."

"I'm not lying. Somewhere around fourteen, you stopped being plain and got gorgeous. Trust me, I'm an artist."

"Flannel merchant, more like. No, I was always in Mondo's shadow in the looks department. I've been thinking about that lately. The things my parents did that I don't want to repeat. If our baby turns out to be a beauty, I don't ever want to make a big issue out of it. I want our child to have confidence, but not that sense of entitlement that's poisoned Mondo."

"You'll get no argument from me on that." He put a hand on the swell of her stomach. "You hear, Junior? No getting big-headed, right?" He leaned down and kissed the top of Lynn's head. "Ziggy dying like that, it's made me scared. All I want is to see my kid grow up, with you by my side. But it's all so fragile. One minute you're here, the next you're gone. All the things Ziggy must have left undone, and now they'll never be done. I don't want that to happen to me."

Lynn gently took his tea from him and put it on the changing table. She drew him into her arms. "Don't be scared," she said. "Everything's going to be all right."

He wanted to believe her. But he was still too close to his own mortality to be entirely convinced.

A huge yawn cracked Karen Pirie's jaw as she waited for the buzzer that signaled the door release. When it came, she pushed the door open and trudged across the hall, nodding to the security guard as she passed his office. God, how she hated the evidence storage center. Christmas Eve, and the rest of the world was girding its loins for the festivities, and where was she? It felt as if her whole life had narrowed to these aisles of archive boxes with their bagged contents telling pathetic stories of crimes perpetrated by the stupid, the inadequate and the envious. But somewhere in here, she was sure there was the evidence that would open her cold case for her.

It wasn't the only route her investigation could take. She knew she'd have to go back and reinterview witnesses at some point. But she knew that in old cases like this, physical evidence was the key. With modern forensic techniques, it was possible that the case exhibits would provide solid proof that would make witness statements largely redundant.

That was all well and good, she thought. But there were hundreds of boxes in the storage facility. And she had to go through every single one. So far, she reckoned she'd covered about a quarter of the containers. The only positive result was that her arm muscles were getting stronger from toting boxes up and down stepladders. At least she had ten glorious days of leave starting tomorrow, when the only boxes she'd be opening would contain something more appealing than the detritus of crime.

She exchanged greetings with the officer on duty and waited while he unlocked the door in the wire cage that enclosed the shelves of boxes. The security protocol was the worst thing about this task. With every box, the routine was the same. She had to get the box off the shelf, and bring it down to the table where the duty officer could see her. She had to write down the case number in the master log, then fill in her name, number and the date on the sheet of paper affixed to the lid. Only then could she open the box and rummage through its contents. Once she'd satisfied herself that it didn't contain what she was looking for, she had to replace it and go through the whole mind-numbing routine again. The only break in the monotony was when another officer turned up to check through one of the boxes. But this was usually a short-lived respite since they were invariably lucky enough to know the whereabouts of what they were looking for.

There was no simple way to narrow it down. At first, Karen had thought the easiest way to conduct the search would be to go through everything that had originally come from St. Andrews. Boxes were filed according to case numbers, which were chronological. But the process of amalgamating all the evidence lockers of all the individual police stations throughout the region had dispersed the St. Andrews boxes through the entire collection. So that possibility was ruled out.

She had started by going through everything from 1978. But that had turned up nothing of interest, apart from a craft knife that belonged to a 1987 case. Then she'd attacked the years on either side. This time, the misfiled item had been a child's gym shoe, a relic of the unsolved disappearance of a ten-year-old boy in 1969. She was fast reaching the point where she feared that she could easily miss the very thing she was looking for because her brain was so dulled by the process.

She popped the top on a can of Diet Irn-Bru, took a swig that set her taste-buds jangling and got started: 1980. Third shelf. She dragged her jaded body to the bottom of the stepladder, still sitting where she'd finished with it the day before. She climbed up, pulled out the box she needed and cautiously descended the aluminium steps.

Back at the table, she did the paperwork then lifted the lid. Great. It looked like a charity-shop reject pile in there. Laboriously, she took out the bags one by one, checking that none had Rosie Duff's case number on its adhesive label. A pair of jeans. A filthy T-shirt. A pair of women's knickers. Tights. A bra. A checked shirt. None of them anything to do with her. The last item looked like a woman's cardigan. Karen lifted out the final bag, expecting nothing.

She gave the label a cursory glance. Then she blinked, unable to believe her eyes. She checked the number again. Not trusting herself, she dug her notebook out of her bag and compared the case number on the cover with the bag she was gripping tightly in her hand.

There was no mistake. Karen had found her early Christmas present.

CHAPTER
TWENTY-NINE

January 2004; Scotland

He'd been right. There was a pattern. It had been disrupted by the festive season, and that had made him fretful. But now the New Year was past, the old routine had reasserted itself. The wife went out every Thursday evening. He watched her framed against the light as the front door of the Bearsden villa opened. Moments later, her car headlights came on. He didn't know where she was going and he didn't care. All that mattered was that she had behaved predictably, leaving her man alone in the house.

He reckoned he had a good four hours to carry out his plan. But he forced himself to be patient. Senseless to take risks now. Best to wait till people had settled down for the evening, slumped in front of the TV. But not for too long. He didn't want someone taking their designer dog for a last pee bumping into him as he made his getaway. Suburbia, predictable as the speaking clock. He hugged the reassurance to himself, trying to stifle the ticking of anxiety.

He turned up the collar of his jacket against the cold and prepared to wait, his heart fluttering in his chest with anticipation. There was no pleasure in what lay ahead, just necessity. He wasn't some sick thrill killer, after all. Just a man doing what he had to do.

. . .

David Kerr swapped DVDs and returned to his armchair.
Thursday nights were when he indulged his semisecret vice.
When Hélène was out with the girls, he was slumped in a
chair glued to the U.S. series that she dismissed as "trash
TV." So far that evening, he'd watched two episodes of *Six
Feet Under* and now he was thumbing the remote to cue up
one of his favorite episodes from the first series of *The West
Wing*. He'd just stopped humming along with the grandiose
swell of the theme tune when he thought he heard the sound
of breaking glass from downstairs. Without conscious
thought, his brain calibrated its coordinates and signaled that
it came from the back of the house. Probably the kitchen.

He jerked upright and hit the mute button on the remote.
More glass tinkled and he jumped to his feet. What the hell
was that? Had the cat knocked something over in the
kitchen? Or was there a more sinister explanation?

David rose cautiously, looking around him for a potential
weapon. There wasn't much to choose from, Hélène being
something of a minimalist when it came to interior design.
He snatched up a heavy crystal vase, slender enough at the
neck to fit neatly into his hand. He crossed the room on tip-
toe, ears straining for a sound, heart racing. He thought he
heard a crunching noise, as if glass were being crushed underfoot. Anger rose alongside fear. Some jakie or junkie was
invading his home looking for the price of a bottle of Buckie
or a wrap of smack. His natural instinct was to call the police
then sit tight. But he was afraid they'd take too long to get
there. No self-respecting burglar would settle for what they
could find in the kitchen; they'd be bound to look for better
pickings and he'd be forced to confront whoever had invaded
his home. Besides, he knew from experience that if he picked
up the phone in here, the extension in the kitchen would
click, revealing what he was up to. And that might really piss
off whoever was raiding his house. Better to try a direct approach. He'd read somewhere that most burglars are cow-
ards. Well, maybe one coward could scare off another one.

Taking a deep breath to still his alarm, David inched open

the living room door. He peered down the hall, but the kitchen door was closed and offered no indication of what might be going on on the other side of it. But now he could hear the unmistakable sounds of someone moving around. The rattle of cutlery as a drawer was pulled open. The slap of a cupboard door closing.

To hell with it. He wasn't going to stand idle while someone trashed the place. He walked boldly down the hall and threw the kitchen door open. "What the hell's going on here?" he shouted into the darkness. He reached for the light switch, but when he flicked it on, nothing happened. In the faint light from outside, he could see glass sparkling on the floor by the open back door. But there was nobody in sight. Had they gone already? Fear made the hair on his neck and naked arms stand on end. Uncertainly, he took a step forward into the gloom.

From behind the door, a blur of movement. David swung round as his assailant cannoned into him. He had an impression of medium height, medium build, features obscured by a ski mask. He felt a blow to the stomach; not enough to make him double over, more like a jab than a punch. The burglar took a step backward, breathing heavily. At the same moment David realized the man was holding a long-bladed knife, he felt a hot line of pain inside his guts. He put a hand to his stomach and wondered stupidly why it felt warm and wet. He looked down and saw a dark spreading stain swallowing the white of his T-shirt. "You stabbed me," he said, incredulity his first reaction.

The burglar said nothing. He drew his arm back and thrust again with the knife. This time, David felt it slice deep into his flesh. His legs gave way beneath him and he coughed, slumping forward. The last thing he saw was a pair of well-worn walking boots. From a distance, he could hear a voice. But the sounds it was making refused to cohere in his head. A jumble of syllables that made no sense. As he drifted away from consciousness, he couldn't help thinking it was a pity.

When the phone rang at twenty to midnight, Lynn expected Alex's voice, apologizing for the lateness of the hour, telling her he was just leaving the restaurant where he'd been entertaining a potential client from Gothenburg. She wasn't prepared for the banshee wail that assaulted her as soon as she lifted the bedside receiver. A woman's voice, incoherent, but clearly anguished. That was all she could make out to begin with.

At the first gulp for breath, Lynn jumped in. "Who is this?" she demanded, anxious and afraid.

More panicked sobs. Then, finally, something that sounded familiar. "It's me—Hélène. God help me, Lynn, this is terrible, terrible." Her voice caught and Lynn heard an incoherent gabble of French.

"Hélène? What's the matter? What's happened?" Lynn was shouting now, trying to cut through the scrambled syllables. She heard a deep intake of breath.

"It's David. I think he's dead."

Lynn understood the words, but she couldn't grasp the sense. "What are you talking about? What's happened?"

"I came home, he's on the kitchen floor, there's blood everywhere and he's not breathing. Lynn, what am I to do? I think he's dead."

"Have you phoned an ambulance? The police?" Surreal. This was surreal. That she was capable of such a thought at a moment like this bemused Lynn.

"I called them. They are on their way. But I had to talk to somebody. I'm afraid, Lynn, I am so afraid. I don't understand. This is terrible, I think I'm going mad. He is dead, my David is dead."

This time, the words penetrated. Lynn felt as if a cold hand was pressing in on her chest, constricting her breathing. This wasn't how things were supposed to happen. You weren't supposed to pick up the phone, expecting your husband, only to hear your brother was dead. "You don't know that," she said helplessly.

"He's not breathing, I can't feel a pulse. And there is so much blood. He's dead, Lynn. I know it. What am I going to do without him?"

"All this blood—has somebody attacked him?"

"What else could have happened?"

Fear hit Lynn like a cold shower. "Get out of the house, Hélène. Wait outside for the police. He could still be in the house."

Hélène screamed. "Oh my God. You think this is possible?"

"Just get out. Call me later, when the police are there." The line went dead. Lynn lay frozen, unable to process what she'd just gone through. Alex. She needed Alex. But Hélène needed him more. In a daze, she speed-dialed his mobile. When he answered, the sounds of a boisterous restaurant in the background seemed incongruous and bizarre to Lynn. "Alex," she said. For a moment nothing else would come.

"Lynn? Is that you? Is everything OK? You're all right?" His anxiety was palpable.

"I'm fine. But I've just had the most awful conversation with Hélène. Alex, she said Mondo's dead."

"Hang on a minute, I can't hear you."

She heard the sound of a chair being pushed back, then a few seconds later the noise subsided. "That's better," Alex said. "I couldn't make out what you were saying. What's the problem?"

Lynn could feel her self-control slip. "Alex, you need to go to Mondo's right away. Hélène's just phoned. Something terrible's happened. She says Mondo's dead."

"What?"

"I know, it's incredible. She says he's lying on the kitchen floor, blood everywhere. Please, I need you to go there, find out what's going on." Tears were on her cheeks now.

"Hélène's there? At the house? And she says Mondo's dead? Jesus Christ."

Lynn choked on a sob. "I can't take it in either. Please, Alex, just go and see what's happened."

"OK, OK. I'm on my way. Look, maybe he's just hurt. Maybe she got it wrong."

"She didn't sound like there was any doubt in her mind."

Aye, well, Hélène's not a doctor, is she? Look, hang in there. I'll call you as soon as I get there."

"I can't believe this." Now the tears were choking her, turning her words into gulps.

"Lynn, you've got to try and stay calm. Please."

"Calm? How can I be calm? My brother's dead."

"We don't know that. Lynn, the baby. You've got to take care of yourself. Getting into a state can't help Mondo, whatever's happened."

"Just get there, Alex," Lynn shouted.

"I'm on my way." She heard Alex's footsteps as the call ended. She'd never wanted him more. And she wanted to be in Glasgow, to be by her brother's side. No matter what had passed between them, he was still bound to her by blood. She hadn't needed Alex's reminder that she was nearly eight months pregnant. She wasn't about to do anything that would put her baby at risk. Groaning softly as she wiped her tears, Lynn tried to make herself physically comfortable. Please God, let Hélène be wrong.

Alex couldn't remember ever having driven faster. It was a miracle that he reached Bearsden without once seeing flashing blue lights in his rear-view mirror. All the way there, he kept telling himself there must be a mistake. The possibility of Mondo's death was one he couldn't entertain. Not so close on the heels of Ziggy's. Sure, terrible coincidences happened. They were the stuff of tabloid ghoulishness and daytime TV shows. But they happened to other people. At least, they always had until now.

His fervent hopes began to disintegrate as soon as he turned into the quiet road where Mondo and Hélène lived. Outside the house, three police cars straggled along the pavement. An ambulance sat in the drive. Not a good sign. If Mondo was alive, he'd be long gone, the ambulance hurtling blues and twos to the nearest hospital.

Alex abandoned his car behind the first police car and ran toward the house. A burly uniformed constable in a fluorescent yellow jacket stepped into his path at the end of the drive. "Can I help you, sir?" he said.

"It's my brother-in-law," Alex said, trying to push past

him. The constable grabbed his arms, firmly preventing his passage. "Please, let me through. David Kerr—I'm married to his sister."

"I'm sorry, sir. Nobody can go in just now. This is a crime scene."

"What about Hélène? His wife? Where's she? She called my wife."

"Mrs. Kerr is inside. She's perfectly safe, sir."

Alex let himself go limp. The constable loosened his grip. "Look, I don't really know what's gone on here, but I do know that Hélène needs support. Can't you radio your boss, get me in?"

The constable looked doubtful. "Like I said, sir, this is a crime scene."

Frustration fizzed in Alex's head. "And this is how you treat the victims of crime? Keep them isolated from their families?"

The policeman put his radio to his mouth with a resigned air. He half turned away, making sure he still blocked access to the house, and muttered something into the radio. It crackled in response. After a brief, muffled exchange, he swung back to face Alex. "Can I see some ID, sir?" he asked.

Impatient, Alex pulled out his wallet and withdrew his driver's license. Thankful that he'd gone for one of the new ones with a photograph, he handed it over. The policeman looked it over and handed it back with a polite nod. "If you'd like to go up to the house, sir, one of my colleagues from CID will meet you at the door."

Alex brushed past him. His legs felt strange, as if his knees belonged to someone else who didn't know how to work them properly. As he reached the door, it swung open and a woman in her thirties swept tired, cynical eyes over him, as if committing his details to memory. "Mr. Gilbey?" she said, stepping back to allow him to enter the vestibule.

"That's right. What's happened? Hélène phoned my wife, she seemed to think Mondo was dead?"

"Mondo?"

Alex sighed, impatient with his own obtuseness. "Nick-name. We've been friends since school. David. David Kerr. His wife said he was dead."

The woman nodded. "I'm sorry to have to tell you that Mr. Kerr has been pronounced dead."

Christ, he thought. *What a way to lay it out.* "I don't understand. What happened?"

"It's too early to be sure," she said. "It appears he was stabbed. There are signs of a break-in at the back of the house. But you'll appreciate, we can't say much at this stage."

Alex rubbed his hands over his face. "This is terrible. Christ, poor Mondo. What a thing to happen." He shook his head, numb and bewildered. "It feels completely unreal. Jesus." He took a deep breath. He'd have time to deal with his reactions later. This wasn't why Lynn had asked him to come. "Where's Hélène?"

The woman opened the inside door. "She's in the living room. If you'd like to come through?" She stood aside and watched as Alex passed her and made straight for the room that overlooked the front garden. Hélène had always referred to it as the drawing room, and he felt a pang of guilt for the times he and Lynn had ridiculed her for that pretentiousness. He pushed the door open and stepped inside.

Hélène was sitting on the edge of one of the vast cream sofas, hunched into herself like an old woman. As he entered, she looked up, her eyes swollen pools of misery. Her long dark hair was tangled around her face, stray strands caught in the corner of her mouth. Her clothes were rumpled, a mocking parody of her normal Parisian chic. She held her hands out to him, beseeching. "Alex," she said, her voice cracked and strained.

He crossed to her side, sitting down and putting his arms around her. He couldn't remember ever holding Hélène this close. Normally, their greetings consisted of a hand lightly placed on an arm, air kisses to either cheek. He was surprised by how muscular her body felt, and even more surprised that he noticed. Shock turned him into a stranger to himself, he was slowly beginning to realize. "I'm so sorry," he said, knowing how pointless words were but unable to avoid them.

Hélène leaned into him, exhausted by grief. Alex was suddenly aware that a uniformed woman constable was sitting discreetly in the corner. She must have brought a chair through from the dining room, he thought irrelevantly. So, no privacy for Hélène in spite of her appalling loss. It didn't take much to work out that she was going to face the same suspicious eyes that had fixed on Paul after Ziggy's death, even though this sounded like a burglary gone horribly wrong.

"I feel as if I'm in some terrible dream. And I just want to wake up," Hélène said wearily.

"You're still in shock."

"I don't know what I am. Or where I am. Nothing feels real."

"I can't believe it either."

"He was just lying there," Hélène said softly. "Blood all over him. I touched his neck, to see if there was a pulse. But you know, I was so careful not to get his blood on me. Isn't that terrible? He was lying there dead and all I could think about was how they turned you four into suspects just because you tried to help a dying girl. So I didn't want to get my David's blood on me." Her fingers convulsively shredded a tissue. "That's terrible. I couldn't bring myself to hold him because I was thinking about myself."

Alex squeezed her shoulder. "It's understandable. Knowing what we know. But nobody could think this had anything to do with you."

Hélène made a harsh sound in the back of her throat and glanced up at the policewoman. *"On parle français, oui?"*

What the hell was this? *"Ça va,"* Alex replied, wondering if his holiday French was up to whatever Hélène wanted to tell him. *"Mais lentement."*

"I'll keep it simple," she said in French. "I need your advice. You understand?"

Alex nodded. "Yes, I understand."

Hélène shivered. "I can't believe I'm even thinking this now. But I don't want to be blamed for this." She clutched his hand. "I'm scared, Alex. I am the foreign wife, I am the suspect."

"I don't think so." He tried to sound reassuring, but his words seemed to flow over Hélène without leaving a trace.

She nodded. "Alex, there is something that will make me look bad. Very bad. Once a week, I went out alone. David thought I met some French friends." Hélène squeezed the tissue into a tight ball. "I lied to him, Alex. I have a lover."

"Ah," Alex said. It felt too much, on top of the news the night had already brought. He didn't want to be Hélène's confidant. He'd never liked her, and he didn't think he was necessarily to be trusted with her secrets.

"David had no idea. God help me, I wish now I had never done this. I loved him, you know? But he was very needy. And it was hard. So, a while back, I met this woman, completely different from David in every way. I didn't mean for it to turn out the way it did, but we became lovers."

"Ah," Alex said again. His French wasn't up to demanding how the hell she could do that to Mondo, how she could claim to love a man she'd consistently betrayed. Besides, it wasn't the best move to start a row in front of a cop. You didn't have to speak a foreign tongue to understand tones of voice and body language. Hélène wasn't the only one who felt like she was in the middle of a bad dream. One of his oldest friends had been murdered, and his widow was confessing to a lesbian love affair? He couldn't take it on board right now. Stuff like this didn't happen to people like him.

"I was with her this evening. If the police find out, they will think, ah, she has a lover, they must be in it together. But that's wrong. Jackie was no threat to my marriage. I didn't stop loving David just because I was sleeping with someone else. So should I tell the truth? Or should I keep quiet and hope they don't find out?" She drew away slightly, so she could direct her anxious gaze into Alex's eyes. "I don't know what to do, and I'm really scared."

Alex felt his grip on reality slipping. What the hell was

she playing at? Was she playing some grotesque double bluff and trying to get him on her side? Was she really as innocent as he'd assumed? He struggled to find the French to express what he needed to say. "I don't know, Hélène. I don't think I'm the right person to ask."

"I need your advice. You've been here yourself, you know what it can be like."

Alex took a deep breath, wishing he was anywhere but here. "What about your friend, this Jackie? Will she lie for you?"

"She won't want to be a suspect anymore than I do. Yes, she will lie."

"Who knows?"

"About us?" She shrugged. "Nobody, I think."

"But you can't be sure?"

"You can never be sure."

"In that case, I think you have to tell the truth. Because if they find it out later, it will look much worse." Alex rubbed his face again and looked away. "I can't believe we're talking like this, and Mondo hardly dead."

Hélène pulled away. "I know you probably think I'm cold, Alex. But I've got the rest of my life to cry for the man I loved. And I did love him, make no mistake about that. But right now, I want to make sure I don't take the blame for something that was nothing to do with me. You of all people should understand that."

"Fine," Alex said, reverting to English. "Have you told Sheila and Adam yet?"

She shook her head. "The only person I spoke to was Lynn. I didn't know what to say to his parents."

"Do you want me to do it for you?" But before Hélène could reply, Alex's mobile chirped cheerfully in his pocket. "That'll be Lynn," he said, taking it out and checking the number on the display. "Hello?"

"Alex?" Lynn sounded terrified.

"I'm here at the house," he said. "I don't know how to tell you this. I'm so, so sorry. Hélène was right. Mondo's dead. It looks like somebody broke in . . ."

"Alex," Lynn interrupted him. "I'm in labor. The contractions started just after I spoke to you before. I thought it was a false alarm, but they're coming every three minutes."

"Oh Jesus." He jumped to his feet, looking around in panic.

"Don't freak out. It's natural." Lynn yelped in pain. "There goes another one. I've called a taxi, it should be here any minute."

"What . . . what . . ."

"Just get yourself to the Simpson. I'll meet you in the labor suite."

"But Lynn, it's too soon." Alex finally managed sense.

"It's the shock, Alex. It happens. I'm fine. Please, don't be scared. I need you not to be scared. I need you to get in your car and drive very carefully to Edinburgh. Please?"

Alex gulped. "I love you, Lynn. Both of you."

"I know you do. I'll see you soon."

The connection broke off and Alex looked helplessly at Hélène. "She's in labor," she said flatly.

"She's in labor," Alex echoed.

"So go."

"You shouldn't be alone."

"I have a friend I can call. You need to be with Lynn."

"Shite timing," Alex said. He thrust his phone back in his pocket. "I'll phone. I'll come back when I can."

Hélène stood up and patted him on the arm. "Just go, Alex. Let me know what happens. Thank you for coming."

He ran from the room.

CHAPTER
THIRTY

Dirty streaks of gray began to materialize in the sodium-smudged city darkness. Alex slumped on a chilly bench by the Simpson Memorial Pavilion, tears chapping his cheeks. Nothing in his life had prepared him for a night like this. He'd gone beyond tiredness into an altered state where he felt he'd never sleep again. The emotional overload was such that he no longer knew what he felt.

He had no recollection of the drive back from Glasgow to Edinburgh. He knew he'd called his parents at some point, had a vague memory of an agitated conversation with his father. Fears tumbled headlong through his head. All the things he knew could go wrong. All the things he didn't know about that he was sure could go wrong with a baby at thirty-four weeks' gestation. He wished he was Weird, so he could place his trust in something less fallible than the medical profession. What the hell would he do without Lynn? What the hell would he do with a baby without Lynn? What the hell would he do with Lynn without a baby? The portents couldn't be worse: Mondo lying dead in some hospital mortuary; Alex not where he should be on the most important night of his life.

He'd abandoned the car somewhere in the Royal Infirmary car park and managed to find the entrance to the maternity wing at the third attempt. He'd been sweating and panting by the time he arrived at the reception desk, grateful that maternity nurses had seen so much that a wild-eyed unshaven man gibbering like a fool didn't even register on their Richter scale.

"Mrs. Gilbey? Ah yes, we've taken her straight up to the delivery suite."

Alex tried to concentrate on the directions, repeating them under his breath as he navigated the corridors of the unit. He pressed the security intercom and looked anxiously into the lens of the video camera, hoping he looked more like an expectant father than an escaped lunatic. After what seemed an eternity, the door buzzed open and he blundered into the delivery suite. He didn't know quite what he'd expected, but it wasn't this deserted foyer and eerie silence. He stood uncertain in the foyer. Just then, a nurse entered from one of the corridors radiating off in all directions. "Mr. Gilbey?" she said.

Alex nodded frantically. "Where's Lynn?" he demanded.

"Come with me."

He followed her back down the corridor. "How is she?"

"She's doing fine." She paused, her hand on the door handle. "We need you to help keep her calm. She's a bit distressed. There have been one or two dips in the fetal heartbeat."

"What does that mean? Is the baby OK?"

"It's nothing to worry about."

He hated it when medical professionals said that. It always felt like a blatant lie. "But it's far too early. She's only thirty-four weeks."

"Try not to worry. They're in good hands here."

The door opened and Alex was confronted with a scene that bore no relationship to the routines they'd practiced at the antenatal classes. It was hard to imagine anything that could be further from his and Lynn's dream of natural childbirth. Three women in surgical scrubs bustled around. A monitor with an electronic display sat next to the bed, a fourth woman in a white coat studying it. Lynn lay on her back, legs apart, her hair plastered to her head with sweat.

Her face was scarlet and damp, her eyes wide and anguished. The thin hospital gown stuck to her body. The tube from a drip stand next to the bed disappeared under her. "Thank fuck you're here," she gasped. "Alex, I'm scared."

He rushed to her side, reaching for her hand. She gripped him tightly. "I love you," he said. "You're doing just fine."

The woman in the white coat glanced across. "Hi, I'm Dr. Singh," she said, acknowledging Alex's arrival. She joined the midwife at the bottom of the bed. "Lynn, we're a wee bit concerned about the baby's heart rate. We're not progressing as fast as I'd like. We might have to consider a section."

"Just get the baby out," Lynn moaned.

Suddenly, there was a flurry of activity. "Baby's stuck," one midwife said. Dr. Singh studied the monitor briefly.

"Heart rate's down," she said. Everything began to happen more quickly than Alex could comprehend as he clung to Lynn's clammy hand. Odd phrases penetrated. "Get her to theater now." "Catheterize her." "Consent form." Then the bed was on the move, the door open, everyone bustling down the corridor toward the theater.

The world turned into a blur of activity. Time seemed alternately to race and to crawl. Then, when Alex had almost stopped hoping, the magic words, "It's a girl. You've got a daughter."

Tears welled up in his eyes and he swung round to see his child. Blood-streaked and purple, frighteningly still and silent. "Oh God," he said. "Lynn, it's a girl." But Lynn was past noticing.

A midwife hastily wrapped the baby in a blanket and hurried off. Alex stood up. "Is she OK?" He was led out of the theater in a daze. What was happening to his child? Was she even alive? "What's going on?" he demanded.

The midwife smiled. "Your daughter's doing great. She's breathing on her own, which is always the big concern with premature babies."

Alex slumped into a chair, his hands over his face. "I just want her to be OK," he said through the tears.

"She's holding her own. She weighs four pounds eight

ounces, which is good. Mr. Gilbey, I've delivered quite a few premature babies, and I'd say your wee girl's one of the strongest I've seen. It's early days, but I think she's going to be just fine."

"When can I see her?"

"You should be able to go down to the neonatal unit and see her in a wee while. You won't be able to pick her up yet, but since she's breathing on her own, you'll likely be able to hold her in a day or so."

"What about Lynn?" he said, suddenly guilty that he hadn't asked sooner.

"They're just stitching her up now. She's had a rough time. When they bring her through, she'll be tired and disorientated. She'll be upset because she won't have her baby with her. So you'll need to be strong for her."

He could remember nothing more except for the single defining moment when he'd looked into the transparent cot and met his daughter for the first time. "Can I touch her?" he'd said, awestruck. Her tiny head looked utterly vulnerable, eyes scrunched shut, threads of dark hair plastered to her scalp.

"Give her your finger to hold," the midwife instructed him.

He'd reached out tentatively, stroking the wrinkled skin on the back of her hand. Her tiny fingers opened and gripped tight. And Alex was a captive.

He had sat with Lynn until she woke, then told her about their miraculous daughter. Pale and exhausted, Lynn had wept then. "I know we agreed we were going to call her Ella, but I want to call her Davina. After Mondo," she said.

It hit him like a train. He hadn't given Mondo a thought since he'd arrived at the hospital. "Oh Jesus," he said, guilt eating into his joy. "That's a good thought. Oh, Lynn, I don't know what to say. My head's all over the place."

"You should go home. Get some sleep."

"I need to make some phone calls. Let people know."

Lynn patted his hand. "That can wait. You need to sleep. You look exhausted."

And so he had left, promising to return later. He'd got no

further than the hospital entrance before realizing he didn't have the strength to make it home. Not just yet. He'd found the bench and collapsed on it, wondering how he was going to get through the next few days. He had a daughter, but his arms were still empty. He had lost another friend, and he couldn't begin to think about the implications of that. And somehow he had to find the resources to support Lynn. Until now, he'd always coasted, safe in the knowledge that Ziggy or Lynn would be there in his corner when push came to shove.

For the first time in his adult life, Alex felt horribly alone.

James Lawson heard the news of David Kerr's death as he drove to work the following morning. He couldn't resist a grim smile of satisfaction as it sank in. It had been a long time coming, but finally Barney Maclennan's killer had got what he deserved. Then his thoughts turned uneasily to Robin and the motive he'd handed him. He reached for the car phone. As soon as he arrived at headquarters, he made for the cold cases squadroom. Luckily Robin Maclennan was the only one in yet. He stood by the coffee maker, waiting for the hot water to filter through the grounds into the jug below. The machine covered Lawson's approach, and Robin jumped when his boss said abruptly, "Did you hear the news?"

"What news?"

"Davey Kerr's been murdered." Lawson narrowed his eyes as he scrutinized the detective inspector. "Last night. In his home."

Robin's eyebrows rose. "You're kidding."

"I heard it on the radio. I phoned Glasgow to double check it was our David Kerr, and lo and behold, it was."

"What happened?" Robin turned away and spooned sugar into a mug.

"At first glance, it looked like a burglary gone sour. But then they realized he had two stab wounds. Now, your average panicking burglar might strike once with a knife, but then he's going to leg it. This one made sure Davey Kerr wasn't going to stick around to tell tales."

"So what are you saying?" Robin asked, reaching for the jug of coffee.

"It's not what I'm saying, it's what Strathclyde Police are saying. They're looking at other possibilities. As they put it." Lawson waited, but Robin said nothing. "Where were you last night, Robin?"

Robin glared angrily at Lawson. "What's that supposed to mean?"

"Calm down, man. I'm not accusing you of anything. But let's face it, if anybody has a motive for killing Davey Kerr, it's you. Now, I know you wouldn't do something like that. I'm on your side. I'm just making sure you're covered, that's all." He put a reassuring hand on Robin's arm. "Are you covered?"

Robin ran a hand through his hair. "Christ, no. It was Diane's mother's birthday and she took the kids across to Grangemouth. They didn't get back till after eleven. So I was home alone." Worry creased his forehead.

Lawson shook his head. "Doesn't look good, Robin. First thing they're going to ask is why you weren't in Grangemouth, too."

"I don't get on with my mother-in-law. Never have. So Diane uses my work as an excuse when I don't show up. But it's not like it was the first time. It's not like I was trying to get out of it so I could drive across to Glasgow and kill Davey Kerr, for Christ's sake." He pursed his lips. "Any other night, I'd be home and dry. But last night . . . Shit. I'm screwed if they get a whisper about what Kerr did to Barney."

Lawson reached out for a mug and poured himself a coffee. "They won't hear it from me."

"You know what this business is like. Bloody gossip central. It's bound to get out. They'll start unraveling Davey Kerr's past, and somebody will remember that my brother died saving him after a stupid suicide attempt. If it was your case, wouldn't you want to talk to Barney's brother? Just in case he'd decided the time was right to settle the score? Like I said, I'm screwed." Robin turned away, biting his lip.

Lawson put a sympathetic hand on his arm. "Tell you what. Anybody from Strathclyde asks, you were with me."

Robin looked shocked. "You're going to lie for me?"

"We're both going to lie. Because we both know you had nothing to do with Davey Kerr's death. Look at it this way. We're saving police time. This way, they're not going to expend time and energy looking at you when they should be looking for the killer."

Reluctantly, Robin nodded. "I suppose so. But . . ."

"Robin, you're a good cop. You're a good man. I wouldn't have you on my team otherwise. I believe in you and I don't want your good name dragged through the mud."

"Thanks, sir. I appreciate your confidence."

"Think nothing of it. Let's just agree that I came round to your house and we had a couple of beers and a few hands of poker. You won about twenty quid off me and I left around eleven. How's that?"

"Fine."

Lawson smiled, chinked his mug against Robin's and walked away. That was the mark of leadership, he believed. Figure out what your team needs and deliver it before they even knew they needed it.

That evening, Alex was on the road again, heading back to Glasgow. He'd eventually made it home, where the phone was ringing off the hook. He'd spoken to both sets of grandparents. His parents had almost seemed embarrassed to be so thrilled, in the light of what had happened in Glasgow. Lynn's mother and father had been incoherent, devastated by the horror of their only son's death. It was still far too soon for them to take any consolation from the birth of their first grandchild. The news that she was in the neonatal unit only seemed another cause for grief and fear. The two phone calls left Alex in a zombie state beyond tiredness. He'd e-mailed their friends and workmates a simple announcement of Davina's birth, then he'd unplugged the phone and crashed out.

When he woke, he couldn't believe he'd only been asleep

for three hours. He felt as refreshed as if he'd been out cold round the clock. Showered and shaved, he'd grabbed a quick sandwich and the digital camera before heading back to Edinburgh. He'd found Lynn down in the neonatal unit in a wheelchair, gazing happily at their child. "Isn't she beautiful?" she'd demanded at once.

"Of course she is. Have you had a hold of her yet?"

"The best moment of my life. But she's so tiny, Alex. It's like holding air." She flashed a look of anxiety at him. "She's going to be OK, isn't she?"

"Of course she is. Gilbeys are all fighters." They held hands, willing him to be right.

Lynn gave him a troubled look. "I feel so ashamed, Alex. My brother's dead, but all I can think of is how much I love Davina, how precious she is."

"I know exactly what you mean. I'm elated, and then something reminds me of what's happened to Mondo, and I come crashing down to earth. I don't know how we're going to get through this."

By the end of the afternoon, Alex too had held his daughter in his arms. He'd taken dozens of photographs, and he'd showed her off to his parents. Adam and Sheila Kerr hadn't been up to the journey, and the fact of their absence reminded Alex that he couldn't stay cocooned in the delights of new parenthood forever. When the auxiliary brought Lynn her evening meal, he'd got to his feet. "I should go back to Glasgow," he said. "I need to make sure Hélène's OK."

"You don't have to take responsibility," Lynn protested.

"I know. But it was us she called," he reminded her. "Her own family's a long way away. She might need some help making the arrangements. Besides, I owe it to Mondo. I wasn't a very good friend to him in recent years, and I can't make up for that. But he was part of my life."

Lynn looked up at him with a sad smile, tears glistening in her eyes. "Poor Mondo. I keep thinking how frightened he must have been at the end. And to die without having any chance to make your peace with the people you love . . . As for Hélène, I can't imagine what it must be like. When I think how I'd feel if anything happened to you or Davina—"

"Nothing's going to happen to me. Or to Davina," Alex said. "I promise you."

He thought of that promise now as he covered the miles between joy and sorrow. It was hard not to feel overwhelmed by the turn his life had taken recently. But he couldn't afford to succumb. There was too much depending on him now.

As he approached Glasgow, he rang Hélène. The answering machine redirected him to her mobile. Cursing, he pulled over and listened to the message again, noting down the number. She answered on the second ring. "Alex? How is Lynn? What's happened?"

He was surprised. He'd always considered Hélène to be too obsessed by her own concerns to care about anyone other than herself and Mondo. That concern for Lynn and the baby had penetrated her grief to the point where it was the first thing she referred to astonished him. "We've got a daughter." They were the biggest words he'd ever uttered. He felt a lump in his throat. "With her being premature, they've got her in an incubator. But she's doing great. And she's beautiful."

"How is Lynn?"

"Hurting. In every sense. But she's OK. And you? How are you?"

"Not good. But I'm coping, I guess."

"Listen, I'm on my way to see you. Where are you?"

"The house is still a crime scene, apparently. I can't go back till tomorrow. I'm staying with my friend, Jackie. She lives in the Merchant City. Do you want to come here?"

Alex really didn't want to face the woman Hélène had betrayed Mondo with. He thought about suggesting neutral ground, but it felt pretty heartless in the circumstances. "Give me directions," he said.

The flat was easy to find. It occupied half of the second floor of one of the converted warehouses that had become the residential badge of success for the city's singles. The woman who opened the door couldn't have looked less like

Hélène. Her jeans were old and faded with rips at the knees, her sleeveless T-shirt proclaimed she was 100% GRRRRL and revealed muscles that Alex reckoned could benchpress her own bodyweight without breaking sweat. Just below each bicep was an intricate tattoo of a Celtic bracelet. Her short dark hair was spiked with gel and the look she gave him was every bit as barbed. Dark eyebrows were drawn down over pale blue-gray eyes and there was no welcoming smile on her wide mouth. "You must be Alex," she said, her Glasgow roots instantly obvious. "You'd better come in."

Alex followed her into exactly the kind of loft apartment that never graced the pages of interiors magazines. Forget sterile modernism, this was the den of someone who knew exactly what she liked and how she liked it. The end wall was floor-to-ceiling bookshelves, crammed untidily with books, videos, CDs and magazines. In front of it was a multigym, dumbbells lying carelessly to one side. The kitchen area had the kind of untidiness that comes with regular use, and the sitting area was furnished with sofas that owed more to comfort than elegance. A coffee table was invisible under stacks of newspapers and magazines. The walls were decorated with big framed photographs of sportswomen, from Martina Navratilova to Ellen MacArthur.

Hélène was curled in the corner of a tapestry sofa whose arms testified to the presence of a cat. He crossed the polished wood floor to his sister-in-law, who raised her face for their customary exchange of air kisses. Her eyes were puffy and shadowed, but other than that, Hélène seemed back in command of herself. "I appreciate you coming," she said. "Thanks for coming when you should be enjoying your new baby."

"Like I said, she's still in neonatal care. And Lynn's exhausted. I thought I might be more use over here. But . . ." he gave Jackie a smile. "I see you're being well looked after."

Jackie shrugged, the hostile expression never wavering. "I'm a freelance journalist, so I can be a bit flexible about my hours. You want a drink? There's beer, whiskey or wine."

"Coffee would be great."

"We're out of coffee. Tea do you?"

Nothing like being made to feel welcome, he thought. "Tea's fine. Milk, no sugar, please." He perched on the far end of the sofa from Hélène. Her eyes looked as if they'd seen far too much. "How are you doing?"

Her eyelids fluttered. "I try not to feel anything. I don't want to think about David, because when I do my heart feels like it's breaking. I can't believe the world can go on and him not be in it. But I need to get through this without cracking up. The police are being horrible, Alex. That dull-looking girl in the corner last night? You remember?"

"The policewoman?"

"Yes." Hélène gave a snort of derision. "It turns out she did French at school. She understood our little conversation last night."

"Oh shit."

"Oh shit, is right. The detective in charge, he was here this morning. He spoke to me first, asking about Jackie and me. He told me there was no point in lying, his officer had heard all about it last night. So I told him the truth. He was very polite, but I could see he is suspicious."

"Did you ask what had happened to Mondo?"

"Of course." Her face tightened in pain. "He said there was very little they could tell me. The glass in the kitchen door was broken, maybe from a burglar. But they haven't found any fingerprints. The knife that was used to stab David was one of a set. From the knife block in the kitchen. He said that, on the surface, it looks as if David heard a noise and came down to investigate. But he stressed those words, Alex. On the surface."

Jackie returned, carrying a mug whose transfer of Marilyn Monroe had suffered some attrition from a dishwasher. The tea it contained was an intense dark tan. "Thanks," Alex said.

Jackie settled on the arm of the sofa, one hand on Hélène's shoulder. "Neanderthals. The wife has a lover, therefore the wife or the lover must want to be rid of the husband. They can't imagine a world where adults can make more complex choices than that. I tried to explain to this cop that you could have sex with someone without wanting to murder their other lovers. Asshole looked at me as if I was from another planet."

Alex was with the cop on this one. Being married to Lynn didn't make him immune to the charms of other women. But it made him repudiate the notion of doing anything about it. In his book, lovers were for people who were with the wrong partner. He could only imagine how distraught he'd feel if Lynn came home and told him she was sleeping with someone else. He felt a stab of pity for Mondo. "I suppose they've got nothing else to go on so they're focusing on you," he said.

"But I am the victim here, not the criminal," Hélène said bitterly. "I didn't do anything to harm David. But it's impossible to prove a negative. You know yourself how difficult it is to dispel suspicion once the finger points. It drove David so crazy he tried to kill himself."

Alex shivered involuntarily at the memory. "It's not going to come to that."

"Damn right, it's not," Jackie said. "I'm going to talk to a lawyer in the morning. I'm not standing for this."

Hélène looked worried. "Are you sure that's a good idea?"

"Why not?" Jackie demanded.

"Aren't you supposed to tell your lawyer everything?" Hélène gave Alex a strange sideways look.

"It's protected by lawyer–client privilege," Jackie said.

"What's the problem?" Alex demanded. "Is there something you're not telling me, Hélène?"

Jackie sighed and rolled her eyes upward. "Christ, Hélène."

"It's OK, Jackie. Alex is on our side."

Jackie gave him a look that said she read him better than her lover.

"What have you not told me?" he asked.

"It's none of your business, OK?" Jackie said.

"Jackie," Hélène protested.

"Forget it, Hélène," Alex got to his feet. "I don't have to

be here, you know," he said to Jackie. "But I'd have thought you needed all the friends you can get right now. Especially among Mondo's family."

"Jackie, tell him," Hélène said. "Otherwise he'll go away thinking we've really got something to hide."

Jackie glared at Alex. "I had to go out for about an hour last night. I was out of dope and we wanted a joint. My dealer's not the sort of guy to give alibis. And even if he did, the police wouldn't believe him. So, technically, either one of us could have killed David."

Alex felt the hair on the back of his neck rising. He remembered the moment the night before when he'd wondered if Hélène was manipulating him. "You should tell the police," he said abruptly. "If they find out you've lied, then they're never going to believe you're innocent."

"Unlike you, you mean?" Jackie challenged him contemptuously.

Alex didn't like the undercurrent of hostility swirling around him. "I came to help, not to be a whipping boy," he said sharply. "Have they said anything about releasing the body?"

"They're doing the post mortem this afternoon. After that, they said we can make the funeral arrangements." Hélène spread her hands. "I don't know who to call. What should I do, Alex?"

"I suppose you'll find an undertaker in the Yellow Pages. Put a notice in the papers, then contact his close friends and relatives. If you like, I can deal with the family end of things?"

She nodded. "That would be a big help."

Jackie sneered. "I don't suppose they'll be very keen to hear from Hélène when they find out about me."

"Better if we can avoid that. Mondo's parents have got enough to cope with," Alex said frostily. "Hélène, you'll need to arrange somewhere for the purvey."

"The purvey?" Hélène said.

"The funeral meal," Jackie translated.

Hélène closed her eyes. "I can't believe we're sitting here

talking about catering when my David is lying on some mortuary slab."

"Aye, well," Alex said. He didn't have to say what he thought; the blame hung in the air between the three of them. "I'd better be getting back."

"Does she have a name yet, your daughter?" Hélène asked, clearly casting around for something uncontroversial to say.

Alex gave her an apprehensive glance. "We were going to call her Ella. But we thought . . . well, Lynn thought she'd like to call her Davina. For Mondo. If you don't mind, that is?"

Hélène's lips trembled and tears trickled from the corners of her eyes. "Oh, Alex. I'm so sorry we never took the time to be better friends with you and Lynn."

He shook his head. "What? So we could feel betrayed as well?"

Hélène recoiled as if from a blow. Jackie moved toward Alex, hands bunching into fists at her side. "I think it's time you left."

"Me, too," Alex said. "See you at the funeral."

CHAPTER
THIRTY-ONE

ACC Lawson pulled the folder across the desk toward him. "I had high hopes of this," he sighed.

"Me, too, sir," Karen Pirie admitted. "I know they didn't pick up any biological samples from the cardigan at the time, but I thought with the sophisticated equipment they've got now there might be a trace of something we could use. Semen or blood. But there's nothing, except those funny drops of paint."

"Which we knew about at the time. And it didn't take us any further forward then." Lawson flipped open the folder dismissively and skimmed the short report. "The problem was that the cardigan wasn't found with the body. If my memory serves me, it was thrown over the hedge into somebody's garden?"

Karen nodded. "Number fifteen. They didn't find it till nearly two weeks had gone past. By which time it had snowed, thawed and rained, which didn't exactly help. Identified by Rosie Duff's mother as the one she was wearing when she went out that night. We never did find her handbag or her coat." She consulted the bulging folder on her lap, flipping through the pages. "A brown below-the-knee swagger coat from C&A with a cream and brown houndstooth-check lining."

"We never found them because we didn't know where to

look. Because we didn't know where she was killed. After she left the Lammas Bar, she could have been taken anywhere within, say, an hour's drive. Over the bridge to Dundee, down through Fife. Anywhere from Kirriemuir to Kirkcaldy. She could have been killed on a boat, in a byre, anywhere. About the only thing we could be reasonably sure of was that she wasn't killed in the house in Fife Park where Gilbey, Malkiewicz, Kerr and Mackie lived." Lawson tossed the forensic report back to Karen.

"Just as a matter of interest, sir . . . were any of the other houses in Fife Park searched?"

Lawson frowned. "I don't think so. Why?"

"It occurred to me that it happened during the university holidays. A lot of people would have already left for Christmas. There might well have been adjacent houses that were standing empty."

"They'd have been locked up. We'd have heard about it if anyone on Fife Park had reported a break-in."

"You know what students are like, sir. In and out of each other's places. It wouldn't be hard to come by a key. Besides, the four of them were in their final year. They could easily have kept a key from another house if they'd lived there previously."

Lawson gave Karen a shrewdly appreciative look. "It's a pity you weren't around for the original investigation. I don't think that line of inquiry was ever pursued. Too late now, of course. So, where are we up to on the exhibits search? Have you not finished it yet?"

"I had some time off over Christmas and New Year," she said defensively. "But I stayed late and finished it last night."

"So that's that, then? The physical evidence relating to Rosie Duff's murder has disappeared without trace?"

"So it would seem. The last person to access the box was DI Maclennan, a week before he died."

Lawson bridled. "You're not suggesting Barney Maclennan removed evidence from a live murder case?"

Karen backtracked hastily. She knew better than to cast aspersions on a fellow officer who had died a hero. "No, that's not what I meant at all, sir. I just meant that, whatever had happened to Rosie Duff's clothes, there's no official paper trail to follow."

He sighed again. "It likely happened years ago. They'll have ended up in the bucket. Honest to God, you have to wonder sometimes. Some of the people we get working for us . . ."

"I suppose the other option is that the DI sent them off for further testing and either they never came back because he wasn't there to chase it up, or the package disappeared into a black hole because DI Maclennan wasn't there to take delivery," Karen suggested cautiously.

"I suppose it's an outside possibility. But, either way, you're not going to find them now." Lawson drummed his fingers on the desk. "Well, that's that, then. One cold case that's going to stay in the deep freeze. I'm not looking forward to telling the son, either. He's been on the phone every other day, asking how we're doing."

"I still can't believe the pathologist missed that she'd given birth," Karen said.

"At your age, I'd have said the same," Lawson admitted. "But he was an old man, and old men make stupid mistakes. I know that now, because I feel like I'm heading in that direction myself. You know, I sometimes wonder if this case has been jinxed from the start."

Karen could sense his disappointment. And she knew how that stung, because it matched her own feelings. "You don't think it's worth me having another crack at the witnesses? The four students?"

Lawson grimaced. "You'll have a job."

"How do you mean, sir?"

Lawson opened his desk drawer and produced a three-day-old copy of the *Scotsman*. It was folded open at the death notices. He pushed it toward her, his finger stabbing the newsprint.

KERR, DAVID MCKNIGHT. The death is announced of Dr. David Kerr, of Carden Grove, Bearsden, Glasgow, dearly beloved husband of Hélène, brother of Lynn and son of Adam and Sheila Kerr of Duddingston Drive, Kirkcaldy. The funeral will take place on Thursday at 2 p.m. at Glasgow Crematorium, Western Necropolis, Tresta Road. Family flowers only.

Karen looked up, surprised. "He couldn't have been more than forty-six, forty-seven? That's pretty young to be dying."

"You should pay more attention to the news, Karen. The Glasgow University lecturer stabbed to death in his kitchen by a burglar last Thursday night?"

"That was *our* David Kerr? The one they called Mondo?"

Lawson nodded. "The crazy diamond himself. I spoke to the DI on the case on Monday. Just to make sure I was right. Apparently, they're far from convinced by the burglary theory. The wife was playing away."

Karen pulled a face. "Nasty."

"Very. So, do you fancy a wee run out to Glasgow this afternoon? I thought we could pay our last respects to one of our suspects."

"You think the other three will turn up?"

Lawson shrugged. "They were best pals, but that was twenty-five years ago. We'll just have to see, won't we? But I don't think we'll be conducting any interviews today. Let it lie for a wee while. We don't want to be accused of insensitivity, do we?"

It was standingroom only at the crematorium. Mondo might have cut himself off from family and old friends, but it looked as if he hadn't had any problem finding replacements. Alex sat in the front pew, Lynn huddled beside him. Two days out of the hospital, she was still moving like an old woman. He had tried to persuade her to stay at home and rest, but she'd been adamant that she couldn't miss her only brother's funeral. Besides, she'd argued, with no baby at home to care for, she would only sit around and brood. Better to be among her family. He didn't have a line of reasoning to counter that. So she sat, holding her shell-shocked father's hand to give comfort, the familiar roles of parent and child reversed. Her mother sat beyond them, her face almost invisible behind the folds of a white handkerchief.

Hélène sat further along the pew, head bowed, shoulders hunched. She looked as if she'd closed in on herself, placing an impenetrable barrier between herself and the rest of the world. At least she'd had the good sense not to arrive at the funeral on Jackie's arm. She shuffled to her feet as the minister announced the final hymn.

The sonorous opening of the Crimond setting of the Twenty-third Psalm brought a lump to Alex's throat. The singing faltered a little as people found the key, then swelled around him. What a cliché, he thought, hating himself for being moved by the traditional funeral hymn. Ziggy's service had been so much more honest, so much more a celebration of the man than this cobbling together of superficialities. As far as he knew, Mondo had never been in a church apart from attending the traditional rites of passage. The heavy curtains slid open and the coffin began its final journey.

The strains of the last verse died away as the curtains closed behind the departing coffin. The minister intoned the blessing, then led the way down the central aisle. The family followed, Alex bringing up the rear with Lynn heavy on his arm. Most of the faces were a blur, but, halfway down, Weird's lanky frame leaped out at him. They acknowledged each other with a brief nod, then Alex was past, heading for the doors. He had his second surprise just as he was leaving. Although he hadn't see James Lawson in the flesh since everybody called him Jimmy, his face was familiar from the media. Bad taste, Alex thought, taking up his station at the end of the meeting-and-greeting line. Weddings and funerals; both required the same etiquette of thanking people for coming.

It seemed to go on forever. Sheila and Adam Kerr appeared utterly bewildered. It was bad enough having to bury a child so savagely despatched without having to try to take in all these condolences from people they'd never seen before and would never see again. Alex wondered if it comforted them to see how many people had turned up to say their last good-byes. All it did for him was to bring home how much distance had separated him and Mondo in recent years. He knew almost nobody.

Weird had hung back almost to the end. He embraced Lynn gently. "I'm so sorry for your loss," he said. He shook Alex's hand, placing his other hand on Alex's elbow. "I'll wait outside." Alex nodded.

At last, the final mourners trickled out. Funny, thought Alex. No Lawson. He must have left by another door. Just as well. He doubted whether he'd have managed to be polite. Alex ushered his in-laws through the subdued crowd to the funeral car. He handed Lynn into her seat, checked everyone else was settled, then said, "I'll see you back at the hotel. I just need to make sure everything's sorted here."

He was ashamed to feel a moment of relief as the car swept off down the drive. He'd left his car here earlier, wanting to make sure he had his own wheels in case anything needed his attention in the immediate aftermath of the service. Deep down, he knew it was because he would want some respite from the suffocating grief of his family.

A hand on his shoulder made him spin round. "Oh, it's you," he said, almost laughing with relief as he saw it was Weird.

"Who else were you expecting?"

"Well, Jimmy Lawson was lurking at the back of the crem," Alex said.

"Jimmy Lawson the cop?"

"Assistant Chief Constable James Lawson, to you," Alex said, moving away from the main entrance toward the area where flowers were displayed.

"So what was he doing here?"

"Gloating? I don't know. He's in charge of the cold case review. Maybe he wanted to check out his prime suspects, see if we were going to get overcome with emotion and fall to our knees and confess."

Weird pulled a face. "I never liked all that Catholic stuff. We should be adult enough to come to terms with our own guilt. It's not God's job to wipe the slate clean so we can go and sin again." He stopped and turned to face Alex. "I wanted to tell you how pleased I am that Lynn was safely delivered of your baby daughter."

"Thanks, Tom." Alex grinned. "See? I remembered."

"Is the baby still in hospital?"

Alex sighed. "She's a wee bit jaundiced, so they're keeping her in for a few days. It's hard. Especially for Lynn. You go through all that, and you come home empty-handed. And then having to deal with what happened to Mondo . . ."

"You'll forget this heartache once you have her home, I promise you. I'll remember you all in my prayers."

"Oh well, that'll make all the difference," Alex said.

"You'd be surprised." Weird said, refusing to take offense where none was intended. They walked on, glancing at the floral tributes. One of the mourners came over, asking Alex for directions to the hotel where the buffet was taking place. When he veered back toward Weird, Alex saw his friend crouching over one of the wreaths. Once he was close enough to see what had attracted Weird's attention, his heart jumped in his chest. It was indistinguishable from the wreath they'd seen in Seattle; a neat, tight circlet of white roses and narrow-leaved rosemary. Weird detached the card and stood up. "The same message," he said, handing it to Alex. "Rosemary for remembrance."

Alex felt his skin turn clammy. "I don't like this."

"You and me both. This is too much of a coincidence, Alex. Ziggy and Mondo both die in suspicious circumstances . . . Hell, no, let's call it what it is. Ziggy and Mondo both get murdered. And the identical wreath turns up at both funerals. With a message that ties all four of us together to the unsolved murder of a girl called Rosemary."

"That was twenty-five years ago. If anybody was going to take revenge, surely they'd have done it a long time ago?" Alex said, trying to convince himself as much as Weird. "It's just somebody trying to scare us."

Weird shook his head. "You've had other things on your mind the past few days, but I've been thinking about this. Twenty-five years ago, everybody was watching. I haven't forgotten the time I got done over. I haven't forgotten the night they dropped Ziggy down the Bottle Dungeon. I haven't forgotten how Mondo got so wound up he tried to kill himself. The only reason it all stopped was because the cops gave Colin and Brian Duff the hard word. They were put on notice to leave us alone. You're the one who told me way back then that Jimmy Lawson said they'd only backed off because they didn't want to give their mother anymore grief. So maybe they decided to wait."

Alex shook his head. "But twenty-five years? Could you nurse a grudge for twenty-five years?"

"I'm the wrong person to ask that question. But there are plenty of people out there who have not taken Jesus Christ as their savior, and you know as well as I do, Alex, that there is nothing these people are not capable of. We don't know what's happened in their lives. Maybe something came up that set all this off again. Maybe their mother died. Maybe the cold case review reminded them they had a score to settle and it was probably safe to do it now. I don't know. All I do know is that this looks very like somebody's out to get us. And whoever it is, they've got time and resources on their side." Weird looked around nervously, as if his nemesis might be among the mourners moving toward their cars.

"Now you're being paranoid." This was not the aspect of Weird's youth that Alex wanted to be reminded of right then.

"I don't think so. I think I'm the one making sense here."

"So what do you suggest we do about it?"

Weird pulled his coat closely around him. "I plan to get on a plane tomorrow morning and head back to the States. Then I plan to send my wife and kids somewhere safe. There's plenty of good Christians who live out in the wilds. Nobody's going to get near them."

"What about you?" Alex could feel himself becoming infected with Weird's suspicions.

Weird gave the old, familiar wolfish grin. "I'm going on retreat. Congregations understand that those who minister to them have to go into the wilderness from time to time to reestablish contact with their spirituality. So that's what I'll be doing. The great thing about a TV ministry is that you can make a video wherever you happen to be. So my flock won't forget me while I'm gone."

"You can't hide forever, though. Sooner or later, you're going to have to go home."

Weird nodded. "I know that. But I'm not going to sit on my hands, Alex. As soon as I get myself and my family out of the firing line, I'm going to hire a private detective and find out just who sent that wreath to Ziggy's funeral. Because when I know that, I'll know who I have to look out for."

Alex exhaled sharply. "You've got this all worked out, haven't you?"

"The more I thought about that first wreath, the more I wondered. And God helps those who help themselves, so I made a plan. Just in case." Weird put a hand on Alex's arm. "Alex, I suggest you do the same. You have more than yourself to consider now." Weird pulled Alex into a hug. "Take care of yourself."

"Very bloody touching," a voice said harshly.

Weird pulled away and swung around. At first he couldn't place the grim-faced man glowering at him and Alex. Then memory erased the years and he was back outside the Lammas Bar, terrified and hurting. "Brian Duff," Weird breathed.

Alex glanced from one to the other. "This is Rosie's brother?"

"Aye, that's right."

The confused emotions that had been tormenting Alex for days suddenly fused into anger. "Come to gloat, have you?"

"Poetic justice, isn't that what they call it? One murderous wee shite sees off another one. Aye, I came to gloat."

Alex lunged forward, stopped short by Weird's firm grip on his arm. "Leave it, Alex. Brian, none of us harmed a hair on Rosie's head. I know you need somebody to blame, but it wasn't one of us. You have to believe that."

"I don't have to believe anything of the kind." He spat on the ground. "I really hoped that the cops were going to nail one of you this time around. Since that's not going to happen, this is the next best thing."

"Of course it's not going to happen. We never touched your sister, and the DNA evidence will prove that," Alex shouted.

Duff snorted. "What DNA evidence? Those fucking idiots have lost the DNA evidence."

Alex's mouth fell open. "What?" he whispered.

"You heard. So you're still safe from the long arm of the law." His lip curled in a sneer. "Didnae save your pal, though, did it?" He turned on his heel and strode off without a backward glance.

Weird shook his head slowly. "You believe him?"

"Why would he lie?" Alex sighed. "I really thought we might finally be in the clear, you know? How could they be so incompetent? How could they lose the one bit of evidence that might have put an end to all this shit?" He waved an arm toward the wreath.

"You're surprised? They hardly covered themselves with glory first time around. Why should this be any different?" Weird tugged at the collar of his coat. "Alex, I'm sorry but I need to head off." They shook hands. "I'll be in touch."

Alex stood rooted to the spot, stunned by the speed at which his world had turned upside down. If Brian Duff was right, was that the reason for those ominous wreaths? And if so, would the nightmare ever end while he and Weird were still alive?

Graham Macfadyen sat in his car and watched. The wreaths had been a master stroke. It paid to make the most of every opportunity. He hadn't been in Seattle to see the effect of the first one, but there was no question that Mackie and Gilbey had got the message this time. And that meant that there was a message to get. Innocent men wouldn't have turned a hair at such a reminder.

Seeing their reaction almost made up for the nauseating parade of hypocrisy he'd had to sit through inside the crematorium. It had been obvious that the minister hadn't known David Kerr in life, so it wasn't surprising that he had done such a good job of whitewashing him in death. But it made him sick, the way everyone had nodded sagely, accepting the bullshit, their pious expressions acceding to this hypocritical fiction.

He wondered how they'd have looked if he'd walked up to the front of the crematorium and told the truth. "Ladies and gentlemen, we are here today to burn a murderer. This man you thought you knew spent all his adult life lying to you. David Kerr pretended to be an upstanding member of the community. But the reality is that many years ago he took part in the brutal rape and murder of my mother, for which he was never punished. So when you thumb through your memories of him, remember that." Oh yes, that would have wiped the looks of reverent sorrow from their faces. He almost wished he'd done it.

But that would have been self-indulgence. It wasn't fitting to gloat. Better to stay in the shadows. Especially since his uncle had turned up out of the blue to make his point for him. He had no idea what Uncle Brian had said to Gilbey and Mackie. But it had rocked the pair of them back on their heels. No chance now of them forgetting what they'd once been part of. They'd be lying awake tonight, wondering when their past was finally going to catch up with them. It was a pleasant thought.

Macfadyen watched Alex Gilbey walk to his car, apparently oblivious to everything around him. "He doesn't even know I'm on the planet," he muttered. "But I am, Gilbey. I am." He started his engine and set off to haunt the fringes of the funeral buffet. It was amazing how easy it was to infiltrate people's lives.

CHAPTER
THIRTY-TWO

Davina was making progress, the nurse told them. She was breathing well without oxygen, her jaundice was responding to the fluorescent lights that shone night and day around her cot. While he held her in his arms, Alex could forget the depression Mondo's funeral had trailed in its wake, and the anxieties Weird's reaction to the wreath had generated. The only thing that could be better than sitting with his wife and daughter in the neonatal unit would be doing exactly the same thing in their own living room. Or so he'd thought until his conversation at the crematorium.

As if she read his mind, Lynn looked up from feeding. "Just a couple of days now, and we'll be bringing her home."

Alex smiled, hiding the uneasiness her words created. "I can't wait," he said.

Driving home afterward, he thought about broaching the subject of the wreath and Brian Duff's revelation. But he didn't want to unsettle Lynn, so he kept quiet. Lynn went straight to bed, exhausted by the day, while Alex opened a particularly good bottle of Shiraz he'd been saving for a night when they deserved indulgence. He brought the wine through to the bedroom and poured them each a glass. "Are you going to tell me what's eating away at you?" Lynn asked as he climbed on top of the duvet next to her.

"Oh, I was just thinking about Hélène and Jackie. I can't

help wondering if Jackie had a hand in Mondo's murder. I'm not saying she killed him. But it sounds like she knows people who might, if the money was right."

Lynn scowled. "I almost wish it was her. That bitch Hélène deserves to suffer. How could she creep around cheating on Mondo and pretend to be the perfect wife?"

"I think Hélène's genuinely suffering, Lynn. I believe her when she says she loved him."

"Don't you start defending her."

"I'm not defending her. But whatever the score is between her and Jackie, she cared about him. It's obvious."

Lynn pursed her lips. "I'll have to take your word for it. But that's not what's bugging you. Something happened after we left the crematorium and before you arrived at the hotel. Was it Weird? Did he say something to wind you up?"

"I swear to God you're a witch," Alex complained. "Look, it was nothing. Just some bee Weird got in his bonnet."

"Must have been the killer bee from Alpha Centauri to have this much effect when you've got so many other important things going on. Why don't you want to tell me? Is it boys' own stuff?"

Alex sighed. He didn't like keeping things from Lynn. He'd never believed that ignorance was bliss, not in a marriage that was supposed to be equal. "In a way. I really don't want to bother you with it, you've got enough on your plate right now."

"Alex, with what I've got on my plate, don't you think anything would be a welcome diversion?"

"Not this, love." He sipped his drink, savoring its warm spice. He wished he could channel all his consciousness into appreciating the wine and lose touch with everything that ailed him. "Some things are better left."

"Why am I having trouble believing you?" Lynn leaned her head against his shoulder. "Come on, spill. You know you'll feel better."

"Actually, I'm not at all sure that I would." He sighed again. "I don't know, maybe I should tell you. You're the sensible one, after all."

"Which is not something any of us could ever have said about Weird," Lynn said dryly.

And so he told her about the funeral wreaths, making as light of it as he could. To his surprise, Lynn made no attempt to dismiss the story as Weird's paranoia. "That's why you're trying to convince yourself Jackie hired a hitman," she said. "I don't like this one little bit. Weird's right to take this seriously."

"Look, it could have a simple explanation," Alex protested. "Maybe somebody that knew them both."

"The way Mondo cut himself off from his past? The only people who could reasonably have known them both must come from Kirkcaldy or St. Andrews. And everybody there knew about the Rosie Duff case. You couldn't forget something like that. Not if you knew them well enough to be sending a wreath to funerals where the announcements said 'family flowers only,'" Lynn pointed out.

"Even so, it doesn't mean somebody's out to get us," Alex said. "OK, someone wanted to get a dig in. That's no reason to suppose that the same person has committed cold-blooded murder twice."

Lynn shook her head in disbelief. "Alex, what planet are you on? I can just about credit that somebody who wanted to get a dig in might have seen the reports of Mondo's death. At least that happened in the same country as Rosie Duff's murder. But how would they have heard about Ziggy's death in time to get flowers to his funeral unless they were involved somehow?"

"I don't know. But it's a small world these days. Maybe whoever sent the wreath had a contact in Seattle. Maybe somebody from St. Andrews moved there and ran across Ziggy through the clinic. It's not exactly a common name, and it's not like Ziggy was Mr. Nobody. You know yourself— whenever we ate out with Ziggy and Paul in Seattle, somebody always came over to say hello. People don't forget the doctor who treated their kid. And if that's how it happened, what would be more natural than to e-mail somebody back home when Ziggy died? A place like St. Andrews, news like that would spread like wildfire. It's not so far-fetched, is it?" Alex's voice grew agitated as he struggled to find something that would mean he didn't have to believe what Weird had suggested.

"It's stretching it a bit, but I suppose you could be right. But you can't just leave it at that. You can't rely on a faint possibility. You've got to do something, Alex." Lynn put down her glass and hugged him. "You can't take risks, not with Davina coming home any day now."

Alex drained his glass, paying no attention to the quality of the wine. "What am I supposed to do? Go into hiding with you and Davina? Where would we go? And what about the business? I can't just walk away from my livelihood, not with a child to support."

Lynn stroked his head. "Alex, take it easy. I'm not suggesting we jump off the deep end like Weird. You told me earlier that Lawson was at the funeral today. Why don't you go and talk to him?"

Alex snorted. "Lawson? The man who tried to con me with lentil soup and sympathy? The man who's carried the torch so long that he came along to see one of us cremated? You think he's going to give me a sympathetic hearing?"

"Lawson might have had his suspicions, but at least he stopped you getting a kicking." Alex slid down the bed, nestling his head against Lynn's stomach. She winced and pulled away. "Mind my wound," she said. He shifted back, settling against her arm.

"He'd laugh in my face."

"Alternatively, he might take you seriously enough to make some inquiries. It's not in his interest to turn a blind eye to vigilante justice, if that's what this is. Apart from anything else, it makes the police look even more crap than they already do."

"You don't know the half of it," Alex said.

"What do you mean?"

"Something else happened after the funeral. Rosie Duff's brother turned up. He made sure Weird and I knew he'd come to gloat."

Lynn looked shocked. "Oh, Alex. That's awful. For all of you. That poor man. Not to be able to let it rest after all this time."

"That's not all. He told us that Fife Police have lost the evidence in Rosie's case. The evidence that we were relying on to produce the DNA that would clear us."

"You're kidding."

"I wish I was."

Lynn shook her head. "All the more reason why you need to talk to Lawson."

"You think he wants me rubbing his nose in it?"

"I don't care what Lawson wants. You need to know for sure what's going on. If there really is someone after you, it might be the realization that they're not going to get justice after all that has set them off. Call Lawson in the morning. Set up an appointment. It would put my mind at rest."

Alex rolled off the bed and started to undress. "If that's what it takes, consider it done. But don't blame me if he decides the vigilante's right and decides to arrest me."

To Alex's surprise, when he called to arrange a meeting with ACC Lawson, the secretary gave him a slot that afternoon. It left him enough time to go to the office for a couple of hours, which left him feeling more out of control than he had previously. He liked to keep a close eye on the day-to-day business, not because he didn't have confidence in his staff but because not knowing what was going on made him feel uneasy. But he'd had his eye off the ball too much lately, and he needed to get up to speed. He copied a stack of memos and reports on to a CD, hoping he'd squeeze some time at home later to get on top of things. Grabbing a sandwich to eat in the car, he headed back to Fife.

The empty office he was shown into was about twice the size of his own. The privileges of rank were always more visible in the public sector, he thought, taking in the big desk, the elaborately framed map of the county and James Lawson's prominently displayed commendations. He sat down in the visitor's chair, noting with amusement that it was much lower than the one behind the desk opposite.

He wasn't kept waiting long. The door behind him opened and Alex jumped up. The years hadn't been kind to Lawson, he thought. His skin was lined and weathered, with two patches of high color on his cheeks, the broken veins the badge of a man who either drank too much or spent too much time exposed to the harsh east winds of Fife. His eyes were still shrewd, however, Alex noted as Lawson took him in from top to toe. "Mr. Gilbey," he said. "Sorry to keep you."

"No problem. I know you must be busy. I appreciate you fitting me in so quickly."

Lawson swept past without offering his hand. "I'm always interested when someone connected with an investigation wants to see me." He settled into his leather chair, tugging at his uniform jacket to straighten it.

"I saw you at David Kerr's funeral," Alex said.

"I had business over in Glasgow. I took the opportunity to pay my last respects."

"I didn't think Fife Police had much respect for Mondo," Alex said.

Lawson made an impatient gesture with one hand. "I presume your visit is connected to our reopening of the Rosemary Duff murder?"

"Indirectly, yes. How is the inquiry going? Have you made any progress?"

Lawson looked irritated by the questions. "I can't discuss operational matters relating to an ongoing case with someone in your position."

"What position is that, exactly? You surely don't still regard me as a suspect?" Alex was more courageous than his twenty-year old self; he wasn't about to let a remark like that pass without challenge.

Lawson shuffled some papers on his desk. "You were a witness."

"And witnesses can't be told what's happening? You're quick enough to talk to the press when you make progress. Why do I have less rights than a journalist?"

"I'm not talking to the press about the Rosie Duff case either," Lawson said stiffly.

"Would that be because you've lost the evidence?"

Lawson gave him a long, hard stare. "No comment," he said.

Alex shook his head. "That's not good enough. After what we went through twenty-five years ago, I think I deserve better than that. Rosie Duff wasn't the only victim back then, and you know it. Maybe it's time I went to the press and told them how I'm still being treated like a criminal by the police after all these years. And while I'm at it, I could tell them how Fife Police have screwed up their review of Rosie Duff's murder by losing the crucial evidence that would have exonerated me and might just have led to the arrest of the real killer."

The threat clearly made Lawson uncomfortable. "I don't respond well to intimidation, Mr. Gilbey."

"Neither do I. Not anymore. You really want to see yourself all over the pages of the papers as the copper who invaded a grieving family's last farewell to their murdered son? The same son whose innocence was still in doubt, thanks to the incompetence of you and your team?"

"There's no need for you to take this attitude," Lawson said.

"Oh no? I think there's every need. You're supposed to be conducting a cold case review here. I'm a key witness. I'm the person who found the body. And yet there's not been a single officer from Fife Police in touch with me. That doesn't exactly smack of zeal, does it? And now I discover you can't even keep a bag of evidence safe. Maybe I should be talking about this with the investigating officer, not some bureaucrat who's hidebound by the past."

Lawson's face tightened. "Mr. Gilbey, it's true there's a problem with the evidence in this case. At some point in the past twenty-five years, Rosie Duff's clothes have gone missing. We're still trying to track them down, but so far, all we've been able to find is the cardigan that was found some

distance away from the crime scene. And that had no biological material on it. None of the clothes that might have been
susceptible to modern forensics are available to us. So at the
moment, we're stymied. Actually, the officer in charge of the
case wanted to have a chat with you, just to go over your
original statement. Perhaps we can arrange that soon?"

"Jesus Christ," Alex said. "Now you finally want to interview me? You really don't get it, do you? We're still twisting
in the breeze. Do you realize two of the four of us have been
murdered in the past month?"

Lawson raised his eyebrows. "Two of you?"

"Ziggy Malkiewicz also died in suspicious circumstances. Just before Christmas."

Lawson pulled a pad toward him and unscrewed a foun-
tain pen. "This is news to me. Where did this happen?"

"In Seattle, where he'd been living for the past dozen
years. An arsonist set a firebomb in his house. Ziggy died in
his sleep. You can check it out with the police over there.
The only suspect they've got is Ziggy's partner, which I have
to tell you is about as dumb as it gets."

"I'm sorry to hear about Mr. Malkiewicz . . ."

"Dr. Malkiewicz," Alex interrupted.

"Dr. Malkiewicz," Lawson corrected himself. "But I still
don't see why you should think these two deaths are connected to Rosie Duff's murder."

"That's why I wanted to see you today. To explain why I
believe there's a connection."

Lawson leaned back in his chair, steepling his fingers.
"You have my full attention, Mr. Gilbey. I'm interested in
anything that might shine a light in this particular dark corner."

Alex explained about the wreaths once more. Sitting here
at the heart of police headquarters, it sounded feeble to his
ears. He could feel Lawson's skepticism across the desk as
he tried to give weight to so slight an occurrence. "I know it
sounds paranoid," he concluded. "But Tom Mackie is convinced enough that he's putting his family into hiding and

going underground himself. That's not something you do lightly."

Lawson gave a sour smile. "Ah yes. Mr. Mackie. Maybe a wee touch of 'too many drugs in the seventies?' I believe hallucinogens can lead to long-term paranoia."

"You don't think we should take this seriously? Two of our friends die in suspicious circumstances? Two men who lived respectable lives, with no criminal connections? Two men who had apparently no enemies? And at both funerals, a wreath turns up that refers directly to a murder investigation where they were both regarded as suspects?"

"None of you was ever publicly named as suspects. And we did our best to protect you."

"Aye. But even after that, one of your officers died as a result of the pressure that was put on us."

Lawson jerked bolt upright. "I'm glad you remember that. Because nobody in this building has forgotten it either."

"I'm sure you haven't. Barney Maclennan was the killer's second victim. And I believe that Ziggy and Mondo were his victims, too. Indirectly, obviously. But I think somebody killed them because they wanted vengeance. And if that's what happened, then my name's on that list, too."

Lawson sighed. "I understand why you're reacting like this. But I don't believe that someone has embarked on a deliberate program of revenge against the four of you. I can tell you that the police in Glasgow are pursuing promising lines of inquiry that have nothing to do with Rosie Duff's murder. Coincidences do happen, and that's what these two deaths are. Coincidence, nothing more. People don't do that kind of thing, Mr. Gilbey. They certainly don't wait twenty-five years to do it."

"What about Rosie's brothers? They were pretty keen to take a pop at us back then. You told me you'd warned them off. That you'd persuaded them not to bring anymore trouble to their mother's door. Is their mother still alive? Are they free from that worry now? Is that why Brian Duff turned up at Mondo's funeral to taunt us?"

"It's true that Mr. and Mrs. Duff are both dead now. But I don't think you've anything to fear from the Duffs. I saw Brian myself a few weeks ago. I don't think vengeance was on his mind. And Colin works out in the Gulf. He was home over Christmas, but he wasn't in the country when David Kerr died." Lawson breathed deeply. "He married one of my fellow officers—Janice Hogg. Ironically, she came to Mr. Mackie's rescue when he was set on by the Duffs. She left the force at the time of the marriage, but I'm pretty sure she wouldn't encourage her husband in law-breaking on this scale. I think you can rest easy on that score."

Alex heard the conviction in Lawson's voice, but it brought him small relief. "Brian wasn't exactly amiable yesterday," he said.

"No, I can see he might not have been. But let's face it, neither Brian nor Colin was what you would call a sophisticated criminal. If they'd decided to kill you and your friends, they'd probably have walked up to you in a crowded bar and blown your heads off with a shotgun. Elaborate planning was never their style," Lawson said dryly.

"So that kind of disposes of the suspects." Alex shifted in his seat, preparing to stand up.

"Not quite," Lawson said softly.

"What do you mean?" Alex asked, apprehension gripping him again.

Lawson looked guilty, as if he'd said too much. "Ignore me, I was just thinking aloud."

"Wait a minute. You can't brush me off like that. What did you mean, 'not quite?' " Alex leaned forward, looking as if he was about to jump across the desk and grab Lawson's immaculate lapels.

"I shouldn't have said that. I'm sorry, I was just thinking like a policeman."

"Isn't that what you're paid to do? Come on, tell me what you meant."

Lawson's eyes flickered from side to side, as if he was looking for a way out that didn't involve passing Alex. He ran a hand over his upper lip then took a deep breath. "Rosie's son," he said.

CHAPTER
THIRTY-THREE

Lynn stared at Alex, never pausing in her gentle rocking of her daughter. "Say again," she commanded.

"Rosie had a son. It never came out at the time. For some reason, the pathologist didn't pick it up at the post mortem. Lawson admitted he was a doddery old sod who liked a drink. But in his defense, he said it was possible the wound itself obscured any traces. Naturally, the family weren't going to tell because they knew that if people found out she'd had an illegitimate kid, she'd instantly be portrayed as a gymslip mum, no better than she should be. She'd be demoted from innocent victim to a lassie who asked for it. They were desperate to protect her good name. You can't blame them for that."

"I don't blame them at all. One look at how viciously the press treated you, and anybody would have done the same. But how come he's surfaced now?"

"According to Lawson, he was adopted. He decided last year to track down his birth mother. He found the woman who ran the home where Rosie had stayed when she was pregnant, and that's when he discovered he wasn't going to have a happy family reunion after all."

Davina gave a small cry and Lynn put her little finger in the baby's mouth, smiling down at her. "That must have been terrible for him. It must take so much courage to go

looking for your birth mother. She's rejected you once—
who knows why—and you're setting yourself up for a second slap in the face. But you must be clinging to the hope
that she's going to welcome you with open arms."

"I know. And then to find out that somebody snatched
that chance away from you twenty-five years before." Alex
leaned forward. "Can I take her for a while?"

"Sure. She's not long had a feed, so she should sleep for a
bit." Lynn gently eased her hands under her daughter, passing her to Alex as if she was the most valuable and fragile
object in the world. He slid his hand beneath her frail neck
and held her to his chest. Davina mumbled softly, then settled. "So, does Lawson think the son is coming after you?"

"Lawson doesn't think anybody's coming after me. He
thinks I'm a paranoid nutter making a mountain out of a
molehill. He got very embarrassed about having let it slip
about Rosie's son, and kept reassuring me that he wouldn't
harm a fly. He's called Graham, by the way. Lawson
wouldn't give me his surname. Apparently he works in the
IT industry. Quiet, stable, very normal," Alex said.

Lynn shook her head. "I can't believe Lawson's taking it
all so lightly. Who does he think sent the wreaths?"

"He doesn't know and he doesn't care. All he's bothered
about is that his precious cold case review is going down the
drain."

"They couldn't run a ménage, far less a murder inquiry.
Did he have any explanation as to how they lost a whole box
of forensic evidence?"

"They didn't lose the whole box. They've still got the
cardigan. Apparently it was found separately. Thrown over
the wall into somebody's garden. They tested it after all the
other stuff, which is probably why it ended up separated
from the rest of the material."

Lynn frowned. "It turned up later? Wasn't there something about a second search they did later at your house? I
vaguely remember Mondo complaining about them being all
over the place weeks after the murder."

Alex struggled with memory. "After they'd done the initial search . . . They came back after the New Year. They scraped paint off the walls and ceilings. And they wanted to know whether we'd done any redecorating." He snorted. "As if. And Mondo said he'd overheard one of them talking about a cardigan. He assumed they were looking for something one of us had been wearing. But they weren't, of course. They were referring to Rosie's cardigan," he finished triumphantly.

"So there must have been paint on her cardigan," Lynn said thoughtfully. "That's why they were taking samples."

"Yeah, but they obviously didn't get a match from our house. Or else we'd have been in even deeper shit."

"I wonder if they've done a fresh analysis. Did Lawson say anything about it?"

"Not specifically. He said they didn't have any of the clothes that would be susceptible to modern forensic analysis."

"That's nonsense. They can do so much with paint these days. I get far more information from the labs now than I did even three or four years ago. They should be testing that. You need to get back to Lawson and insist that they look again at it."

"An analysis isn't any use without something to compare it with. Lawson's not going to jump just because I say so."

"I thought you said he wanted to solve this case?"

"Lynn, if there was anything to be gained, they'd have done it."

Lynn flushed with sudden anger. "Christ, Alex, listen to yourself. Are you just going to sit back and wait for something else to blow up in the middle of our lives? My brother's dead. Somebody walked into his house bold as brass and murdered him. The only person who might have been any use to you thinks you're paranoid. I don't want you to die, Alex. I don't want your daughter to grow up without a single memory of you."

"You think I want that?" Alex hugged his daughter to his chest.

"Stop being so bloody spineless, then. If you and Weird

are right, the person who killed Ziggy and Mondo is going to come after you. The only way you're going to get off the hook is if Rosie's killer is finally exposed. If Lawson won't do it, maybe you should give it a try. You've got the best motivation in the world there in your arms."

He couldn't deny it. He'd been awash with emotion since Davina's birth, perpetually astonished at the depth of his feelings. "I'm a greetings card manufacturer, Lynn, not a detective," he protested weakly.

Lynn glared at him. "And how often have miscarriages of justice been overturned because some punter wouldn't stop digging?"

"I haven't got a clue where to start."

"Do you remember that series about forensic science on the telly a couple of years back?"

Alex groaned. His wife's fascination with thrillers on TV and film had never infected him. His usual response to a two-hour special featuring Frost, Morse or Wexford was to pick up a pad and start working on ideas for greetings cards.

"Vaguely," he said.

"I remember one of the forensic scientists saying how they often leave stuff out of their reports. Trace evidence that can't be analyzed, that sort of thing. If it's not going to be of any use to the detectives, they don't bother including it. Apparently, the defense might use it to create confusion in the minds of the jury."

"I don't see where that gets us. Even if we could get our hands on the original reports, we wouldn't know what was left out, would we?"

"No. But maybe if we tracked down the scientist who put it together in the first place, he might remember something that meant nothing at the time but might mean something now. He might even have kept his own notes." Her anger had been swallowed by her enthusiasm now. "What do you think?"

"I think your hormones have addled your brain," Alex said. "You think if I ring up Lawson and ask him who did the forensic report, he's going to tell me?"

"Of course he's not." Her lip curled in distaste. "But he'd tell a journalist, wouldn't he?"

"The only journalists I know are the ones who write lifestyle features for the Sunday supplements," Alex protested.

"Well, ring round and ask them to find one of their colleagues who can help." Lynn spoke with an air of finality. When she was in this kind of mood, there was no point in trying to argue with her, he knew. But as he resigned himself to creeping round his contacts, the glimmer of an idea came into his mind. It might, he thought, kill two birds with one stone. Of course, it might also rebound painfully. There was only one way to find out.

Hospital car parks were good places for surveillance, Macfadyen thought. Plenty of comings and goings, always people sitting in their cars waiting. Good lighting, so you were sure of seeing your quarry arriving and leaving. No one gave you a second look; you could hang around for hours without anybody thinking you were dodgy. Not like your average suburban street where everybody wanted to know your business.

He wondered when Gilbey would get to take his daughter home. He'd tried ringing the hospital for information, but they'd been cagey, refusing to say much other than that the baby was doing well. Everybody with responsibility for kids was so security-conscious these days.

The resentment he felt toward Gilbey's child was overwhelming. Nobody was going to turn their back on this child. Nobody was going to hand it over and let it take its chances with strangers. Strangers who would bring up a child in a state of permanent anxiety that he'd do something that would bring arbitrary wrath down on his head. His parents hadn't abused him, not in the sense of beating him. But they'd made him feel constantly wanting, constantly at fault. And they hadn't hesitated to lay the blame for his inadequacies at the door of his bad blood. But he'd missed out on so much more than tenderness and love. The family stories that had been fed to him as a child were other people's stories, not his. He was a stranger to his own history.

He would never be able to look in the mirror and see an echo of his mother's features. He would never be aware of those strange congruences that happen in families, when a child's reactions replicate those of their parents. He was adrift in a world without connections. The only real family he had still didn't want him.

And now this child of Gilbey would have everything that had been denied him, even though its father was one of those responsible for what he'd lost. It rankled with Macfadyen, biting deep to the core of his shriveled soul. It wasn't fair. It didn't deserve the secure, loving home he knew it was going to.

It was time to make plans.

Weird kissed each of his children as they got into the family van. He didn't know when he'd see them again and saying good-bye in these circumstances felt like ripping a hole in his heart. But he knew this hurt was infinitesimal compared to how he'd feel if he did nothing and, by his inaction, left any of them in harm's way. A few hours driving would see them safe in the mountains, behind the stockade of an evangelical survivalist group whose leader had once been a deacon in Weird's church. He doubted the federal government could get to his kids there, far less a vengeful killer working on his own.

Part of him thought he was overreacting, but that wasn't the part he was prepared to listen to. Years of talking to God had left him with little self-doubt when it came to decision-making. Weird folded his wife into his arms and held her close. "Thanks for taking this seriously," he said.

"I've always taken you seriously, Tom," she murmured, stroking the silk of his shirt. "I want you to promise me you'll take as good care of yourself as you're taking of us."

"I've got one phone call to make, then I'm out of here. Where I'm going, I won't be easy to follow or to find. We lay low for a while, trust to God, and I know we'll overcome this threat." He leaned down and kissed her long and hard. "Go with God."

He stood back and waited while she climbed aboard and started the engine. The kids waved goodbye, their faces excited at the thought of an adventure that would take them out of school. He didn't envy them the harsh weather up in the mountains, but they'd do OK. He watched the van to the end of the street, then hurried back inside the house.

A colleague in Seattle had put him on to a reliable, discreet private investigator. Weird dialed the cellphone number and waited. "Pete Makin here," the voice on the other end said in a slow Western drawl.

"Mr. Makin? My name is Tom Mackie. Reverend Tom Mackie. I was given your name by Reverend Polk."

"I do like a minister who puts work in the way of his flock," Makin said. "How can I be of service to you, Reverend?"

"I need to find out who was responsible for sending a particular wreath to a funeral I attended recently in your area. Would that be possible?"

"I guess. Do you have any details?"

"I don't know the name of the florist who made it up, but it was a very distinctive arrangement. A circlet of white roses and rosemary. The card said, 'Rosemary for remembrance.' "

"Rosemary for remembrance," Makin repeated. "You're right, it is unusual. I don't think I've ever come across anything quite like that. Whoever made it should remember it. Now, can you tell me when and where this funeral took place?"

Weird passed on the information, carefully spelling Ziggy's name. "How long will it take you to come up with an answer?"

"That depends. The funeral home may be able to give me a list of the florists who usually supply them. But if that doesn't pan out, I'm going to have to canvas a pretty wide area. So it could be a few hours, could be a few days. If you give me your contact details, I'll keep you posted."

"I'm not going to be very easy to reach. I'll call in daily, if that's all right with you?"

"That's fine by me. But I'll need a retainer from you before I can begin work, I'm afraid."

Weird gave an ironic smile. These days, not even a man of the cloth could be trusted. "I'll wire it to you. How much do you need?"

"Five hundred dollars will be sufficient." Makin gave Weird his payment details. "Soon as the money is with me, I'll be on the case. Thank you for your business, Reverend."

Weird replaced the phone, strangely reassured by the conversation. Pete Makin hadn't wasted time asking why he wanted the information, nor had he made the job sound tougher than it was. He was, Weird thought, a man who could be trusted. He went upstairs and changed out of his clerical clothes into a comfortable pair of jeans, a cream Oxford cloth shirt and a soft leather jacket. His bag was already packed; all it lacked was the Bible that sat on his bedside table. He tucked it into a flap pocket, looked around the familiar room, then closed his eyes in prayer for a brief moment.

Several hours later, he was walking out of the long-stay car park at Atlanta airport. He was in good time for his flight to San Diego. By nightfall, he'd be across the border, anonymous in some cheap motel in Tijuana. It wasn't an ambience he'd normally choose, which made it even safer.

Whoever was out to get him, they weren't going to find him there.

Jackie glowered at Alex. "She's not here."

"I know. It's you I wanted to see."

She snorted, arms folded across her chest. Today, she was dressed in leather jeans and a tight black T-shirt. A diamond twinkled in her eyebrow. "Warning me off, eh?"

"What makes you think that's any of my business?" Alex said coolly.

She raised her eyebrows. "You're Scottish, you're male, she belongs to your family."

"That chip on your shoulder's going to leave one hell of a grease stain on your T-shirt. Look, I'm here because I think you and I can do each other a favor."

Jackie tilted her head at an insolent angle. "I don't do boys. Hadn't you worked that one out by now?"

Exasperated, Alex turned to go. He wondered why he'd risked Lynn's anger for this. "I'm wasting my time here. I just thought you might appreciate a suggestion that could get you off the hook with the police."

"Wait a minute. Why are you offering me a way out?"

He paused, one foot on the stairs. "It's not because of your natural charm, Jackie. It's because it also offers me peace of mind."

"Even if you do think I might have killed your brother-in-law."

Alex grunted. "Believe me, I'd sleep a lot easier in my bed at night if I believed that."

Jackie bristled. "Because then the dyke would have got what she deserved?"

Irritated, Alex snapped, "Could you put your prejudices away for five minutes? The only reason I'd be glad if you'd killed Mondo is that it would mean I was safe."

Jackie tilted her head to one side, intrigued in spite of herself. "That's a very strange thing to say."

"You want to talk about it on the landing?"

She gestured to the door and stepped back. "You'd better come in. What do you mean, 'safe'?" she asked as he walked to the nearest chair and sat down.

"I've got a theory about Mondo's death. I don't know if you know, but another friend of mine was killed in suspicious circumstances a few weeks ago."

Jackie nodded. "Hélène mentioned it. This was someone you and David were at university with, right?"

"We grew up together. Four of us. We were best friends at school and we all went on to university together. One night, coming home drunk from a party, we stumbled over a young woman—"

"I know about that, too," Jackie interrupted.

Alex was surprised at how relieved he felt at not having to go over all the details of the aftermath of Rosie's murder. "Right. So you know the background. Now, I know this is going to sound crazy, but I think the reason Mondo and Ziggy are dead is that someone is taking revenge for Rosie Duff. That's the girl that died," he added.

"Why?" In spite of herself, Jackie was all attention now, head forward, elbows on her knees. The whiff of a good story was powerful enough to put her hostility on hold.

"It sounds so insignificant," Alex said, then told her about the wreaths. "Her full name was Rosemary," he finished off.

She raised her eyebrows. "That's creepy shit," she said. "I've never come across a wreath like that. It's hard to interpret it except as a reference to this woman. I can see why it would do your head in."

"The police couldn't. They acted like I was a little old lady afraid of the dark."

Jackie made a scornful noise in the back of her throat. "Well, we both know how smart the police are. So what is it you think I can do?"

Alex looked embarrassed. "Lynn had this notion that, if we could find out who really killed Rosie all those years ago, then whoever is taking it out on us will see they have to stop. Before it's too late for the two of us that are left."

"It makes sense. Can't you persuade the police to reopen the case? With the techniques they have nowadays . . ."

"It's already been reopened. Fife Police are doing a review of cold cases, and this is one of them. But they seem to have hit a brick wall, mostly because they've lost the physical evidence. Lynn has this idea that if we can track down the forensic scientist who did the original report, he might be able to tell us more than he put in it."

Jackie nodded, understanding. "Sometimes they leave things out to avoid giving the defense any leverage. So you want me to track this guy down and interview him?"

"Something like that. I thought you might be able to pretend you were going to do an in-depth feature on the case, focusing on the original investigation. Maybe you could persuade the police to give you access to material they wouldn't readily show me?"

She shrugged. "It's worth a try."

"Then you'll do it?"

"I'll be honest with you, Alex. I can't say I've got any great interest in saving your skin. But you're right. I've got something at stake here, too. Helping you find who killed David gets me off the hook. So, who should I speak to?"

CHAPTER
THIRTY-FOUR

The message on James Lawson's desk simply said, "The cold case team would like to see you asap." It didn't sound like news of disaster. He walked into the squadroom with an air of cautious optimism, which was immediately vindicated by the sight of a bottle of Famous Grouse and half a dozen plastic cups in the hands of his detectives. He grinned. "This looks very like a celebration to me," he said.

DI Robin Maclennan stepped forward, offering the ACC a whiskey. "I've just had a message from Greater Manchester Police. They arrested a guy on suspicion of rape a couple of weeks ago in Rochdale. When they ran the DNA results through the computer, they got a hit."

Lawson stopped in his tracks. "Lesley Cameron?" Robin nodded.

Lawson took the whiskey and raised his cup in a silent toast. As with the Rosie Duff case, Lawson would never forget Lesley Cameron's murder. A student at the university, she'd been raped and strangled on her way back to her halls of residence. As with Rosie, they'd never found her killer. For a while, the detectives had tried to link the two cases, but there weren't sufficient similarities to justify the connection. It wasn't enough simply to say that there were no other rape-murders in St. Andrews during the period in question. He'd been a junior CID detective then and he remembered the debate. Personally, he'd never gone for the linkage theory. "I remember it well," he said.

"We ran DNA tests on her clothes, but there was no match in the system then," Robin continued, his lean face revealing previously unseen laughter lines. "So I put it on the back burner and carried on checking out subsequent sex offenders. Got nowhere. But then we got this call from GMP. Looks like we might have got a result."

Lawson clapped him on the shoulder. "Well done, Robin. You'll be going down to do the interview?" he asked.

"You bet. I can't wait to see the look on this scumbag's face when he hears what I want to question him about."

"That's great news." Lawson beamed at the rest of the team. "You see? All it takes is that one lucky break and you've got a success on your hands. How are the rest of you doing? Karen, did you get anywhere tracking down Rosie Duff's ex-boyfriend? The one we think is Macfadyen's father?"

Karen nodded. "John Stobie. The local lads had a word with him. And they got a result of sorts too. Turns out Stobie has the perfect alibi. He broke his leg in a motorbike accident at the end of November, 1978. The night Rosie was murdered, he had a stookie from thigh to toe. There's no way he was running around St. Andrews in the middle of a blizzard."

Lawson raised his eyebrows. "Christ, anybody would think Stobie had brittle bones. Presumably they checked his medical records?"

"Stobie gave them permission. And it looks like he was telling the truth. So that's the end of that."

Lawson turned slightly, cutting himself and Karen off from the others. "As you say, Karen." He sighed. "Maybe I should put Macfadyen on to Stobie. It might get him off my case."

"He still hassling you?"

"A couple of times a week. I'm beginning to wish he'd never come out of the woodwork."

"I've still got to interview the other three witnesses," Karen said.

Lawson pulled a face. "Actually, there's only two. Apparently, Malkiewicz died in a suspected arson just before Christmas. And Alex Gilbey has got it into his head that now David Kerr's been murdered, too, there's some mad vigilante out there picking them off one by one."

"What?"

"He came in to see me a couple of days ago. It's paranoia run mad, but I don't want to encourage him. So maybe it's best if you just leave the witness interviews. I can't see that they'd be any use after all this time."

Karen thought about objecting. Not that she expected anything significant to turn up by talking to her witnesses, but she was too dogged a detective to be comfortable leaving any avenue unexplored. "You don't think he could be right? I mean, it's a bit of a coincidence. Macfadyen appears on the scene, finds out we've no hope of catching his mother's killer, then two of the original suspects wind up murdered."

Lawson rolled his eyes. "You've been stuck in this investigation room for too long, Karen. You're starting to hallucinate. Of course Macfadyen isn't going around doing a Charles Bronson. He's a respectable professional man, for heaven's sake, not some demented vigilante. And we're not going to insult him by interrogating him about two murders that didn't even happen on our patch."

"No, sir," Karen said, sighing.

Lawson put a paternal hand on her arm. "So let's forget about Rosie Duff for the time being. It's going nowhere." He moved back into the main group. "Robin, isn't Lesley Cameron's sister an offender profiler?"

"That's right. Dr. Fiona Cameron. She was involved in the Drew Shand case in Edinburgh a few years back."

"I remember now. Well, maybe you should give Dr. Cameron a courtesy call. Let her know we're questioning a suspect. And make sure the press office knows too. But only after you've spoken to Dr. Cameron. I don't want her reading it in the papers before she hears it from the horse's mouth." It was clearly the end of the conversation. Lawson knocked back his whiskey and headed for the door. He paused on the threshold and turned back. "Great result, Robin. This makes us all look good. Thank you."

Weird pushed his plate away from him. Greasy tourist food, and in helpings large enough to feed an entire family of poor Mexicans for a day or two, he thought miserably. He hated being wrenched from his daily round like this. All the things that made his life enjoyable felt like a distant dream. There were limits to the comfort that could be extorted from faith alone. Proof, if ever he needed it, that he fell far short of his own ideals.

As the waiter cleared away the debris of his burrito special, Weird pulled out his phone and called Pete Makin. Greetings over, he cut straight to the chase. "Have you made any progress," he asked.

"Only of the negative kind. The funeral home gave me the names of three stores who normally supply their floral tributes. But none of them ever created a wreath like the one you described to me. They all agreed it sounded unusual, distinctive. Something they'd recall if it had been one of theirs."

"What now, then?"

"Well," Makin drawled. "There are maybe five or six florists in the immediate area. I'm going to do the rounds of them, see what I come up with. But it may take a day or two. I'm in court tomorrow, testifying in a fraud case. It could run over to the next day. But, rest assured, Reverend. I'll get back to this just as soon as I can."

"I appreciate you being so straightforward with me, Mr. Makin. I'll give you a ring in a couple of days and see how you're getting on." Weird put his phone back in his pocket. It wasn't over yet. Not by a long chalk.

Jackie put fresh batteries in her tape recorder, checked she had a couple of pens in her bag, then left her car. She'd been pleasantly surprised by the helpfulness of the police press officer she'd called after Alex's visit.

She'd had her pitch ready. She was writing a major magazine article comparing the methods the police used in a murder inquiry twenty-five years ago with how they ran an investigation now. It had struck her that the easiest way to get a handle on an old investigation would be to piggyback a cold case review such as Fife were running. That way, she'd be dealing with an officer who was completely current with the details of the case. She'd emphasized that there was no question of criticizing the police; this was to be purely about the changes in procedure and practice that had been brought about by scientific developments and legal changes.

The press officer had called her back the following day. "You're in luck. We've got a case from almost exactly twenty-five years ago. And it so happens that our Assistant Chief Constable was the first police officer at the scene. And he's agreed to give you an interview about that. I've also arranged for you to meet DC Karen Pirie, who's been working on the case review. She's got all the details at her fingertips."

So here she was, breaching the bastion of Fife Police. Jackie didn't normally feel nervous before an interview. She'd been in the game long enough for it to hold no terrors for her. She'd dealt with every kind of interviewee; the shy, the brash, the excited, the frightened, the self-publicizing and the blasé, the hardened criminal and the raw victim. But today, there was definitely a buzz of adrenaline in her blood. She hadn't been lying when she'd told Alex that she had something at stake here, too. She'd lain awake for hours after they'd talked, keenly aware of how much damage suspicion over David Kerr's death could do to her life. So she'd prepared herself for today, dressing conservatively and deliberately trying to look as unthreatening as possible. For once, there were more holes in her ears than rings.

It was hard to see the young police constable in ACC Lawson, she thought as she settled herself opposite him. He looked like one of those people who have been born with the cares of the world on their shoulders, and today they seemed to weigh particularly heavy on him. He couldn't have been much over fifty, but he looked as if he'd be more at home on a bowling green than running criminal investigations throughout Fife. "Funny idea, this story of yours," he said, once the introductions were done with.

"Not really. People take so much for granted now in police investigations. It's good to remind them how far we've traveled in a relatively short period of time. Of course, I need to learn much more than I'll ever be able to use in my final article. You always end up throwing away about ninety percent of the research."

"And who's this article for?" he asked conversationally.

"*Vanity Fair*," Jackie said definitely. It was always better to lie about commissions. It reassured people that you weren't wasting their time.

"Well, here I am at your disposal," he said with forced cheerfulness, spreading his hands wide.

"I appreciate it. I know how busy you must be. Now, can we go back to that December night in 1978? What brought you into the case?"

Lawson breathed heavily through his nose. "I was working the night shift in the patrol car. That meant I was out on the road all night, except for refreshment breaks. I didn't drive around all night, you understand." One corner of his mouth rose in a half-smile. "We had budgetary restraints even then. I wasn't supposed to drive more than forty miles on a shift. So I'd cruise around the town center when the pubs were closing, then I'd find a quiet spot and park there until I got called out on a shout. Which didn't happen that often. St. Andrews was a fairly quiet town, especially during the university holidays."

"It must have been pretty boring," she sympathized.

"You're not kidding. I used to take a transistor radio with me, but there was never much worth listening to. Most nights I'd park up by the entrance to the Botanic Gardens. I liked it up there. It was nice and quiet, but you could be anywhere in the town in minutes. That night, the weather was hellish. It had been snowing on and off all day, and by the middle of the night it was lying pretty thick. I'd had a quiet night as a result. The weather was keeping most folk in their own homes. Then, around four o'clock, I saw this figure looming up through the snow. I got out of the car and, I'll be honest with you, I wondered for a moment if I was going to be attacked by a drunken maniac. This young lad was heaving for breath, blood all over him, sweat running down his face. He blurted out that there was a lassie on Hallow Hill who had been attacked."

"You must have been shocked," Jackie prompted him.

"I thought at first it was some drunken student wind-up. But he was very insistent. He told me he'd stumbled over her in the snow and that she was bleeding badly. I realized pretty quickly that he was genuinely in a state, not putting it on. So I radioed back to base and told them I was investigating a report of an injured woman on Hallow Hill. I got the lad into the car . . ."

"This was Alex Gilbey, right?"

Lawson raised his eyebrows. "You've done your homework." ❦

She shrugged. "I read the newspaper cuttings, that's all. So, you took Gilbey back to Hallow Hill? What did you find there?"

Lawson nodded. "By the time we got there, Rosie Duff was dead. There were three other young men around the body. It then became my job to secure the scene and radio for backup. I called for uniform and CID back-up and moved the four witnesses away from the scene, back down the hill. I freely admit, I was all at sea. I'd never seen anything like this, and I didn't know at that point if I was standing in the middle of a blizzard with four killers."

"Surely, if they'd killed her, the last thing they would have done was run for help?"

"Not necessarily. They were intelligent young men, perfectly capable of coming up with the double bluff. I saw it as my job to say nothing that would indicate I had any suspicions, for fear that they'd run off into the night and leave us with an even bigger problem. After all, I had no idea who they were."

"Presumably you succeeded, since they waited for your

colleagues to arrive. What happened then? Procedurally, I mean?" Jackie dutifully listened while Lawson ran through everything that had happened at the crime scene, up to the point where he had taken the four young men back to the police station.

"That was really the extent of my direct involvement with the case," Lawson concluded. "All the subsequent inquiries were dealt with by CID officers. We had to draft in men from other divisions, we didn't have the staffing levels to cover a case like this ourselves." Lawson pushed back his chair. "Now, if you'll excuse me, I'll have DC Pirie come up and get you. She's better placed than me to run through the case with you."

Jackie picked up her tape recorder but didn't turn it off. "You've got very good recall of that night," she said, letting admiration seep into her voice.

Lawson pressed the button on his intercom. "Ask Karen to come up, would you, Margaret?" He gave Jackie the sort of smile that reveals vanity satisfied. "You've got to be meticulous in this job," he said. "I always kept careful notes. But you have to remember, murder is a pretty rare occurrence in St. Andrews. We've only had a handful of instances in my ten years stationed there. So naturally it sticks in my mind."

"And you never came near to arresting anyone?"

Lawson pursed his lips. "No. And that's a very hard thing for police officers to live with. The finger pointed at the four lads who found the body, but there was never anything more than circumstantial evidence against any of them. Because of where the body was found, I had a hunch it might have been some sort of pagan ritual killing. But nothing ever came of that idea, and nothing like it ever happened again on our patch. I'm sorry to say that Rosie Duff's killer went free. Of course, men who commit this kind of crime often go on to repeat it. So for all we know he may be behind bars for another murder."

There was a knock at the door and Lawson called, "Come in." The woman who walked in was the diametric opposite to Jackie. Where the journalist was fluid and lithe, Karen Pirie was solid and graceless. What united them was the obvious spark of intelligence each recognized in the other. Lawson performed the introductions then skilfully steered them toward the door. "Good luck with your article," he said as he closed the door firmly behind them.

Karen led the way up one flight of stairs to the cold cases review room. "You're based in Glasgow?" she asked as they climbed.

"Born and bred. It's a great city. All human life is here, as they say."

"Handy for a journalist. So what got you interested in this case?"

Jackie swiftly ran through her cover story again. It seemed to make sense to Karen. She pushed open the door of the squadroom and led the way inside. Jackie looked around, noting the pinboards covered with photographs, maps and memos. A couple of people sitting behind computers glanced up as they walked in, then returned to their work. "It goes without saying, by the way, that anything you see or hear in this room relating to current investigations or to any other case should be treated as confidential. Are you clear about that?"

"I'm not a crime reporter. I have no interest in anything other than what we are here to discuss. So no sneaky stuff, OK?"

Karen smiled. She'd encountered a fair few journalists in her time, and most of them she wouldn't trust not to steal an ice-cream from a toddler. But this woman seemed different. Whatever she was hungry for, it wasn't a quick, devious hit and run. Karen showed Jackie to a long trestle table set against one wall where she'd arranged the material from the original investigation. "I don't know how much detail you want," she said dubiously, eyeing the stack of files in front of them.

"I need to have a sense of how the investigation progressed. What avenues were explored. And of course"—

Jackie pulled a self-deprecating expression out of her bag of tricks—"because this is journalism and not history, I need the names of the people concerned, and any background you have on them. Police officers, pathologist, forensic scientists. That sort of thing." She was so smooth, water would have slithered off her like rain on a duck's feathers.

"Sure, I can give you names. Background I'm a bit sketchy on. I was only three when this case hit the bricks running. And of course, the senior investigating officer, Barney Maclennan, died during the investigation. You knew that, right?" Jackie nodded. Karen continued. "The only one of the players I've ever met is David Soanes, the forensics guy. He did the work, though it was actually his boss that signed off on the report."

"Why was that?" Jackie asked nonchalantly, trying not to show her elation at getting what she wanted so easily and quickly.

"Standard practice. The person who actually signs off on the reports is always the head of the lab, even though he might never have touched any of the exhibits. It impresses the jury."

"So much for expert testimony," Jackie said sardonically.

"You do what it takes to put the bad guys away," Karen said. It was clear from her weary tone that she couldn't be bothered going on the defensive over such a self-evident point. "Anyway, in this instance, we couldn't have been better served. David Soanes is one of the most painstaking guys I've ever come across." She smiled. "And these days, he's the guy who signs off on other people's reports. David's the Professor of Forensic Science at Dundee University now. They supply all our forensic services."

"Maybe I could talk to him."

Karen shrugged. "He's a pretty approachable guy. So, where should we start?"

Two mostly tedious hours later, Jackie managed to make her escape. She knew more than she could possibly want to about police procedure in Fife in the late 1970s. There was nothing more frustrating than getting the information you needed at the start of an interview and then having to carry on regardless, for fear of revealing a hidden agenda.

Of course, Karen hadn't let her see the original forensic report. But Jackie hadn't expected that. She'd got what she came for. Now it was up to Alex.

CHAPTER
THIRTY-FIVE

Alex stared down into the moses basket. She was here, where she belonged. Their daughter, in their house. Loosely swaddled in a white blanket, her face scrunched up in sleep, Davina made his heart sing. She'd lost that pinched look that had frightened him so much in the first few days of her life. Now, she looked like other babies, her face growing more individual. He wanted to draw her every day of her life, so he'd never miss a single nuance of the changes she'd go through.

She filled his senses. If he leaned down close and held his breath, he could hear the faint susurration of her breathing. His nostrils trembled at the unmistakable smell of baby. Alex knew he loved Lynn; but he'd never felt this overwhelming protective passion in his heart before. Lynn was right; he had to do whatever he could to make sure he'd be there to see his daughter grow up. He decided to call Paul later, to share this momentous evening. He'd have done it if Ziggy had still been alive, and Paul deserved to know he was still part of their lives.

The distant sound of the doorbell interrupted his devotions. Alex gave his sleeping daughter the lightest of touches, then walked backward out of the room. He reached the front door seconds behind Lynn, who looked thunderstruck to see Jackie standing on the doorstep. "What are you doing here?" she demanded.

"Didn't Alex tell you?" Jackie drawled.

"Tell me what?" Lynn rounded on Alex.

"I asked Jackie to help me," Alex said.

"That's right." Jackie seemed more amused than offended.

"You asked *her*?" Lynn made no attempt to disguise her contempt. "A woman who had a motive for murdering my brother and the kind of contacts to get it done? Alex, how could you?"

"Because she's got something to gain, too. Which means I could trust her not to rat us out for the sake of a page lead," he said, trying to calm Lynn down before Jackie took the huff and marched off into the night without revealing what she'd learned.

"I'm not having her in my house," Lynn said categorically.

Alex held his hands up. "Fine. Just let me get my coat. We'll go to the pub, if that's all right with you, Jackie?"

She shrugged. "Whatever. But you're buying."

They walked down the gentle slope to the pub in silence. Alex didn't feel inclined to apologize for Lynn's hostility and Jackie couldn't be bothered to make an issue of it. When they were settled with a couple of glasses of red wine, Alex raised his eyebrows interrogatively. "Well? Any joy?"

Jackie looked smug. "I have the name of the forensic scientist who carried out the work on the Rosie Duff case. And the beauty of it is that he's still in the game. He's a professor at Dundee. His name is David Soanes, and apparently he's shit hot."

"So when can you go and see him?" Alex asked.

"I'm not going to go and see him, Alex. That's your job."

"My job? I'm not a journalist. Why would he talk to me?"

"You're the one with something at stake here. You throw yourself on his mercy and ask for any information he can give you that might help move the case forward."

"I don't know how to conduct an interview," Alex protested. "And why would Soanes tell me anything? He's not going to want it to look as if there were things he overlooked before."

"Alex, you talked me into going out on a limb for you,

and frankly I don't like you or your offensive, small-minded wife. So I think you can probably talk David Soanes into telling you what you want to know. Especially since you're not asking about things he overlooked. You'll be asking about things that might not have been susceptible to analysis, things he justifiably didn't include in his report. If he cares about his work, then he should want to help. He's also a lot less likely to talk to a journalist who could make him look incompetent." Jackie swallowed some wine, made a face and got to her feet. "Let me know when you've got something that gets me off the hook."

Lynn sat in the conservatory, watching the lights on the estuary. They were faintly haloed with damp air, investing them with more mysteriousness than they merited. She heard the front door close and Alex's cry of, "I'm back." But before he could join her, the doorbell pealed out again. Whoever it was, she wasn't in the mood.

Mumbled voices grew more distinct as they approached, but still she couldn't tell who their latest visitor was. Then the door opened and Weird strode in. "Lynn," he cried. "I hear you have a beautiful daughter to show me."

"Weird," Lynn exclaimed, astonishment on her face. "You're the last person I expected to see."

"Good," he said. "Let's hope that's how everybody else is thinking." He looked down at her with concern. "How are you holding up?"

Lynn leaned into his hug. "I know it sounds stupid, given how little we saw of Mondo, but I miss him."

"Of course you do. We all do. And we always will. He was part of us, and now he isn't anymore. Knowing he's with the Lord is a small consolation for what we've lost." They were quiet for a moment, then Lynn moved away.

"But what are you doing here?" she asked. "I thought you went straight back to America after the funeral?"

"I did. I packed my wife and kids off to the mountains, somewhere they'll be safe from anybody who has an issue with me. And then I made myself disappear. I crossed the border into Mexico. Lynn, never go to Tijuana unless you have a cast-iron stomach. The food is the worst in the world, but what really gives the soul indigestion is the collision between the extravagant riches of America and the grinding poverty of those Mexicans. I was ashamed of my adopted countrymen and women. Do you know, the Mexicans even paint their donkeys in stripes, like zebras, so the tourists can have their pictures taken with them? That's how far we've driven them."

"Spare us the sermon, Weird. Cut to the chase," Lynn complained.

Weird grinned. "I'd forgotten quite how forthright you can be, Lynn. Well, I felt pretty uneasy after Mondo's funeral. So I hired a private eye in Seattle. I wanted to find out who sent that wreath to Ziggy's funeral. And he came back with an answer. An answer that gave me good reason to come back here. Plus, I figured this was the last place that anybody looking for me would expect to find me. Way too near to home."

Alex rolled his eyes. "You really have learned a few theatrical tricks over the years, haven't you? Are you going to tell us what you found out?"

"The man who sent the wreath lives right here in Fife. St. Monans, to be precise. I don't know who he is, or how he's connected to Rosie Duff. But his name is Graham Macfadyen."

Alex and Lynn exchanged a look of anxiety. "We know who he is," Alex said. "Or we can at least make an educated guess."

Now it was Weird's turn to look puzzled and frustrated. "You do? How?"

"He's Rosie Duff's son," Lynn said.

Weird's eyes widened. "She had a son?"

"Nobody knew about him at the time. He was adopted at birth. He must have been three or four when she died," Alex said.

"Oh my," Weird said. "Well, that makes sense, doesn't it? I take it he only found out about his mother's murder recently?"

"He went to see Lawson when the cold case review was

launched. He'd only started trying to trace his birth mother a few months before that."

"There's your motive, if he thought you four were responsible for her murder," Lynn said. "We need to find out more about this Macfadyen."

"We need to find out if he was in the States the week Ziggy died," Alex said.

"How do we do that?" Lynn said.

Weird raised a hand. "Atlanta is Delta's hub. One of my flock has a pretty senior position there. I'd guess he can maybe get hold of passenger manifests. The airlines swap information like that all the time, apparently. And I have Macfadyen's credit-card details, which might speed things up. I'll call him later, if I may?"

"Of course," Alex said. Then he cocked his head. "Is that Davina I can hear?" He headed for the door. "I'll bring her through."

"Well done, Weird," Lynn said. "I'd never have put you down for the methodical researcher."

"You forget, I was a mathematician and a damn good one. All the other stuff, that was just a desperate bid not to be my father. Which, thank the Lord, I managed to avoid."

Alex returned, Davina whimpering in his arms. "I think she needs to be fed."

Weird stood up and peered down at the tiny bundle. "Oh my," he said, his voice soft as milk. "She is a beauty." He looked up at Alex. "Now you understand why I'm so determined to come out of this alive."

Out under the bridge, Macfadyen stared down at the scene below. It had been an eventful evening. First, the woman had turned up. He'd seen her at the funeral, watched the widow Kerr leave in her car. He'd followed them to a flat in the Merchant City, then, a couple of days later, he'd followed Gilbey to the same flat. He wondered what her connection was, where she fit into the complex pattern. Was she just a friend of the family? Or was she more than that?

Whatever she was, she hadn't been made welcome. She

and Gilbey had gone to the pub, but they'd barely been there long enough to have a single drink. Then, when Gilbey had gone back to the house, the real surprise had walked in. Mackie was back. He should have been safely ensconced in Georgia, ministering to his flock. But here he was, in Fife again, and in the company of his co-conspirator. You didn't walk away from your life unless you had good reason.

It was proof. You could tell from the expressions on their faces. This was no cheerful reunion of friends. This was no blithe gathering to celebrate the return from the hospital of Gilbey's daughter. These two had something to hide, something that drew them together in this time of crisis. Fear had brought them into each other's orbit. They were terrified that whatever nemesis had caught up with their fellow killers was about to visit them. And they were huddling together for safety.

Macfadyen smiled grimly. The cold hand of the past was reaching inexorably for Gilbey and Mackie. They wouldn't sleep easy in their beds tonight. And that was how it should be. He had plans for them. And the more afraid they were now, the better it would be when those plans came to fruition.

They'd had twenty-five years of peace, which was more, far more than his mother had enjoyed. Now, it was over.

CHAPTER
THIRTY-SIX

Morning dawned dreich and gray, the view from North Queensferry obscured by a dismal haar. Somewhere in the distance a foghorn boomed its miserable warning like a cow mourning a dead calf. Unshaven and dazed with broken sleep, Alex leaned his elbows on the breakfast table and watched Lynn feeding Davina. "Was that a good night or a bad one?" he asked.

"I think it was about average," Lynn said through a yawn. "They need to feed every few hours at this age."

"One o'clock, half-past three, half-past six. Are you sure that's a baby and not a gannet?"

Lynn grinned. "How quickly the first bloom of love fades," she teased.

"If that was true, I'd have pulled the pillow over my head and gone back to sleep instead of getting up to make you tea and change her nappy," Alex said defensively.

"If Weird wasn't here, you could sleep in the spare room."

Alex shook his head. "I don't want to do that. We'll see how we go."

"You need your sleep. You've got a business to run."

Alex snorted. "That would be when I'm not running about the country talking to forensic scientists, right?"

"Right. Are you OK about Weird being here?"

"Why wouldn't I be?"

"I just wondered. I've got a naturally suspicious nature. You know I always thought he was the only one of the four of you who could possibly have killed Rosie. So I suppose I'm a bit uneasy about him turning up like this."

Alex looked uncomfortable. "Surely that's the very thing that absolutely lets him off the hook over Rosie? What possible motive could he have for killing the rest of us after twenty-five years?"

"Maybe he heard about the cold case review and was afraid that, after all this time, one of the four of you might point the finger."

"You always push things to the limit, don't you? He didn't kill her, Lynn. He's not got it in him."

"People do terrible things when they're on drugs. As I recall, Weird was always up for anything in that department. He had the Land Rover; she probably knew him well enough to take a lift off him. And then there was that sudden dramatic conversion. Could have been about guilt, Alex."

He shook his head. "He's my friend. I'd have known."

Lynn sighed. "You're probably right. I do get carried away with myself. I'm really edgy just now. Sorry."

As she spoke, Weird walked in. Showered and shaved, he looked the picture of health and strength. Alex took one look and groaned. "Oh God, it's Tigger."

"That's a great bed," Weird said, looking round the room and clocking the coffeemaker. He crossed the kitchen and started opening cupboards until he found the mugs. "I slept like a baby."

"I don't think so," Lynn said. "Not unless you woke up crying every three hours. Aren't you supposed to have jet lag?"

"Never suffered from it in my life," Weird said cheerfully, pouring out his coffee. "So, Alex, when are we leaving for Dundee?"

Alex stirred himself. "I'll have to ring up and make an appointment."

"Are you crazy? Give the guy the chance to say no?" Weird said, rooting around in the breadbin. He took out a triangular farl and smacked his lips. "Mmm. I've not had one of these for years."

"Make yourself at home," Alex said.

"I am," Weird said, raiding the fridge for butter and cheese. "No, Alex. No phone calls. We just turn up and make it clear we're not going anywhere until Professor Soanes finds a window."

"What? So he can jump?" Alex couldn't resist the chance to poke fun at Weird's adoption of American idiom. It sounded so bizarre delivered in an accent that had become markedly more Scottish overnight.

"Ha ha." Weird found plate and knife and settled at the table.

"You don't think that might piss him off just a smidge?" Lynn asked.

"I think it tells him we're serious," Weird said. "I think it's what two guys in fear of their lives would do. This isn't the time for being polite, douce and obedient. It's time to say, 'We're truly scared and you can help us.'"

Alex winced. "Are you sure you really want to come with me?" The repressive look Weird gave him would have stopped even a teenager in his tracks. Alex held his hands up in submission. "OK. Give me half an hour."

Lynn watched him go, her eyes concerned.

"Don't worry, Lynn. I'll look after him."

Lynn snorted with laughter. "Oh please, Weird. Let that not be my only hope."

He swallowed a mouthful of his farl and considered her. "I'm really not the person you remember, Lynn," he said seriously. "Forget the teenage rebellion. Forget the excessive drinking and the drugs. Think about the fact that I always did my homework and got my essays in on time. It only ever looked like I was going off the rails. Underneath it all, I was as much a solid citizen as Alex. I know you all laugh up your sleeve at having a TV evangelist on your Christmas card list—and very nice cards they are, too. But underneath the pizzazz, I'm very serious about what I believe and what I do.

When I say I'll look after Alex, you can trust that he'll be as safe with me as he could be with anyone."

Chastened but without her residual suspicion entirely stilled, Lynn swapped her daughter from one breast to the other. "There you go, darling." She winced at the still unfamiliar sensation as the hard gums clamped down on her nipple. "I'm sorry, Weird. It's just hard to move past the time when I knew you best."

He finished his coffee and stood up. "I know. I still think of you as a silly wee lassie dreaming of David Cassidy."

"Bastard," she said.

"I'm going to spend some time in prayer now," he said, heading for the door. "Alex and I need all the help we can get."

The exterior of the Old Fleming Gymnasium was about as far from Alex's image of a forensic laboratory as it was possible to get. Tucked away down a narrow wynd, its Victorian sandstone was heavily stained with a century of pollution. It wasn't an unattractive building, its single story well proportioned with tall, Italianate arched windows. It just didn't look like somewhere that housed the cutting edge of forensic science.

Weird clearly shared his impression. "You sure this is the place?" he asked, hesitating at the mouth of the lane.

Alex gestured across the street. "There's the OTI café. According to the university Web site, that's where we turn off."

"Looks more like a bank than a gymnasium or a laboratory." Nevertheless, he followed Alex down the wynd.

The reception area didn't give much away. A young man with a bad case of psoriasis and a dress code modeled on a 1950s beatnik sat behind a desk, tapping at a computer keyboard. He peered at them over the heavy black rims of his glasses. "Can I help you?" he said.

"We were wondering if it would be possible to have a word with Professor Soanes," Alex said.

"Have you got an appointment?"

Alex shook his head. "No. But we'd really appreciate it if he could see us. It's about an old case he worked on."

The young man moved his head sinuously from side to side like an Indian dancer. "I don't think that will be possible. He's a very busy man," he said.

"So are we," Weird cut in, leaning forward. "And what we want to talk about is a matter of life and death."

"My," said the young man. "The Tommy Lee Jones of Tayside." It should have sounded rude, but he invested it with an amused air of admiration that undercut any malice.

Weird gave him a hard stare. "We can wait," Alex interjected before hostilities could break out.

"You'll have to. He's giving a seminar right now. Let me take a look at his schedule for today." He rattled over the keyboard. "Can you come back at three?" he asked after a few seconds.

Weird scowled. "Spend five hours in Dundee?"

"That's great," Alex said, glaring at Weird. "Come on, Tom." They left their names, the details of the case and Alex's mobile number and retreated.

"Mr. Charm," Alex said as they walked back toward the car.

"We got a result, though. If it had been down to Mr. Supplicant here, we'd have been lucky to get slotted in before the end of term. So what are we going to do for the next five hours?"

"We could go to St. Andrews," Alex said. "It's only across the bridge."

Weird stopped in his tracks. "Are you kidding?"

"No. Never been more serious. I don't think it would hurt to remind ourselves of the terrain. It's not as if anybody's going to recognize us after all these years."

Weird's hand went to the place on his chest where his cross would normally hang. He tutted at himself as his fingers brushed empty cloth. "OK," he said. "But I'm not going anywhere near the Bottle Dungeon."

Driving into St. Andrews was a strange, dislocating experience. For one thing, they'd never had access to a car as undergraduates, so they'd never experienced the town from the perspective of a motorist. For another, the road into town led past buildings that hadn't been there when they were students. The concrete sprawl of the Old Course Hotel; the neoclassical cylinder of the St. Andrews University Museum; the Sea Life Center behind the eternally unbending Royal and Ancient clubhouse, the temple of golf itself. Weird stared out of the window, uneasy. "It's changed."

"Of course it's changed. It's been nearly a quarter of a century."

"I suppose you've been back often enough?"

Alex shook his head. "Haven't been near the place in twenty years." He drove slowly along The Scores, finally squeezing his BMW into a slot vacated by a woman in a Renault.

They got out in silence and started tracking the once familiar streets on foot. It was, Alex thought, very like seeing Weird again after all these years. The basic bone structure was the same. There was no question of mistaking him for someone else, or someone else for him. But the surface was different. Some changes were subtle, others gross. So it was walking around St. Andrews. Some of the shops were still in the same place, their façades identical. Paradoxically, they were the ones that looked out of kilter, as if they'd somehow avoided slipping through a time warp that had engulfed the rest of the town. The sweetie shop was still there, a monument to the national appetite for sugar. Alex recognized the restaurant where they'd eaten their first Chinese meal, the tastes alien and confusing to palates blunted by good plain cooking. They'd been a foursome then, light-hearted and confident, without the slightest sense of foreboding. *And then there were two.*

There was no escaping the university. In this town of sixteen thousand souls, a third of the inhabitants earned their living from it, and if its buildings had mysteriously turned to dust overnight, it would have left a gap-toothed village in its wake. Students hurried the streets, the occasional distinctive red flannel gown wrapped round its owner against the chill. It was hard to believe they'd once done the same thing. Alex had a momentary flash of memory; Ziggy and Mondo in the smart men's outfitters, trying on their new gowns. Alex and Weird had had to settle for secondhand, but they'd made the most of the opportunity to misbehave in a good cause, pushing the patience of the shop staff to its limits. It all felt strange and distant now, as if it were a movie, not a memory.

As they neared the West Port, they glimpsed the familiar frontage of the Lammas Bar through the stone arches of the massive gateway. Weird stopped abruptly. "This is doing my head in. I can't handle this, Alex. Let's get out of here."

Alex wasn't exactly unhappy at the suggestion. "Back to Dundee, then?"

"No, I don't think so. Part of the reason I came back was to front up this Graham Macfadyen about the wreaths. St. Monans isn't that far, is it? Let's go and see what he has to say for himself."

"It's the middle of the day. He'll be at his work," Alex said, speeding up to keep pace with Weird as he strode back toward the car.

"At least we can take a look at his house. And maybe we can go back after we've seen Professor Soanes." There was no arguing with Weird in this mood, Alex realized with resignation.

Macfadyen couldn't figure out what the point was. He'd been stationed outside Gilbey's house from seven that morning and had felt a warm glow of gratification when the car had left with the pair of them. The partners in crime were clearly up to something. He'd trailed them across Fife and into Dundee and followed them up Small's Wynd. As soon as they were inside the old sandstone building, he'd hurried in their wake. The sign by the door said DEPARTMENT OF FORENSIC SCIENCE, which gave him pause. What were they looking for? Why were they here?

Whatever it was, it didn't take them long. They were out on the street inside ten minutes. He almost lost them on the approach to the Tay Bridge, but managed to stay in touch as they slowed to turn on to the St. Andrews road. Parking had been a slight problem, and he'd ended up leaving the car blocking someone's drive.

He'd kept them in sight as they walked up through the town. There seemed to be no particular objective to their progress. They doubled back on themselves a couple of times, criss-crossing North Street, Market Street and South Street. Luckily, Mackie was tall enough to stand out on the street, so it wasn't too hard to trail them. Then, suddenly, he realized this apparently aimless wander was taking them closer and closer to the West Port. They were going to the Lammas Bar. They actually had the brass neck to walk through the door and revisit the place where they'd first targeted his mother.

Sweat broke out on Macfadyen's upper lip in spite of the damp cold of the day. The pointers to their guilt were multiplying by the hour. Innocence would have kept them well away from the Lammas Bar, innocence and respect. But guilt would draw them like a magnet, he was sure of it.

He was so lost in his thoughts that he almost walked straight into them. They'd stopped unexpectedly in the middle of the pavement, and he'd kept walking. His heart banging in his chest, Macfadyen sidestepped them, head turned away. He dodged into a shop doorway and looked back, clenching his clammy hands in his pocket. He couldn't believe his eyes. They'd bottled it. They'd turned their backs on the West Port and were striding back down South Street in the direction they'd come from.

He almost had to break into a trot to keep them in sight as they cut down a series of vennels and wynds. Their choice of narrow thoroughfares instead of the wider streets seemed to shriek guilty conscience at Macfadyen. Gilbey and Mackie were hiding from the world, taking cover from the accusing eyes they must imagine on every street.

By the time he made it back to his own car, they were already driving toward the cathedral. Cursing, Macfadyen got behind the wheel and gunned the engine. He'd almost caught up with them when the fates dealt him a cruel blow.

At the bottom of Kinkell Braes there were roadworks, the single carriageway controlled by traffic lights. Gilbey shot through just as the light turned from amber to red, as if he knew he needed to make his getaway. If there had been no vehicle between them, Macfadyen would have taken the risk and gone through on red. But his way was blocked by an auto-spares van. He brought his fist down savagely on the steering wheel, fuming as the minutes ticked by before the green light glared out again. The van crawled up the hill, Macfadyen tailgating it. But it was a good couple of miles before he was able to pass it, and he knew in his heart there was no chance of catching Gilbey's BMW.

He could have wept. He had no idea where they were headed. Nothing in their perplexing morning offered any clues. He thought about going home, checking his computers to see if there was any fresh news. But he couldn't see the point. The Internet wasn't going to tell him where Gilbey and Mackie were.

The only thing he could be sure of was that sooner or later they'd return to North Queensferry. Cursing himself for his inadequacy, Macfadyen decided he might as well make his way back there.

At the moment Graham Macfadyen was passing the turn-off that would have taken him home, Weird and Alex were sitting outside his house. "Happy?" Alex said. Weird had already stalked up the path and hammered on the door to no avail. Then he'd walked round the house, peering in at the windows. Alex was convinced that the police would turn up at any moment, alerted by some nosy neighbor. But this wasn't the sort of development where people were at home all day.

"At least we know where to find him," Weird said. "It looks like he lives alone."

"What makes you think that?"

Weird gave him a look that said, *Duh*.

"No feminine touches, eh?"

"Not a one," Weird said. "OK, you were right. It was a waste of time." He glanced at his watch. "Let's go and find a decent pub, grab a bite of lunch. And then we can go back to bonnie Dundee."

CHAPTER
THIRTY-SEVEN

Professor David Soanes was a chubby butterball of a man. Rosy-cheeked, with a fringe of curling white hair round a gleaming bald pate and blue eyes that actually twinkled, he bore a disconcerting resemblance to a clean-shaven Father Christmas. He ushered Alex and Weird into a tiny cubicle that barely had room enough for his desk and a couple of visitors' chairs. The room was spartan, its only decoration a certificate that proclaimed Soanes a freeman of the city of Srebrenica. Alex didn't want to think about what he might have had to do to earn that honor.

Soanes waved them to the chairs and settled in behind his desk, his round belly butting up against the edge. He pursed his lips and considered them. "Fraser tells me you gentlemen wanted to discuss the Rosemary Duff case," he said after a long moment. His voice was as rich and plummy as a Dickensian Christmas pudding. "I have one or two questions for you first." He glanced down at a piece of paper. "Alex Gilbey and Tom Mackie. Is that right?"

"That's right," Alex said.

"And you're not journalists?"

Alex fished out his business card and passed it over. "I run a company that makes greetings cards. Tom is a minister. We're not journalists."

Soanes scrutinized the card, tilting it to check the embossing was real. He raised one bushy white eyebrow. "What is your interest in the Rosemary Duff case?" he asked abruptly.

Weird leaned forward. "We are two of the four guys who discovered her dying body in the snow twenty-five years ago. You probably had our clothes under your microscope."

Soanes inclined his head slightly to one side. The wrinkles at the corners of his eyes tightened almost imperceptibly. "That was a long time ago. Why are you here now?"

"We think we're on somebody's hit list," Weird said.

This time, both of Soanes's eyebrows rose. "You've lost me. What has that to do with me or Rosemary Duff?"

Alex put a hand on Weird's arm. "Of the four of us who were there that night, two are dead. They died within the past six weeks. They were both murdered. I know that could just be coincidence. But at both funerals, there was an identical wreath saying, 'Rosemary for remembrance.' And we believe those wreaths were sent by Rosie Duff's son."

Soanes frowned. "I think you're in the wrong place, gentlemen. You should be talking to Fife Police, who are currently conducting a review which includes this very case."

Alex shook his head. "I've already tried that. ACC Lawson as good as told me that I'm paranoid. That coincidences happen and I should go away and stop worrying. But I think he's wrong. I think someone is killing us because they're convinced we murdered Rosie. And the only way I can see to get myself off the hook is to find out who really did."

An impenetrable expression flickered across Soanes's face at the mention of Lawson's name. "All the same, I still don't quite understand what has brought you here. My personal involvement with the case ended twenty-five years ago."

"That would be because they've lost the evidence," Weird interrupted, unable to do without the sound of his own voice for long.

"I think you must be mistaken. We recently carried out some tests on an item. But our tests for DNA were negative."

"You got the cardigan," Alex said. "But the important

things, the clothes with the blood and semen on, they've gone missing."

There was no mistaking the upsurge in Soanes's interest. "They've lost the original exhibits?"

"That's what ACC Lawson told me," Alex said.

Soanes shook his head in disbelief. "Terrifying," he said. "Though not entirely astonishing under this command." His forehead wrinkled in a disapproving frown. Alex wondered what else Fife Police had done that had failed to impress Soanes. "Well, without the principal physical evidence, I'm really not sure what you think I can do to help."

Alex took a deep breath. "I know you did the original work on the case. And I understand that forensic experts don't always include every detail in their reports. I wondered if there was anything that maybe you hadn't written up at the time. I'm thinking particularly about paint. Because the one thing they haven't lost is the cardigan. And after they found that, they came and took paint samples from our house."

"And why would I tell you about anything like that, always supposing there were anything like that? It's scarcely normal practice. After all, one could say you were suspects."

"We were witnesses, not suspects," Weird said angrily. "And you should do it because if you don't and we are murdered, you'll have a difficult time squaring matters with God and your conscience."

"And because scientists are supposed to care about the truth," Alex added. *Time to go out on a limb*, he thought. "And I get the feeling that you're a man who sees truth as his province. As opposed to the police, who generally just seem to want a result."

Soanes leaned an elbow on the desk and fingered his lower lip, revealing its inner moist fleshiness. He looked at them as if he was considering long and hard. Then he sat up decisively and flipped open the cardboard folder that was the only other item on his desk. He glanced at the contents then looked up and met their expectant eyes. "My report dealt principally with blood and semen. The blood was all Rosie Duff's, the semen was assumed to belong to her killer. Because whoever deposited the semen was a secretor, we were able to establish his blood group." He flipped over a couple of pages. "There was some fiber evidence. Cheap brown industrial carpet and a couple of fibers from a charcoal-gray carpet used by several vehicle manufacturers in their mid-range cars. Some dog hairs that were compatible with the springer spaniel belonging to the landlord of the pub where she worked. All of that was covered fully in my report."

He caught Alex's look of disappointment and gave a small smile. "And then there are my notes."

He pulled out a sheaf of handwritten notes. He squinted at them for a moment, then took a pair of gold-rimmed half-moon glasses from his waistcoat pocket and perched them on his nose. "My writing has always been something of a trial," he said dryly. "I've not looked at this for years. Now, where are we . . . ? Blood . . . semen . . . mud." He turned a couple of pages covered in a tiny, dense script. "Hairs . . . Here we go—paint." He stabbed the page with a finger. He looked up. "What do you know about paint?"

"Emulsion for walls, gloss for woodwork," Weird said. "That's what I know about paint."

Soanes smiled for the first time. "Paint consists of three principal components. There's the carrier, which is normally some sort of polymer. That's the solid stuff that ends up on your overalls if you don't clean it off straight away. Then there's the solvent, which is usually an organic liquid. The carrier is dissolved in the solvent to create a coating with a consistency suitable for a brush or roller. The solvent seldom has any forensic significance because it will usually have evaporated long since. Finally, there's the pigment, which is what gives the color. Among the most commonly used pigments are titanium dioxide and zinc oxide for white, phthalocyanines for blue, zinc chromate for yellow and copper oxide for red. But every batch of paint has its own microscopic signature. So it's possible to analyze a paint stain and say what kind of paint it is. There are whole libraries of paint samples that we can compare individual examples to.

"And of course, as well as the paint itself, we look at the physical stain. Is it a spatter? Is it a drop? Is it a scraping?" He held up his finger. "Before you ask anymore, I'm no expert here. This is not my area of specialism."

"You could have fooled me," Weird said. "So what do your notes say about the paint on Rosie's cardie?"

"Your friend does like to get to the point, does he not?" Soanes said to Alex, thankfully more amused than irritated.

"We know how valuable your time is, that's all," Alex said, wincing inside at his sycophancy.

Soanes returned to his notes. "True," he said. "The paint in question was a pale blue aliphatic polyurethane enamel. Not a common house paint. More the sort of thing you'd find on a boat, or something made of fiberglass. We didn't get any direct matches, though it did resemble a couple of marine paints in our reference library. What was most interesting about it was the profile of the droplets. They were shaped like minuscule teardrops."

Alex frowned. "What does that mean?"

"It means that the paint wasn't wet when it made its way on to the clothing. These were tiny, tiny drops of dried paint that were undoubtedly transferred to her clothes from a surface on which she was lying. Probably a carpet."

"So somebody had been painting something in the place where she was lying? And they'd got paint on the carpet?" Weird asked.

"Almost certainly. But I have to come back to the odd shape. If paint drips from a brush, or spatters on a carpet, the droplets would not look like this. And all of the droplets we looked at in this case shared the same profile."

"Why didn't you put all that in your report?" Alex asked.

"Because we couldn't explain it. It's very dangerous to the prosecution case to have an expert witness in the box answering, 'I don't know.' A good defense advocate would leave the questions about the paint to last, so what the jury would remember most clearly would have been my boss shaking his head and admitting he didn't know the answers." Soanes pushed his papers back into the folder. "So we left it out."

Now for the only question that mattered, thought Alex. "If you looked at that evidence again, would you be able to come up with a different answer?"

Soanes gazed at him over his glasses. "Me personally? No. But a forensic paint expert might well be able to provide a more useful analysis. Of course, your chances of finding a match twenty-five years later is negligible."

"That's our problem," Weird said. "Can you do it? Will you do it?"

Soanes shook his head. "As I said, I'm very far from being an expert in the area. But even if I were, I couldn't authorize tests without a request from Fife Police. And they didn't ask for tests on the paint." He closed his folder with an air of finality.

"Why not?" Weird asked.

"I would presume because they thought it was a waste of money. As I said, the chances of finding a match at this late stage are infinitesimal."

Alex slumped down in his chair, deflated. "And I'm not going to be able to change Lawson's mind. Great. I think you just signed my death warrant."

"I didn't say it was impossible to have some tests conducted," Soanes said gently. "What I said was that they couldn't be conducted here."

"How can they be conducted anywhere else?" Weird said belligerently. "Nobody's got any samples."

Soanes pulled at his lip again. Then he sighed. "We don't have any of the biological samples. But we do still have the paint. I checked before you came." He opened the folder again and took out a plastic sheet divided into pockets. Tucked inside were a dozen microscope slides. Soanes removed three of them and lined them up on the desk. Alex stared down at them hungrily. He couldn't quite believe his eyes. The specks of paint were like tiny flakes of blue cigarette ash.

"Somebody could analyze these?" he said, barely daring to hope.

"Of course," Soanes said. He took a paper bag from his drawer and placed it on top of the slides, pushing them a little closer to Alex and Weird. "Take them. We have others we can analyze independently, should anything come of it. You'll need to sign for them, of course."

Weird's hand snaked out and enveloped the slides. He gently put them in the bag and slid it into his pocket. "Thanks," he said. "Where do I sign?"

As Weird scribbled his name on the bottom of a log sheet, Alex looked curiously at Soanes. "Why are you doing this?" he said.

Soanes took off his glasses and put them away carefully. "Because I hate unsolved puzzles," he said, getting to his feet. "Almost as much as I hate sloppy police work. And besides, I should hate to have your deaths on my conscience should your theory prove correct."

"Why are we turning off?" Weird asked as they hit the outskirts of Glenrothes and Alex signaled a right turn.

"I want to tell Lawson about Macfadyen sending the wreaths. And I want to try and persuade him to get Soanes to test the samples he's got."

"Waste of time," Weird grunted.

"No more than going back to St. Monans to knock on the door of an empty house."

Weird said nothing more, letting Alex drive to police headquarters. At the front desk, Alex asked to see Lawson. "It's in connection with the Rosemary Duff case," he said. They were directed to a waiting area, where they sat reading the posters about Colorado Beetle, missing persons and domestic violence. "Amazing how it makes you feel guilty, just being here," Alex muttered.

"Not me," Weird said. "But then, I answer to a higher authority."

After a few minutes, a stocky woman came across to them. "I'm DC Pirie," she said. "I'm afraid ACC Lawson is unavailable. But I'm the officer in charge of the Rosemary Duff case."

Alex shook his head. "I want to see Lawson. I'll wait."

"I'm afraid that won't be possible. He's actually on a couple of days' leave."

"Gone fishing," Weird said ironically.

Karen Pirie, caught by surprise, said, "Yes, as it happens. Loch—" before she could stop herself.

Weird looked even more surprised. "Really? I was just using a figure of speech."

Karen tried to cover her confusion. "It's Mr. Gilbey, isn't it?" she said, looking intently at Alex.

"That's right. How did you . . . ?"

"I saw you at Dr. Kerr's funeral. I'm sorry for your loss."

"That's why we're here," Weird said. "We believe the same person who killed David Kerr is planning to kill us."

Karen took a deep breath. "ACC Lawson briefed me on his meeting with Mr. Gilbey. And as he told you then," she continued, looking at Alex, "there really is no basis for your fears."

Weird gave a snort of exasperation. "What if we told you that Graham Macfadyen sent those wreaths?"

"Wreaths?" Karen seemed puzzled.

"I thought you said you'd been briefed?" Weird challenged her.

Alex intervened, wondering momentarily how the sinners coped with Weird. He told Karen about the curious floral tributes and was gratified when she appeared to take them seriously.

"That is strange, I'll grant you. But it's not an indication that Mr. Macfadyen is going around killing people."

"How else would he know about the murders?" Alex asked, genuinely seeking an answer.

"That's the question, isn't it?" Weird demanded.

"He'd have seen Dr. Kerr's death in the papers. It was widely reported. And I imagine it wouldn't be hard to find out about Mr. Malkiewicz. The Internet has made it a very small world," Karen said.

Alex felt that sinking feeling all over again. Why was everyone so resistant to what seemed obvious to him? "But why would he send the wreaths unless he thought we were responsible for his mother's death?"

"Believing you to be responsible is a long way from murder," Karen said. "I realize you feel under pressure, Mr. Gilbey. But there's nothing in what you've told me that leads me to think you're at risk."

Weird looked apoplectic. "How many of us have to die before you start to take this seriously?"

"Has anyone threatened you?"

Weird scowled. "No."

"Have you had any unexplained telephone hang-ups?"

"No."

"And have you noticed anyone hanging round your home?"

Weird looked at Alex, who shook his head.

"Then I'm sorry, there's nothing I can do."

"Yes, there is," Alex said. "You can ask for a new analysis of the paint that was found on Rosie Duff's cardigan."

Karen's eyes widened in astonishment. "How do you know about the paint?"

Frustration lent an edge to Alex's voice. "We were witnesses. Suspects, in all but name. You think we didn't notice when your colleagues scraped our walls and stuck Sellotape all over our carpets? So how about it, DC Pirie? How about actually trying to find out who killed Rosie Duff?"

Needled by his words, Karen drew herself up straight. "That's exactly what I've been doing for the past couple of months, sir. And the official view is that a paint analysis would not be cost effective, given the remoteness of the possibility of finding any sort of match after all this time."

The anger Alex had been buttoning down for days suddenly welled up in him. "Not cost effective? If there's any possibility, you should pursue it," he shouted. "It's not as if you've got any other expensive forensic testing to do, is it? Not now you've lost the only evidence that might finally have cleared our names. Do you have any idea what you people did to us back then because of your incompetence? You tainted our lives. He got beaten up—" He pointed at Weird. "Ziggy got dumped down the Bottle Dungeon. He could have died. Mondo tried to kill himself, and Barney Maclennan died because of it. And if Jimmy Lawson hadn't come along at the right moment, I would have had the crap beaten out of me, too. So don't stand here and talk to me about cost effectiveness. Just do your bloody job." Alex turned on his heel and marched out.

Weird stood his ground, not taking his eyes off Karen Pirie. "You heard the man," he said. "Tell Jimmy Lawson to reel in his line and keep us alive."

CHAPTER
THIRTY-EIGHT

James Lawson slit open the belly and plunged his hand into the cavity, his fingers closing on the slippery guts. His lips twisted into a moue of distaste, the slithering of vital organs against his skin an offense against his basic fastidiousness. He drew the entrails out, making sure the blood and mucus stayed within the confines of the newspaper he'd spread out in preparation. Then he added the trout to the other three he'd caught that afternoon.

Not a bad result for the time of year, he thought. He'd fry a couple for his tea and put the others in the caravan's tiny fridge. They'd make a good breakfast before he set out for work in the morning. He got up and switched on the pump that supplied the little sink with a stream of cold water. He reminded himself to bring a couple of replacement five-gallon bottles the next time he came out to his bolthole on the shores of Loch Leven. He'd emptied the spare into the tank that morning, and although he could always rely on the local farmer who rented him the pitch in an emergency, Lawson didn't like to impose on his goodwill. He'd always kept to himself in the twenty years since he'd moved the caravan up here. That was the way he liked it. Just him and the radio and a pile of thrillers. A private place where he could escape the pressures of work and family life, a place to renew his energies.

He opened a tin of new potatoes, drained them and diced them. While he waited for the big frying pan to heat up for the fish and potatoes, he folded the newspaper fussily around the fish guts and thrust it into a plastic bag. He'd add the skin and bones after his meal, then tie the handles tightly and leave it on the caravan steps for removal in the morning. There was nothing worse than sleeping in the stink of the detritus of his catch.

Lawson dumped a chunk of lard in the pan, watched it sizzle into translucency then added the potatoes. He stirred them around, then, as they started to brown, he carefully placed the two trout in the pan, adding a squeeze of juice from a Jif lemon. The familiar sizzle and crackle cheered him up, the smell a promise of the delight to come. When it was done, he tipped his meal onto a plate and settled in at the table to enjoy his dinner. Perfect timing. The familiar theme tune of *The Archers* bounded out of the radio as his knife slid under the crispy skin of the first trout.

He was halfway through his meal when he heard something he shouldn't have. A car door slammed. The radio had covered the sound of the approaching engine, but the closing of the door was loud enough to be heard over the everyday story of country folk. Lawson froze momentarily then reached for the radio and turned it off, straining his ears to catch any sound from outside. Stealthily, he eased the curtain back a fraction. Just beyond the gate into the field, he could make out the shape of a car. Small- to medium-sized hatchback, he thought. A Golf, an Astra, a Focus. Something like that. It was hard to be more accurate in the dark. He scanned the gap between the gate and his caravan. No movement.

The rap at the door made his heart leap in his chest. Who the hell was this? As far as he was aware, the only people who knew exactly where his fishing lair was were the farmer and his wife. He'd never brought colleagues or friends here. When they'd gone fishing, he'd met them farther along the shore in his boat, determined to maintain his privacy.

"Just a minute," he shouted, rising to his feet and moving toward the door, pausing only to palm his razor-sharp gutting knife. There were plenty of criminals who might feel they had a score to settle, and he wasn't going to be caught unprotected. Keeping one foot behind the door, he opened it a crack.

In the sliver of light that spilled out on to the steps stood Graham Macfadyen. It took Lawson a moment to recognize him. Since their last meeting, he'd lost weight. His eyes burned feverish above hollow cheeks and his hair was lank and greasy. "What the hell are you doing here?" Lawson demanded.

"I need to talk to you. They said you were having a couple of days off, so I thought you must be here." Macfadyen's tone was matter-of-fact, as if there were nothing unusual about a member of the public turning up on the doorstep of the Assistant Chief Constable's fishing caravan.

"How the hell did you find me here?" Lawson demanded, anxiety making him belligerent.

Macfadyen shrugged. "You can find out anything these days. You gave an interview to the *Fife Record* last time you were promoted. It's on their Web site. You said you liked fishing, that you had a place up at Loch Leven. There's not many roads that go close to the waterside. I just drove around till I spotted your car."

There was something in his manner that chilled Lawson to the bone. "This isn't appropriate," he said. "Come and see me at the office if you want to discuss police business."

Macfadyen looked annoyed. "This is important. It won't wait. And I'm not talking to anybody else. You understand my position. You're the one I need to talk to. I'm here now. So why not listen to me? You need to listen to me, I'm the man who can help you."

Lawson started to close the door, but Macfadyen raised a hand and pressed against it. "I'll stand outside and shout if you won't let me in," he said. The nonchalance of his tone was at odds with the determination in his face.

Lawson weighed up the odds. Macfadyen didn't strike him as potentially violent. But you never knew. However, he did have the knife if it came to it. Better to hear the man out and get rid of him. He let the door swing open and stepped back, never turning his back on his unwelcome visitor.

Macfadyen followed him inside. In a dislocating perversion of normal discourse, he grinned and said, "You've made it very cozy in here." Then his glance fell on the table and he looked apologetic. "I've disturbed you at your tea. I'm really sorry."

"It's OK," Lawson lied. "What was it you wanted to talk to me about?"

"They're gathering. They're huddling together to try to avoid their fate," Macfadyen said, as if it were an explanation.

"Who's gathering?" Lawson asked.

Macfadyen sighed, as if frustrated at dealing with a particularly slow trainee. "My mother's killers," he said. "Mackie's back. He's moved in with Gilbey. It's the only way they feel safe. But they're wrong, of course. That won't protect them. I never believed in fate before, but there's no other way to describe what's happened to that foursome lately. Gilbey and Mackie must feel it, too. They must be afraid time is running out for them like it has for their friends. And of course, it is. Unless they pay the proper price. Them coming together like this—it's a confession. You must see that."

"You might well be right," Lawson said, going for conciliation. "But it's not the sort of confession that works in a court of law."

"I know that," Macfadyen said impatiently. "But they're at their most vulnerable. They're afraid. It's time to use that weakness to drive a wedge between them. You have to arrest them now, make them tell you the truth. I've been watching them. They could crack at any time."

"We've no evidence," Lawson said.

"They'll confess. What more evidence do you need?" Macfadyen never took his eyes from the policeman.

"People often think that. But in Scots law, a confession on its own isn't enough to convict someone. There needs to be corroborative evidence."

"That can't be right," Macfadyen protested.

"It's the law."

"You've got to do something. Get them to confess, then find the evidence that will make it stand up in court. That's your job," Macfadyen said, his voice rising.

Lawson shook his head. "That's not how it works. Look, I promise I'll go and talk to Mackie and Gilbey. But that's all I can do."

Macfadyen clenched his right hand into a fist. "You don't care, do you? Not any of you."

"Yes, I do care," Lawson said. "But I have to operate inside the law. And so do you, sir."

Macfadyen made a strange noise in the back of his throat, like a dog choking on a chicken bone. "You were supposed to understand," he said coldly, grabbing the door handle and pulling it open. The door swung right back and banged against the wall.

Then he was gone, swallowed by the darkness outside. The damp chill of the night invaded the cozy fug of the caravan, smothering the smell of stale cooking and replacing it with the tang of marshes. Lawson stood in the doorway long after Graham Macfadyen's car had reversed erratically up the track, his eyes dark pools of worry.

Lynn was their ticket into Jason McAllister. And she wasn't leaving Davina with anyone, not even Alex. And that was why what should have been an easy forenoon run out to Bridge of Allan had turned into a major operation. It was amazing what had to travel with a baby, Alex thought as he made his third and final trip to the car, listing under the combined weight of the baby seat and Davina. Buggy. Backpack containing nappies, wipes, muslin squares, two changes of clothes just in case. Spare blankets, also just in case. A clean jumper for Lynn, because projectile vomit didn't always land on the muslin square. The baby sling. He was mildly amazed he'd gotten away with leaving the kitchen sink plumbed in.

He threaded the rear seatbelt through the restraints on the portable seat and tested its security. He'd never worried about the strength of seatbelts before, but now he found himself wondering just how reliable they might be under impact. He leaned into the car, straightened Davina's fleece hat and kissed his sleeping daughter, then held his breath in apprehension as she stirred. Please let her not scream all the way to Bridge of Allan, he prayed. He didn't think he could cope with the guilt.

Lynn and Weird joined him and they all piled into the car. A few minutes later they were on the motorway. Weird tapped him on the shoulder. "You're supposed to go faster than forty miles an hour on a motorway," he said. "We're going to be late."

Stifling his concerns for his valuable cargo, Alex obediently put his foot down. He was every bit as keen as Weird to drive their investigation forward. Jason McAllister sounded just the man to take them the next part of the journey. Lynn's work as a restorer of paintings for the national galleries of Scotland meant she'd become an expert in the sort of paint that artists used at different periods. It also meant she'd had to find her own expert who could analyze the samples from the original so she could make her match as accurate as possible. And of course there were times when there were question marks over the authenticity of a particular work of art. Then the paint samples had to be evaluated to check whether they were from the right time frame and whether they were consistent with the materials used by the same painter in other works whose provenance was not in doubt. The man she'd found to do the scientific end of the investigations was Jason McAllister.

He worked in a private forensic lab near Stirling University. Most of his working life was spent analyzing paint fragments from road-traffic accidents, either for the police or for insurance companies. Occasionally he'd have an interesting diversion into murder, rape or serious assault, but that happened too seldom to provide enough variation for Jason's talents.

At a private preview of a Poussin exhibition, he'd tracked Lynn down and told her he was passionate about paint. At first, she'd thought this slightly geeky young man was being pretentious, claiming kinship with great art. Then she'd realized he meant precisely what he'd said. No more, no less. What infused him with enthusiasm was not what was depicted on the canvas; it was the structure of the stuff used to make the painting. He gave her his card and made her promise she'd call him the next time she had a problem. He assured her several times that he'd be better than whoever she was using.

As it happened, Jason had struck lucky that night. Lynn was fed up with the pompous prat she'd previously been forced to rely on. He was one of the Edinburgh old school who couldn't stop themselves condescending to women. Even though his status was effectively that of a lab technician, he treated Lynn as if she was a menial whose opinion was of no importance. With a major restoration on the horizon, Lynn had been dreading working with him again. Jason felt like a gift from the gods. Right from the start, there had never been any question of him talking down to her. If anything, the problem was the opposite. He tended to assume she was his equal, and she'd lost count of the times she'd had to tell him to slow down and speak in something approaching English. But that was infinitely preferable to the alternative.

When Alex and Weird had come home with the bag of paint samples, Lynn had been on the phone to Jason within ten minutes. As she'd expected, he'd reacted like a child who's just been told he's spending the summer at Disneyland. "I've got a meeting first thing, but I'll be clear of that by ten."

As Alex had suggested, she'd tried to tell him they'd pay his fee privately. But he'd waved away her offer. "What are pals for?" he'd demanded. "Besides, I'm up to my back teeth with car paint. You'll be saving me from dying of boredom. Bring it on, woman."

The lab was a surprisingly attractive modern single-story building set off the main road in its own grounds. The windows were set high up in the brown brick walls, and CCTV cameras covered every angle of approach. They had to be buzzed through two sets of security doors before they reached the reception. "I've been in prisons with less security," Weird commented. "What do they do here? Manufacture weapons of mass destruction?"

"They do freelance forensic work for the Crown Office. And for the defense," Lynn explained as they waited for Jason to join them. "So they've got to be able to demonstrate that any evidence they take custody of will be held securely."

"So they do DNA and all that?" Alex asked.

"Why? Are you having doubts about your paternity?" Lynn teased him.

"I'll wait till she turns into the teenager from hell for that," Alex said. "No, I'm just curious."

"They do DNA and they do hair and fiber evidence as well as paint," Lynn told him. As she spoke, a burly man approached and clapped an arm round her shoulder.

"You brought the baby," he said, leaning over to peer into the carrier. "Hey, she's gorgeous." He grinned up at Lynn. "Most babies look like the dog sat on their faces. But she looks like a proper wee person." He straightened up. "I'm Jason," he said, looking uncertainly from Weird to Alex.

They introduced themselves. Alex took in the Stirling Albion shirt, the cargo pants with bulging pockets and the spiked hair, its tips bleached a blond never found in nature. On the surface, Jason looked as if he'd be home in any Friday-night pub, bottle of designer lager in his hand. But his eyes were sharp and watchful, his body still and controlled. "Come away through," Jason instructed them. "Here, let me carry the baby," he added, reaching for the carrier. "She is a beauty."

"You might not say that at three in the morning," Lynn said, her maternal pride obvious.

"Maybe not. By the way, I was sorry to hear about your brother," he said, glancing awkwardly over his shoulder at Lynn. "That must have been hellish."

"It's not been easy," Lynn said as they followed Jason down a narrow corridor, the walls painted eggshell blue. At the end, Jason led them into a daunting laboratory. Mysterious equipment gleamed in every corner. Worktops were neat and tidy, and the technician peering down the barrel of something Alex thought might be a futuristic microscope didn't move a muscle as they bustled in. "I feel like I'm contaminating the place just by breathing," he said.

"It's less of an issue with paint," Jason said. "If I was in DNA, you'd be getting nowhere near the sharp end. So, tell me again exactly what it is you've got for me."

Alex ran through what Soanes had revealed the previous afternoon. "Soanes thinks there's not much chance of finding a match for the paint, but maybe you can tell something new from the shape of the drops," he added.

Jason peered at the slides. "Looks like they've kept them in good condition, which is a plus."

"What is it you'll do with them?" Weird asked.

Lynn groaned. "I wish you hadn't said that."

Jason laughed. "Ignore her, she just likes to pretend she's ignorant. We've got a range of techniques that analyze the carrier and pigment. As well as using microspectrophotometry to establish the color, we can go more in-depth to nail down the composition of the paint samples. Fourier Transform Infrared Spectrometry, Pyrolysis Gas Chromatography and Scanning Electron Microscopy. Stuff like that."

Weird looked dazed. "Which tells you what?" Alex asked.

"Lots of things. If it's a chip, what type of surface it came from. With car paint, we analyze the different layers and we've got a database we can refer to and discover the make, model and year of manufacture. With droplets, we can do pretty much the same, though of course we don't get the surface details because the paint was never stuck to a surface."

"How long is all of this going to take?" Weird asked. "Only, we're kind of up against it, time-wise."

"I'll be doing it in my own time. A couple of days? I'll be as quick as I can. But I don't want to do anything less than the best possible job. If you're right about this, we could all end up in court testifying about it, and I'm not taking any shortcuts. I'm also going to give you a receipt to say I got these samples from you, just in case anybody tries to say otherwise somewhere down the line."

"Thanks, Jason," Lynn said. "I owe you."

He grinned. "I do like that in a woman."

CHAPTER
THIRTY-NINE

Jackie Donaldson had written on occasion about the knock on the door in the early hours, the hustle to the waiting po- .lice car, the fast drive through empty streets and the utterly unnerving wait in a cramped room that tasted of other people. It had never crossed her mind that one day she'd be experiencing it rather than chronicling it.

She'd been woken from sleep by the intercom's buzzing. She'd registered the time—03:47—then stumbled to the door, dragging her dressing gown on. When Detective Sergeant Darren Heggie had announced himself, her first thought was that something terrible had happened to Hélène. She couldn't understand why he was demanding to be let in at this hour. But she didn't argue. She knew that would be a waste of time.

Heggie had clattered into her flat with a woman in plain-clothes and two uniformed officers, who shuffled in at the rear looking faintly uncomfortable. Heggie wasted no time on small talk. "Jacqueline Donaldson, I am detaining you on suspicion of conspiracy to murder. You can be detained for up to six hours without arrest, and you have the right to communicate with a solicitor. You do not have to say anything other than your name and address. Do you understand the reason for your detention?"

She gave a small, scornful snort. "I understand you've got the right. But I don't understand *why* you're doing this."

Jackie had disliked Heggie on sight. His pointed chin, his small eyes, his bad haircut, his cheap suit and his swagger. But he had been polite, even somewhat apologetic at their previous encounters. Now, he was all brusque efficiency. "Please get dressed. The female officer will remain with you. We will wait outside." Heggie turned away and shooed the uniformed men on to the landing.

Discomfited but determined not to show it, Jackie returned to the sleeping area of the apartment. She grabbed the first T-shirt and jumper in the drawer and snatched up a pair of jeans from the chair. Then she dropped them. If this all went wrong, she could be appearing in front of a sheriff before she got the chance to change. She rummaged in the back of her wardrobe for her one decent suit. Jackie turned her back to the woman officer, who refused to take her eyes off her, and dressed. "I need to go to the bathroom," she said.

"You'll have to leave the door open," the woman said stolidly.

"You think I'm going to shoot up or something?"

"It's for your own protection," she replied, sounding bored.

Jackie did what she had to, then slicked her hair back with a handful of cold water. She looked into the mirror, wondering when she'd be able to do that again. Now she knew what those she'd written about had felt. And it was horrible. Her stomach jittered as if she hadn't slept for days and her breath seemed to catch in her throat. "When do I get to call my lawyer?" she asked.

"When we get to the police station," came the reply.

Half an hour later, she was shut in a small room with Tony Donatello, a third-generation criminal solicitor she'd known since her first months as a reporter in Glasgow. They were more accustomed to meeting in bars than in cells, but Tony had the grace not to say so. He was also sensitive enough not to remind her that the last time he'd represented her at a police station, she'd ended up with a record. "They want to question you about David's death," he said. "But I suppose you'd worked that out for yourself?"

"It's the only murder I've been remotely connected to. Did you call Hélène?"

Tony gave a small, dry cough. "Turns out they've lifted her, too."

"I should have figured that out for myself. So, what's our strategy?"

"Is there anything that you've done in the recent past that could be misconstrued as connecting to David's death?" Tony asked.

Jackie shook her head. "Nothing. This is not some sleazy conspiracy, Tony. Hélène and I had nothing to do with David's murder."

"Jackie, you don't speak for Hélène here. You're my client and it's your actions I'm concerned with. If there's anything at all—a chance remark, a flippant e-mail, whatever—that might make you look bad, then we won't answer any questions. Just stonewall. But if you're certain there's nothing you have to worry about, we'll answer. What's it to be?"

Jackie fiddled with her eyebrow ring. "Look, there's something you should know. I wasn't with Hélène the whole time. I nipped out for an hour or so. I had to go out and see somebody. I can't say who it was, but take it from me, he's not alibi material."

Tony looked worried. "That's not good," he said. "Maybe you should go 'no comment.'"

"I don't want to. You know how bad it'll make me look."

"It's your decision. But, in the circumstances, I think silence would be the better option."

Jackie thought long and hard. She didn't see how the police could know about her absence. "I'll talk to them," she said finally.

The interview room held no surprises for anyone versed in the grammar of TV cop drama. Jackie and Tony sat opposite Heggie and the female detective who had accompanied him to the flat. At this proximity, Heggie's aftershave smelled rancid. Two cassettes spooled in tandem in the machine at the end of the table. After the formalities were over,

Heggie dived straight in. "How long have you known Hélène Kerr?"

"About four years. I met her and her husband at a party given by a mutual friend."

"What is the nature of your relationship?"

"First and foremost, we are friends. We are also occasional lovers."

"How long have you been lovers?" Heggie's eyes looked hungry, as if the thought of Jackie and Hélène together was potentially as satisfying as any criminal confession.

"For about two years."

"And how often did this take place?"

"We spent an evening together most weeks. We had sex on most of those occasions. Though not always. As I said, friendship is the most important component of our relationship." Jackie found it harder than she'd expected to stay cool and clinical under the assessing gaze of her interrogators. But she knew she had to stay calm; any outburst would be interpreted as evidence of something more than nerves.

"Did David Kerr know you were sleeping with his wife?"

"I don't believe so."

"It must have been galling for you that she stayed with him," Heggie offered.

A shrewd observation, she thought. And one that was uncomfortably close to the truth. Scratch the surface, and Jackie knew she wasn't sorry David Kerr was dead. She loved Hélène and she was bitterly tired of the scraps her lover granted her. She'd wanted a lot more for a long time. "I knew from the word go she wasn't going to leave her husband. That was fine by me."

"I find that hard to believe," he said. "You were being rejected in favor of her husband and it didn't bother you?"

"It wasn't a rejection. The arrangement suited both of us." Jackie leaned forward, aiming for open body language to fake candor. "Just a bit of fun. I like my freedom. I don't want to be tied down."

"Really?" He looked at his notes. "So the neighbor that

heard the pair of you screaming and fighting because she wouldn't leave her husband is lying?"

Jackie remembered the row. There had been few enough in their time together for it to be memorable. A couple of months before, she'd asked Hélène to come to a friend's fortieth birthday party. Hélène had looked at her in disbelief. It was outside the ground rules, not a subject they should even be discussing. All Jackie's frustrations had overflowed and a blazing argument had erupted. It had changed tack abruptly when Hélène had threatened to walk out and never come back. That was a prospect Jackie couldn't endure, and she'd surrendered. But she wasn't about to share any of that with Heggie and his sidekick. "They must be," she said. "You can't hear a bloody thing through the walls of those lofts."

"Apparently you can if the windows are open," Heggie said.

"When is this alleged conversation supposed to have taken place?" Tony interrupted.

Another glance at the notes. "Toward the end of November."

"Are you seriously suggesting that my client had her windows open at the end of November in Glasgow?" he said scornfully. "Is that all you've got? Gossip and tittle-tattle from nosy and overimaginative neighbors?"

Heggie stared at him for a long moment before he spoke. "Your client has a history of violence."

"No, she doesn't. She has one conviction for assaulting a police officer while she was reporting an anti–poll tax demonstration where one of your colleagues enthusiastically mistook her for one of the demonstrators. That's hardly a history of violence."

"She punched a policeman in the face."

"After he'd dragged her along the ground by the hair. If it had been that violent an assault on a police officer, do you not think the sheriff would have given her more than six months probation? If you've nothing more than this, I don't see you have any reason to hold my client."

Heggie glared at them both. "You were with Mrs. Kerr on the night her husband died?"

"That's right," Jackie said cautiously. This was where the thin ice started. "It was our usual night for seeing each other. She arrived about half-past six. We ate a fish supper I went out for, we drank some wine and we went to bed. She left around eleven. Exactly as usual."

"Can anyone verify that?"

Jackie raised her eyebrows. "I don't know about you, Inspector, but when I make love with someone, I don't invite the neighbors round. The phone rang a couple of times, but I didn't answer it."

"We have a witness who claims to have seen you walking to your car at approximately nine P.M. that evening," Heggie said triumphantly.

"They must have got the wrong night," Jackie said. "I was with Hélène all evening. Is this another one of my homophobic neighbors you've been coaching in incriminating testimony?"

Tony shifted in his chair. "You've heard my client's answer. If you've got nothing new to bring to the table, I really do suggest we end this now."

Heggie breathed heavily. "If you'll bear with me, Mr. Donatello, I'd like to introduce a witness statement we took yesterday."

"Can I see that?" Tony asked.

"All in good time. Denise?"

The other detective opened a folder she'd held on her lap and placed a sheet of paper in front of him. Heggie licked his lips and spoke. "We arrested a small-time drug dealer yesterday. He was eager to offer up anything that might lead us to view his case in a more favorable light. Ms. Donaldson, do you know Gary Hardie?"

Jackie's heart jolted in her chest. What did this have to do with anything? It hadn't been Gary Hardie she'd met that night, nor any of his buddies. "I know who he is," she stalled. Hardly an admission; anyone who read a newspaper or watched TV in Scotland would have recognized the name.

A few weeks previously, Gary Hardie had sensationally walked free from the High Court in Glasgow after one of the highest-profile murder cases the city had seen for some years. In the course of the trial, he'd been variously called a drug lord, a man with no regard for human life, and an utterly ruthless criminal mastermind. Among the allegations the jury had heard was the claim that he had paid a hitman to have a business rival eliminated.

"Have you ever met Gary Hardie?"

Jackie felt sweat in the small of her back. "In a purely professional context, yes."

"Would that be your profession or his?" Heggie demanded, shifting his chair closer to the table.

Jackie rolled her eyes in derision. "Oh, please, Inspector. I am a journalist. It's my job to talk to people in the news."

"How many times have you met Gary Hardie?" Heggie pressed her.

Jackie breathed out through her nose. "Three times. I interviewed him a year ago for a feature I wrote for a magazine about contemporary Glasgow gangland. I interviewed him while he was awaiting trial for an article I planned to write after the trial was over. And I had a drink with him a couple of weeks ago. It's important to me to maintain contacts. That's how I get stories that nobody else gets."

Heggie looked skeptical. He glanced down at the statement. "Where did that meeting take place?"

"In Ramblas. It's a café bar in . . ."

"I know where Ramblas is," Heggie interrupted. He glanced again at the paper in front of him. "At that meeting, an envelope changed hands. From you to Hardie. A bulky envelope, Ms. Donaldson. Would you care to tell us what was in that envelope?"

Jackie tried not to show her shock. Tony stirred at her side. "I'd like to speak to my client in private," he said hastily.

"No, it's OK, Tony," Jackie said. "I have nothing to hide. When I spoke to Gary to arrange the meeting, he told me someone had shown him the magazine article, and he'd liked the photograph they'd used. He wanted some copies for himself. So I had prints made and I took them to Ramblas with me. If you don't believe me, you can check with the photo lab. They don't process much black and white. They might remember. I also have the receipt in my accounts file."

Tony leaned in. "You see, Inspector? Nothing sinister. Just a journalist trying to keep a good contact happy. If that's the extent of your new material, then there is no reason for my client to be held here a moment longer."

Heggie looked mildly put out. "Did you ask Gary Hardie to have David Kerr killed?" he asked.

Jackie shook her head. "No."

"Did you ask Gary Hardie if he could put you in touch with someone who would murder David Kerr?"

"No. It never crossed my mind." Jackie's head was up now, chin out, fear battened down.

"You never once thought how much more pleasant life would be without David Kerr? And how easily you could arrange that?"

"This is bullshit." She slammed her hands palm down on the table. "Why are you wasting your time with me when you should be doing your job?"

"I am doing my job," Heggie said calmly. "That's why you're here."

Tony glanced at his watch. "Not for much longer, Inspector. Either arrest my client or let her go. This interview is over." He placed a hand over Jackie's.

A minute feels like a very long time in a police interview room. Heggie held the pause, his eyes never leaving Jackie. Then he pushed his chair back. "Interview terminated at six twenty-five. You're free to go," he said, his voice grudging. He hit the button that switched off the tape recorders. "I don't believe you, Ms. Donaldson," he said as he got to his feet. "I think you and Hélène Kerr conspired to have David Kerr killed. I think you wanted her for yourself. I think you went out that night to pay off your hitman. And that's what I intend to prove." At the door, he turned back. "This is just the beginning."

As the door closed behind the detectives, Jackie covered her face with her hands. "Jesus Christ," she said.

Tony gathered his things together, then put an arm round her shoulders. "You handled that well. They've got nothing."

"I've seen people tried on thinner evidence. They've got their teeth into this. They're not going to stop till they've got somebody who can put me outside my flat that night. Jesus. I can't believe Gary Hardie came out of the woodwork just now."

"I wish you'd mentioned that to me before," Tony said, loosening his tie and stretching.

"I'm sorry. I'd no idea it was going to come up. It's not like I think about Gary Hardie every day. And it's not like he had anything to do with this. You do believe me, don't you, Tony?" She looked anxious. If she couldn't convince her lawyer, she stood no chance against the police.

"What I believe doesn't matter. It's what they can prove. And right now, they've got nothing that a good advocate wouldn't demolish in minutes." He yawned. "Great way to spend the night, eh?"

Jackie stood up. "Let's get out of this shithole. Even the air feels contaminated."

Tony grinned. "Somebody should give Heggie a decent bottle of aftershave for his next birthday. Whatever he was wearing smelled like a polecat in heat."

"It would take more than Paco Rabane to grant him membership to the human race," Jackie snarled. "Are they holding Hélène here, too?"

"No." Tony took a deep breath. "It's probably a good idea if you two don't see much of each other just now."

Jackie gave him a look that mingled hurt and disappointment. "Why not?"

"Because if you stay away from each other, it's harder to demonstrate that you're in cahoots. Being together might look as if you're discussing strategies to keep your stories straight."

"That's stupid," she said firmly. "We're friends, for fuck's sake. Lovers. Where else do you go for support and comfort? If we avoid each other, it looks as if we've got something to be uncomfortable about. If Hélène wants me, she's got me. No question."

He shrugged. "Your choice. You pay for the advice whether you take it or not." He opened the door and ushered her out into the corridor. Jackie signed for the return of her belongings, and they made for the exit together.

Tony pushed open the doors that led to the street then stopped short. In spite of the earliness of the hour, three cameramen and a handful of journalists were huddled on the pavement. As soon as they saw Jackie, the cries went up. "Hey, Jackie, have they arrested you?" "Did you and your girlfriend hire a hitman, Jackie?" "What's it feel like to be a murder suspect, Jackie?"

It was the kind of scene she'd participated in countless times, though never from this perspective. Jackie had thought nothing could feel worse than being rousted from her bed in the middle of the night and treated like a criminal by the police. Now she knew she was wrong. Betrayal, she had just discovered, tasted infinitely more bitter.

CHAPTER
FORTY

The darkness of Graham Macfadyen's study was kept at bay by the ghostly light of monitors. On the two screens he wasn't using at that moment, screensavers showed a slideshow of images he'd scanned into his computer. Grainy newspaper photographs of his mother; moody shots of Hallow Hill; the gravestone in Western Cemetery; and the photographs he'd snatched of Alex and Weird in recent days.

Macfadyen sat at his PC, composing a document. He'd originally planned simply to make a formal complaint about the inaction of Lawson and his officers. But a trip to the Web site of the Scottish Executive had demonstrated the futility of that. Any complaint he made would be investigated by Fife Police themselves, and they were hardly going to criticize the actions of their Assistant Chief Constable. He wanted satisfaction, not to be fobbed off.

So he'd decided to lay out the whole story and send copies to his Westminster MP, his MSP and to every major news medium in Scotland. But the more he wrote, the more he began to worry that he'd just be dismissed as another conspiracy theorist. Or worse.

Macfadyen chewed the skin round his fingernails and considered what he should do. He'd finish writing his devastating critique of the incompetence of Fife Police and their refusal to take seriously the presence of a pair of murderers on their patch. But he needed something else that would make people sit up and take notice. Something that would make it impossible to ignore his complaints or to disregard the way that fate had pointed an undeniable finger at the culprits in his mother's murder.

Two deaths should have been enough to produce the result he craved. But people were so blind. They couldn't see what was staring them in the face. After all this, justice still had not been served.

And he remained the only person in a position to see that it was.

The house was beginning to feel like a refugee camp. Alex was accustomed to the flow of life that he and Lynn had developed over the years: companionable meals, walks along the shore, visits to exhibitions and movies, socializing occasionally with friends. He acknowledged a lot of people would think them dull, but he knew better. He liked his life. He'd understood that things would change with the arrival of a baby, and he welcomed that change wholeheartedly, in spite of not knowing all it might mean. What he hadn't bargained for was Weird in the spare room. Nor the arrival of Hélène and Jackie, the one distraught and the other incandescent with rage. He felt invaded, so buffeted by everyone else's pain and anger that he no longer knew what he himself felt.

He'd been stunned to find the two women on the doorstep looking for sanctuary from the press camped outside their homes. How could they have imagined they'd be welcome here? Lynn's first instinct had been to tell them to check into an hotel, but Jackie had been adamant that this was the one place nobody would be looking for them. Just like Weird, he'd thought wearily.

Hélène had burst into tears and apologized for betraying Mondo. Jackie had reminded Lynn forcefully that she'd been willing to take a chance and help Alex. And still Lynn had been insistent that there was no place for them there.

Then Davina had started wailing. And Lynn had shut the door in their faces and stormed off to her child, giving Alex a look that dared him to let the two women in. Weird slipped past him and caught up with them as they were getting into their car. When he returned an hour later, he revealed he'd booked them into a nearby motel under his name. "They've got a wee chalet in among the trees," he'd reported. "Nobody knows they're there. They'll be fine."

Weird's apparent chivalry had got the evening off to an awkward start, but their common purpose gradually overcame their discomfort, assisted by liberal quantities of wine. The three adults sat round the kitchen table, blinds closed against the evening dark, the wine bottles emptying as they talked round in circles. But it wasn't enough to talk about what ailed them; they needed action.

Weird was all for confronting Graham Macfadyen, demanding an explanation of the wreaths at the funerals of Ziggy and Mondo. He'd been shouted down by the other two; without evidence of his involvement in the murders, they would only alert Macfadyen to their suspicions rather than provoke a confession.

"I don't mind if he's alerted," Weird had said. "That way he might just quit while he's ahead and leave us two in peace."

"Either that or he'll go away and come up with even more subtle approaches next time. He's not in any hurry, Weird. He's got his whole life to avenge his mother," Alex pointed out.

"Always supposing it is him and not Jackie's hitman that killed Mondo," said Lynn.

"Which is why we need Macfadyen to confess," Alex said. "It doesn't help clear anybody's name if he just retreats into the shadows."

They chased their conversational tails, the dead-ends enlivened only by Davina's occasional wailing as she woke up ready for yet another feeding. Now they were reliving the past again, Alex and Weird running over the damage done to their lives by the toxic rumors that had enveloped their final year at St. Andrews.

It was Weird who first lost patience with the past. He drained his glass and stood up. "I need some fresh air," he announced. "I'm not going to be intimidated into hiding behind locked doors for the rest of my life. I'm going for a walk. Anybody want to keep me company?"

There were no takers. Alex was about to cook dinner and Lynn was feeding Davina. Weird borrowed Alex's waxed jacket and set off toward the shore. Against all odds, the clouds that had shrouded the sky all day had cleared. The sky was clear, a gibbous moon hanging low in the sky between the bridges. The temperature had dropped several degrees and Weird hunched into the collar of the jacket as a squall of chill wind gusted up from the Firth. He veered off toward the shadows under the railway bridge, knowing that if he climbed up on the headland, he'd earn himself a great view down the estuary toward the Bass Rock and the North Sea beyond.

Already, he felt the benefit of being outside. A man was always closer to God in the open air, without the clutter of other people. He thought he'd made his peace with his past, but the events of the past few days had left him uneasily aware of his connection to the young man he had once been. Weird needed to be alone, to restore his belief in the changes he'd made. As he walked, he considered how far he had come, how much cumbersome baggage he'd shed on the way thanks to his belief in the redemption offered by his religion. His thoughts grew brighter, his heart lighter. He'd call the family later tonight. He wanted the reassurance of their voices. A few words with his wife and kids and he'd feel like a man waking from a nightmare. Nothing practical would change. He knew that. But he'd be better able to cope with whatever the world threw at him.

The wind was picking up now, blustering and whooping around his head. He paused for breath, aware of the distant hum of traffic crossing the road bridge. He heard the clatter of a train on the approach to the rail bridge and he leaned back, craning his neck to watch it make its toytown progress a hundred and fifty feet above his head.

Weird neither saw nor heard the blow that brought him to his knees in a terrible parody of prayer. The second blow caught him in the ribs and propelled him crashing to the ground. He had a vague impression of a dark figure toting what looked like a baseball bat before a third blow across his shoulders sent his scattered thoughts reeling with pain. His fingers scrabbled for purchase on the rough grass as he tried to crawl out of range. A fourth blow struck him across the back of the thighs, making him collapse on his stomach, beyond escape.

Then, as suddenly as the attack had begun, it was over. It felt like a flashback to twenty-five years before. Through a miasma of pain and dizziness, Weird was vaguely aware of shouting and the incongruous sound of a small dog yapping. He smelt warm, stale breath, then felt a rough wet tongue slobbering over his face. That he could feel anything at all was such a blessing, he let the tears flow. "You have preserved me from mine enemies," he tried to say. Then everything went dark.

"I'm not going to the hospital," Weird insisted. He'd said it so many times, Alex was beginning to think it was incontrovertible evidence of concussion. Weird sat at the kitchen table, rigid with pain, and equally inflexible on the subject of medical care. His face was drained of color and a long welt stretched from his right temple to the back of his skull.

"I think you've got broken ribs," Alex said. Not for the first time either.

"Which they won't even strap up," Weird said. "I've had broken ribs before. They'll just give me some painkillers and tell me to keep taking them till I'm better."

"I'm more worried about concussion," Lynn said, bustling in with a mug of strong, sweet tea. "Drink it. It's good for shock. And if you throw up again, you're probably concussed and we're going to take you to the hospital in Dunfermline."

Weird shuddered. "No, not Dunfermline."

"He's not that bad if he can still crack wise about Dunfermline," Alex said. "Is anything coming back about the attack?"

"I didn't see a thing before the first blow. And after that, my head was reeling. I saw a dark shape. Probably a man. Maybe a tall woman. And a baseball bat. How stupid is that? I had to come all the way back to Scotland to get beaten up with a baseball bat."

"You didn't see his face?"

"I think he must have been wearing some kind of mask. I didn't even see the pale shape of a face. The next thing I knew, I'd fainted. When I came round, your neighbor was kneeling beside me, looking absolutely terrified. Then I threw up over his dog."

In spite of the affront to his Jack Russell, Eric Hamilton had helped Weird to his feet and supported him the quarter of a mile back to the Gilbeys' house. He'd muttered something about disturbing a mugger then brushed off their effusive thanks and melted back into the night without so much as an appreciative whiskey.

"He already disapproves of us," Lynn said. "He's a retired accountant and thinks we're bohemian artists. So don't worry, you've not ruined a beautiful friendship. However, we do need to call the cops."

"Let's wait till morning. Then we can speak directly to Lawson. Maybe now he'll take us seriously," Alex said.

"You think this was Macfadyen?" Weird asked.

"This isn't Atlanta," Lynn said. "It's a quiet wee village in Fife. I don't think anybody's ever been mugged in North Queensferry. And if you were going to mug someone, would you pick on a giant in his forties when there's pensioners walking their dogs on the foreshore every night? This wasn't random, this was meant."

"I agree," Alex said. "It follows the pattern of the other murders. Dress it up to look like something else. Arson, burglary, mugging. If Eric hadn't come along when he did, you'd be dead now."

Before anyone could respond, the doorbell rang. "I'll get it," Alex said.

When he returned, he was trailed by a police constable. "Mr. Hamilton reported the attack," Alex said in explanation. "PC Henderson has come along to take a statement. This is Mr. Mackie," he added.

Weird managed a tight smile. "Thanks for coming over," he said. "Why don't you sit down?"

"If I can just take some details," PC Henderson said, taking out a notebook and settling down at the table. He unfastened his bulky uniform waterproof, but made no move to take it off. They were probably specially trained to withstand the heat rather than lose the impression of size the jacket provided, Alex thought irrelevantly.

Weird gave his full name, and address, explaining he was visiting his old friends Alex and Lynn. When he revealed he was a minister, Henderson looked uncomfortable, as if embarrassed that a mugger on his patch had walloped a man of the cloth. "What exactly happened?" the constable asked.

Weird recounted the scant details he could remember of the attack. "Sorry I can't tell you more. It was dark. And I was caught unawares," he said.

"He didn't say anything?"

"No."

"No demand for money or your wallet?"

"Nothing."

Henderson shook his head. "A bad business. It's not the sort of thing we expect in the village." He looked up at Alex. "I'm surprised you didn't call us yourself, sir."

"We were more concerned with making sure Tom was all right," Lynn butted in. "We were trying to persuade him to go to the hospital, but he seems determined to be stoic about it."

Henderson nodded. "I think Mrs. Gilbey's right, sir. It wouldn't do any harm to have a doctor take a look at your injuries. Apart from anything else, it means there's an official record of the extent of the damage if we catch whoever did it."

"Maybe in the morning," Weird said. "I'm too tired to face it now."

Henderson closed his notebook and pushed the chair back. "We'll keep you informed of any developments, sir," he said.

"There is something else you can do for us, officer," Alex said.

Henderson gave him an interrogative look.

"I know this is going to sound totally off the wall, but can you arrange for a copy of your report to be sent to ACC Lawson?"

Henderson seemed bemused by the request. "I'm sorry, sir, I don't quite see . . ."

"I don't mean to patronize you, but it's a very long and complicated story and we're all too tired to go into it now. Mr. Mackie and I have been dealing with ACC Lawson on a very sensitive matter, and there's a chance this isn't just a casual mugging. I'd like him to see the report, just so he's aware of what's happened here tonight. I'll be speaking to him about it in the morning anyway, and it would be helpful if he was up to speed." No one who had ever seen Alex persuading his staff the extra mile would have been surprised by his quiet assertiveness.

Henderson weighed his words, uncertainty in his eyes. "It's not normal procedure," he said hesitantly.

"I realize that. But this isn't a normal situation. I promise you, it's not going to rebound on you. If you'd rather wait for the Assistant Chief Constable to contact you . . ." Alex let the sentence trail off.

Henderson made his decision. "I'll send a copy to headquarters," he said. "I'll mention you requested it."

Alex saw him out. He stood on the doorstep and watched the police car nose out of the drive and into the street. He wondered who was out there in the dark, watching for his moment. A shiver ran through him. But not from the cold night air.

CHAPTER
FORTY-ONE

The phone rang just after seven. It wakened Davina and gave
Alex a jolt. After the attack on Weird, the slightest sound had
penetrated his consciousness, requiring analysis and risk assessment. There was someone out there stalking him and
Weird, and his every sense was on the alert. As a result, he'd
hardly slept. He'd been aware of Weird moving around in
the night, probably searching for more painkillers. It wasn't
a normal night noise, and it had made his heart hammer before he'd worked it out.

He grabbed the phone, wondering if Lawson was at his
desk already, Henderson's report in his in-tray. He wasn't
prepared for the jollity of Jason McAllister. "Hi, Alex," the
forensic paint expert greeted him cheerfully. "I know new
parents are always up with the lark so I figured you wouldn't
mind me calling so early. Listen, I've got some information
for you. I can come over now, and run it past you before I go
into work. How would that be?"

"Great," Alex said heavily. Lynn pushed the duvet back
and blearily crossed to the moses basket, lifting her daughter
with a grunt.

"Smashing. I'll be with you in half an hour."

"You know the address?"

"Sure. I've had meetings with Lynn there a couple of

times. See you." The phone went dead and Alex pushed himself up the bed as Lynn returned with the baby.

"That was Jason," Alex said. "He's on his way. I'd better get in the shower. You didn't tell me he was second cousin to the Jolly Green Giant." He leaned over and kissed his daughter's head as Lynn put her to the breast.

"He can be a bit much," Lynn agreed. "I'll feed Davina, then I'll throw on a dressing gown and join you."

"I can't believe he's got a result so quickly."

"He's like you were when you first started the business. He adores what he does so he doesn't mind how much time he spends on it. And he wants to share his delight with everybody else."

Alex paused, hand reaching for his dressing gown. "I was like that? It's a miracle you didn't file for divorce."

Alex found Weird in the kitchen looking terrible. The only color in his face came from the bruising that spread like greasepaint round both eyes. He sat awkwardly, hands wrapped round a mug. "You look like shit," Alex said.

"I feel like it, too." He sipped coffee and winced. "Why don't you have decent painkillers?"

"Because we don't make a habit of getting hammered," Alex said over his shoulder as he left to answer the door. Jason bounced into the room on the balls of his feet, jazzed with excitement, then did a double-take that was almost comic as he took in Weird's appearance. "Shit, man. What the hell happened to you?"

"A man with a baseball bat," Alex said succinctly. "We weren't joking when we said this might be a matter of life and death." He poured a coffee for Jason. "I'm impressed that you've got something for us so soon," he said.

Jason shrugged. "When I got to it, it wasn't such a big deal. I did the microspectrophotometry to establish the color, then I ran it through the gas chromatograph for the composition. It didn't match anything in my database, though."

Alex sighed. "Well, we were expecting that," he said.

Jason held up a finger. "Now, Alex. I am not a man without resources. A couple of years ago, I met this guy at a conference. He is the world's biggest paint head. He works for the FBI, and he reckons that he's got most extensive paint database in the known universe. So I got him to run my results against his records, and bingo! We got it." He held his arms out wide, as if expecting applause.

Lynn walked in just in time to hear his conclusion. "So what was it?" she asked.

"I won't bore you with the technical spec. It was made by a small manufacturer in New Jersey in the mid-seventies for use on fiberglass and certain types of molded plastic. The target market was boat builders and boat owners. It gave a particularly tough finish that was hard to scratch and wouldn't flake even in extreme weather conditions." He opened his backpack and rummaged around, eventually producing a computer-generated color chart. A swatch of pale blue was outlined in black marker. "That's what it looked like, he said, passing the sheet around. "The good news about the quality of the finish is that if by some miracle your crime scene has survived, the chances are that you could still make a match. The paint was mostly sold on the Eastern Seaboard of the U.S., but they did export into the U.K. and the Caribbean. The company went belly-up in the late eighties, so there's no way of telling where it ended up over here."

"So the chances are that Rosie was killed on a boat?" Alex asked.

Jason made a dubious smacking noise with his lips. "If she was, it must have been a fair-sized boat."

"Why do you say that?"

He pulled some papers out of his backpack with a flourish. "This is where the shape of the paint drops comes into play. Tiny tears, that's what we've got here. And one or two very small fiber fragments, which look a lot like carpet tile to me. And this tells me a story. These drops came off a brush while something was being painted. This is a very motile paint, which means that it came off in minute droplets. The person doing the painting probably didn't even notice. Typically, it's the kind of fine spray that you'd get if you were working over your head, especially at full stretch. And because there's almost no variation in the shape of the droplets, that suggests all the paint was applied overhead and at an equal distance. None of this fits with painting a hull. Even if you had the hull upside down to paint the inside, you wouldn't be doing it somewhere carpeted, would you? And the droplets would vary in size because some of the surface would be nearer to you, wouldn't it?" He paused, looking round the room. Everyone was shaking their heads, spellbound by his enthusiasm.

"So what are we left with? If it was a boat, then your man was probably painting the cabin roof. The inside of the cabin roof. Now, I did some experiments with a very similar paint and, to get this effect, I needed to be reaching quite high. And small boats don't have much headroom. So I guess your man had a pretty big boat."

"If it was a boat," Lynn said. "Couldn't it have been something else? The inside of a trailer? Or a caravan?"

"Could be. You probably wouldn't get carpet in a trailer, though, would you? It could have been a shed, or a garage too. Because paints that are designed for fiberglass are pretty good on asbestos as well, and there was a lot more of that around back in the seventies."

"The bottom line is that it doesn't take us any further forward," Weird said, disappointment in his voice.

The conversation veered off in several directions. But Alex had stopped listening. His brain was ticking, a train of thought triggered by what he'd just heard. Connections were forming in his mind, links between apparently unconnected pieces of information forging into a chain. Once you gave space to the first unthinkable thought, so many things made sense. The question now was what to do about it.

He suddenly realized he'd been out of it. Everyone was looking at him expectantly, waiting for an answer to some unheard question. "What?" he said. "Sorry, I was miles away."

"Jason asked if you wanted him to write a formal report," Lynn said. "So you can show it to Lawson."

"Yeah, great idea," Alex said. "That's brilliant, Jason, really impressive."

As Lynn showed Jason to the door, Weird gave Alex a penetrating look. "You've got an idea, Gilly," he said. "I know that look."

"No. I was just racking my brains, trying to think of anybody from the Lammas that had a boat. There were a couple of fishermen, weren't there?" Alex turned away and busied himself, popping a couple of slices of bread in the toaster.

"Now you come to mention it . . . We should remind Lawson about that," Weird said.

"Yeah. When he calls, you can tell him."

"Why? Where are you going to be?"

"I need to go into the office for a few hours. I've been neglecting the business. It doesn't run itself. There's a couple of meetings this morning I really need to go to."

"Should you be driving around alone?"

"I've no choice," Alex said. "But I think I'm pretty safe in broad daylight on the road into Edinburgh. And I'll be back long before it's dark."

"You'd better be." Lynn walked through the door carrying the morning papers. "Looks as if Jackie was right. They're plastered all over the front pages."

Alex munched his toast, lost in thought, as the others went through the papers. While they were occupied, he picked up the color chart Jason had left behind and tucked it into his trouser pocket. He seized a lull in the conversation to announce his departure, kissed his wife and sleeping baby and left the house.

He eased the BMW out of the garage and onto the street, heading for the motorway that would take him over the bridge to Edinburgh. But when he reached the roundabout, instead of turning south on the M90, he took the northbound slip road. Whoever was after them was on his turf now. He had no time to waste sitting in meetings.

. . .

Lynn got behind the wheel of her car with a sense of relief she wasn't proud of. She was starting to feel claustrophobic in her own home. She couldn't even retreat to her studio and regain her calm by working on her latest painting. She knew she shouldn't be driving, not so soon after a C section, but she had to get away. The need to shop had provided the perfect excuse. She promised Weird she'd get one of the supermarket staff to do all the heavy lifting. Then she'd wrapped Davina up warmly, tucked her into her carrier and escaped.

She decided to make the most of her freedom and drive up to the big Sainsburys at Kirkcaldy. If she had enough energy after shopping, she could always pop in to see her parents. They'd not seen Davina since she'd come home from hospital. Maybe a visit from their new granddaughter would help lift their gloom. They needed something to give them a bigger stake in the future than in the past.

As she left the motorway at Halbeath, the fuel warning light appeared on her dashboard. Rationally, she knew she had more than enough petrol to get her to Kirkcaldy and back again, but she wasn't taking any chances with the baby on board. She flicked the indicator at the turn-off for the services and cruised down to the pumps, entirely oblivious to the car that had been on her tail since she'd left North Queensferry.

Lynn fueled up the car, then hurried inside to pay. As she waited for her credit card to be accepted, she glanced out to the forecourt.

At first, she couldn't take it in. The scene outside was wrong, all wrong. Then it sank in. Lynn screamed at the top of her lungs and stumbled toward the door, her bag hitting the floor and scattering its contents as she ran.

A silver VW Golf was parked behind her car, engine running, driver's door wide open. The passenger door of her car was also ajar, shielding whoever was leaning in from sight. As she hauled open the heavy door of the service area, a man straightened up, thick black hair falling over his eyes.

He was clutching Davina's carrier. He cast a glance in her direction then ran for the other car. Davina's shrieks pierced the air like a blade.

He half-threw, half-pushed the baby carrier into his passenger seat, then jumped in. Lynn was almost upon him. He slammed the car into gear and took off, his tires screaming on the tarmac.

Indifferent to the pain from her half-healed scar, Lynn threw herself at the wildly swerving Golf as it careered past her. But her desperate fingers connected with nothing they could cling to, and her momentum carried her forward on to her knees. "No," she screamed, banging her fists on the ground. "No." She tried to stand up, to get to her car, to give chase. But her legs wouldn't hold her and she collapsed on the ground, anguish wracking her.

Exultation swelled inside Graham Macfadyen as he hammered along the A92 away from the Halbeath services. He'd done it. He had the baby. He snatched a quick look, making sure it was OK. It had stopped that banshee screaming as soon as they'd hit the dual carriageway. He'd heard babies liked the sensation of being driven in a car, and this one certainly seemed to. Its blue eyes looked up at him, uncurious and calm. At the end of the dual carriageway, he'd cut off onto back roads, to avoid the police. He'd stop then and strap it in properly. He didn't want anything bad to happen to it yet. It was Alex Gilbey he wanted to punish, and the longer the baby was alive and apparently well, the worse his suffering would be. He'd keep the baby hostage for just as long as it was of use to him.

It had been laughably easy. People really should take better care of their children. It was astonishing that more of them didn't fall into the hands of strangers.

This would make people listen to him, he thought. He'd take the baby home and lock the doors. A siege, that's what it would be. The media would turn up mob-handed and he'd have the chance to explain why he'd been forced to take such extreme action. When they heard how Fife Police were shielding his mother's killers, they'd understand why he'd been driven to something so out of character. And if that still didn't work, well, he had one final card to play. He glanced down at the drowsy baby.

Lawson was going to regret not listening to him.

CHAPTER
FORTY-TWO

Alex had left the motorway at Kinross. He'd driven through the quiet market town and out the far side, heading toward Loch Leven. When she'd let slip that Lawson was off fishing, Karen Pirie had said "Loch" before she stopped herself. And there was only one loch in Fife where a serious fisherman would ply his rod. Alex couldn't stop thinking about his recent revelation. Because he knew deep down none of them had done it, and because he couldn't imagine Rosie wandering around in a blizzard alone, easy prey for a stranger, he'd always tended to believe she'd been killed by her mystery boyfriend. And if you were planning to seduce a lassie, you didn't take her to a shed or a garage. You took her to the place where you lived. And then he'd remembered a throwaway line in one of the previous day's conversations. The unthinkable had suddenly been the only thing that made sense.

The looming bulk of the Bishop reared up on his right-hand side like a sleeping dinosaur, cutting him off from a signal on his mobile phone. Oblivious to what was happening elsewhere, Alex was on a mission. He knew exactly what he was looking for. He just didn't know where he might find it.

He drove slowly, turning off on every farm track and side road that led down toward the shores of the loch. A light mist clung to the surface of the steel-gray water, blanketing sound and adding an unwelcome eeriness to his quest. Alex pulled up in every gateway he came to, getting out of the car and leaning into fields lest he miss his quarry. As the long grass soaked his ankles, he wished he'd dressed more sensibly. But he hadn't wanted to alert Lynn to the fact that he was going anywhere other than the office.

He took his time, moving methodically along the lochside. He spent the best part of an hour prowling round a small caravan site, but what he was looking for wasn't there. That didn't really surprise him. He didn't expect to find the object of his hunt anywhere that ordinary punters had access to.

Around the time his distraught wife was giving her initial statement to detectives, Alex was drinking coffee in a roadside tearoom, spreading butter on a homemade scone, trying to get some warmth back in his bones after the caravan site. He had not the slightest inkling that anything was wrong.

The first officer at the scene had found an incoherent woman with dirt on her hands and the knees of her jeans wailing on the forecourt. The distraught attendant was standing helpless at her side while frustrated motorists arrived and then left when they found they couldn't get served.

"You get Jimmy Lawson here, now," she'd kept screaming at him while the attendant explained what had happened.

The policeman had tried to ignore her demands, radioing in for urgent assistance. Then she'd grabbed his jacket and sprayed him with saliva, all the while demanding the presence of the ACC Crime. He tried to fend her off, suggesting she might want to call her husband, a friend, anyone.

Lynn pushed him away contemptuously and stormed back inside the garage. From the scattered pile of her possessions, she grabbed her mobile. She tried Alex's number, but the irritating voice of the service told her the number was unavailable. "Fuck," Lynn yelled. Her fingers fumbling over the keys, she managed to ring home.

When Weird answered, she wailed, "Tom, he's taken Davina," Lynn wailed. "The bastard's taken my daughter."

"What? Who's taken her?"

"I don't know. Macfadyen, I suppose. He's stolen my baby." Now the tears came, cascading down her cheeks and choking her.

"Where are you?"

"The services at Halbeath. I only stopped for petrol. I was only away a minute . . ." Lynn gagged on her words and dropped the phone at her feet. She crouched down, leaning against a confectionery display. She wrapped her arms over her head and sobbed. She had no idea how much time passed before she heard the soft, reassuring tones of a woman's voice. She looked up into a stranger's face.

"I'm Detective Inspector Cathy McIntyre," the woman said. "Can you tell me what happened?"

"His name's Graham Macfadyen. He lives in St. Monans," Lynn said. "He stole my baby."

"Do you know this man?" DI Mcintyre asked.

"No. I don't. But he's got it in for my husband. He thinks Alex killed his mother. But of course, he's wrong. He's deranged. He's already killed two people. Don't let him kill my baby." Lynn's words tumbled over themselves, making her sound unhinged. She tried to take a deep breath and hiccupped. "I know I sound crazy, but I'm not. You need to contact the Assistant Chief Constable James Lawson. He knows all about it."

DI McIntyre looked dubious. This was way outside her league and she knew it. All she'd managed to arrange so far was to radio all cars and foot patrols to tell them to be on the lookout for a silver Golf driven by a dark-haired man. Maybe calling the ACC in would be her ticket out of humiliation. "Leave it with me," she said, heading back out to the forecourt to consider her options.

Weird sat in the kitchen, fuming at his incapacity. Prayer was all very well, but a man needed a far higher level of internal calm to achieve anything useful with prayer. His imagination was galloping, running movies of his own children in the hands of an abductor. He knew he'd be beyond the reach of any rational response in Lynn's shoes. What he needed to do was come up with something concrete that might help.

He'd tried to get hold of Alex. But his mobile wasn't responding, and Alex's office denied having seen him or heard from him at all that morning. So Alex was on the missing list, too. Weird wasn't entirely surprised; he'd been convinced Alex had something on his mind he intended to deal with.

He reached for the phone, wincing at even such a small movement, and asked directory inquiries for the number of Fife Police. It took him all his powers of persuasion to get as far as Lawson's secretary. "I really need to speak to the Assistant Chief Constable," he said. "It's urgent. You have a child abduction going on, and I have vital information," he told the woman, who was clearly as adept at stonewalling as he was at sweet-talking.

"Mr. Lawson is in a meeting," she said. "If you'll leave me your name and number, I'll ask him to contact you when he has the chance."

"You're not hearing me, are you? There's a baby out there whose life is in the balance. If anything happens to that baby, you can bet your pension that I'm going to be talking to the press and TV within the hour, letting them know how you guys fell down on the job. If you don't get Lawson on the line now, you're going to be the scapegoat."

"There's no need for that attitude, sir," the woman said coldly. "What was your name again?"

"The Reverend Tom Mackie. He'll talk to me, I promise you."

"Hold the line, please."

Weird raged inwardly to the soundtrack of a frenetic concerto grosso. After what felt an interminable wait, a voice he recognized down the years sounded in his ears. "This better be good, Mr. Mackie. I've been dragged out of a meeting with the Chief Constable to talk to you."

"Graham Macfadyen has snatched Alex Gilbey's baby. I can't believe you were sitting in a meeting while this is going on," Weird snapped.

"What did you say?" Lawson said.

"You've got a child abduction on your hands. About quarter of an hour ago, Macfadyen kidnapped Davina Gilbey. She's only a couple of weeks old, for crying out loud."

"I know nothing about this, Mr. Mackie. Can you tell me what you know?"

"Lynn Gilbey stopped for petrol at Halbeath services. While she was paying, Macfadyen stole the baby from Lynn's car. Your guys are there now, why has nobody told you?"

"Did Mrs. Gilbey recognize Macfadyen? Has she met him?" Lawson demanded.

"No. But who else would want to hurt Alex like this?"

"Children are kidnapped for all sorts of reasons, Mr. Mackie. It may not be personal." The voice was soothing, but it had no effect.

"Of course it's personal," Weird shouted. "Last night, somebody tried to beat me to death. You should have a report about that on your desk. And this morning, Alex's kid is abducted. You going to play the coincidence card again? Because we're not buying it. You need to get off your arse and find Macfadyen before anything happens to that baby."

"Halbeath services, you say?"

"Yes. You get down there right now. You've got the authority to get things moving."

"Let me speak to my officers on the ground. Meanwhile, Mr. Mackie, try to stay calm."

"Yeah, right. That'll be easy."

"Where is Mr. Gilbey?" Lawson asked.

"I don't know. He was supposed to be going to his office, but he's not turned up there. And his mobile's not responding."

"Leave this with me. Whoever has the baby, we'll find them. And we'll bring her home."

"You sound like the worst kind of TV cop, you know that, Lawson? Just get things moving. Find Macfadyen." Weird slammed down the phone. He tried to tell himself he'd achieved something, but it didn't feel like it.

It was no use. He couldn't sit here doing nothing. He

reached for the phone again and asked directory inquiries for a taxi number.

Lawson stared at the phone. Macfadyen had crossed the line. He should have seen it coming but he had failed. Now it was too late to put him out of circulation. This had all the potential to spiral out of control. And who knew what might happen then? Struggling to maintain the semblance of calm, he called the force control room and asked for a report on what was going on at Halbeath.

As soon as he heard the words, "Silver Volkswagen Golf," his brain replayed the walk up Macfadyen's path, the car parked in the drive. No question about it. Macfadyen had lost it.

"Patch me through to the officer in charge at the scene," he ordered. He drummed his fingers on the desk till the connection was made. This was the scenario from hell. What the hell was Macfadyen playing at? Was he taking revenge on Gilbey for the supposed wrong against his mother? Or was he playing a deeper game? Whatever the agenda, the child was at risk. Normally, when babies were snatched, the abductor's motivation was simple. They wanted a child of their own. They would take care of the child, smothering it with love and attention. But this was different. This child was a pawn in whatever sick game Macfadyen was playing, and if murder was what he thought he was avenging, then murder might be his endgame. The consequences of this scenario didn't bear thinking about. Lawson's stomach contracted at what it could mean. "Come on," he muttered.

Eventually, a voice crackled on the line. "This is DI McIntyre," he heard. At least it was a woman DI who was on the ground, Lawson thought with relief. He remembered Cathy McIntyre. She'd been a sergeant in CID when he'd been a uniformed superintendent at Dunfermline. She was a good officer, always did things by the numbers.

"Cathy, it's ACC Lawson here."

"Yes, sir. I was just about to call you. The mother of the kidnapped baby, a Mrs. Lynn Gilbey? She's been asking for you. She seems to think you will know what this is all about."

"It was a silver VW Golf that the abductor drove off in, is that right?"

"Yes, sir. We're trying to get an index number from the CCTV footage, but we've only got footage of the car in motion. He parked right up behind Mrs. Gilbey, you can't see his number plates when the car was stationary."

"Keep someone on it for now. But I think I know who's responsible for this. Graham Macfadyen is his name. He lives at 12 Carlton Way, St. Monans. And I suspect that's where he's taken the child. I think a hostage situation is what he's aiming for. So I want you to meet me there, at the end of the road. Don't come mob-handed but have someone bring Mrs. Gilbey in a separate car. Radio silence with her. I'll organize the hostage negotiation team at this end, and brief you fully when I get there. Don't hang around, Cathy. I'll see you in St. Monans."

Lawson ended the call, then clenched his eyes tight in concentration. The freeing of hostages was the hardest task police officers faced. Dealing with the bereaved was a cakewalk by comparison. He called the control room again and ordered the mobilization of the hostage negotiation team and an armed-response unit. "Oh, and get a Telecom engineer there, too. I want his access to the outside world terminated." Finally, he rang Karen Pirie. "Meet me in the car park in five minutes," he barked. "I'll explain on the way."

He was halfway to the door when his phone rang. He debated whether to answer it, then turned back. "Lawson," he said.

"Hallo, Mr. Lawson. It's Andy down in the press office here. I've just had the *Scotsman* on with a very peculiar tale. They say they've just had an e-mail from a guy who claims he's abducted a baby because Fife Police are shielding the murderers of his mother. It specifically blames you for the situation. It's apparently a very long and detailed e-mail. They're going to forward it on to me. They're asking if it's true, basically. Do we have a child abduction in progress?"

"Oh Christ," Lawson groaned. "I had a horrible feeling something like this was going to happen. Look, we've got a very sensitive situation going on here. Yes, a baby has been abducted. I don't have the full story myself yet. You need to talk to the control room, they can give you chapter and verse. I suspect you're going to get a lot of calls on this, Andy. Give them as much of the operational detail as you can. Call a press conference for as late in the afternoon as you can get away with. But go strong on the line that this guy is mentally disturbed and they shouldn't give credence to his ramblings."

"So the official line is that he's a nutter," Andy said.

"Pretty much. But we're treating it very seriously. A child's life is at stake here, I don't want irresponsible reporting sending this guy over the edge. Is that clear?"

"I'm on it. Talk to you later."

Lawson cursed under his breath then hurried toward the door. This was going to be the day from hell.

Weird asked the taxi driver to make a diversion to the retail park in Kirkcaldy. When they got there, he handed the driver a wad of notes. "Do me a favor, pal. You can see the state I'm in. Go and buy me a mobile phone. One of those pay-as-you-go jobs. And a couple of top-up cards. I need to be connected to the world."

Quarter of an hour later, they were back on the road. He fished out the sheet of paper on which he'd scribbled the mobile numbers for Alex and Lynn. He tried Alex again. Still no response. Where in the name of heaven was he?

Macfadyen stared at the baby in perplexity. It had started crying almost as soon as he'd brought it indoors, but he hadn't had time to deal with it then. He had e-mails to fire off, to tell the world what was going on. Everything was prepared. He only had to get online and, with a few mouse clicks, his message would go out to every news organization in the country and most of the Internet news sites. Now they'd have to pay attention.

He left the computers and returned to the living room, where he'd left the baby carrier on the floor. He knew he should stay with it to prevent the police separating them in an assault on the house, but its cries had driven him to distraction and he'd moved it so that he could concentrate. He'd drawn the curtains there, as he had in every other room in the house. He'd even nailed a blanket over the bathroom window, whose frosted glass was normally uncurtained. He knew how sieges worked; the less the cops knew about what was going on inside the house, the better for him.

The baby was still crying. Its wails had died away to a low grizzle, but as soon as he'd walked in, it had started screaming again. The sound went through his head like a drill, making it impossible to think. He had to shut it up. He lifted it up gingerly and held it to his chest. The cries intensified, to the point where he could feel them resonating in his chest. Maybe it had a dirty nappy, he thought. He laid it on the floor and unwrapped the blanket that swaddled it. Underneath was a fleece jacket. He undid that then opened the poppers that ran up the insides of its legs, then unfastened the vest underneath. How many layers did the fucking kid need? Maybe it was just too hot.

He fetched a roll of kitchen towel and knelt down. He unpeeled the tapes that held the nappy secure around the child's belly and recoiled. God, that was revolting. It was green, for Christ's sake. Wrinkling his nose in disgust, he removed the dirty nappy and scrubbed away the remains from its bottom. Hastily, before anything fresh could erupt, he dumped the baby on a thick wad of kitchen towel.

All that, and it was still crying. Jesus Christ, what did it take to shut the little bastard up? He needed it alive, at least for a while yet, but this noise was driving him crazy. He slapped the scarlet face and earned a brief moment's respite. But as soon as the shocked child had filled its lungs again, the screams intensified.

Maybe he should feed it? He went back to the kitchen and tipped some milk into a cup. He sat down, cradling the baby awkwardly in the crook of his arm as he'd seen people do on

TV. He poked a finger between its lips and tried to dribble some liquid in. Milk trickled down its chin and onto his sleeve. He tried again, and this time it struggled against him, the tiny hands fists, the legs kicking. How could the little bastard not know how to swallow? How come it acted like he was trying to poison it? "What the fuck is wrong with you?" he shouted. It went rigid in his arms, wailing even more.

He struggled for a while longer, without success. But all of a sudden, the crying stopped. The baby fell asleep instantly, as if someone had turned off a switch. One minute, it was whinging, the next its eyes were shut and it was spark out. Macfadyen inched off the sofa and placed it back in the carrier, forcing himself to be gentle. The last thing he could stand right now was a reprise of that hellish noise.

He went back to his computers, planning to log on to a couple of Web sites to see if they were running the story yet. He wasn't entirely surprised to see his screens displaying the message, "Connection lost." He'd expected them to cut off his phone lines. As if that would stop him. He took a mobile off its charger and connected it to his laptop with a short cable, then dialed up. OK, it was like going back to traveling on a mule after you'd driven a Ferrari. But even though it took a criminally long time to download anything, he was still online.

If they thought they could shut him up that easily, they had another think coming. He was in this for the long haul, and he was in it for victory.

CHAPTER
FORTY-THREE

Alex's enthusiasm was growing thin. All that kept him going was a dogged conviction that the answer he so desperately sought was out there somewhere. It had to be. He'd covered the south side of the loch and now he was working his way round to the north shore. He'd lost count of the number of fields he'd looked into. He'd been stared at by geese, by horses, by sheep and even, once, by a llama. He vaguely remembered reading somewhere that shepherds put them in with their flocks to act as a defense against foxes, but he couldn't for the life of him figure out how a big lazy lump with eyelashes a model would die for was going to deter anything as fearless as the average fox. He'd bring Davina out here and show her the llama one day. She'd like that when she was bigger.

The track he was driving down passed a pathetic-looking farm. The buildings were down at the heel, guttering sagging and window frames peeling. The farmyard resembled a graveyard for machinery that had been moldering quietly into rust for generations. A skinny collie with a mad look strained against a chain, barking furiously and fruitlessly at his passage. A hundred yards past the farm gate, the ruts deepened and grass straggled feebly up the middle. Alex splashed through the puddles, wincing as a rock crunched against his chassis.

A gateway loomed up in the high hedge to his left, and Alex pulled in wearily. He walked around the front of his car and leaned over the metal bars. He looked to his left and saw a handful of dirty brown cows mournfully chewing the cud. He gave a cursory glance to his right and gasped. He couldn't believe his eyes. Was this really it?

Alex fumbled with the rusty chain that held the gate shut. He let himself into the field, and looped the links back around the post. He picked his way down the field, not caring about the mud or the dung that clung to his expensive American loafers. The closer he got to his goal, the more certain he was that he'd found what he was looking for.

He hadn't seen the caravan for twenty-five years, but his memory told him this was the one. Two-tone, like he remembered. Cream on top, sage green below. The colors had faded, but it was still possible to match them to his recollection. As he grew closer, he could see it was still in decent repair. Breeze blocks piled at either end kept the tires above the ground, and there was no moss clinging to the roof or the sills. The brittle rubber round the windows had been treated with some sort of sealant to keep it watertight, he saw as he circled it cautiously. There was no sign of life. Light-colored curtains were drawn across the windows. About twenty yards beyond the caravan, a wicket gate in the fence led to the lochside. Alex could see a rowing boat drawn up on the shore.

He turned back and stared. He could hardly believe his eyes. What were the chances of this, he wondered. Probably not as remote as it might at first seem. People got rid of furniture, carpets, cars. But caravans lived on, assuming an existence of their own. He thought of the elderly couple who lived opposite his parents. They'd had the same tiny two-berth caravan since he'd been a teenager. Every summer Friday evening, they hitched it to their car and headed off. Nowhere far, just up the coast to Leven or Elie. Sometimes they'd really go for it and cross the Forth to Dunbar or North Berwick. And on Sunday evening, they'd return, as thrilled with themselves as if they'd crossed the North Pole. So really, it wasn't such a surprise that PC Jimmy Lawson had hung on to the caravan he'd lived in while he'd built his house. Especially since every angler needs a retreat. Most people would likely have done the same.

Except, of course, that most people wouldn't have been hanging on to a crime scene.

"Now do you believe Alex?" Weird demanded of Lawson. The effect of his words was tempered by the fact that he was huddled into himself, his arm across his ribs trying to stop them grating against each other in spasms of agony.

The police hadn't been far ahead of Weird, and he'd arrived to find apparent chaos. Men in bulletproof vests with field caps and rifles milled around, while other officers bustled hither and thither on obscure tasks of their own. Curiously, nobody seemed to be paying him much attention. He limped out of the taxi and surveyed the scene. It didn't take him long to spot Lawson, leaning over a map spread on a car bonnet. The woman cop he and Alex had talked to at police headquarters was at his side, a mobile to her ear.

Weird approached, anger and apprehension acting as painkillers. "Hey, Lawson," he called from a few feet away. "You happy now?"

Lawson spun round, a guilty thing surprised. His jaw dropped as recognition filtered through the damage to Weird's face. "Tom Mackie?" he said uncertainly.

"The same. Now do you believe Alex? That maniac has his kid in there. He's already killed two people and you're just standing by in the hope he'll make it easy for you by making it three."

Lawson shook his head. Weird could see the anxiety in his eyes. "That's not true. We're doing everything we can to get the Gilbeys' baby back safely. And you don't know that Graham Macfadyen is guilty of anything else except this offense."

"No? Who the hell else do you think killed Ziggy and Mondo? Who the hell else do you think did this to me?" He raised a single finger toward his face. "He could have killed me last night."

"You saw him?"

"No, I was too busy trying to stay alive."

"In that case, we're exactly where we were before. No evidence, Mr. Mackie. No evidence."

"Listen to me, Lawson. We've lived with Rosie Duff's death for twenty-five years. Suddenly, her son turns up out of the blue. And the next thing that happens is that two of us are murdered. For pity's sake, man, why are you the only one who can't see that's cause and effect?" Weird was shouting now, oblivious to the fact that several cops were now staring at him with watchful, impassive eyes.

"Mr. Mackie, I'm trying to mount a complex operation here. You standing here throwing out unfounded allegations really doesn't help. Theories are all very well, but we operate on evidence." Lawson's anger was obvious now. At his side, Karen Pirie had ended her call and was moving unobtrusively closer to Weird.

"You don't find evidence unless you start looking for it."

"It's not my job to investigate murders that are outside my jurisdiction," Lawson snapped. "You're wasting my time, Mr. Mackie. And, as you point out, a child's life may be at stake."

"You are going to pay for this," Weird said. "Both of you," he added, turning to include Karen in his condemnation. "You were warned and you did nothing. If he harms a hair on that child's head, I swear, Lawson, you are going to wish you had never been born. Now, where's Lynn?"

Lawson shuddered inwardly, remembering Lynn Gilbey's arrival at the scene. She'd hurtled out of the police car and thrown herself at him, raining blows on his chest and screaming incoherently. Karen Pirie had stepped in smartly, wrapping her arms round the frantic woman.

"She's in that white van over there. Karen, take Mr. Mackie over to the armed-response unit vehicle. And stay with him and Mrs. Gilbey. I don't want them running around like loose cannons when we've got marksmen all over the place."

"See, when this is all over?" Weird said as Karen steered him away. "You and me are going to have a reckoning."

"I wouldn't bank on it, Mr. Mackie," Lawson said. "I'm a senior police officer and threatening me is a serious offense. Away you go and lead a prayer meeting. You do your job and I'll do mine."

Carlton Way looked like a backstreet in a ghost town. Nothing stirred. It was always quiet during the day, but today it was preternaturally hushed. The night-shift worker at number seven had been rousted from his bed by a hammering at the back door. Befuddled, he'd been persuaded to get dressed and to accompany the two police officers on his doorstep over the fence at the bottom of his garden and through the playing fields to the main road, where he'd been told of events so unlikely that he'd have thought it was a wind-up if not for the overwhelming presence of the police and the roadblock that cut off Carlton Way from the rest of the world.

"Is that all the houses empty now?" Lawson asked DI McIntyre.

"Yes, sir. And the sole communication into Macfadyen's house is a dedicated phone line for our use only. All the armed response team officers are deployed round the house now."

"Right. Let's do it."

Two marked police cars and a van drove single-file into Carlton Way. They parked in a line outside Macfadyen's house. Lawson got out of the lead vehicle and joined the hostage negotiator, John Duncan, behind the van, out of sight of the house. "We're sure he's in there?" Duncan said.

"So the techies say. Thermal-imaging, or something. He's in there with the baby. They're both still alive."

Duncan handed Lawson a set of headphones and picked up the phone handset that would give him a line into the house. The phone was answered on the third ring. Silence. "Graham? Is that you?" Duncan said, his voice firm but warm.

"Who's that?" Macfadyen sounded surprisingly relaxed.

"My name's John Duncan. I'm here to see what we can do to resolve this situation without anyone getting hurt."

"I've nothing to say to you. I want to speak to Lawson."

"He's not here right now. But anything you say to me, I'll pass on to him."

"It's Lawson or nobody." Macfadyen's tone was pleasant and casual, as if they were talking about the weather or the football.

"Like I said, Mr. Lawson isn't here right now."

"I don't believe you, Mr. Duncan. But let's pretend you're telling me the truth. I'm in no hurry. I can wait till you find him." The line went dead. Duncan looked at Lawson. "End of round one," he said. "We'll give him five minutes then I'll try him again. He'll start talking eventually."

"You think so? He sounded pretty cool to me. Don't you think I should maybe talk to him? That way, he might feel that he's going to get what he's asking for."

"It's too early for concessions, sir. He has to give us something before we give him anything in return."

Lawson sighed deeply and turned away. He hated the feeling of being out of control. This was going to be a media circus and the potential for an atrocious outcome was far, far greater than the alternative. He knew about sieges. They almost always ended badly for someone.

Alex contemplated his options. In any other set of circumstances, the sensible course of action would be to walk away now and go to the police. They could send in their forensic team and take the place apart in search of the single drop of blood or the teardrop of paint that would make the inevitable connection between this caravan and Rosie Duff's death.

But how could he do that when the caravan in question belonged to the Assistant Chief Constable? Lawson would stop any investigation in its tracks, kill it dead before it even got started. The caravan would doubtless go up in flames, laid at the door of vandals. And then what would there be? Nothing more than coincidence. Lawson's presence so close to the place where Alex had stumbled over her body. At the time, nobody had thought twice about it. Back in the late seventies in Fife, the police were still above suspicion, the good guys keeping the bad things at bay. Nobody had even questioned why Lawson hadn't seen the killer driving Rosie's body to Hallow Hill, even though he was parked facing the most obvious route. But this was a new world, a world where it was possible to question the integrity of men like James Lawson.

If Lawson had been the mystery man in Rosie's life, it made sense that she would keep his identity secret. Her troublemaking brothers would have hated her seeing a copper. Then there was the way that Lawson always seemed to turn up when he or his friends were under threat, as if he had appointed himself their guardian angel. Guilt, Alex thought now. Guilt would do that to a man. In spite of having killed Rosie, Lawson still retained enough decency not to want someone else to pay the price for his crime.

But none of those circumstances was any kind of proof. The chance of going back to witnesses after twenty-five years and finding someone who had seen Rosie with Jimmy Lawson was nil. The only solid evidence was inside that caravan, and if Alex didn't do something about it now, it would be too late.

But what could he do? He wasn't versed in the techniques of burglary. Breaking into cars as a teenager was light years away from picking a lock, and if he forced the door, Lawson would be alerted. At any other time, he might put it down to kids or some homeless wanderer. But not now. Not with so much interest in the Rosie Duff case. He couldn't afford to treat it as anything other than significant. He might just torch the place.

Alex stepped back and considered. There was, he noticed, a skylight on the roof. Maybe he could squeeze in there? But how to get up to the roof? There was only one possibility. Alex trudged back to the gate, wedged it open and drove into the boggy field. For the first time in his life, he wished he was the kind of moron who drove a big fuck-off four-wheel drive around the city. But no, he had to be Mr. Flash with his BMW 535. What would he do if he got stuck in the mud?

He cruised slowly down to the caravan and stopped parallel with one end. He opened the boot and unfastened the car's standard-issue toolkit. Pliers, a screwdriver, a spanner. He pocketed everything that looked as if it might be useful, took off his suit jacket and his tie then closed the boot. He clambered over the bonnet and onto the car roof. From there, it wasn't far to the top of the caravan. Scrabbling for purchase, Alex somehow managed to launch himself onto the roof.

It was disgusting up there. The roof was slippery and slimy. Particles of dirt clung to his clothes and his hands. The skylight was a raised plastic dome about thirty inches by twelve. It was going to be a very tight squeeze. He jammed the screwdriver under the edge and tried to lever it up.

At first, it wouldn't budge. But after repeated attempts at various points along the rim, it slowly shifted, creaking upward. Sweating, Alex wiped the back of his hand over his face and peered in. There was a pivoting metal arm with a screw adjustment that kept the skylight in place, so it could be raised and lowered from within. It also prevented the skylight from opening more than a few inches at one end. Alex groaned. He was going to have to unscrew the metal arm and then replace it.

He fumbled to get the right angle. It was hard to get any purchase on the screws, which hadn't been moved since they were first put in more than a quarter of a century before. He strained and struggled until, eventually, first one screw and then the other shifted in their moorings. At last, the skylight swung free.

Alex looked down. It wasn't as bad as it might have been. If he lowered himself carefully, he reckoned he could reach the bench seat that ran along one side of the living area. He took a deep breath, gripped the edge and let go.

He thought his arms would fly free from their sockets as the jolt of his full weight traveled upward. His feet bicycled madly, trying for purchase, but after a few seconds, he just let himself drop.

In the dim light, it looked as if little had changed since he'd sat here all those years ago. He'd had no intuition then that he was sitting in the very place where Rosie had met her violent end. There was no tell-tale smell, no giveaway blood smears, no psychic stain to set his nerves jangling.

He was so close to an answer now. Alex could hardly bear to look up at the ceiling. What if Lawson had repainted it a dozen times since? Would there still be evidence? He let his heart rate subside to something approaching normal, then, muttering a prayer to Weird's God, he tilted his head back and looked up.

Shit. The ceiling wasn't blue. It was cream. All this, and for nothing. Well, he wasn't going away empty-handed. He climbed up on the bench seat and chose a spot right in the corner, where it wouldn't be noticed. With the sharp blade of the screwdriver, he chipped away at the paint, catching the flakes in an envelope he'd taken from his briefcase.

When he had gathered a decent amount, he climbed back down and picked out a decent-sized chip. It was cream on one side, and blue on the other. Alex's legs trembled and he sat down heavily, overcome with a turmoil of emotion. From his pocket, he pulled the color chart Jason had left behind and looked at the blue oblong that had jogged his visual memory of twenty-five years ago. He lifted the edge of the curtain to let daylight in and placed the flake of paint on the swatch of pale blue. It almost disappeared.

Tears pricked at Alex's eyes. Was this the final answer?

CHAPTER
FORTY-FOUR

Duncan had made three further attempts to talk to Graham Macfadyen, but he had steadfastly refused to budge on his demand to speak to Lawson, and Lawson only. He'd allowed Duncan to hear Davina's cries, but that had been the single concession he'd made. Exasperated, Lawson decided he'd had enough.

"Time's rolling on. The baby's distressed, we've got the media breathing down our necks. Give me the phone. I'm doing the talking now," he said.

Duncan took one look at his boss's flushed face and handed over the receiver. "I'll help you keep it on track," he said.

Lawson made the connection. "Graham? It's me. James Lawson. I'm sorry it's taken me so long to get here. I understand you want to talk to me?"

"Damn right I want to talk to you. But before we get into it, I should tell you that I'm recording this. As we speak, it's going out live via a webcast. The media have all got the URL, so they're probably hanging on our every word as we speak. There's no point in trying to close down the site, by the way. I've got it set up to jump from server to server. Before you can even find where it's coming from, it'll be somewhere else."

"There's no need for this, Graham."

"There's every need. You thought you could close me down by cutting the phone lines, but you think like last century's man. I'm the future, Lawson, and you're history."

"How's the baby?"

"Pain in the arse, actually. It just cries all the time. It's doing my head in. But it's fine. So far, anyway. It's come to no harm yet."

"You're harming her just by keeping her from her mother."

"It's not my fault. It's Alex Gilbey's fault. Him and his friends, they kept me from my mother. They murdered her. Alex Gilbey, Tom Mackie, David Kerr and Sigmund Malkiewicz murdered my mother, Rosie Duff, on 16 December 1978. First they raped her and then they murdered her. And Fife Police never charged them with the crime."

"Graham," Lawson interrupted, "that's in the past. What we're concerned about now is the future. Your future. And the sooner we end this, the better your future will be."

"Don't talk to me as if I'm stupid, Lawson. I know I'm going to be sent to prison for this. It doesn't make any odds whether I give up my hostage or not. Nothing's going to change that, so don't insult my intelligence. I've got nothing left to lose, but I can make damn sure that other people take a hit, too. Now, where was I? Oh yes. My mother's murderers. You never charged them. And when you reopened the case recently, with a big fanfare of trumpets about how DNA would solve old crimes, you found you'd lost the evidence. How could you do that? How could you lose something so important?"

"We're losing control," Duncan whispered. "He's calling the baby, 'it.' That's not good. Get back to the baby."

"Kidnapping Davina isn't going to change that, Graham."

"It's stopped you sweeping my mother's murder under the carpet. Now the whole world's going to know what you've done."

"Graham, I'm as committed as I could be to dealing with whoever killed your mother."

A hysterical laugh crackled down the line. "Oh, I know that. I just don't believe in your way of dealing with them. I want them to suffer in this world, not the next. They're dying like heroes. What they really were is being swept under the carpet. That's what comes of doing it your way."

"Graham, we need to talk about your situation as it is now. Davina needs her mother. Why don't you bring her out now and we'll talk about your complaints. I promise we'll listen."

"Are you crazy? This is the only way to get your attention, Lawson. And I plan to make the most of it before this is over." The call ended abruptly with the crashing down of the phone at the other end.

Duncan tried to hide his frustration. "Well, at least we know now what's eating him."

"He's off his head. We can't negotiate with him if he's broadcasting it to the world. Who knows what crazy allegations he's going to come up with next? The man should be sectioned, not humored." Lawson slammed his hand against the side of the van.

"Before we can do that, we need to get him and the baby out of there."

"Fuck that," Lawson said. "It'll be dark in an hour. We'll storm the place."

Duncan looked stunned. "Sir, that's way outside the rules of engagement."

"So is kidnapping a baby," Lawson called over his shoulder as he stalked back to his car. "I'm not standing by while a child's life is at risk."

Alex hit the track with an overwhelming sense of relief. There had been a couple of moments when he'd seriously doubted he'd ever get out of the field without a tractor. But he'd made it. He picked up his phone, planning to call Jason and tell him he was on his way with something very interesting. No signal. Alex tutted and drove carefully up the rutted lane toward the main road.

As he neared Kinross, his phone rang. He grabbed it. Four messages. He thumbed the keys and summoned them. The first was from Weird, a terse message telling him to call home as soon as he picked it up. The second was also from Weird, passing on a mobile number. The fourth and fifth were from journalists asking him to return their calls.

What the hell was going on? Alex pulled into a pub car park on the outskirts of the town and called Weird's number. "Alex? Thank the Lord," Weird gasped. "You're not driving, are you?"

"No, I'm parked up. What's going on? I've got these messages . . ."

"Alex, you have to be calm."

"What is it? Davina? Lynn? What's happened?"

"Alex, something bad has happened. But everybody's OK."

"Weird, just fucking tell me," Alex roared, panic thudding in his chest.

"Macfadyen has taken Davina," he said, speaking slowly and clearly. "He's holding her hostage. But she's OK. He hasn't hurt her."

Alex felt as if someone had reached inside his body and ripped his heart out. All the love he'd discovered in himself seemed to transmute into a mixture of fear and rage. "What about Lynn? Where is she?" he choked out

"She's here with us, outside Macfadyen's house in St. Monans. Hang on, I'll let you speak to her." A moment passed, then he heard a forlorn shadow of Lynn's voice.

"Where have you been, Alex? He stole Davina. He took our baby, Alex." He could hear the tears hovering beneath the hoarseness.

"I was in a black spot. No reception. Lynn, I'm coming. Hold on. Don't let them do anything. I'm coming, and I know something that'll change everything. Don't let them do anything, you hear? It's going to be all right. You hear? It's going to be OK. Put Weird back on, please?" As he spoke, he was starting the engine and pulling out of the car park.

"Alex?" He could hear the strain in Weird's voice. "How soon can you be here?"

"I'm in Kinross. Forty minutes? Weird, I know the truth. I know what happened to Rosie and I can prove it. When

Macfadyen hears this, he'll understand he doesn't need to take any more revenge. You've got to stop them doing anything that puts Davina at risk until I can tell him what I know. This is dynamite."

"I'll do my best. But they've got us shut away from the action."

"Whatever it takes, Weird, do it. And look after Lynn for me, please?"

"Of course. Get here fast as you can, eh? God bless you."

Alex jammed his foot to the floor and drove as he'd never driven. He almost wished to be stopped for speeding. That way he'd get a police escort. Blues and twos all the way to the East Neuk. That was what he needed right now.

Lawson looked around the church hall they'd commandeered. "The technical support team can identify which rooms Macfadyen and the baby are in. So far, he's spent most of his time in a room at the back of the house. The baby is sometimes with him and sometimes in the front room. So it should be straightforward. We wait till they're separated, then one team goes in the front and gets the baby. The other team goes in the back and closes down Macfadyen.

"We wait till it's dark. The streetlights will be off. He won't be able to see a damn thing. I want this to go like clockwork. I want that baby out of there alive and unharmed.

"Macfadyen is another matter. He's mentally unstable. We have no idea whether he is armed or not. We have reason to believe he has already killed twice. Only last night, he is believed to have committed a serious assault. If he hadn't been disturbed then, it's my belief he would have killed again. He said himself he has nothing left to lose. If he shows any sign of reaching for a weapon, I am authorizing you to open fire. Does anyone have any questions?"

The room was silent. The officers in the armed-response group had honed their skills for an operation like this. The room had become a vessel for testosterone and adrenaline. This was the moment when fear was given another name.

.   .   .

Macfadyen tapped the keys and clicked his mouse. The connection over the mobile phone was abominably slow, but he'd managed to upload his conversation with Lawson to the Web site now. He sent out a follow-up e-mail to the news outlets he'd contacted earlier, telling them they could get a front-row seat at the siege by linking to his site, where they could hear for themselves what was going on.

He was under no illusion that he could control the outcome. But he was determined to stage-manage what he could, and to do whatever was necessary to make this front-page news. If that cost the baby's life, so be it. He was ready. He could do it, he knew he could. No matter whether it meant his name would be synonymous with evil in the tabloids. He wasn't going to come out of this as the only bad guy. Even if Lawson had called for a news blackout, the information was out there now, in the wild. He couldn't gag the Internet, couldn't stop those facts spawning. And Lawson must know by now that Macfadyen had an ace in the hole.

Next time they called, he'd lay it out. He'd reveal the full extent of the police duplicity. He'd tell the world how low justice had stooped in Scotland.

It was judgment day.

Alex was halted at a police roadblock. He could see the massed emergency vehicles ahead, could just make out the red-and-white barriers at the mouth of Carlton Way. He rolled down the window, aware that he looked filthy and disheveled. "I'm the father," he told the police officer who leaned down to speak to him. "It's my baby in there. My wife's here somewhere, I need to be with her."

"Have you got some ID, sir?" the constable asked.

Alex produced his driving license. "I'm Alex Gilbey. Please, let me through."

The constable compared his face to the picture on the license, then turned away to speak into his radio. He came back a moment later. "I'm sorry, Mr. Gilbey. We have to be

careful. If you'd just park on the verge there, one of the officers will take you to your wife."

Alex followed another yellow-jacketed officer to a white
minibus. He opened the door and Lynn leaped out of her
seat, falling into his arms on the steps. Her body was trem-
bling and he could feel her heart thudding against him.
There were no words for what ailed them. They simply
clung to each other, their anguish and fear palpable.

For a long time, no one spoke. Then Alex said, "It's going
to be OK. I can end this now."

Lynn looked up at him, eyes red-rimmed and swollen.
"How, Alex? You can't fix this."

"I can, Lynn. I know the truth now." He looked over her
shoulder and saw Karen Pirie sitting by the door, next to
Weird. "Where's Lawson?"

"He's at a briefing," Lynn said. "He'll be back soon. You
can talk to him then."

Alex shook his head. "I don't want to talk to him. I want
to talk to Macfadyen."

"That won't be possible, Mr. Gilbey. It's being dealt with
by trained negotiators. They know what they're doing."

"You don't understand. There are things he needs to
hear that only I can tell him. I don't want to threaten him. I
don't even want to plead with him. I just need to tell him
something."

Karen sighed. "I know you're very upset, Mr. Gilbey. But
you could do a lot of harm thinking you're doing good."

Alex gently disengaged himself from Lynn's arms. "This
is about Rosie Duff, right? This is happening because he
thinks I had something to do with Rosie Duff's murder,
isn't it?"

"That would appear to be the case, sir." Karen spoke
cautiously.

"What if I told you that I can answer his questions?"

"If you have information pertaining to the case, I'm the
one you should be talking to."

"All in good time, I promise. But Graham Macfadyen deserves to be the first to hear the truth. Please. Trust me. I've

got my reasons. It's my daughter's life that's at stake here. If you won't let me talk to Macfadyen, I'm walking away from here and telling the press what I know. And believe me, you don't want me to do it that way."

Karen weighed up the situation. Gilbey seemed calm. Almost too calm. She wasn't trained in dealing with situations like this. Normally, she'd pass it up the line. But Lawson was busy elsewhere. Maybe the person to deal with this was the hostage negotiator. "Let's go and talk to Inspector Duncan. He's been speaking to Macfadyen."

She climbed out of the van and called one of the uniformed officers over. "Please stay with Mrs. Gilbey and Mr. Mackie."

"I'm going with Alex," Lynn said mutinously. "I'm not leaving his side."

Alex took her hand. "We go together," he said to Karen.

She knew when she was beaten. "OK, let's go," she said, leading the way toward the cordon that blocked the entrance to Macfadyen's street.

Alex had never felt so alive. He was conscious of the movements of his muscles with every step he took. His senses seemed heightened, every sound and smell amplified almost beyond bearing. He would never forget this short walk. This was the most important moment of his life and he was determined to do the right thing, the right way. He'd rehearsed the conversation on his helter-skelter drive to St. Monans and he was sure he'd found the words to win his daughter's freedom.

Karen brought them to a white van parked outside the familiar house. In the gathering dusk, everything seemed overlaid with gloom, reflecting the spirits of those involved in the siege. Karen banged on the side of the van and the door slid open. John Duncan's head appeared in the gap. "DC Pirie, isn't it? What can I do for you?"

"This is Mr. and Mrs. Gilbey. He wants to speak to Macfadyen, sir."

Duncan's eyebrows rose in alarm. "I don't think that's a good idea. The only person Macfadyen wants to speak to is

ACC Lawson. And he's given orders for no more calls till he gets back."

"He needs to hear what I have to say," Alex said heavily. "He's doing this because he wants the world to know who killed his mother. He thinks it was me and my friends. But he's wrong. I found out the truth today and he should be the first person to hear it."

Duncan failed to hide his astonishment. "You're saying you know who killed Rosie Duff?"

"I do."

"Then you should be making a statement to one of our officers," he said firmly.

A tremor of emotion flickered across Alex's face, betraying how tightly he was holding himself in. "That's my daughter in there. I can end this now. Every minute you delay letting me talk to him is a minute when she's at risk. I'm not talking to anybody but Macfadyen. And if you won't let me talk to him, I'm going to the press. I'm going to tell them I have the means to finish this siege and you won't let me use them. Do you really want that to be your professional epitaph?"

"You don't know what you're doing here. You're not a trained negotiator." Alex could tell it was Duncan's last throw of the dice.

"All your training doesn't seem to have done you much good, does it?" Lynn interjected. "Alex spends all his working life negotiating with people. He's very good at it. Let him try. We'll take full responsibility for the outcome."

Duncan looked at Karen. She shrugged. He took a deep breath and sighed. "I'll be listening in," he said. "If I think the situation is getting out of control, I'll end the call."

Relief made Alex dizzy. "Fine. Let's do it," he said.

Duncan brought out the phone and clamped headphones over his ears. He handed a pair to Karen and the receiver to Alex. "It's all yours."

The phone rang. Once. Twice. Three times. Halfway through the fourth ring, it was picked up. "Back for more, Lawson?" the voice on the other end said.

He sounded so ordinary, Alex thought. Not like a man who would kidnap a baby and dangle its life in the balance. "This isn't Lawson. This is Alex Gilbey."

"I've got nothing to say to you, you murdering bastard."

"Give me a minute of your time. I've got something to tell you."

"If you're going to deny you killed my mother, save your breath. I won't believe you."

"I know who killed your mother, Graham. And I have proof. It's here in my pocket. I've got paint flakes that match the paint on your mother's clothes. I took them this afternoon from a caravan by Loch Leven." No response other than a sharp intake of breath. Alex soldiered on. "There was someone else there that night. Someone nobody paid any attention to because he had a reason to be there. Someone who met your mother after work and took her back to his caravan. I don't know what happened, but I suspect she probably refused to have sex with him and he raped her. When he came to his senses, he realized he couldn't let her go to tell her tale. It would be the end of everything for him. So he stabbed her. And he took her up to Hallow Hill and left her there to die. And nobody ever suspected him because he was on the side of the law." Karen Pirie was staring at him now, open-mouthed and horror-struck as she grasped the implications of what he was saying.

"Say his name," Macfadyen whispered.

"Jimmy Lawson. It was Jimmy Lawson who murdered your mother, Graham. Not me."

"Lawson?" It was almost a sob. "This is a trick, Gilbey."

"No trick, Graham. Like I said, I've got proof. What have you got to lose by believing me? End this now, you get the chance to see justice done at last."

There was a long silence. Duncan edged forward, poised to take the phone from Alex. Alex deliberately turned away, gripping the handset tighter. Then Macfadyen spoke.

"I thought he was doing it because it was the only way of getting some kind of justice. And I didn't want it his way because I wanted you to suffer. But he was doing it to cover his back," Macfadyen said, his words meaning nothing to a bewildered Alex.

"Doing what?" Alex said.

"Killing you guys."

CHAPTER
FORTY-FIVE

A pall of darkness hung over Carlton Way. Within the gloom, darker shapes moved, semiautomatic weapons held close to their bulletproof vests. They covered the terrain with the silent delicacy of a lion stalking an antelope. As they approached the house, they fanned out, crouching to stay below window sills, then regrouping on either side of front and back doors. Each man fought to keep his breathing soft and steady, heart pounding like a drum calling him to battle. Fingers checked that earpieces were in place. None wanted to miss the clarion call to action when it came. If it came. This was no time for ambivalence. When the word sounded, they'd demonstrate their commitment.

Above their heads, the helicopter hovered, the technicians glued to their thermal-imaging screens. Theirs was the responsibility for making sure the moment was right. Sweat prickled their eyes and dampened their palms as they focused on the two bright shapes. As long as they stayed apart, they could give the go-ahead. But if they merged into one, everyone stayed on pause. There was no room for error here. Not with a life at stake.

Now it was all in the hands of one man. Assistant Chief Constable James Lawson walked down Carlton Way, knowing this was the last throw of the dice.

. . .

Alex struggled to make sense of Macfadyen's words. "What do you mean?" he asked.

"I saw him last night. With the baseball bat. Under the bridge. Hitting your pal. I thought he wanted justice. I thought that's why he was doing it. But if Lawson killed my mother . . ."

Alex clung to the one thing he knew to be true. "He killed her, Graham. I've got the evidence." Suddenly the line went dead. Baffled, Alex rounded on Duncan. "What the fuck?" he said.

"Enough," Duncan said, wrenching the headphones from his head. "I'm not having this broadcast to the world. What the hell is this, Gilbey? Some kind of pact between you and Macfadyen to fit up Lawson?"

"What are you talking about?" Lynn demanded.

"It was Lawson," Alex said.

"I heard you, Lawson killed Rosie," Lynn said, gripping his arm.

"Not just Rosie. He killed Ziggy and Mondo, too. And he tried to kill Weird. Macfadyen saw him," Alex said wonderingly.

"I don't know what you think you're playing at . . ." Duncan began. He was stopped in his tracks by the arrival of Lawson. Pale and sweating, the ACC looked around the group, puzzled and clearly angry.

"What the hell are you two doing here?" he demanded, pointing at Alex and Lynn. He rounded on Karen. "I told you to keep her in the ARU van. Christ, this is a fucking circus. Get them out of here."

There was a moment of silence, then Karen Pirie said, "Sir, some very serious allegations have been made that we need to talk about . . ."

"Karen, this is not a fucking debating society. We're in the middle of a life-and-death operation," Lawson shouted. He raised his radio to his lips. "Is everyone in position?"

Alex dashed the radio from Lawson's hand. "Listen to me, you bastard." Before he could say more, Duncan was grappling him to the ground. Alex wrestled the policeman, dragging his head free to shout, "We know the truth, Lawson. You killed Rosie. And you killed my friends. It's over. You can't hide any longer."

Lawson's eyes blazed fury. "You're as mad as he is." He bent down and retrieved his radio as a couple of uniformed officers dived on top of Alex.

"Sir," Karen said urgently.

"Not now, Karen," Lawson exploded. He turned away, his radio to his face again. "Is everyone in position?"

The replies crackled back through his earpiece. Before Lawson could respond, he heard the voice of the technical-support commander in the helicopter. "Hold fire. Target with hostage."

He hesitated for only a second. "Go," he said. "Go, go, go."

Macfadyen was ready to face the world. Alex Gilbey's words had restored his faith in the possibility of justice. He would give the man his daughter back. To ensure safe passage, he'd take a knife with him. One final insurance policy to get him safely out the door and into the arms of the waiting police.

He was halfway to the front door, Davina tucked under his arm like a parcel, a kitchen knife in his free hand, when his world exploded. Doors caved in front and back. Men shouted, a deafening cacophony. Brilliant white flares exploded, blinding him. Instinctively, he pulled the child round to his chest. The hand holding the knife came up toward her. Through the chaos, he thought he heard someone shout, "Drop her."

He felt paralyzed. He couldn't let go.

The lead marksman saw a child's life at risk. He spread his feet, steadied his gun hand and aimed for the head.

CHAPTER
FORTY-SIX

April 2004; Blue Mountains, Georgia

The spring sunshine shimmered over the trees as Alex and Weird emerged onto the ridge. Weird led the way to an out-cropping of rock that jutted over the slope and clambered up, settling down with his long legs dangling over the edge. He reached into his backpack and came out with a small pair of binoculars. He trained them down the hillside then passed them over to Alex.

"Straight down, then slightly to your left."

Alex adjusted the focus and ranged over the territory be-low. All of a sudden, he realized he was looking at the roof of their cabin. The figures running around outside were Weird's kids. The adults sitting by the picnic table were Lynn and Paul. And the baby kicking on the rug at her feet was Davina. He watched as his daughter spread her arms wide and chuckled up at the trees. His love for her pierced him like stigmata.

He'd come so close to losing her. When he'd heard the gunshot, he thought his heart would explode. Lynn's scream had echoed in his head like the end of the world. An eternity had passed before one of the armed cops had emerged with Davina in his arms, and even that had been no relief. As they approached, all he could see was blood.

But the blood had all been Macfadyen's. The marksman

had hit his target unflinchingly. Lawson's face could have been carved from granite for all the expression he showed.

In the mayhem that had followed, Alex had torn himself away from his wife and daughter long enough to grab Karen Pirie. "You need to secure that caravan."

"What caravan?"

"Lawson's fishing caravan. Up at Loch Leven. That's where he killed Rosie Duff. The paint on his ceiling matches the paint on Rosie's cardigan. You never know, there might even be blood traces still."

She'd looked at him with distaste. "You expect me to take that shit seriously?"

"It's the truth." He pulled the envelope out of his pocket. "I've got the paint that will prove I'm right. If you let Lawson get back to the caravan, he'll destroy it. The evidence will go up in smoke. You've got to stop him doing that. I'm not making this up," he said, desperate to make her believe him. "Duncan heard Macfadyen, too. He saw Lawson attacking Tom Mackie last night. Your boss will stop at nothing to cover his tracks. Take him into custody and secure that caravan."

Karen's face had remained expressionless. "You're suggesting I arrest my Assistant Chief Constable?"

"Strathclyde Police took Hélène Kerr and Jackie Donaldson into custody on a lot less evidence than you've heard here this afternoon." Alex struggled to stay calm. He couldn't believe this was all slipping away from him now. "If Lawson wasn't who he is, you wouldn't be hesitating."

"But he is who he is. He's a highly respected senior police officer."

"Caesar's wife, officer. All the more reason why you should take this seriously. You think this isn't going to be all over the papers tomorrow morning? If you think Lawson's clean, then show him to be clean."

"Your wife's calling you, sir," Karen had said icily. She'd walked away, leaving him stranded.

But she'd taken his words on board. She hadn't arrested

Lawson, but she had gathered a couple of uniformed officers and unobtrusively left the scene. Next morning, Alex had had a call from Jason, exultantly informing him that he'd heard on the forensic grapevine that his colleagues in Dundee had taken possession of a caravan late the previous night. Game on.

Alex lowered the glasses. "They know you spy on them?"

Weird grinned. "I tell them God sees everything, and I have a direct line to him."

"I bet you do." Alex lay back, letting the sun dry the sweat from his face. It had been a steep and breathless climb up here. No time for talking. This was the first chance he'd had alone with Weird since they'd arrived the previous day. "Karen Pirie came to see us last week," he said.

"How was she?"

It was, Alex had come to understand, a typical Weird question. Not, "What did she have to say for herself?" but rather, "How was she?" He'd underestimated his friend too often in the past. Now perhaps he'd have the chance to make up for that. "I think she's still pretty shaken up. Her and most of the cops in Fife. It's a bit of a stunner when you find out that your Assistant Chief Constable's a rapist and a multiple murderer. The reverberations are pretty serious. I think half the force still believes that Graham Macfadyen and I made the whole thing up between us."

"So Karen came to debrief you?"

"Sort of. It's not her case anymore, of course. She had to hand over the Rosie Duff investigation to officers from an outside force, but she's made pals with one of their team. Which means she's still got an inside track. Credit to her, she wanted to come and fill us in on the latest."

"Which is what?"

"All the forensics have been completed on the caravan. As well as the paint matches, they found some tiny spots of blood where the bench seat meets the floor. They took blood samples from Rosie's brothers and from Macfadyen's body, because of course there's nothing left of Rosie's DNA for comparison so they have to go with close relatives. And the overwhelming odds are that the blood in Lawson's caravan came from Rosie Duff."

"That's incredible," Weird said. "After all this time, he gets caught by a flake of paint and a drop of blood."

"One of his former colleagues has come forward with a statement that Lawson used to boast about passing the time on the night shift by taking lassies back to his caravan and having sex with them. And our evidence puts him very close to where the body was found. Karen says the fiscal's office were a bit wobbly at first, but they decided to go ahead with a prosecution. When he heard that, Lawson just crumbled. She said it was as if he just couldn't carry the load any longer. Apparently, it's not an uncommon phenomenon. Karen told me that, when they're cornered, it's not unusual for murderers to feel the need to unburden themselves of every single bad thing they've ever done."

"So why did he do it?"

Alex sighed. "He'd been going out with her for a few weeks. And she wouldn't go the whole way. He says she would only ever go so far, then no further. And she drove him beyond control. He raped her. According to him, she said she was going straight to the police. And he couldn't handle that, so he picked up his filleting knife and stabbed her. It was already snowing, he thought there would be nobody around, so he dumped her on Hallow Hill. He meant it to look like it had been a ritual killing. He's saying he was horrified when he realized we were being suspected. Obviously, he didn't want to be caught himself, but he claims he didn't want anybody else fitted up for the crime."

"Very high-minded of him," Weird said cynically.

"I think that's the truth. I mean, with one little lie, he could have dumped one of us right in the shit. Once Maclennan knew about the Land Rover, all Lawson had to do was to say it had slipped his mind that he'd seen it earlier. Either on the way to Hallow Hill or outside the Lammas at closing time."

"The Lord alone knows the truth, but we can give him the benefit of the doubt, I suppose. You know, he must have thought he was home and dry after all this time. Never so much as a whisper of suspicion."

"No. We were the ones who carried that can. Lawson had twenty-five years of living an apparently blameless life. And then the Chief Constable announces a cold case review. According to Karen, Lawson had ditched the physical evidence the first time DNA was used successfully in court. It was still held at St. Andrews then, so he'd have had no trouble accessing it. The cardigan was genuinely misfiled at some point when the evidence was moved from one location to another, but the rest of the clothes, the stuff with the biological samples, he got rid of himself."

Weird frowned. "How come the cardigan ended up in a completely different place from the body?"

"When he was going back to his panda car, Lawson found the cardie lying in the snow. He'd dropped it carrying the body up the hill. He just stuffed it into the nearest hedge. It was the last thing he wanted sitting around in his police car. So with all the relevant evidence missing, he must have thought he could still ride out the review safely."

"And then Graham turns up out of the woodwork. The one factor he'd never been able to take account of because of her family's craving for respectability. Here was somebody who really had a stake in Rosie's death, demanding answers. But what I still don't see is why he decided to start killing us off," Weird said.

"According to Karen, Macfadyen was on Lawson's back constantly. Demanding he reinterview witnesses. Particularly us. He was convinced we were the guilty men. Among the stuff on his computer, there was an account of his conversations with Lawson. At one point, he comments that it surprised him that Lawson hadn't seen anything suspicious, sitting in his patrol car. When he put that to Lawson, he seemed very edgy about it, which Macfadyen assumed was because it sounded like he was being critical. But of course, what was really behind it was that Lawson didn't want anyone focusing on what he'd been doing that night. Everyone had taken his presence at the scene for granted, but once you took us out of the equation, the only person we know for sure was in the area that night was Lawson himself. If he hadn't been a cop, he'd have been the prime suspect."

"Even so. Why decide to go for us after all this time?"

Alex shifted uncomfortably on the rock. "This is the bit that's hard to take. According to Lawson, he was being blackmailed."

"Blackmailed? Who by?"

"Mondo."

Weird looked thunderstruck. "Mondo? You're kidding. What kind of sick line is Lawson shooting now?"

"I don't think it's a line. You remember the day Barney Maclennan died?"

Weird shuddered. "How could I forget?"

"Lawson was the front man on the rope. He saw what happened. According to him, Maclennan was hanging onto Mondo, but Mondo panicked and kicked him off the rope."

Weird closed his eyes momentarily. "I wish I could say I don't believe it, but it's exactly how Mondo would react. Still, I don't understand what that has to do with Lawson being blackmailed."

"After they pulled Mondo up, it was chaos. Lawson took charge of Mondo. He went in the ambulance with him. He told Mondo he'd seen what had happened and promised that he would make sure Mondo paid the full legal price for what he'd done. And that's when Mondo dropped his wee bombshell. Mondo claimed that he'd seen Rosie getting into Lawson's patrol car one night outside the Lammas. Well, Lawson knew that he'd be in deep shit if that came out. So he did a deal. If Mondo kept quiet about what he'd seen, Lawson would do the same."

"Not so much blackmail as mutually assured destruction," Weird said harshly. "What went wrong?"

"As soon as the cold case review was announced, Mondo went to see Lawson and told him that the price of his continued silence was to be left alone. He didn't want his life blown apart a second time. And he told Lawson he had insurance. That he wasn't the only one who knew what he'd seen. Only, of course, he didn't specify which one of us he'd allegedly told. That's why Lawson was so insistent that Karen concentrate on the physical evidence rather than interviewing us again. It bought him time while he killed off anyone who might know the truth. But then he got too clever by half. He wanted to make Robin Maclennan look like a suspect in Mondo's murder, so he told him how Barney had really died. But before he could kill Mondo, Robin Maclennan got in touch with Mondo, who panicked and went to see Lawson again." Alex gave a wry smile. "That was the bit of business he had over in Fife the night he came to see me. Anyway, Mondo accused Lawson with breaking his end of the bargain. Older and wiser, or so he thought. He said he'd get his side of the story in first so that Lawson's claim that he killed Barney Maclennan would look like the desperate mud-slinging of a cornered man." Alex rubbed a hand over his face.

Weird groaned. "Poor, silly Mondo."

"The irony is that, if it hadn't been for Graham Macfadyen's obsession with the case, Lawson might well have succeeded in killing all four of us."

"What do you mean?"

"If Graham hadn't been tracking us all via the Internet, he'd never have found out about Ziggy's death and he wouldn't have sent that wreath. Then we'd never have made a connection between the two murders and Lawson would have been able to pick us off at his leisure. Even then, he muddied the waters as much as he could. He carefully made sure I knew all about Graham, even though he pretended he'd accidentally let it slip. And of course, he told Robin Maclennan how Mondo had killed his brother. That way, he could give himself a bit of insurance. After Mondo was killed, the sly bastard went to Robin and offered him an alibi. Which Robin agreed to, not thinking for a minute that it worked the other way too—that he was giving an alibi to the real killer."

Weird shivered and pulled his legs up, hugging his knees to his chest. He felt a twinge in his ribs, the shadow of a former pain. "But why did he come after me? He must have realized that neither of us knew what Mondo had seen or else we'd have confronted him with it after Mondo's death."

Alex sighed. "By that time, he'd dug himself in too deep. Because of Macfadyen's wreaths, we'd made the connection between two killings that were supposed to look completely unrelated. His only hope was to make Macfadyen look like the killer. And Macfadyen wouldn't have stopped at two, would he? He'd have gone on until he'd taken us all out."

Weird shook his head sadly. "What a terrible mess. But why did he kill Ziggy first?"

Alex groaned. "It's so banal it would make you weep. Apparently he'd already booked his holiday in the States before the cold case review was announced."

Weird licked his lips. "So it could just as easily have been me?"

"If he'd decided to go fishing on your side of the country, yes."

Weird closed his eyes, steepling his fingers in his lap. "What about Ziggy and Mondo? What's happening about that?"

"Not so good, I'm afraid. In spite of the fact that Lawson's singing like the proverbial bird, they've got no corroborative evidence that ties Lawson into Mondo's murder. He was very, very careful. He's got no alibi, but he claims he was up at his caravan that night, so even if they can find a neighbor to confirm his car wasn't at his house, he's covered."

"He's going to get away with it, isn't he?"

"It looks that way. Under Scots law, a confession has to be corroborated before a prosecution can succeed. But the cops in Glasgow are giving Hélène and Jackie a wide berth, which is a result of sorts."

Weird slammed the flat of his hand against the rock in frustration. "What about Ziggy? Have the Seattle police done any better?"

"A little. But not much. We know Lawson was in the U.S. the week before Ziggy died. He was supposedly on a game-fishing trip in Southern California. But here's the thing.

When he took his rental car back, it had about two and a half thousand miles more on the clock than you'd get from local driving."

Weird kicked out at the rock beneath his feet. "And that's a round trip from Southern California to Seattle, right?"

"Right. But again, there's no direct evidence. Lawson's too smart to have used his credit card anywhere other than where he was supposed to be. Karen says the Seattle police have been showing his photo around hardware stores and motels, but no luck so far."

"I can't believe he's going to get away with murder again," Weird said.

"I thought you believed in a judgment more powerful than humans can provide?"

"God's judgment doesn't absolve us from the duty to operate in a moral universe," Weird said seriously. "One of the ways we show love for our fellow human beings is to protect them from their own worst impulses. Sending criminals to jail is just an extreme example of that."

"I'm sure they feel loved," Alex said sardonically. "Karen did have one other piece of news. They've finally decided not to charge Lawson with attempted murder for his attack on you."

"Why the heck not? I told them back then that I was willing to come back and testify."

Alex sat up. "Without Macfadyen, there's no direct evidence that it was Lawson who did you over."

Weird sighed. "Oh well. At least he's not going to be able to wriggle off the hook over Rosie. I guess it doesn't much matter whether he faces charges over what he tried to do to me. You know, I've always prided myself on being streetwise," he mused. "But I walked out of your house that night full of bravado. I wonder if I'd have been so brave or stupid if I'd known there was not just one person but two on my tail."

"Be grateful for that. If Macfadyen hadn't been spying on us, we'd never have been able to place Lawson and his car at the scene."

"I still can't believe he didn't intervene when Lawson started beating me to a pulp," Weird said bitterly.

"Maybe he was forestalled by Eric Hamilton appearing on the scene." Alex sighed. "I suppose we'll never know."

"I guess what matters most is that we finally got the answer to who took Rosie's life," Weird said. "It's been a thorn in our flesh for twenty-five years, and now we can put it to rest. Thanks to you, we managed to neutralize the poison that infected the four of us."

Alex gave him a curious look. "Did you ever wonder . . . ?"

"If it really was one of us?"

Alex nodded.

Weird considered. "I knew it couldn't have been Ziggy. He had no interest in women, and even back then, he didn't want to be cured. Mondo wouldn't have had the nerve to keep his mouth shut if it had been him. And you, Alex . . . Well, let's just say I couldn't figure out how you would have got her up to Hallow Hill. You never had the Land Rover keys."

Alex was shocked. "That's the only reason you decided it couldn't have been me?"

Weird smiled. "You were strong enough to have kept your own counsel. You've got the capacity for tremendous coolness under pressure, but when you blow, you blow like a volcano. You were taken with the lassie . . . I'll be honest. It did cross my mind. But as soon as they told us she'd been attacked somewhere else and dumped on the hill, I knew it couldn't be you. You were saved by the logistics."

"Thanks for your confidence," Alex said, wounded.

"You did ask. And you? Who did you suspect?"

Alex had the grace to look embarrassed. "You did cross my mind. Especially when you got God. It seemed like the sort of thing a guilty man might have done." He gazed out over the treetops to the distant horizon where mountains folded into each other in a blue haze. "I often wonder how different my life would have been if Rosie had accepted my invitation and come to the party that night. She'd still be alive. So would Mondo and Ziggy. Our friendship would have survived in much better nick. And we'd have lived without guilt."

"You might have ended up marrying Rosie instead of Lynn," Weird commented wryly.

"No." Alex frowned. "That would never have happened."

"How not? Don't underestimate how slender are the threads that bind us to the life we have. You fancied her."

"It would have worn off. And she would never have settled for a boy like me. She was far too grown up. Besides, I think I knew even then that Lynn was the one who would save me."

"Save you from what?"

Alex smiled, a small, private smile. "From anything and everything." He stared down toward the cabin and the clearing where his heart was held hostage. For the first time in twenty-five years, he had a future, not just the millstone of a past. And it felt like a gift that he'd finally earned.

Just because you hear voices, it doesn't mean you're mad. You don't have to be well bright to know that. And nobody has ever accused you of being anything other than thick as pigshit. But you're bright enough to know you're not a nutter. All sorts of people have other voices in their heads, you know that. It's how they make a living. People that write books, they're always making up conversations. Faking it. The same with the telly. Even though you can believe it when you're watching it, everybody knows it's not real. And somebody's got to have dreamed it up in the first place, all that nattering, without them ending up where you have. Stands to reason.

So you're not worried. Well, not very worried. OK, they said you were insane. The judge said your name, Derek Tyler, and he tagged you with the mad label. But even though he's supposed to be a smart bastard, that judge didn't know he was following the plan. The way to avoid the life sentence that they always hand down when somebody does what you did. If you make them believe you were off your head when you did it, then it isn't you that did the crime, it's the madness in you. And if you're mad, not bad, it stands to reason you can be cured. Which is why they lock you up in the nuthouse instead of the nick. That way the doctors can poke around in your head and have a crack at fixing what's broke.

Of course, if nothing's broke in the first place, the best thing you can do is keep your mouth zipped. Not let on you're as sane as them. Then when the time is right, you can start talking. Make it look like they've somehow worked their magic and turned you into somebody they can let out on the street again.

It sounded really easy when the Voice explained it to you. You're pretty sure you got it right, because the Voice went over it so many times you can replay the whole spiel just by closing your eyes and mouthing the opening words. 'I am the Voice. I am your master. Whatever I tell you to do is for the best. I am the Voice. This is the plan. Listen very carefully.' That's the trigger. The words you recite to make everything go away. That's all it takes. The intro that makes the whole tape play in your head. The seductive message is still there, implanted deep inside your brain. And it still makes sense. Or at least, you think it does.

Only, it's been a long time now. It's not easy, staying on the wrong side of silence day after day, week after week, month after month. But you're pretty proud of the way you've hung on to it. Because there's all the other stuff interfering with the Voice. Therapy sessions where you have to struggle to blot out what the real nutters are going on about. Counselling sessions where the doctors try to trick you into words. Not to mention the screaming and shouting when somebody goes off on one. Which happens a lot more than you think is right. They should do something about it, they really should. Then there's all the background noise of the day room, the TV and the music rumbling round your head like interference.

All you have to fight back with is the Voice and the promise that the word will come when the time is right. And then you'll be back out there, doing what you've discovered you do best.

Killing women.

It's amazing how little we actually need to survive, I've been thinking about that a lot lately. We're constantly bombarded by messages from the media with their litany of spurious necessities. If a Martian arrived here and spent a week watching TV and reading magazines and lifestyle supplements, he'd end up believing that human beings had a list of absolute requirements that include Manolo Blahniks; a bunch of kooky friends; several restaurant meals, a trip to the cinema, a dose of culture at an exhibition or museum, a night's clubbing, a live gig and a dozen bottles of supermarket plonk every week; oh, and regular sex, preferably with someone who isn't your partner.

But they'd be wrong. I've learned these past three months how far back you can strip your life and still be glad to be here. And I've got history on my side. Look at Alexander Selkirk. Look at Shackleton. We're survivors, if we allow ourselves to be.

I've done all the things the counsellors would shudder at. I've cut myself off from my former friends. I've refused to use work as a panacea. I've resolutely avoided talking about what splintered my certainties and shattered my illusions about my impregnability. And you know what? I'm still standing. I'm still myself.

Carol Jordan's mouse pointer hovered over the <send> button. But, as she'd done so many times in the previous three months, she moved it to <delete>. "Do you want to save this message as a text file?" the screen prompt asked her. She clicked <yes>. She'd come back to it later. Sometimes she followed through and sent these messages to the one person she believed she could still open up to. But more often, she held back.

The accumulated text files were the nearest thing to a diary she had ever maintained. On the bad days, she would go back and reread some of the earlier entries. They offered balm to her bruised heart. They were incontrovertible evidence that she was capable of forward movement. They were the promise that she had a future that was not conditional on anyone but herself.

Carol ran her fingers through her hair. One of the first things she'd done when she'd returned to London after the worst week of her life had been to visit the hairdresser and demand a new cut that would alter the shape of her face. Oliver, her stylist, had cropped it short at the sides and back, then swept the thick blonde fringe away from her forehead. Even now it felt unnatural to her touch. But when she looked in the mirror every morning, Carol still experienced a moment of surprised gratitude when she saw how little she resembled the woman she'd been. Apart from the familiar grey eyes, there was almost nothing to anchor this face to her past. That face had belonged to a different Detective Chief Inspector Carol Jordan. That face had been the catalyst for the chain of events that had nearly destroyed her. A chance, uncanny resemblance spotted by someone whose ambition and ruthlessness obliterated any concern for her well-being had sent her abroad on an undercover mission that had cast her adrift from all her resources. It had ended up almost costing her life.

Carol shivered at the recollection, willing the flashbacks to close down. She closed down the email program and pushed back from her desk. Her visitor was due in ten minutes and she didn't expect him to be late. She regarded it as a major victory that she'd been able to arrange the meeting in her flat. The only man she'd been alone with inside these four walls since her return had been her brother, and even that had felt threatening enough to dry her mouth and set her heart galloping. Even when she'd spent time with the one person she could still trust, that had been on neutral ground, and that at his suggestion. One corner of Carol's mouth twitched in a wry smile. How very like him to have understood without being told.

But then, everyone who knew what had happened was treating her with an unaccustomed sensitivity. Though of course they never spelled out why. They were embarrassed by what had happened to her. They didn't know what to say. It wasn't like asking how someone's pregnancy or cancer treatment was going. There was no neat social formula that allowed for, "So, how are you recovering from being hung out to dry by your bosses? How's the post-traumatic stress today? Think you'll ever have sex again?"

Today's appointment, for example. The email he'd sent suggesting they meet had had none of the casual assumption of authority he had every right to make. John Brandon had been the last boss she'd trusted, first in Bradfield then in Seaford. She'd done the best work of her career under his guidance. They'd become not quite friends but more than colleagues. She'd eaten dinner with his family, been on first-name terms with his wife. But even he had sidestepped the "r" word. She knew his words by heart. "Dear Carol, I understand you're still on leave. I don't mean to intrude, but I'm going to be in London next week, and I'd very much like to see you. I have a proposition that might interest you, but I'd rather discuss it face to face. You've been in our thoughts lately—Maggie sends her best, as do I. Let me know if we can meet. Yours, John Brandon."

Tactful, sympathetic without being unctuous or voyeuristic. And oddly, in spite of pussyfooting round the realities, he'd hit the perfect note and the perfect moment. Any sooner and she'd have refused. She'd felt so comprehensively betrayed by the people who were supposed to be on her side that it had poisoned her against the job that had been her world since she'd left university. But in the last couple of weeks, her inactivity had started to feel like a kind of prison. And Carol wasn't a woman who found constraint a relief from the difficulties of making her own choices. She might not be able to contemplate working again with the elite cohort she'd finally managed to attain. But that wasn't the only option. There were other ways to carry out the job she loved. She'd done it before, and with distinction. She could do it again.

John Brandon's email had reminded her of that. She had no idea what he had in mind for her, but it had to be worth listening to. A fresh start was what she needed. Somewhere her history wasn't common currency, a constant reproach to those who had failed in their duty of care. Somewhere she could replace the nightmares with dreams.

The entryphone buzzed, firing the adrenaline like a live wire in the blood. Fight or flight? There was still an option.

She could pretend not to be home, send Brandon back north with the taste of failure in his mouth. Or she could give her courage the chance to fail further down the line. Carol clenched her hands into fists and stared at the handset. Was she really ready for this?

Dr. Tony Hill balanced a bundle of files on the arm carrying his battered briefcase and pushed open the door of the faculty office. He had enough time before his seminar group to collect his mail and deal with whatever couldn't be ignored. The psychology department secretary stuck her head round the door of her inner office at the sound of the door closing. "Dr. Hill," she said, sounding unreasonably pleased with herself.

"Morning, Mrs. Stirrat," Tony mumbled, dropping files and briefcase to the floor while he reached for the contents of his pigeonhole. Never, he thought, was a woman more aptly named. He wondered if that was why she'd chosen the husband she had.

"The Dean's not very pleased with you," Janine Stirrat said, leaning against the door jamb and folding her arms across her ample chest.

"Oh? And why might that be?" Tony asked.

"The cocktail party with SJP yesterday evening? You were supposed to be there."

With his back to her, Tony rolled his eyes. "I was engrossed in some work. The time just ran away from me."

"They're a major donor to the behavioural psychology research programme," Mrs. Stirrat scolded. "They wanted to meet you."

Tony grabbed his mail in an unruly pile and stuffed it into the front pocket of his briefcase. "I'm sure they had a wonderful time without me," he said, grabbing his files and backing towards the door.

"The Dean expects all academic staff to support fundraising, Dr. Hill. It's not much to ask, that you give up a couple of hours of your time . . ."

"To satisfy the prurient curiosity of the executives of a pharmaceutical company?" Tony snapped. "To be honest,

Mrs. Stirrat, I'd rather set my hair on fire and beat the flames out with a hammer." Using his elbow to manipulate the door handle, he escaped into the corridor without waiting to check out the affronted look he knew would be plastered across her face.

Temporarily safe in the haven of his own office, Tony slumped in the chair behind his computer. What the hell was he doing here? He'd managed to bury his unease about the academic life for long enough to accept the Reader's job at St. Andrews, but ever since his brief and traumatic excursion back into the field in Germany, he'd been unable to settle. The growing realisation that the university had hired him principally because his was a sexy name on the prospectus hadn't helped. Students enrolled to be close to the man whose profiles had nailed some of the country's most notorious serial killers. And donors wanted the vicarious, voyeuristic thrill of the war stories they tried to cajole from him. If he'd learned nothing else from his sojourn in the university, he'd come to understand that he wasn't cut out to be a performing seal. Whatever talents he possessed, pointless diplomacy had never been among them.

This morning's encounter with Janine Stirrat had been the last straw. Tony pulled his keyboard closer and began to compose a letter of resignation.

Three hours later, he was struggling to recover his breath. He'd set off far too fast and now he was paying the price. He crouched down and felt the rough grass at his feet. Dry enough to sit on, he decided. He sank to the ground and lay spreadeagled till the thumping in his chest eased off. Then he wriggled into a sitting position and savoured the view. From the top of Largo Law, the Firth of Forth lay before him, glittering in the late spring sunshine. He could see right across to Berwick Law, its volcanic cone the prehistoric twin to his own vantage point, separated now by miles of petrol blue sea. He checked off the landmarks; the blunt thumb of the Bass Rock, the May Island like a basking humpback whale, the distant blur of Edinburgh. They had a saying in this corner of Fife. "If you can see the May Island, it's going

to rain. If you can't see the May Island, it's already raining."
It didn't look like rain today. Only the odd smudge of cloud
broke the blue, like soft streamers of aerated dough pulled
from the middle of a morning roll. He was going to miss this
when he moved on.

But spectacular views were no justification for turning his
back on the true north of his talent. He wasn't an academic.
He was a clinician first and foremost, then a profiler. His resignation would take effect at the end of term, which gave him
a couple of months to figure out what he was going to do next.

He wasn't short of offers. Although his past exploits
hadn't always endeared him to the Home Office establishment,the recent case he'd worked on in Germany and Hol-
land had helped him leapfrog the British bureaucracy. Now
the Germans, the Dutch and the Austrians wanted him to
work for them as a consultant. Not just on serial murder, but
on other criminal activity that treated international fron-
tiers as if they didn't exist. It was a tempting offer, with a
guaranteed minimum that would be just about enough to live
on. And it would give him the chance to return to clinical
practice, even if it was only part-time.

But had had another offer on the table. He'd also been approached by Europol to spearhead a new initiative on cross-
border intelligence profiling. It was, he thought, the ultimate
irony. Carol Jordan had aspired to such a role, but the very
people who should have grabbed her gifts with both hands
had shattered her dream with an operation of calculated duplicity that had come perilously close to destroying them
both. And now they wanted him to spread his wares before
their officers, to train them to do what Carol could have done
with her eyes closed. The most tormenting aspect of their
proposal was that it tempted him in a way that almost nothing else could have done.

However, there was Carol to consider. As always when
she came into his thoughts, his mind veered away from direct confrontation. His natural instinct was to reach out to
her, to give her all the support he could. But he couldn't escape the knowledge that the reason she was so damaged now

was because his pathetic efforts to take care of her previously had backfired. He'd been so eager to rush to her side in Germany, so arrogantly convinced that he could give her the support she needed to get her through her isolated undercover operation. But he wasn't a cop. He didn't think like a cop. And his carelessness had been responsible for Carol making the crucial mistake that had exposed her to the violence that had almost destroyed her. He didn't think she saw it like that, but he couldn't escape the guilt. Somehow, he had to find a way to atone for what had happened to her, without her ever knowing that was what he was trying to do.

And so far, he had no idea how he could achieve that.

John Brandon climbed the steps up from the Barbican station. The dirty yellow bricks seemed to sweat and even the concrete underfoot felt hot and sticky. The air was stuffy with the thick, mingled smells of humanity. The tube had been stifling and Brandon had silently chided himself for his paradoxically proud assumption of humility. He could have come to London in an official car, a driver bringing him to Carol's door in air-conditioned splendor. He couldn't even remember now why he'd thought it would be such a good idea to travel like a civilian. Something about keeping in touch with ordinary people, that was it. Experiencing the world as they saw it, not cocooned behind smoked glass or a uniform.

Maybe he should have saved that for another day, when he had something less demanding to face than an interview with Carol Jordan. No matter how much he'd tried to prepare himself for their meeting, he knew he didn't really have a clue what he'd find. He was certain of only two things: he had no idea how she felt about what had happened to her; and work would be her salvation.

He'd been appalled when he'd heard about the botched mission that had ended with the violent assault on Carol. His informant had tried to stress the significance of what she'd achieved, as if that were somehow a counterbalance to what had been done to her. But Brandon had cut impatiently across the rationale. He understood the demands of command. He'd given his adult life to the police service and he'd reached the top of the tree with most of his principles intact. One of those was that no officer should ever be exposed to unnecessary risk. Of course danger was part of the job, particularly these days, with guns as much a fashion accessory in some social groups as iPods were in others. But there was acceptable risk and unacceptable risk. And in Brandon's view, Carol Jordan had been placed in a position of intolerable, improper risk. He simply did not believe there was any end that could have justified such means.

But it was pointless to rage against what had happened. Those responsible were too well insulated for even a Chief Constable to make much of a dent in their lives. The only thing John Brandon could do now for Carol was to offer her a lifeline back into the profession she loved. She'd been probably the best detective he'd ever had under his command, and all his instincts told him she needed to be back in harness.

He'd discussed it with his wife Maggie, laying out his plans before her. "What do you think?" he asked. "You know Carol. Do you think she'll go for it?"

Maggie had frowned, stirring her coffee thoughtfully. "It's not me you should be asking that, it's Tony Hill. He's the psychologist."

Brandon shook his head. "Tony is the last person I'd ask about Carol. Besides, he's a man, he can't understand the implications of rape the way a woman can."

Maggie's mouth twisted in acknowledgement. "The old Carol Jordan would have bitten your hand off. But it's hard to imagine what being raped will have done to her. Some women fall to pieces. For some women, it becomes the defining moment of their lives. Other women lock it away and pretend it never happened. It sits there like a time bomb waiting to blow a hole in their lives. And some find a way to deal with it and move forward. If I had to guess, I'd say Carol would either bury it or else work through it. If she's burying it, she'll probably be gung ho to get back to serious work, to prove to herself and the rest of the world that she's sorted. But she'll be a loose cannon if that's what she's try-

ing to do, and that's not what you need in this job. However . . . " She paused. "If she's looking for a way through,
you might be able to persuade her."

"Do you think she'd be up to the job?" Brandon's blood-
hound eyes looked troubled.

"It's like what they say about politicians, isn't it? The
very people who volunteer for the job are the last ones who
should be doing it. I don't know, John. You're going to have
to make your mind up when you see her."

It wasn't a comforting thought. Brandon squared his
shoulders and headed for the concrete labyrinth where Carol
Jordan waited at the epicentre like a sibylline riddle.

*Find them in the first six hours or you're looking for a
corpse. Find them in the first six hours or you're looking for
a corpse.* The missing children mantra mocked Detective Inspector Don Merrick. He was looking at sixteen hours and
counting. And counting was just what the parents of Tim
Golding were doing. Counting every minute that took them
farther from their last glimpse of their son. He didn't have to
think about what they were feeling; he was a father and he
knew the visceral fear waiting to assail any parent whose
child is suddenly, unaccountably not where they should be.
Mostly, it was history in a matter of minutes when the child
reappeared unscathed, usually grinning merrily at the panic
of its parents. But it was history that left its mark bone deep.

And sometimes there was no relief. No sudden access of
anger masking the ravages of ill-defined terror when the
child reappeared. Sometimes it just went on and on and on.
And Merrick knew the dread would continue screaming inside Alastair and Shelley Golding until his team found their
son. Alive or dead. He knew because he'd witnessed the
same agony in the lives of Gerry and Pam Lefevre, whose
son Guy had been missing now for just over four months.
Merrick had been the bagman on that inquiry, which was the
main reason why he'd been assigned to Tim Golding. He
had the knowledge to see whether there were obvious links
between the cases.

He leaned against the roof of his car and swept the long curve of the railway embankment with binoculars. Every available body was down there, combing the scrubby grass for any trace of the eight-year-old boy who had been missing since the previous evening. Tim had been playing with two friends, some complicated game of make-believe involving a superhero that Merrick vaguely remembered his own son briefly idolising. The friends had been called in by their mother and Tim had said he was going down the embankment to watch the freight trains that used this spur to bring roadstone from the quarry on the outskirts of the city to the railhead.

Two women heading for the bus stop and bingo thought they'd caught a glimpse of his canary yellow Bradfield Victoria shirt between the trees that lined the top of the steep slope leading down to the tracks. That had been around twenty to eight. Nobody else had come forward to say they'd seen the boy.

His face was already etched on Merrick's mind. The school photograph resembled a million others, but Merrick could have picked out Tim's sandy hair, his open grin and the blue eyes crinkled behind Harry Potter glasses from any line-up. Just as he could have done with Guy Lefevre. Wavy dark brown hair, brown eyes, a scatter of freckles across his nose and cheeks. Seven years old, tall for his age, he'd last been seen heading for an overgrown stand of trees on the edge of Downton Park, about three miles from where Merrick was standing now. It had been around seven on a damp spring evening. Guy had asked his mother if he could go out for another half-hour's play. He'd been looking for birds' nests, mapping them obsessively on a grid of the scrubby little copse. They'd found the grid two days later, on the far edge of the trees, crumpled into a ball. That had been the last anyone had seen of anything connected to Guy Lefevre. And now another boy seemed also to have vanished into thin air. Merrick sighed and lowered the binoculars. Time to round up the usual suspects.

He pulled out his mobile and called his sergeant, Kevin Matthews. "Kev? Don here. Start bringing the nonces in."

"No sign, then?"

"Not a trace. I've even had a team through the tunnel half a mile up the tracks. No joy. It's time to start rattling some cages."

"How big a radius?"

Merrick sighed again. Bradfield Metropolitan Police area stretched over an area of forty-four square miles, protecting and serving somewhere in the region of 900,000 people. According to the latest official estimates he'd read, that meant there were probably somewhere in the region of three thousand active paedophiles in the force area. Fewer than ten percent of that number was on the register of sex offenders. Rather less than the tip of the iceberg. But that was all they had to go on. "Let's start with a two-mile radius," he said. "They like to operate in the comfort zone, don't they?" As he spoke, Merrick was painfully aware that these days, with people commuting longer distances to work, with so many employed in jobs that kept them on the road, with local shopping increasingly a thing of the past, the comfort zone was, for most citizens, exponentially bigger than it had ever been even for their parents' generation. "We've got to start somewhere," he added, his pessimism darkening his voice.

He ended the call and stared down the bank, shielding his eyes against the sunshine that lent the grass and trees below a blameless glow. The brightness made the search easier, it was true. But it felt inappropriate, as if the weather was insulting the anguish of the Goldings. This was Merrick's first major case since his promotion, and already he suspected he wasn't going to deliver a result that would make anybody happy. Least of all him.

John Brandon was shaken to see the change in Carol Jordan. The woman who waited in the doorway for him to emerge from the lift bore almost no resemblance to his memory of her. He might well have passed her in the street. Her hair was radically different, it was true, but she had altered in more fundamental ways. The flesh seemed to have melted from her face, giving it a new arrangement of planes and hollows. Where there had been an expression of intelligent interest in her eyes, now there was a blank wariness. She radiated tension rather than the familiar confidence. In spite of the warmth of the early summer day, she was dressed in a shapeless polo neck sweater and baggy trousers instead of the sharply tailored suits Brandon was used to seeing her in.

He paused a couple of feet from her. "Carol," he said. "It's good to see you."